A TALE OF TWO FAMILIES

Written and Edited
by
Susan Lemieux Marsolais
and
Harold Raymond Marsolais

Published by:
Right Coast Productions

in conjunction with:

AuthorHouse™
1663 Liberty Drive
Bloomington, IN 47403
www.authorhouse.com
Phone: 1-800-839-8640

Revised November, 2010
First published by AuthorHouse 12/29/2010

ISBN: 978-1-4567-1339-3 (sc)

Library of Congress Control Number: 2010919234

Printed in the United States of America
Bloomington, Indiana

This book is printed on acid-free paper.

TABLE OF CONTENTS

Photo Albums

Appendices
    A. Legend for End Papers – 1655 Map of Rouen
    B. List of Society of New France
    C. List of Residences

Bibliography

DEDICATION

For the children
        and all the children to come.

ACKNOWLEDGEMENTS

This work would not have been possible without my husband, Hal Marsolais, who, among other things, financed the research of this material. So many documents were needed to compile and verify this information---the only way to assure accuracy. Initially, this meant sending for records from the archives of Ohio, New York and Canada and, finally, hiring a researcher in France to locate and send copies of the medieval documents from the archives in Normandy for both the Lemieux and Marsolais lineages. Over the years we continued to replace our computers with upgraded equipment which was the best way for me to store all the information, organize it into a book and publish it myself.

During the research, I discovered *Les Descendants des Lemieux d'Amerique*, a family association. Through my membership in the association, I found they had done thorough research on the Lemieux family and provided all the information I needed through Canada and back to our origins in France. Cousin Jacques Lemieux, the historian of *Lemieux d'Amerique* in Québec, researched and published an extraordinary edition of the Lemieux family history in French. This revealed to me that the Lemieux and Marsolais have always been together. *Les Descendants des Lemieux d'Amerique* did all that work and showed me the way to complete the Marsolais history. They have also been good friends. Additionally, Cousin Jacques gave me a copy of his revised draft even before he completed his updated book, making it possible for me to make current revisions. Cousin Guy Lemieux recently published an English version of Jacques's work with his own emphasis on the migrations of the Lemieux, which clarified many things for me.

Discovering the ancient link between the Lemieux and Marsolais families increased our passion for the research. We arranged trips to France and Canada so we could see first-hand and photograph where our ancestors had been---together. Hal carried all the luggage. He also provided emotional support from editing drafts and giving advice, to preparing meals so I could complete this book.

It was so rewarding to share this project with Hal and have the end result mean as much to both of us. This research has resulted in a new favorite pastime…traveling in France and Canada. We also collect antique maps from the ancestors' eras and use them to decorate our home and illustrate this book. It was so generous of Hal to share France with Shelly and Bill, Ray and Nicole in the summer of 2002. In the summer of 2003, he arranged a family reunion in Québec, which resulted in our finding the complete line of ancestors for his mother's Chamberland lineage back to France. This meant a trip to Poitou to look into the Chamberland's region of France. We also prepared another Québec family reunion for 2008, which celebrated the 400th anniversary of Champlain's founding of Québec as the capital city of New France. When Champlain sailed into Québec in 1608, Nicolas Marsolet was standing beside him.

For the last edition, Hal researched Nicolas Marsolet online and through many published editions. He revised the entire chapters on Nicolas in France and New France, bringing incredible detail to the Marsolet line.

I want to thank everyone who loaned or gave me family pictures. That generosity made the book so much better and enabled me to share them with the rest of the family.

Finally, I want to thank Steve Meyers for serving as an editor and providing the final polish which was so important and for which I will always be grateful.

PREFACE

Susan Lemieux Marsolais

I began this project because my children were grown and getting ready to leave home. We had moved so often during Hal's military career that they had grown up without frequent contact with their cousins and all the family stories. I wanted to make sure they knew where they fit in the family tree. I made Shelly and Ray their own photo albums illustrating their lives with their favorite family pictures. I placed a family tree in the back of each album but it was limited mostly to the information found in the Lemieux family Bible.

As I became immersed in the research, I found a wealth of information. In Québec's first 100 years, the Jesuits wrote about their small parishes, keeping records of the marriages, baptisms and burials of their members. And during his reign, Napoleon Bonaparte had required the churches to submit their records for duplicating by the French government. I have been able to document our families as far back as there are records---until more may be found.

In order to share this information with the rest of the family, I decided to present it in book form. I wanted to have it completed to give as wedding gifts so Shelly's and Ray's spouses would understand the family they had joined. I missed this deadline when Shelly married Bill O'Brien but it was completed before Ray married Nicole Bryant.

Because we have so much family history, deciding how to tell it is challenging in order for it to be readable and enjoyable, as well as enriching. This was the most difficult task. Typically, teenagers begin evaluating their lives, thinking about their futures and deciding the direction they want to go. During this time, they also become curious about their family roots to help them understand their own identities---and perhaps their own destinies. This material is presented for them. It is an adventure story of how our ancestors came to be in America---because of and in spite of all the historical events surrounding them.

This is a never-ending story and the next chapters will be determined by future generations.

Les Descendants des Lemieux d'Amérique

LES DESCENDANTS DES LEMIEUX D'AMERIQUE

A une réunion du Conseil d'Administration, tenue le 83 01 22 13:30 au 960, rue St Georges, local 1325, C.E.G.E.P. de Drummondville.

Sont présents : Messieurs: Jacques Lemieux, Jean-Jacques Lemieux, André Lemieux, Gérard Lemieux, Antoine Lemieux, Félix Lemieux, Jean-Guy Lemieux, Jean-Marie Lemieux, Noel Lemieux et Mademoiselle Pauline Lemieux, sous la présidence de Monsieur Pierre Lemieux.

Absence motivée : Madame Marielle Lemieux-Tardif.

Blason

Il est proposé par Monsieur Pierre Lemieux et secondé par Monsieur André Lemieux de reconnaître les armoiries du Sieur HENRI DE MIEUX déclarées le 6 juillet 1700 et la description du blason, à savoir: "d'azur, au chevron d'or, accompagné de trois trèfles du même, deux en chef et un en pointe", comme étant le blason des Descendants des Lemieux d'Amérique et d'en informer qui de droit.

ADOPTE.

Vraie copie conforme en date du 83 03 29.

Le Secrétaire

Marielle Lemieux-Tardif

Marielle Lemieux-Tardif

HONNEUR SUIS

DE MIEUX

Armoiries déclarées le 16 juillet 1700, par

HENRI DE MIEUX, ÉCUYER, SIEUR DU HAMEAU
GARDE DE LA MANCHE DE SA MAJESTÉ, CONSEIL-
LER DU ROY, LIEUTENANT GÉNÉRAL DE LA PRÉ-
VOSTÉ DE HAUTE ET BASSE NORMANDIE.

Blason : *D'azur, au chevron d'or, accompagné de trois trèfles du même, deux en chef et un en pointe.*

(Extrait de l'Armorial général de France, Normandie, Alençon, p. 541.)

Family Name History

MARSOLAIS

The French surname Marsolais is of patronymic origin, deriving from the personal name of the father of the original bearer of the name. In this instance, the surname derives from the name Marcel, which further derives from the Latin "Marcellus", a variant of "Marcus", from "Mars Martis", meaning "sacred or dedicated to the god Mars". According to Roman religion, Mars was the god of agriculture and of war. He was considered to be the most important deity after Jupiter and, as the father of Romulus, was a progenitor of the Roman race. Mars was so significant as a war god that his name became synonymous with "bellum", the Latin word for "war". The month of March, called "Martius", was sacred to Mars. The surname Marsolais thus means, "son or descendant of Marcel". During the Middle Ages, parents frequently named their children after saints and Biblical figures. The name Marcel spread because of devotion to several saints who bore the name, particularly Saint Marcellus, a first century Roman martyr, and Saint Marcellus I, a fourth century pope. It is interesting to note that the name Marcel became quite popular in France during the Revolutionary period. In addition, the name is found in other European countries, as shown by the Portuguese name Marcelo and the Italian name Marcello. Variants of the surname Marsolais include Marcel, Marcelet, Marcelon, Marcelot, Marceleau, Marcellier, and Marcelier. References to the surname Marcelais or to its variants include the record of a coat of arms being granted to a noble family bearing the surname Marcellier from the region of Languedoc. In addition, records show that a noble family bearing the surname Marcelier resided in the region of Dauphine, where the name of one Francois Marcelier, a lawyer and member of parliament.

BLAZON OF ARMS: Gules, two towers argent; a
                    chief azure, charged with three
                    mullets or.
CREST: A mullet of the arms.
Source Ref: Rietshap's Armorial General.
ORIGIN: FRANCE

Marsollet

Armorial Bearings

Arms

Azure, chaussé-ployé or; the azure charged
with a round mirror argent, within a bordure pommetée
of sixteen pieces or.
Crest: Upon a wreath of the colours,
a rock argent shaded gules, and on the rock, a Red-winged Blackbird,
rising with wings addorsed, proper. Above the crest, gules letters, set upon an undulating
banderole or bear the name of the honoured organism: *Association des Familles Lemire d'Amérique*.
Supporters: Two myrtle branches, leaved and flowered proper, tiges saltirwise.
Motto: *Nisi sapiens, liber est nemo*, gules on a fillet or.

Meaning

The mirror is a traditional utensil worthy of adoption as the symbol of the Lemire name,
considering the phonetic similarity of the two. The mirror, of antique style, appears in a place
of honour, on the azure part of the escutcheon, and invites one to explore the profound values
inscribed in a grand name throughout the history of Nouvelle-France.

Just above the escutcheon lies the crest of Cap-Rouge Rock, the reminiscence of a promising land,
a home base and a launching ground for families dedicated to the development of Québec,
Canada and America. Thus, in the period of the formidable French expeditions, the Lemire family
spread its name across America, and it is on the site of Cap-Rouge which the very first of its
members, François Lemire, landed as early as 1542 and where our first ancestor, Jean Lemire,
lived in approximately 1660.

On the summit of Cap-Rouge Rock stands the Red-winged Blackbird,
reflecting the aspiration to attain noble ideals.

Two myrtle branches support, protect and decorate the escutcheon.
The myrtle is a centuries-old symbol attached to Lemire heraldries by reason of their phonetic
similarities and by the fact that the myrtle is a medicinal plant; in old French, *mire* carries the
meaning of *médecin*, physician.

The motto, *Nisi sapiens, liber est nemo*, translates as "Without wisdom, one is not free".
It is attributed to the great Roman orator Cicero.

Above the escutcheon, the banderole is reminiscent of the large Lemire gathering at Baie-du-Febvre
held in 1988, the occasion at which the *Association des Familles d'Amérique was founded*.

Lemire

Introduction

Understanding our family history is made easier by first understanding our ancestral homeland and the historic events which helped to shape the style, customs and traditions which, through hundreds of years, have become a part of our lives, resulting in the people we are today. This book is concerned with the way in which individual lives were played out in the context of epoch-defining historical events. I hope it not only introduces you to your ancestors, but in turn, it makes history and geography come to life in a personal way.

I make no claim to originality with this material. The bibliography lists all the history books and art books that were the sources for the information and illustrations used in this publication. My goal was to gather and consolidate all the data I thought relevant to our family history and make it simple and direct to attract young readers.

It is also important to understand that spelling was not an exact science and was done phonetically for the most part. The notary had only a basic education and was one of the few literate people in a medieval town. Many records misspelled places and peoples' names---even by the person himself. In one marriage contract, the name Marsolais is spelled three different ways: Marsolet, Marcelais, Marsolais. If three different sources were available for a birth record, often there were three different dates. Clerical errors were common --- as they are today.

In the case of Champlain's writings, serious researchers are cautious. He dictated his writings some 20 years after the events took place. As a consequence, the dates and details of events are often tainted by a fading memory. Additionally, Champlain was influenced by the actions and events that transpired over a 20-year period and his descriptions and opinions on individuals and events are colored by those biases.

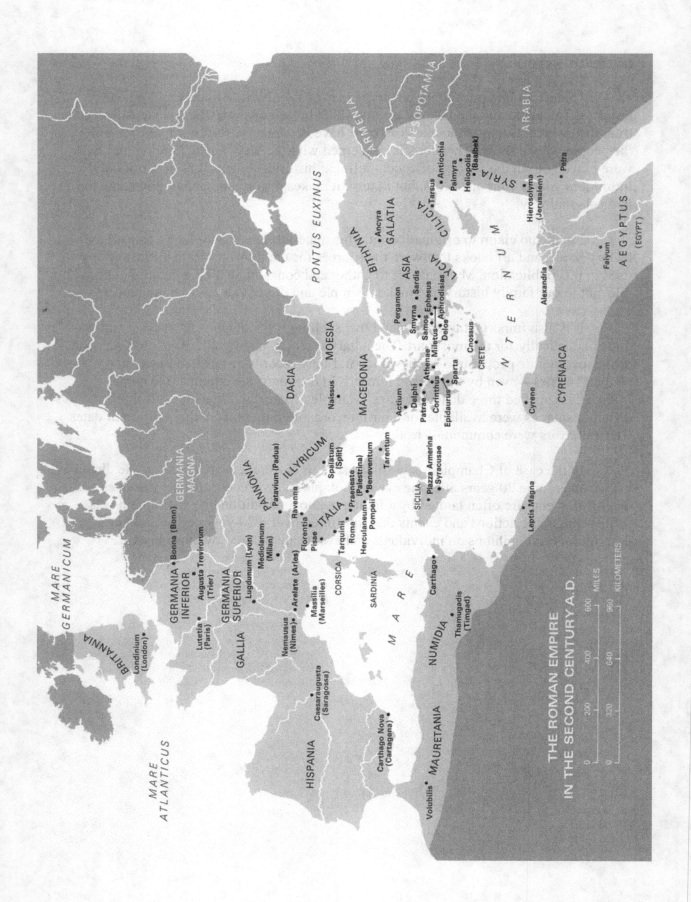

THE ROMAN EMPIRE
IN THE SECOND CENTURY A.D.

France

rance is a beautiful and diverse country. From its craggy northern coastline along the English Channel to its sunny Mediterranean beaches in the South, its beauty astounds. Its location makes it Europe's natural crossroad. Through the centuries, its temperate climate, fertile soil and network of rivers and streams attracted many diverse settlers to choose it as their home.

Initially inhabited by various cavemen, Cro-Magnon man came to the Dordogne region and left the gift of some of the most awe-inspiring cave paintings ever seen.

Cro-Magnon cave paintings at Lascaux, Perigord Region, France

Other wandering tribes including the Celts, Gauls and even the Greeks, who are credited with founding Marseille, subsequently settled France.

The Romans had conquered all the countries around the Mediterranean Sea as well as England. Under their control cities were founded, roads were built, architecture was introduced, as was the rule of law, the conduct of commerce, and Latin was the language of the day. They were the conquerors who had the most impact on France. In fact, the name **Marsolais** is derived from the Roman "Marcellus," meaning young Marcus.

Pont du Gard - Roman aqueduct in France was used for 400 years to bring water 31 miles from Uzes to Nimes.

MEDIEVAL ENGLAND, FRANCE, AND THE HOLY ROMAN EMPIRE

The Roman Empire began to slowly deteriorate and the void created by its eventual decline and fall was filled by the Franks migrating from what is now Germany. The Romans called the foreign warriors barbarians because they were largely uneducated and rough in their ways. These invasions divided the once great Roman Empire into several smaller kingdoms. Roman written law gave way to German law based on oral traditions. Farming replaced trade and towns that had once thrived through industry were abandoned. In the 8th Century, France was once again invaded---this time by the dreaded Vikings who eventually settled in what is now Normandy. The **Lemieux** are descended from those Vikings who settled the Cotentin Peninsula of Normandy near Cherbourg.

Medieval times, also known as the Middle Ages, the period from 400 to 1500 AD, can be thought of as the time between ancient and modern life in Western Europe. Feudal lords controlled the land and the Christian Church had great power. European populations were small and people often suffered from disease, war and famine. It was during this time that much of Europe as we know it today was formed.

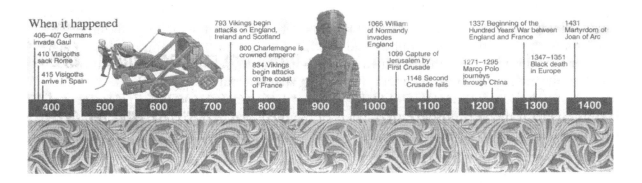

The Holy Roman Empire, a political entity of lands in western and central Europe, was founded by Charlemagne in AD 800 and dissolved by Emperor Francis II in 1806. The extent and strength of the empire largely depended on the military and diplomatic skill of its emperors, both of which fluctuated considerably during the empire's thousand-year lifetime. However, the principal area of the empire was the German states. From the 10th Century, its leaders were German kings who usually sought but did not always receive coronation as emperor by the popes in Rome.

At its peak in the 12th Century, the empire comprised most of the territory of modern-day Germany, Austria, Switzerland, eastern France, Belgium, the Netherlands, western Poland, the Czech Republic and Italy. By the later Middle Ages, however, the emperors' power had become increasingly symbolic, with real legal and administrative power exercised at the territorial and municipal levels. When the last Holy Roman emperor resigned in 1806, the realm had long matched Voltaire's famous description of it as "neither Holy, nor Roman, nor an Empire."

By the 800s Western Europe was in disarray, fragmented and localized. Ruled by a few rich landowners (land barons or lords) who controlled vast estates called manors, they could make local laws and declare themselves king over their districts. Even French kings reigned only 20 to 30 miles outside Paris. Most people worked the land as peasants for the landowner. A manor village was self-sustaining and could grow or manufacture everything it needed for survival. This system of organized agricultural labor and the economic relationship between the lord of a manor and his peasant tenants is called manorialism.

Unlike manorialism, which was an economic/agricultural system, feudalism was a political and military system used by noblemen and aristocrats. This system filled the turbulent void left by the fall of the Roman Empire. The word feudal is from the Latin word "fief," which referred to land given as payment for service or loyalty. Only noblemen and aristocrats took part in feudalism. A king or lord owned and ruled the land. Noble tenants or servants, called vassals, worked and protected their lord's lands and castles. The lord rewarded vassals for outstanding service with gifts of land, money and marriage. A vassal's primary service to his lord was martial, and he swore an oath to protect and remain faithful to his lord. Eventually, it became the vassal's duty to provide his lord with knights. Vassals rewarded knights with gifts of land and they, in turn, became vassals, until the community had banded together for their common good. Each fief or feudal estate was self-contained and self-supporting. Under feudalism, Europe took on its medieval appearance with fortified castles surrounded by moats.

One of the most fascinating aspects of the medieval period is the often romanticized idea of castles and knights. A castle was built by a king or a nobleman and served as a home in times of peace and a fortress in times of war. Peasants in nearby villages relied on the castle for protection against invading armies. Wars were usually fought for profit and power; that is, to win land, castles and towns. Wars were expensive and fought mostly during the summer - few could afford to equip an army year-round. Knighthood was a rich man's game. Chivalry was a code or a set of rules for war and served as a guide for knightly behavior during war but greed and the heat of battle could make a knight forget those rules.

With a lack of central authority, these were violent times. Laying siege to a town or castle was one of the best ways to capture it. Catapults and archers equipped with long bows were effective in a siege. Surrounding a castle cut off supplies, while a barrage of heavy rocks, flaming arrows and battering rams stormed the walls and gates.

Hunting was generally a sport of kings and noblemen. In many lands it was against the law for anyone but a king to hunt in parks or forests. Poachers were people who broke that law and, if caught, paid with their lives. Hunting was a way to practice riding and weaponry but it also put food on the table. Dogs, hawks and falcons were trained to help in the hunt. Wild boars and fallow deer provided the best sport but roe deer, badgers and wildcats were also hunted.

During the medieval period, more than 90 percent of the European people lived on and worked the land in an entrenched class system. The life of a peasant was one of extreme poverty. Known as serfs, peasants were little more than slaves. They did not own anything; they worked the land for their lord and gave him most of what they grew. They were oppressed by their lords for taxes to pay for wars, as well as by roaming tribes and warlords; they were robbed of money, food and animals. They could not marry or move away without permission. When an estate changed ownership, serfs were sold or given away as part of the property. Serfdom was inherited through the mother's line. The only way to gain freedom was to marry a free person or somehow save enough money to buy land. The Church taught peasants that they should not complain about their lives and accept that this was they way things should be. Their reward would come in the next life.

A Medieval Castle: The Bastion of Feudal Lords
This view of the medieval fortress at Carcassonne in southern France dramatically illustrates the kind of security that its owner could offer to those who were his vassals. And it likewise suggests how defiant that same owner and his followers could be in the face of those who claimed authority over them.

Medieval medical knowledge was very limited and living conditions were generally dirty and overcrowded. Disease, famine and war took their toll and the average life span was about 30 years. When the Bubonic Plague (or Black Death) swept through Europe between 1347 and 1351, it killed about one-third of the European population. It was transmitted by the fleas of infected rats. Early signs of infection were black boils. Fever, thirst, delirium and death soon followed. In winter the disease seemed to disappear, but only because fleas--which carried it from person to person--were dormant then. Each spring, the Plague attacked again. Smaller outbreaks continued, not just for years, but for centuries, and did not disappear until the 1600s. Medieval society never recovered from the results of the Plague. So many people had died that there were serious labor shortages. This led workers to demand higher wages, but landlords refused those demands. By the end of the 1300s, peasant revolts broke out.

The Plague
This painting captures the terror inflicted on the population of a city by the Black Death. Even while shrouding the dead for burial, people were suddenly struck down, as is the man shown falling to the ground. Neither the prayers of the clergy nor the pleas of the saints, represented by St. Sebastian, could help.

Many wars fought during the Middle Ages were in the name of religion. Christians brought Holy Wars upon the Muslims over control of the Holy Land. Pope Urban called for the Crusades in an attempt to unify the Christian West and stop the violence in Europe. Christians, knights and kings, thought they could secure their place in heaven by helping to fight these Holy Wars. There were eight major Crusades, beginning in 1095 and lasting for almost 200 years.

Christian missionaries traveled across Europe and converted many non-Christians to Christianity. The Church took on a vital role in the lives of peasants, lords and kings. It also helped to reintroduce Roman ideas of law and government and became a unifying element throughout Europe. Church leaders began to collect taxes and establish courts of law. Cathedrals and monasteries were more than places to worship; they also served as hospitals, schools and inns. It was the Church that kept art and education alive during this period.

Medieval technology brought improved farm equipment. The windmill, water wheel, better plows and crop rotation brought an improvement in agriculture. With an increase in food production, there was an increase in the population. Agricultural changes caused a relaxation of the feudal system. Labor services, which the peasants performed in return for their holdings, were giving way to paid labor and rent. The French lords needed money if they were to go on crusade. The feudal system was slackening.

Medieval Farming
From the beginning of the 11ᵗʰ Century forests were cleared, marshland drained and the countryside became a checkerboard of fields and hedgerows. Farming methods improved and were a cooperative effort. Peasants combined their labor, their draft animals and their equipment to till the manor fields. The heavy moldboard plow was a major technological advance of the Middle Ages, efficient in cutting through and turning heavy soil. Producing sufficient yields to feed both people and livestock was a major problem.

By the end of the 13ᵗʰ Century, France was a country of small towns and local capitals. Towns flourished, as they could now import more food from rural areas. Paris and Rouen on the Seine River had even more advantages as they were ports and distribution centers. The people who went to live in these towns were mainly artisans and traders.

A new class of society was forming as people became inhabitants of the towns. They were called burghers, the *bourgeois*, to distinguish them from the residents of the old burgs who were called *castellani,* castle-dwellers.

The retailers and craftsmen who handled the same products formed guilds and many of them became wealthy merchants. Many towns grew into rich cultural centers. The increased cash in circulation due to trade brought a boom to city life, paying for churches, docks, marketplaces, roads, bridges, hospitals and, shortly, the first universities. The chief towns in France at the time were Paris and Rouen.

These new towns offered many new opportunities for work and profit, attracting craftsmen from nearby villages: free peasants discouraged with farming, unfree serfs escaping economic bondage, small traders and local peddlers, as well as drifters and shady characters from all over Europe. This trend toward urban life and commercialism created a social revolution fatal to feudalism---it was called a "renaissance" (rebirth) or "the age of enlightenment."

But the 14th Century was a period of disaster. The larger population became a great strain on the resources of the land, famines became more frequent and, by the middle of the century, the Black Plague ravaged the country. It is estimated that between 1350 and 1450 France lost between a third and a half of her population. Under feudalism, the land was divided too many ways, among too many lords to be efficient. The primitive economic system made too many demands for the lords who inherited them and their ambitions were too great. Even the Church had two, sometimes three Popes, further complicating the lives of an already overburdened population. Also, civil revolts compounded by wars with England increased the devastation.

The Hundred Years' War can be considered a prolonged attempt of the English kings and the Anglo-Norman dukes to repossess their homeland, Normandy. During this era, the kings of England, who were Norman feudal lords, resented French royal infringement on their jurisdiction. In 1328, Edward III of England claimed the French throne on the basis of inheritance and in 1340 declared himself King of France. These conflicts resembled civil war until 1429, when the French, led by Joan of Arc, stopped the English at Orleans.

THE LATE MIDDLE AGES, 1300–1500

THE HUNDRED YEARS' WAR

Joan of Arc, *Jehanne, La Pucelle* (Joan, the Maid) as she called herself, hearing the voices of Michael, the Archangel, St. Catherine and St. Margaret, left her home in Domremy in 1427 at the age of fifteen. She secured an interview with Charles VII, the Valois King, and convinced him that she would see him anointed King of France at Reims. Jehanne raised a siege, won a battle at Orleans and helped Charles VII, the *Dauphin*, march through his own domain from the Loire into Champagne and had him crowned at Reims. She was captured and turned over to the English Bishop Cauchon at Rouen, the most English of Norman cities, where she was tried as a witch, convicted and on May 30, 1431, burned at the stake in the Old Market Place in Rouen. Charles VII made no attempt to save her. The English wanted her used as an example to discourage French uprisings and the Church wanted her used as an example to discourage a split in the Church. It took twenty more years to drive the English out of France. When Cherbourg fell in 1450, the Hundred Years' War ended. Charles VII eventually cleared her name, she was canonized a saint in 1920 and she remains a symbol of France.

Charles VII proved to be a good administrator, creating a standing army supported by regular taxes and reconstituting the Parlement of Paris. In 1446, toward the end of the conflict, Charles VII ordered a tabulation of all the parishes and a listing of all inhabitants. This census, called a Hearth Tax, listed the names and surnames of all heads of families. These changes marked the end of the feudal system and created a more centralized administration.

As France began to normalize and prosper again, it also experienced a cultural flowering, centered primarily in Paris and the royal court. The French language reappeared and spread throughout the land because it was the language of the King. A majority of the French people were now able to understand each other. The printing press, established in Paris and Lyons during the 1470s, accelerated change by getting printed material to the common people. By the mid-1500s, French became the official, administrative and literary language of all France as well as the language of medicine, science and history. But France was not just a geographical expression---there was now a sense of nationalism.

In addition to more war, assassination, conspiracy, and rebellion, there were years of major harvest failures. An increase in wheat prices impacted the whole pattern of economic and social life causing the so-called depression of the 17th Century from approximately 1620-1640. This seems to have resulted due to a reduction in the quantity of precious metal coming from America as well as by a climatic change in which both the winters and summers became colder. From 1619 to 1632, the Black Plague returned in full force and, from 1647 to 1651, there were catastrophic crop failures. The combination of poverty, hunger and fear, added to the constantly increasing taxes to pay for more royal wars, resulted in more rebellions.

The acquisition of colonies, encouraged by Minister of Finance Colbert and Cardinal Richelieu, meant that France possessed vast territories in North America as well as important trading opportunities in Africa, India, and colonies in the West Indies. The colonial trade was extremely profitable and, as merchant ships improved, ports such as Bordeaux, Nantes, Rouen, Honfleur and Dieppe now had a promising future.

Monument to Joan of Arc, Paris

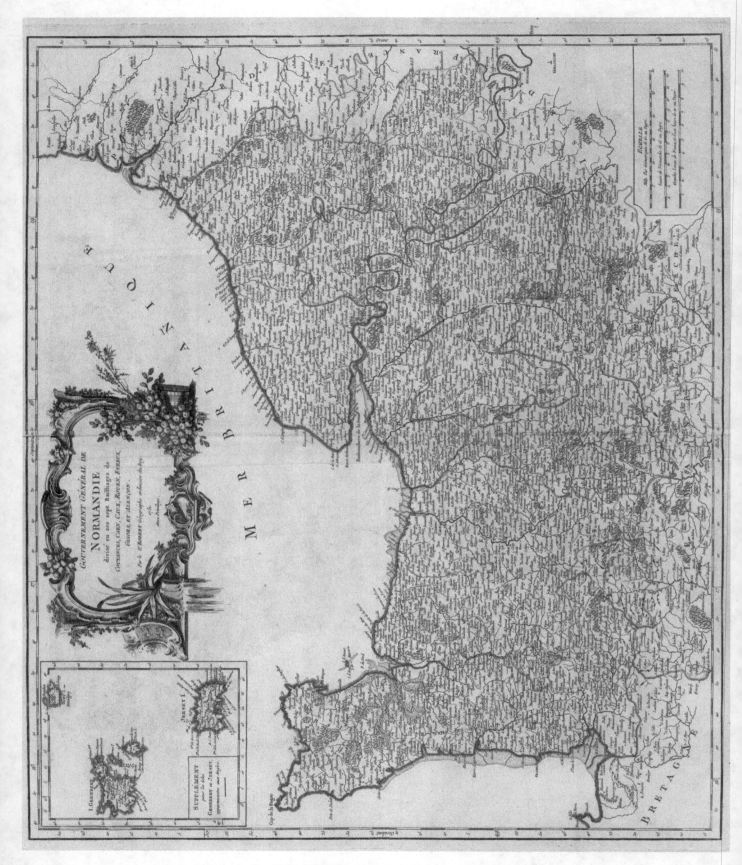

Normandie, 1751, by Gilles Robert de Vaugondy 1688 - 1766;
and Didier Robert de Vaugondy, 1723 – 1786, father and son,
cartographers to the King, from an atlas

12

II

Normandy

$\mathcal{N}$ormandy is an especially beautiful province. Monet, one of the most famous and talented artists in history, painted throughout Europe, but he made Normandy his home and it was his greatest love. His paintings of Normandy capture the power of the rugged cliffs, a mild summer day at the beach at Deauville, the perfect Gothic architecture of Rouen's Notre Dame Cathedral, poplars along the Epte, fields of poppies, mornings on the Seine and the gardens of his own design.

The open Norman countryside is both practical and elegant. Apple orchards are more than a cash crop---the apple trees in bloom both adorn and symbolize Normandy. The homes range from great formal chateaux, to rustic timbered homes with thatched roofs of the Anglo-Norman influence. Even the oldest homes are still in use. The rolling hills at Les Andelys still have the ruins of Richard the Lionheart's medieval castle, Château Gaillard, to explore. The religious monument of Mont St-Michel is unforgettable, as are the monuments for those who died on the Normandy beaches in World War II.

Normandy's cool, rainy climate and soil are not good for growing grapes, but are perfect for apple orchards. Therefore, the traditional drink of the Normans is not wine, but cider. This is also distilled into a brandy called *Calvados*. The farmland is rich and fertile, dotted with Norman dairy cows grazing in lush pastures thinking buttery thoughts. With so much of the province running along the Northern coast, seafood is a major staple of the Norman diet. The salt marshes where sheep graze, give their lamb dishes a distinctive flavor. All this abundance results in the freshest Norman dishes; meats, seafood, fruits and vegetables, all made most often with rich cream, butter and cheeses, such as the local Camembert---served with a glass of *cidre brut*. Dessert is apple tart with *crème fraische*. The meal ends with a glass of *Calvados*---everyone makes their own. Normandy is a delicious experience for the eye as well as the palate.

One of the Vikings' permanent settlements was Normandy---named for the Normans. Attempting to bring peace to the area, in 911 A.D. King Charles of France gave large feudal estates around the mouth of the Seine to the Viking leader, Rollo the Marcher. This earned the King the name of "Charles the Simple." Vikings also settled the Cotentin peninsula surrounding the city of Cherbourg. The **Lemieux** were Vikings, coming to Normandy at the time of the Danish and Norwegian invasions, and settling on the Cotentin Peninsula. Cotentin means "country of Coutances"---slang for Constantinus.

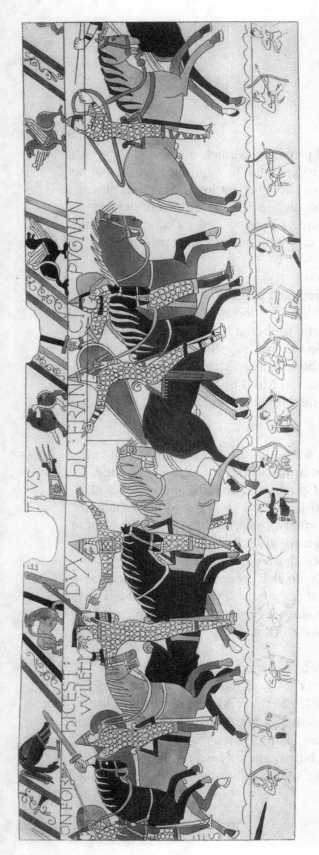

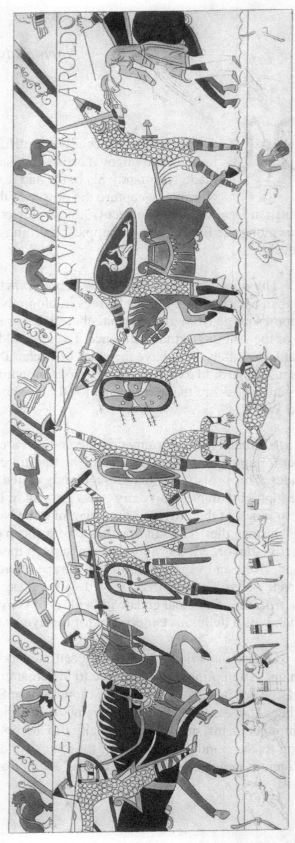

The Bayeux Tapestry: Here, Duke William refutes the rumor of his death by raising his visor. He encourages his men, who begin to inflict grievous losses on Harold's army. William brought from France infantry, cavalry and archers to fight at the Battle of Hastings.

The blend of Roman, Germanic, Viking and Christian cultures resulted in what became the "style" of the Norman province. Each province had its own components of nationalities, each blending and moderating the legal and popular religious systems with a trend toward unity and a common "customary" culture.

Under the old Frankish system there had been a static adherence to tradition. Subsistence farming, the deterioration of trade and currency and the dangers and difficulty of travel divided the West into minor worlds. Borders, closed to outsiders, restricted the exchange of ideas.

For all the damage and upheaval caused by the Norman invasions, they brought a constructive revolution to a decaying Frankish system. Normans were organizers as well as conquerors and the duchy of Normandy became the most highly organized and militarily efficient state in Europe. Trial by jury was originated by the Franks but developed by the Normans. The commerce that the Viking ships developed covered the western European seaboard, becoming more important than the Mediterranean. Normans played a leading role in restoring order to the shattered political structure, adding a genius for trade. Viking commerce headed west, covering the western European seaboard, the Baltic Sea and the Atlantic to the New World.

The Battle of Hastings, one of the battles that changed the medieval world, was fought in 1066 for the throne of England because King Edward the Confessor died childless and was undecided as to whom he wanted to succeed him: Harold, his brother-in-law, or William, Duke of Normandy, his illegitimate nephew. At Edward's death, Harold assumed the throne and William led an invading army from Normandy to Hasting to fight for his right to be king. Harold was killed in battle and "William the Bastard" became "William the Conqueror" and assumed the English crown. The Norman Conquest is important in European history because it wiped out Saxon rule and introduced the feudal system, changing the course of England forever. From this point the cultures of England and Norman France would be interchangeable until the end of the Hundred Years War. For example, Richard the Lionheart, son of the English king, Henry II, and French queen, Eleanor of Aquitaine, was king of England from 1189 until 1199 and was feudal lord of Normandy, Aquitaine and Poitou regions of France.

The Bayeux Tapestry, the embroidered 231 foot-long story of the Battle of Hastings, is displayed at the Museum of Queen Matilda, Bayeux, Normandy. Legend says that it was made by William's wife, Matilda, to tell the story of his conquest but Odo, William's half-brother and Bishop of Bayeux, is depicted in the tapestry and may have commissioned it.

An even more remarkable monument is the Domesday Book which testifies to the Norman genius for administration. Compiled (1085-86) by order of William the Conqueror, it was a complete survey of the land, its holdings, tenures and services, wealth, population, animals, resources and taxable capacity. Some historians have called the Domesday Book the greatest record of medieval Europe. The English hated the Domesday Book, Norman taxation and harsh Norman rule.

Chateau de Beaumesnil

Sheep grazing in salt marsh near Mont-St-Michel

Siméon Manor

Norman cows grazing under apple trees in bloom,
thinking buttery thoughts

ROUEN.

18

III

Rouen

Rouen is a beautiful, historic, yet modern city and plays an important role in the history of the Lemieux and Marsolet families. The first Celtic settlement was called Ratumakos which meant a "place of exchange." The Romans came in 57 BC, changing the name to Rotomagus. In the 8ᵗʰ Century when the Vikings came to stay, Duke Rollo and his men made Rouen their capital and converted to Christianity. Thanks to the extraordinary role of Frenchwomen as wives, within a few decades the Normans were as "French" as everyone else.

The Norman capital's historic civic pride breathes from every stone, every timber-frame lovingly restored or reconstructed after the fierce bombing raids of WWII. After all, this is the ancient center of Normandy's thriving textile and faience industries and the place of Joan of Arc's martyrdom---a symbol of national resistance to tyranny.

Hugging a loop in the Seine, the left bank is a bustling modern port which has always prospered through world-wide trade, bringing exotic products and wealth to the city. But it was also open to the accompanying health risks. The Black Plague ravaged Rouen from 1348-1394 and devastated the population again in 1621. The city was subjected to the Religious Wars, sacked by the Calvinists and besieged for six months by Royal Troops.

The right bank is the charming medieval and renaissance center around the Notre Dame Cathedral. Monet's many impressionistic light studies of its façade made this one of France's most famous cathedrals. Its lantern tower is called the Butter Tower because it was financed by people who paid a fee to be able to eat butter during Lent.

The 17ᵗʰ Century saw spectacular development here. Removed from the main path of invasion and spared by wars, Rouen grew rapidly with new industries creating new jobs. From the late 1500s through the mid-1600s, this was the town where the Marsolets and the Lemieux, like other bourgeois, came to make their fortune.

The Lemieux were related by marriage to the LeMaistre family who were traditionally godparents to the Marsolets; the activities of the two families were intertwined. They knew each other socially, lived in the same neighborhoods and were members of the same parishes. It is still possible to visit most of the neighborhoods where the families lived and the churches where they were baptized and married. Rouen was an important waypoint for both families before they made their way to the New World and made their mark on another continent with a completely different culture.

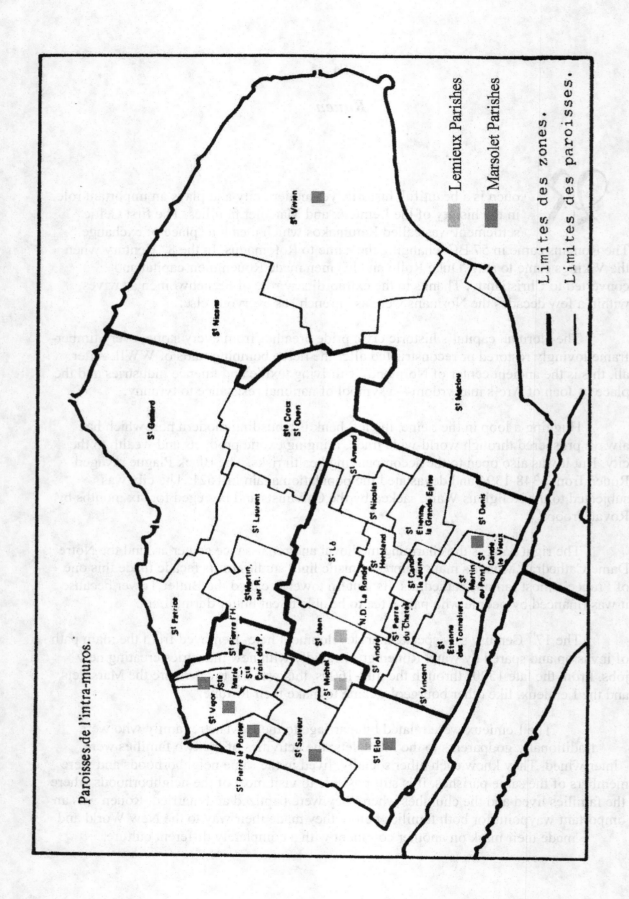

Paroisses de l'intra-muros.

Limites des zones.

Limites des paroisses.

Lemieux Parishes

Marsolet Parishes

St Vivien

St Nicaise

St Godard

Ste Croix
St Ouen

St Maclou

St Amand

St Nicolas

St Laurent

St
Etienne
la Grande Eglise

St
Herbland

St Lô

St Denis

St
Candé
le Vieux

St Martin
au Pont

St
Candé
le Jeune

St Martin,
sur R.

N.D. La Ronde

St Pierre
du Châtel

St
Etienne
des Tonneliers

St Patrice

St Pierre l'H.

Ste
Croix des P.

Ste
Marie

St Jean

St André

St Vincent

St Vigor

St Michel

St Pierre le Portier

St Sauveur

St Eloi

20

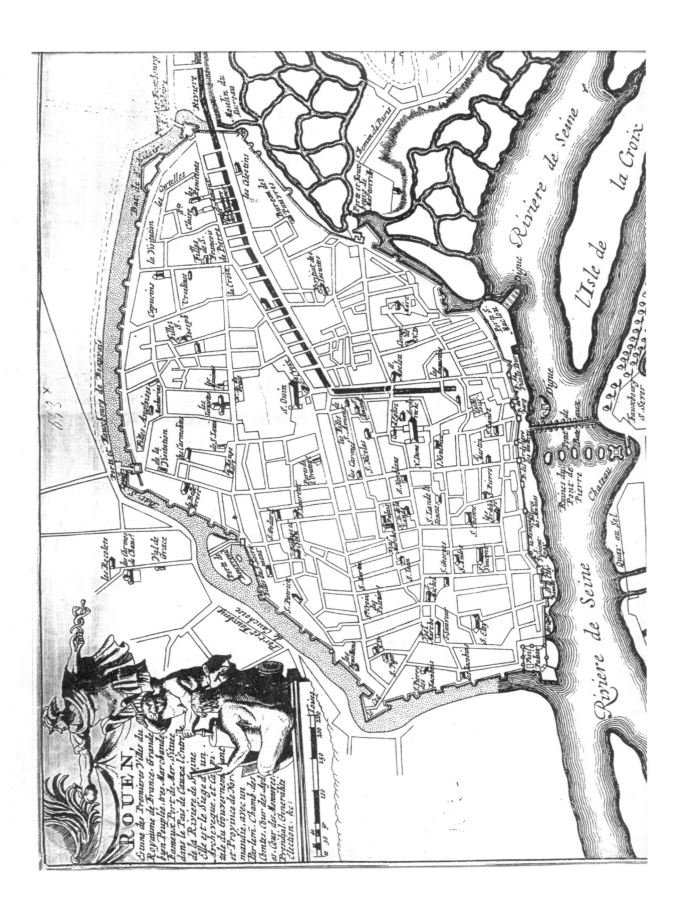

21

Le Gros Horloge, Rouen

The cathedral of Rouen

Saint-Pierre, Canteloup, Normandie, France

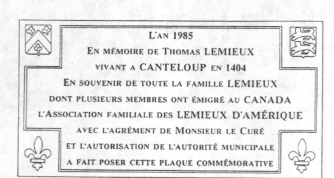

L'AN 1985
EN MÉMOIRE DE THOMAS LEMIEUX
VIVANT A CANTELOUP EN 1404
EN SOUVENIR DE TOUTE LA FAMILLE LEMIEUX
DONT PLUSIEURS MEMBRES ONT ÉMIGRÉ AU CANADA
L'ASSOCIATION FAMILIALE DES LEMIEUX D'AMÉRIQUE
AVEC L'AGRÉMENT DE MONSIEUR LE CURÉ
ET L'AUTORISATION DE L'AUTORITÉ MUNICIPALE
A FAIT POSER CETTE PLAQUE COMMÉMORATIVE

THE YEAR 1985
IN MEMORY OF THOMAS LEMIEUX
LIVING AT CANTELOUP IN 1404
IN REMEMBERING ALL THE LEMIEUX FAMILY
WHOSE SEVERAL MEMBERS EMIGRATED TO CANADA
THE FAMILY ASSOCIATION OF LEMIEUX OF AMERICA
WITH THE APPROVAL OF MONSIEUR CURÉ
AND THE AUTHORIZATION OF THE MUNICIPAL AUTHORITY
TO PLACE THIS COMMEMORATIVE PLAQUE

IV

Lemieux in France

The Lemieux lived in Canteloup near Cherbourg on the Cotentin peninsula of Normandy. The oldest documents show the Lemieux lands were located near the small village of Canteloup---Chante/loup---"the place where the wolf sings." Near Canteloup is a hamlet called Hameau es Mieux (Hamlet of the Lemieux) and a farm called *La Mieuserie*. The Lemieux lands came under "la Commanderie de Valcanville" which was controlled by the noble and religious order of St. John of Jerusalem, the Jerusalem Templars, whose members were knights and monks.

La Mieuserie, Canteloup

The Hameau es Mieux has carried the name from ancient times. The current houses date back to the beginning of the 18th Century. Some architectural elements, such as beveled doorjambs, are even older. This hamlet is on the road from Canteloup to Valcanville and consists of a dozen houses. The Lemieux lived on these lands in the Hameau des Mieux until 1876. The last to live here was Marie Lemieux, born in 1797, who lived to be seventy-nine years old.

25

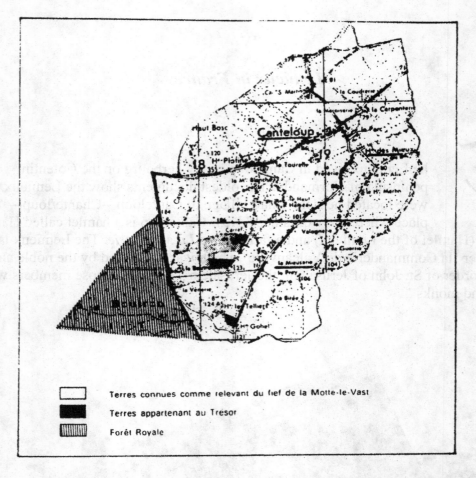

Terres connues comme relevant du fief de la Motte-le-Vast

Terres appartenant au Tresor

Forêt Royale

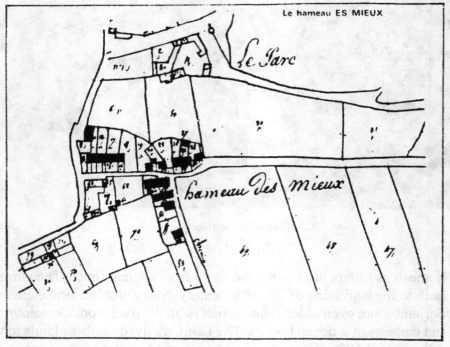

Le hameau ES MIEUX

Le Parc

hameau des mieux

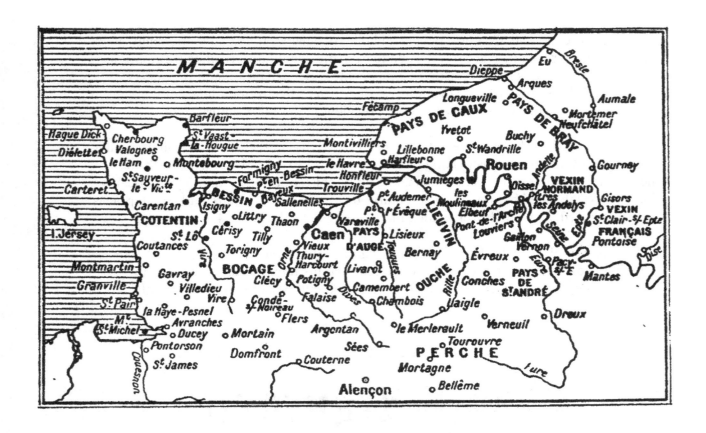

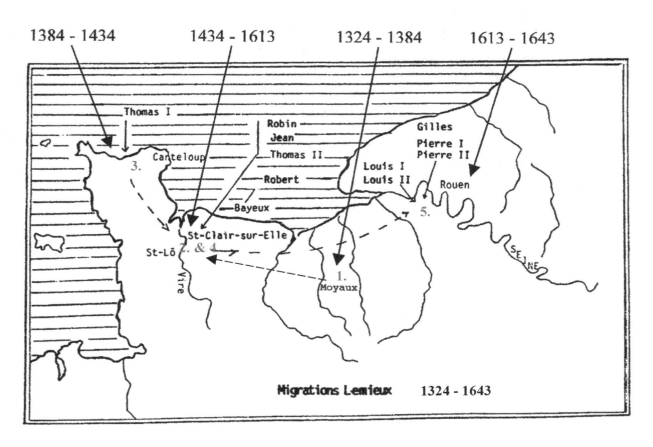

1384 - 1434   1434 - 1613   1324 - 1384   1613 - 1643

Thomas I

Robin
Jean

Gilles
Pierre I
Pierre II

Thomas II

Louis I
Louis II

Rouen

Canteloup

3.

Robert

Bayeux

5.

St-Clair-sur-Elle

St-Lô

2. & 4

1.
Moyaux

Vire

SEINE

Migrations Lemieux   1324 - 1643

27

Before the 10th Century, people had only one name. Eventually, too many people had the same first name and there needed to be some way to differentiate them. Some attached their father's name (O'Brien), a nickname (Short), a profession (Cooper) or a location (Hill). Some lords began adding to their names that of their lands or domains as a surname, a practice which became more prevalent in the 11th Century.

It would not be possible to trace our lineage without the use of surnames. Under the reign of Philippe-Auguste, King of France from 1180 – 1223, surnames became hereditary but were still unreliable since no civil register of births, marriages or deaths had been established before the 15th Century. In 1406 a synod required all parish priests to register births, to which were added marriages and deaths in 1464.

Not until 1539 did King François I legally enforce these registrations with the Ordinance of Viller-Cotterêts. Every child received his father's surname for birth, marriage and death registrations which were required to be in French in place of Latin.

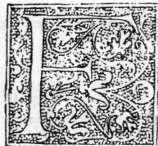

Première page des Ordonnances de Villers-Cotterets (1539) par lesquelles fut prescrit l'emploi exclusif du français au lieu du latin dans les actes judiciaires.

C'est à partir de cette ordonnance que les noms de famille furent ajoutés aux prénoms sur les actes de baptême, de mariage et de sépulture.

Rôle de Moyaux.

Despite the lack of registers, it has been possible to trace our lineage back beyond 1406, thanks to old tax rolls and legal acts. At Moyaux, near Lisieux, a first Lemieux (Jehan, born circa 1324, deceased before 1398) was listed as father of Guillaume (born circa 1354, deceased before 1446). Guillaume would become the father of Thomas 1, born circa 1384 in St-Clair-sur-Elle, deceased after 1434 in Canteloup, and who is mentioned in a 1404 legal act as tenant of a piece of land in Canteloup.

Though no lineage can be established with any certainty further back, two names appear in documents in 1295 and 1297, Pierre Le Mies and Gobert Limies, who may be part of our ancestry, given the numerous variations found in the surnames at the time.

If we accept the theory of our name coming from a location, as with Lemieux and the Mieux Hamlet, we find: Henri de Mieux, Squire, Sieur of the Hamlet, Guard of the Channel of his Majesty, Counselor of the King, who on 16 July 1700, adopted a coat of arms which read: "Of azure, a chevron of gold, accompanied by three trefoils of the same, two on top and one at the point." This Mieux was Lieutenant General of the Provost of Upper and Lower Normandy. As mentioned, when people began using last names, lords frequently took the name of their feudal estate. This could have also applied to the vassals who farmed the land generation after generation such as our ancestors.

In the days of Thomas Lemieux, Canteloup was part of a "knightery," land granted to Knights Templar to support their crusades in the Middle East, particularly the Holy Land, in the 12th Century. These knights were originally soldiers who went on to become monks. The Order of the Temple, founded in 1099 by Hugues de Payns, became active in banking and money exchange.

A knight exercised full judiciary powers over his "knightery," produced his own currency, had exclusive operation of mills and also exclusive hunting rights over his domain. His feudal tenants had to erect an eight-pointed cross on their houses, pay an annual rent and perform military service at their lord's request.

Philippe le Bel, King of France, maintained good relations with the Templars from 1285 to 1304. But over the years he accumulated considerable debt with the Order, which had become a financial multinational. King Philippe dissolved the Order, seized all its holdings and brought it to court.

In Valcanville, on October 13, 1307, the King's officers arrested Jean Vassal, monk of the Order and parish priest of Valcanville. Pope Clément V officially dissolved the Order in 1312. The confiscated properties were devolved to another group of soldier/monks, the Hospitalier Knights of Saint-Jean de Jérusalem. One of the "knighteries" of this group was located on the land cultivated in 1404 by our ancestor, Thomas Lemieux.

In addition to farming feudal lands, the Lemieux were traditionally "*tonneliers*," or barrel-makers. At that time, Canteloup was a large area of oak forests, supplying the wood for barrels, as well as extensive apple orchards for producing cider brandy, *Calvados*, to sell in the barrels. They also probably produced a beverage called hydromel which is a drink made of fermented honey and water. The name, Le Mieux, may have evolved from Le Miel--honey--used in this context.

Research of the origins of the name Lemieux goes back into the 13th and 14th Century. In medieval French it was common to use the expression "*bailler es mielz*" (leasing of honey) the land of royal domain. The modern term, "*louer au mieux*" (lease of the best), means "to offer the most." Possibly our ancestors had given the best offer in rental transactions.

During the Hundred Years' War, this horrendously unstable time, families attempted to make a life. Our steady genealogical line begins with Thomas Lemieux (1384-1435) who had land in Canteloup in 1404 and must have been about 20 years old at that time.

As decreed by Charles VII, the Cotentin Peninsula was to be evacuated to deny the invading English anything of value for armament or forage. Thomas had retreated with other inhabitants of North Cotentin before 1404 and again between 1434 and 1450 until the final French victory at Formigny. Relocating to St-Clair-sur-Elle, near St-Lo, the place of his birth, it isn't known exactly where Thomas and his family lived. They not only survived the war, the Plague and the famine but he also sired our line through his three sons: Robin, **Geoffroy** and Colin who were born during his time at Saint-Clair. It is understandable that he decided to return to his lands in Canteloup. After so many years of chaos, it must have felt like a promise of stability. Robin, Geoffroy and Colin, having never known or seen Canteloup, decided to stay behind and establish themselves at Saint-Clair because their roots and many attachments were centered there.

Thomas's return to Canteloup during the truce of 1434 was made during a very dangerous time. English soldiers and sailors, when not soldiering, lived off the land by pillaging, stealing and raping. Wandering in small groups, they tried to survive until a battle was imminent. The Normans, furious over the soldiers' behavior, never missed an opportunity to attack them. Each village placed a guard in the belfry of the church to warn of their approach. These wandering soldiers were considered destructive beasts and were treated as such. When Charles VII managed to pay his soldiers, it brought an end to the pillaging and gave him the support of the Norman people. Thomas Lemieux again made it through the turmoil because according to the records of the "knightery" he still held property in Canteloup in 1434 at which time he must have been about 50 years old.

In 1379 Charles V charged a one-time-only tax of one franc for each hearth called "rolles des fouages." In 1388 Charles VI augmented the tax under the same name for each fireplace, house or family, and his successor, Charles VII, perpetuated the tax to list the head of each household. Unfortunately, as no wives were named, we will never know the names of the mothers from this era. From the tax roll at Saint-Clair-sur-Elle, we know there were only three Lemieux living there, and in 1421, there was only one under Thomas Lemieux, therefore, Robin, Geoffroy and Colin would have to be the sons of Thomas of Canteloup.

After the Hundred Years' War, Thomas, the most documented ancestor of all the Lemieux, clearly returned to the Canteloup area, as indicated by records, and was there from 1384 to 1446. The Hearth Tax of 1446-1447 for Saint-Clair indicates the Lemieux of our line inhabited the region from 1409 until 1588, about a century and a half before establishing themselves at Rouen. They had, during the years of relative calm, prospered and given birth to new generations.

Pierre
Le Mies
Tax List: 1295

Gobert
Limies
Tax List: 1297
Normandie, FRANCE

Jean
Lemioux
b: Abt. 1324 in Moyaux canton
de Lisieux, Normandie,
FRANCE
d: Bef. 1398

Guillaume
Lemioux
b: Abt. 1354 in Moyaux canton
de Lisieux
d: Bef. 1446

Thomas
Le Mioux
b: Abt. 1384 in St-Clair-sur-Elle,
Normandie, FRANCE
d: Aft. 1434 in Canteloup,
Normandie, FRANCE
Witness: 1404
Cantaloup, Normandie,
FRANCE

Geoffroy
Le Mioux
Witness: 1467
St-Clair-sur-Elle, Normandie,
FRANCE

Jehan "l'aine" : the
elder
b: Abt. 1440 in St-Clair-sur-Elle,
Normandie, FRANCE
o: (aine in 1494)

Cont. p. 2

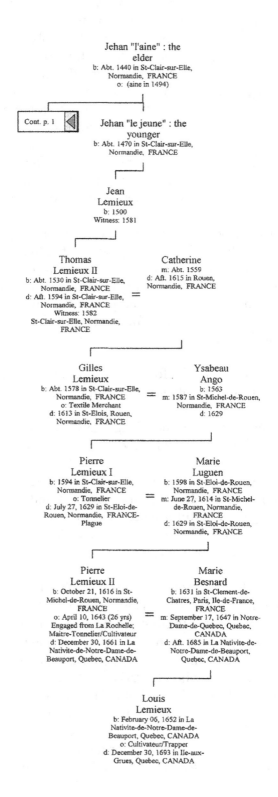

Jehan "l'aine" : the elder
b: Abt. 1440 in St-Clair-sur-Elle, Normandie, FRANCE
o: (aine in 1494)

Cont. p. 1

Jehan "le jeune" : the younger
b: Abt. 1470 in St-Clair-sur-Elle, Normandie, FRANCE

Jean Lemieux
b: 1500
Witness: 1581

Thomas Lemieux II
b: Abt. 1530 in St-Clair-sur-Elle, Normandie, FRANCE
d: Aft. 1594 in St-Clair-sur-Elle, Normandie, FRANCE
Witness: 1582 St-Clair-sur-Elle, Normandie, FRANCE
=

Catherine
m: Abt. 1559
d: Aft. 1615 in Rouen, Normandie, FRANCE

Gilles Lemieux
b: Abt. 1578 in St-Clair-sur-Elle, Normandie, FRANCE
o: Textile Merchant
d: 1613 in St-Elois, Rouen, Normandie, FRANCE
=

Ysabeau Ango
b: 1563
m: 1587 in St-Michel-de-Rouen, Normandie, FRANCE
d: 1629

Pierre Lemieux I
b: 1594 in St-Clair-sur-Elle, Normandie, FRANCE
o: Tonnelier
d: July 27, 1629 in St-Eloi-de-Rouen, Normandie, FRANCE-Plague
=

Marie Luguen
b: 1598 in St-Eloi-de-Rouen, Normandie, FRANCE
m: June 27, 1614 in St-Michel-de-Rouen, Normandie, FRANCE
d: 1629 in St-Eloi-de-Rouen, Normandie, FRANCE

Pierre Lemieux II
b: October 21, 1616 in St-Michel-de-Rouen, Normandie, FRANCE
o: April 10, 1643 (26 yrs) Engaged from La Rochelle; Maitre-Tonnelier/Cultivateur
d: December 30, 1661 in La Nativite-de-Notre-Dame-de-Beauport, Quebec, CANADA
=

Marie Besnard
b: 1631 in St-Clement-de-Chatres, Paris, Ile-de-France, FRANCE
m: September 17, 1647 in Notre-Dame-de-Quebec, Quebec, CANADA
d: Aft. 1685 in La Nativite-de-Notre-Dame-de-Beauport, Quebec, CANADA

Louis Lemieux
b: February 06, 1652 in La Nativite-de-Notre-Dame-de-Beauport, Quebec, CANADA
o: Cultivateur/Trapper
d: December 30, 1693 in Ile-aux-Grues, Quebec, CANADA

Selling Indulgences

Following the Hundred Year's War the Norman Church needed physical reconstruction and spiritual revival. A provincial Council was convened to address popular superstitions and practices, but more importantly, problems with the clergy. The Council drew attention to the fact that too many priests lived in adultery; many used the offer of masses as payment of goods, and the power of excommunication to force payment of tithes and other dues. There was a serious lack of preparation of candidates for the priesthood. It was not surprising that people showed a lack of respect for the clergy, and contested its authority. The Protestant Reform could not have come at a better time.

Reform had already been called for in the 1400s in England by John Wycliffe and in Bohemia by John Huss. In 1517 Martin Luther posted his proposals on the door of the Church of Wittenberg. His purpose was to generate an academic debate but, due to the advent of printing, his proposals quickly spread throughout Europe. They were used to consolidate power, and to free craftsmen and peasants from religious oppression. The term "Protestant work ethic" comes from the fact that Protestants could work on Sunday and Catholics were forbidden.

Jean Calvin introduced the Reform in France and the questionable behavior of the clergy and a propensity of the people for criticism and contention made the new ideas quite appealing. Soon, half the nobility had embraced the Reform, including, Prince Antoine de Bourbon, father of the future King Henri IV. But King François I felt this wave of conversions threatened his authority as well as state security.

After some executions in 1523, François I authorized open war against the Calvinists (Huguenots) in 1545. Repression intensified under Henri II and his wife, Catherine de Médici. Again, the Reform served as a vehicle for political ambitions, including those of the Dukes de Condé and de Guise. With the nobility divided, the scene was set for political carnage across Europe.

Between 1554 and 1591, many Lemieux became Protestant, and inevitably became involved in the Religious Wars. The area around St-Lo and St-Clair served as the center of Protestantism due to its proximity to the coast of England and the Norman islands of Jersey and Guernsey where people could find quick refuge when things went badly. During this period the country was crisscrossed and devastated by armies of both sides. In 1572, the Protestants, invited to Paris for the wedding of Henry of Navarre, a Huguenot, and Marguerite de Valois, Catholic daughter of Catherine de Médici, were assassinated on St-Barthelemy's Day. At Rouen, a massacre killed 500.

In January 1572, the Edict of Saint-Germain guaranteed the freedom of Protestants, bringing a truce, but forbade access for Protestants to any public office or to

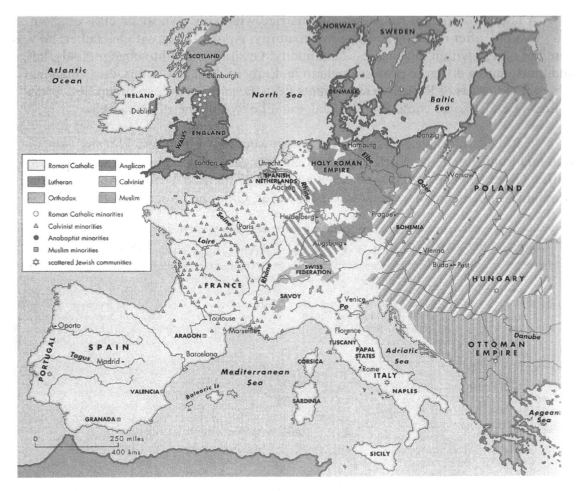

Reformation, circa 1560

certain professions. Under the pressure and spreading terror, a number of Protestants abjured and returned to the Catholic Church. Among those listed was Claude Le Myeux of Saint-Clair. It was important to the Lemieux because it allowed them to become masters in certain careers. Royal troops reoccupied the Cotentin; their pillaging, in addition to the Plague from 1575 to 1598, devastated the population.

In April 1598, Henry IV introduced religious freedom to Protestants with the Edict of Nantes in an effort to end the conflicts. The Protestant community became quite influential in Rouen with about 7,500 Calvinists/Huguenots. They were better educated and more cosmopolitan as they shared the same faith as the English, Dutch, Germans Swedes and others, which also fostered international business connections.

Rouen was a supermarket for all of Upper Normandy. In addition to all the tradesmen and craftsmen, the textile industry alone involved more than a quarter of the population. It also supported manufacturing and export industries in lace, embroidery, tapestry, clothing, spinning, weaving, and more. The Lemieux were involved in the haberdasher-draper field. As a major port city, the outer harbor of Paris, international traders of every field were abundant.

A bourgeois man of Rouen usually married within his own social class at about 25 or 26 years old, after reaching professional maturity. Apprenticing with his father, he was assured of access within his business community. Or, if he wished to change fields, he could marry into a different professional circle. Early in the 17th Century more than half the household heads of Rouen were migrants from the surrounding communities. Gilles and Louis Lemieux had come from St-Clair-sur-Elle to seek their fortunes also.

In Rouen, marriages outside of the parish were few in number. Thomas's sons, **Gilles** and Louis Lemieux married the most Norman and prosperous of Protestant families. Gilles became a textile merchant and in 1587 married Ysabeau Ango, daughter of Romain Ango, an architect and mason. However, Gilles and Ysabeau's first child,

Françoise, born October 4, 1588, was baptized in the Catholic Church of St-Michel-de-Rouen on October 11. Later, on January 16, 1595, Louis married Madeleine Lemaitre, the daughter of a Magistrate and haberdasher, François Lemaitre or Le Maistre--- traditionally godparents to the Marsolet and Ango families, but the marriage took place in the Catholic Church of St-Vincent-de-Rouen. Notary records confirm that the Lemieux of St-Clair were involved in trades and were financially well off, due in part to Thomas's business acumen and their sufficient education to succeed.

In 1685, Louis XIV revoked the Edict of Nantes which destroyed the economic network developed by the Protestants. The reforms placed pressures on the population such as the obligatory baptisms of children and adults, the kidnapping of children and entrusting them to Catholic convents. There are records of baptisms without parents present, and with godparents selected by the Church. As a result, two out of three Protestants chose exile and freedom over conversion. The remainder changed religions as needed.

Under siege for three years, Rouen had lost one-third of its population and 30% of its textile trade. Henri IV restored peace and commerce. During the turbulent times Gilles and Louis moved between St-Clair and Rouen frequently, and when peace was restored, they settled in Rouen permanently in 1594. The Cauchoise district where Gilles and Louis's families lived was in the southwest corner of the city in the parishes of St-Elois (Protestant) and St-Michel-de-Rouen (Catholic) and near the Marsolets.

In 1613 Gilles died at 59 after a long illness. Ysabeau was widowed with three children: **Pierre I**, 19, Madeleine, 17 and Thomas III, 10. Pierre was now the head of the family and on June 27, 1614 he married Marie Luguan at St-Michel-de-Rouen. Marie was the daughter of Jean Luguan or Luguen or Le Quen, a cooper in St-Michel Parish, which must be the reason Pierre entered the profession. Coopers were highly regarded in that society and were important craftsmen in the world of trade. To enter this field one needed a good education in math and business accounting. Pierre was most likely educated in one of the Jesuit schools and apprenticed by Jean Luguan.

Pierre and Marie had four children:
1. Jehan, baptized October 1,1615, who died three years later
2. **Pierre II**, baptized October 21, 1616
3. Claude, baptized June 1, 1624 and died July 7
4. Marie, baptized June 27, 1629

Records describe the Black Death of 1348, and its conclusion in 1394. At the beginning of the 1600s it seemed to have completely disappeared, however, it returned in full force from 1619 to 1632. In 1621, the population of Rouen had diminished by one-third and many left the city. Port activity declined and the lack of business for barrel-makers during this period led them to search for employment elsewhere. An informal study tracking the timeline of the Plague in conjunction with trade routes, found it followed most closely with the textile trade.

Of all the remedies available to fight the disease at the time, Marie and Pierre Lemieux chose the best---they left Rouen. In fact, from 1617 to 1624, there is no recorded birth in the family of the barrel merchant. In 1624, Claude was born but did not survive and, in 1629, Marie was the last child.

In 1624, the year that Claude was born, the Plague seemed to diminish, 58 died in August, 62 in September and 144 in October. Pierre and Marie must have believed that the worst was over and it was behind them. It was not true. In 1629 Ysabeau, Pierre's 76-year-old mother, and his brother, Thomas III, 26, became gravely ill, and died.

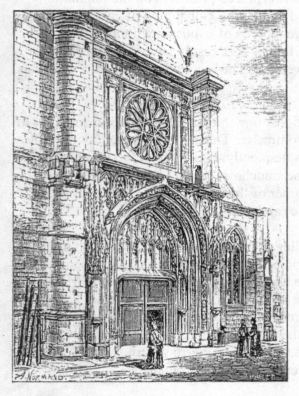

Portail de Saint-Eloi, dessin de Normand, d'après le croquis de M. A. Marguery

After the death of Ysabeau and Thomas, Pierre I also became sick. He was being nursed at home, and finally, at the hospital by Doctor Lamperiere, the doctor in charge of epidemic diseases. L'Abbe Jehan Luguan, a relative of the family, named priest of contagious diseases, prepared the way for Pierre's death at the age of 35. Overwhelmed and pregnant, Marie decided to accept the offer of her cousins, Louis and Jehanne, to have her come live with them in St-Elois Parish. A month after her husband's death, Marie gave birth to a daughter she named Marie.

During this string of disasters, Pierre II was only 13 years old. We can only imagine the disillusionment of a young adolescent who, within a few months, lost his grandmother, his uncle and, worst of all, his father. He was forced to move from one house to another and change parishes. Eventually, his mother remarried to his father's cousin, Louis Lemieux.

Pierre II continued his studies at the Jesuit school. Becoming a barrel merchant like his father required that he also be able to read, write, do mathematics and conduct business. The role he would play in the future in the business of the Company of the One Hundred Associates in Québec shows that he mastered these skills well. His signature on his contract is firm, clear and even elegant, showing that he received a good education and used it wisely. Like his father and grandfather, he had from childhood learned the basics of the barrel-making trade. Unfortunately, because of his father's death, he would not be able to inherit a business and was forced to apprentice the trade in someone else's shop.

There is no trace of little sister Marie's marriage or death records which would describe her life. It's likely that she became the cherished and spoiled child of the family and, in time, the confidant of Gabriel, their cousin, who came to live with them.

Thomas Lemieux III, brother of Pierre I, was engaged to Anne Le Cornu in 1629, but he died of the Plague before they could marry. Anne was pregnant and gave birth to Gabriel in April 1630. Gabriel's baptism from St-Etienne La Grande Église says:

> *This Wednesday, tenth day of April 1630, was baptized the son of Anne Le Cornu, before Jean le Cornu, her father, said Anne having had carnal relation on the verbal promise of marriage with Thomas Le Mieux, now deceased, the infant being named Gabriel by Anne le Cornu, [godmother?] widow of Jean le Parent, aunt of said Anne, mother of the child, and by Guillaume Baniguot, father of the second wife of said Jean le Cornu, godfather.*

This was a difficult situation for Anne and her family. To remedy this, since Marie Luguen, mother of Pierre II, had remarried to Louis Lemieux, Gabriel came to live with his aunt and uncle, who reared him as their own and took care of his training.

All of their lives, Pierre and Gabriel would be together and were considered brothers. They would go to North America and would experience great adventures together. Under the influence of Pierre, Gabriel eventually chose the same career as his grandfather. Judging by his life in New France, Gabriel was also independent and adventurous.

Training to be a cooper was a fortunate choice for Pierre II, considering the status of Rouen as an important seaport and the need for barrels, casks, and shipping containers. A daily stroll along the wharves would also allow him to meet ship-owners and crews familiar with sailing the English Channel, the Baltic and the Atlantic.

Tonneliers

In 1635, at the age of 19 years, Pierre II acted as Master Valet aboard the ships crossing between France and New France. With experience as a cooper, a Master Valet would have been responsible for loading and unloading the shipping containers. In the chain of command, Master Valet came after Captain and Boatswain. In 1638 Pierre already had a three-year contract with the Company of the Hundred Associates, as a cargo manager aboard the ships sailing from Dieppe. He was responsible for loading, checking and storage of goods and equipment both onboard and on the docks. This helped him earn the status of Master Cooper. This adventurous young man had already established ties to his new life in Québec, which he knew was a trading post exchanging furs for merchandise and food imported from France.

The greatest impact on our ancestors was that throughout Louis XIII's reign, heavy taxes were imposed to support reforms, but mainly for war, causing frequent rioting. In 1639, Normandy revolted. Craftsmen and merchants of Rouen took to the streets, ransacked the tax offices, and refused to pay more taxes because it would cause their financial ruin. Cardinal Richelieu sent armed troops to quash the rebellion, dissolved the Parliament and put its members under house arrest. One man was sent to the wheel, four were hanged and two hundred exiled. It's likely that Pierre was in Quebec during this event but surely it influenced his decision to return to Quebec again.

The French government did not aggressively recruit settlers to strengthen the colonies. This was done by the Company of New France and The One Hundred Associates, private investors who hoped to become wealthy from the riches of New France. Men of trade and commerce, Bourdon, Marsolet, Couillard, Le Tardif and Couture, recruited new associates through the partner system. Québécois who came at the request of merchants were partners even before they crossed the Atlantic.

Pierre II and Gabriel's reason for leaving for New France simply may have been that they were receptive to the inducements of recruiters. Neither Pierre nor Gabriel were farmers, but artisans, skilled craftsmen and members of the business world. It would take two generations on Canadian soil for the Lemieux to return reluctantly to the land. At the invitation of merchants associated with the One Hundred Associates, possibly Nicolas Marsolet, Pierre and Gabriel came to the New World.

In 1643, Pierre Lemieux II decided to accept Le Tardif's offer to come to New France. It may not have been a difficult decision to leave his life in Rouen because he already had a three-year contract with the Hundred Associates as a Master Valet aboard French vessels, and had traveled to New France. He was familiar with the situation in Québec and knew he could return to Rouen as he had before. Perhaps he thought there was a better chance for success as a Master *Tonnelier* in Québec rather than being just another barrel merchant in Rouen. It was a calculated risk, but he was ready to make the transition to New France.

Pierre Lemieux, *tonnelier* of Rouen, at 26.6 years, of age signed a three-year contract of engagement at La Rochelle with Antoine Cheffault de la Reynardière, Parisian attorney for the One Hundred Associates Company, on April 10, 1643. He would have an annual salary of 100 livres with 80 livres payable in advance.

10 April 1643

Engagement
Lemieux
to
Cheffault

Personally establishing Pierre Lemieux, tonnelier of the city of Rouen, of one part and noble man Antoine Cheffault, long of the directors of the Company of the New France and of the one of Québec, of the other part. Between these parties this was done and suited the said Lemieux.

It is known that the said Lemieux promises and obliges himself to embark at the first Requisition that he will do this by the said Sieur Cheffault to go to Québec, country of New France, serving the Messieurs of the said company in his said trade of tonnelier and all other things that he finds himself capable.

Monsieur le Governor in his lieutenance being at the said country to which the said one has ceded faith and promised to obey during the space of three successive years that will begin on the day that he arrives in the said country and likewise the following days. Renouncing for and with the sum of one hundred livres for each of the said years on the first of each one the said Sieur Cheffault presently paid in advance to the said Lemieux the sum of eighty livres in good money according to the order of this contract with the aforementioned Cheffault, who promises and is obliged to pay the remainder of the said year together with the price of the two years at the end of the one at which time the aforementioned Cheffault will be held to do the return trip to these sections in France deducting that done now what would have been received in said country. And this expressly ….. …. the aforementioned Lemieux is of the said country…. He will be paid the sum of twenty livres for each year with the said sum of hundred livres meeting the dictates two sums at the sum of two hundred livres…. the contract under pain of all damage and interest between the said parties. These for the accomplishment of those present are obliged. A clause……. presents and following three years or pay by check lower city to know the aforementioned Cheffault in the house of Nicolas of the escuyer the…. remain and the one of the Royal notary undersigned for….. and renouncing and….

This done at la Rochelle in the study of said notary before noon, the tenth day of April the year one thousand six hundred forty-three. Present Mathieu Bouvat and Renaud Paillac, Clerk residing in this city, one thousand six hundred forty-three.

Signees

Cheffault   P. Lemieux   P. Bouvat
                      ——————————
            Teuléron, Notaire Royal

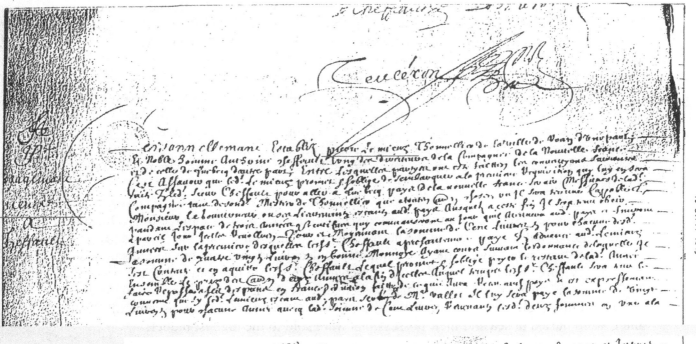

10 avril 1643

10. 04. 1643

The Harbor of Saint-Malo, France, had witnessed Jacques Cartier and the fishermen of the 16th Century leaving and Honfleur hailed the departure of Samuel de Champlain taking Nicolas Marsollet to his destiny. But in the 17th Century, it was the working ports of La Rochelle and Dieppe that saw the future settlers embarking for New France. Why travel overland 250 miles with all your belongings to La Rochelle rather than sail from Rouen? Because privateers paid by England patrolled the English Channel, departure from La Rochelle rather than Rouen offered more room at sea to avoid potential attacks.

Pierre, being from Rouen and having worked aboard ships, knew his way around these port cities. With his previous valet experience he must have been busy packing and loading containers and assisting with all the preparations for departure. In addition to the regular crew there was usually a carpenter, a caulker, and sometimes a surgeon, a writer and a priest. Due to weather conditions on this side of the Atlantic, ships would usually sail in late May or early June.

While waiting, other travelers often spent part of their money in the inns. During the day they filled the streets and the harbor, trying to find out if their ship would sail soon. The ship captains were the sole authority to decide when their ship would sail and would only leave when fully loaded, all passengers were on board and if the tide was high and winds were right. The average passenger was not accustomed to the rough seas, dirty conditions, sleeping in hammocks, poor food and water, and many became ill. Some died, were buried at sea and their possessions were sold to the highest bidder.

Pierre boarded the *Saint-Francois*, 130 tons, Master: J. Barraud, departing for his new life in Kebec on April 10, 1643 and arrived in August. Gabriel, only 13 at the time, followed later.

La Rochelle, est venu Pierre Cenleux a monter le Saint-Francois: 130 tonneaux. le Ma tre: J. Barraud. Ils sont partis 10 avril 1643 et arrive au Quebec en aout.

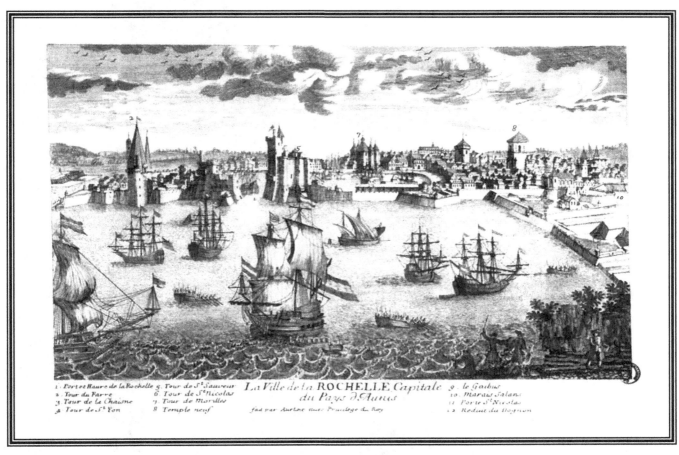

La Rochelle Harbor
Pierre Lemieux's departure point on April 10, 1643

Eglise Saint-Jean-Baptiste built from 1170 to 1406 at Bec-Thomas, Normandie, France

V

Marsollet in France

ll indications are that the Marsollet family originated in Normandy near Rouen. The first record of Marsollet information is from the notary or scrivener of Rouen, about a family who inhabited the pastoral village of Bec-Thomas (Louviers, canton d'Amfreville-la-Campagne), and was fixed at Rouen in the second half of the 16th Century.

A document lists, Nicolas (he signed Collas Marchollet) and Etienne (cousin?), laborers of the hamlet of Bosc Heroult, parish of Bec-Thomas, these sold, September 17, 1581, three crown (obsolete coin formerly worth 3 francs) and two third of rent to Guillebert Marsollet, Sergeant Royal of Rouen, in the presence of Guillaume Viel, notary of the parish of Vreville, and of Massine Alix, their mother and widow of Etienne.

Nicolas Marsolet I was probably born in Bec-Thomas and baptized at Saint Jean-Baptiste there. It is known that he was married to Laurence Griffon in 1569 at St-Eloi Protestant parish and again on September 25, 1572 in Ste-Marie-la-Petite Catholic Parish, both in Rouen. Their four children were named Marie, Jeanne, Nicolas and Roulant Marsolet. They were members of the parish of St-Vigor in Rouen in 1568 when Nicolas I died and in 1600 when Laurence died.

Nicolas Marsollet II was born and baptized March 19, 1570 in Sainte-Marie-la-Petite, Rouen. His marriage to Marguerite de Planes is documented in 1600 in St-Sauveur in Rouen which was, again, likely to have been a conversion back to the Catholic religion. He was known to be a regular attendant at the French Court probably through his uncle Guillebert, a Sergeant Royal. For many years he discreetly kept himself informed in hopes of finding a suitable place for his young enterprising son in the employ of the King. His patience was rewarded when he found King Henri IV needed reliable people to use as interpreters in *la Nouvelle-France*. His young son, Nicolas III, was the first interpreter signed with the *Compagnie du Canada*.

Even at age 12, Nicolas III showed promise with languages, having enough natural ability to have learned Latin, Italian, Spanish, English and Dutch. His temperament showed not only resourcefulness but also endurance, courage and integrity and the fact that his father was the King Henri's faithful servant was enough recommendation for the assignment as interpreter. In 1599, Henri IV signed him as a *Drogman* (from an Arab word *tordgeman* which became *truchement* in French, meaning interpreter) for the newly founded *Compagnie du Canada*. The family was also well connected to the One Hundred Associates as evidenced by the number of Associates that served as witnesses to the many baptisms, marriages, and deaths of the Marsolet family.

Samuel de Champlain

According to the historian Sulte and others, Nicolas Marsolet accompanied Champlain from Honfleur in 1608 to assist in the founding of Québec. Entrusted very young to the Indian tribes, he learned to perfection the Algonquin and Montagnaise languages. Marsolet was a young boy in the eyes of the founder of Québec. In July 1629 the Governor mentioned three interpreters: Brûlé, Marsolet and Raye. And addressing Brûlé and Marsolet, he noted, "You have been excellent young men in this position."

All were of value to the *Compagnie des Cent Associes* who, next to the Church, quickly garnered a principal role in New France. The charter conferred on the Company the whole of the North American Continent from Florida to the farthest northern point and from the Atlantic seaboard to the western sources of the St. Lawrence River. The fur trade was to belong to them exclusively for all time and they were to control the trade of the colony, with the exception of the coast fisheries, for a term of fifteen years. No duty would be charged on the goods they would import to France. In return the Associates were to send three hundred people to Canada each year and to bring the total to four thousand within fifteen years.

"It was provided that the members of the nobility might become associates without any prejudice to the dignities which formerly had excluded them from participation in trade. On the other hand, twelve patents of nobility were to be distributed among the men of lesser degree, the merchants and the shipping heads. All settlers were to be French and Catholic. The government was to stand back of the company and to provide immediately two warships fully equipped for service."

Unfortunately, the delighted leaders of New France did not have the forethought to see the drawbacks in this new formation. This document would determine every aspect of the lives of the men and women who braved the rigors of life on this new continent. Every detail of the *habitants'* existence would be dictated. Free will was to be denied to everyone. The *habitant* would not be allowed to determine his own destiny. Even the act of marriage would be subject to king-made controls and restrictions.

In early 1628, much of the fleet sent to New France by the Company was captured by the English. This fleet, heavily loaded with supplies and settlers, contained items desperately needed by the current *habitants* for survival during the long, harsh winter. Life in New France seemed hopeless.

However, unknown to the current *habitants* and leaders, this defeat had brought the *Compagnie des Cent Associes* to the brink of bankruptcy. Further examination showed that the Company had been hovering on the brink of bankruptcy almost from the beginning. Reorganization attempts were unsuccessful and the Company's fate was obvious. The "beaver wars" with the Iroquois in the early 1640s sealed this fate. The

Company was forced to relinquish their exclusive hold on the fur trade to the more powerful inhabitants of New France. At this point, the *coureurs des bois* (couriers of the woods) came into existence. The *coureurs des bois*, who were able to see the advantage of self-sufficiency, began raking in large profits. There was no turning back at this point. In 1663, the *Compagnie des Cent Associes* closed its books and, finally, its doors.

Marsollet

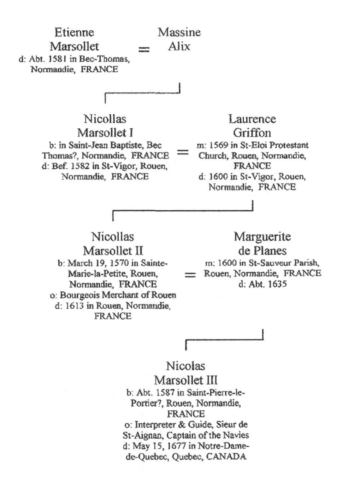

Etienne Marsollet = Massine Alix
d: Abt. 1581 in Bec-Thomas, Normandie, FRANCE

Nicollas Marsollet I
b: in Saint-Jean Baptiste, Bec Thomas?, Normandie, FRANCE
d: Bef. 1582 in St-Vigor, Rouen, Normandie, FRANCE
=
Laurence Griffon
m: 1569 in St-Eloi Protestant Church, Rouen, Normandie, FRANCE
d: 1600 in St-Vigor, Rouen, Normandie, FRANCE

Nicollas Marsollet II
b: March 19, 1570 in Sainte-Marie-la-Petite, Rouen, Normandie, FRANCE
o: Bourgeois Merchant of Rouen
d: 1613 in Rouen, Normandie, FRANCE
=
Marguerite de Planes
m: 1600 in St-Sauveur Parish, Rouen, Normandie, FRANCE
d: Abt. 1635

Nicolas Marsollet III
b: Abt. 1587 in Saint-Pierre-le-Portier?, Rouen, Normandie, FRANCE
o: Interpreter & Guide, Sieur de St-Aignan, Captain of the Navies
d: May 15, 1677 in Notre-Dame-de-Quebec, Quebec, CANADA

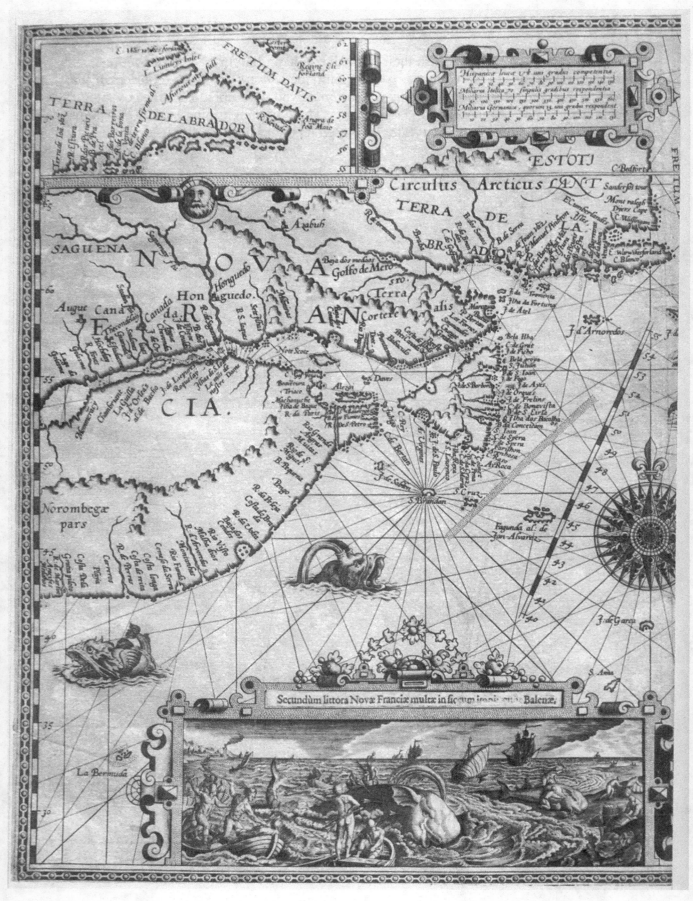

Nova Francia

VI

New France

hen Champlain returned to Quebec as governor in 1633, he found seventy-five people living there. The French population of North America ebbed and flowed at low levels, with no sustained growth and scarcely any natural increase. Despite Champlain's dream of an established settlement in New France, for thirty years most French inhabitants were solitary men who stayed briefly. He would now resume his efforts to bring families to the community.

During this period Champlain also had an impact on the development of the seigneurial system, which was designed as an engine of population growth. His general pattern of seigneurial grants became the standard way of organizing the land in New France. In its simplicity, each grant was defined by a survey line commonly at right angles to the St-Lawrence and other rivers, most adaptable to the terrain. Seigneurs received land and feudal privileges in return for a commitment to bring colonists to Canada at their expense. It was a society built on networks of kinship and patronage.

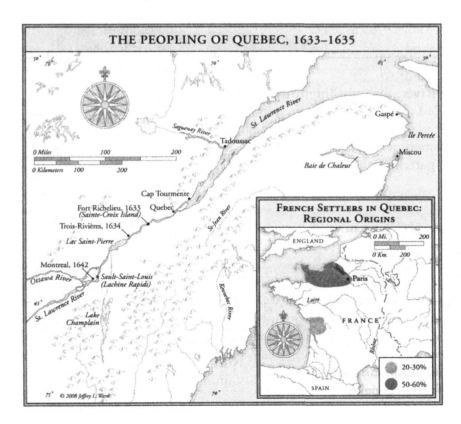

From about 1633 to 1635, immigrant ships to Quebec came mostly from Norman ports and many from the west-center of France around La Rochelle and Poitou. Once started, there continued a pattern of chain-migration---families, friends, and neighbors who followed others they knew in America---such as Marsolet and Lemieux from the same parishes of St-Sauveur and St-Eloi in Rouen.

The *seigneurial* system of land tenure was imported to Canada in a more flexible form than the old feudal system. The *seigneur* was most often just a worthy person, not a nobleman, who was granted by royal deed a large piece of land. He was dependent on his tenants to develop their small division of property and they were charged rent for a few cents and the rest in goods produced from the land. The tenant was a free *habitant* who could sell out and buy another tenancy at will.

The *seigneur* was a "*gentilhomme*," a militia officer or a middle class professional who hoped to better his prospects by putting down roots in a new land. He was head of the local community and the guardian of its law and order. Disgruntled tenants could sue him if unsatisfied and could appeal directly to the central administration in Québec.

Like the *seigneur*, the tenant preferred to have his hundred or so

A Canadien in snowshoes going to war in the snow

acres on the St. Lawrence River, the only "highway" for nearly a century. Since his property was equally divided among his children, in time the strips of land grew narrower and the little houses by the waterfront grew closer together. The average *seigneur's* whitewashed house was sometimes indistinguishable, except in size, from the tenant's one story log cabin with a garret for the children.

The kings of France attempted to control colonization and the monopoly of the fur trade, but even with the threat of serious punishment, this proved difficult. The difference between the English and French systems of colonizing the New World was significant. England encouraged settlers to go to North America and become self-sustaining.

France, on the other hand, had not encouraged settlement, considered the colony an expensive luxury, and kept the few unprepared settlers dependent on the home country for supplies. Unlike the English, the French faced two major issues in their colonies: the *seigneurial* system and the *coureurs des bois.*

The French *coureurs des bois* were carefree, fearless and beyond control. They were remarkable woodsmen and the kings' major competitors in the fur trade. Their courage, curiosity and restlessness, gave them the instinct for adventure and the capacity for adapting themselves to any environment.

To challenge the fur trade monopoly, illicit traders would stay out in the woods for four years at a time counting on official forgetfulness to escape penalties on their return. When this technique eventually failed, they established small settlements north of Montréal and Three Rivers and never came into larger posts at all. Here they became serious competitors because they could intercept the Indian canoes on their way to the bigger markets. They were always ready to trade brandy for pelts---a perfect lure.

The King and his advisers tried to meet the challenge of the *coureurs des bois* with the fur fairs called *Rendezvous.* Towns would set aside two weeks so merchants could bring goods and set up booths. Like a carnival, dancers, jugglers and magicians entertained in the streets for pennies. The Indians would come painted and feathered in a huge flotilla, sometimes four or five hundred canoes at a time, fully aware of their impact. There was shouting and singing and quarreling as they landed and set up their camp and for two weeks everyone mingled, celebrated and did the business of getting the furs to market.

Canada was not a country that could be easily settled. The French faced bitter winters. For more than five months of the year farming came to a dead stop and ice in the St. Lawrence River blocked communication between Québec and France. For twenty years, beginning in the 1640s, with a new ferocity, the Iroquois ravaged the line of French settlements along the St. Lawrence as far as Québec, coming close to paralyzing the fur trade. The Indians constantly assaulted the settlers, usually on their own farms, threatening to eliminate the entire colony. By 1663, New France only had 2,500 settlers, most of whom were confined to three small settlements at Québec, Three Rivers and Montréal. Both the Lemieux and Marsolets are listed among the first one hundred families in Canada and they are still found in these original settlements.

In the earlier days of river settlements, the religious needs of the people had been met by roving priests who made their rounds in canoes. The Jesuits had also been sending their journal, *Relations*, back to France and traveling the rivers converting the Indians. But in time, little churches were springing up and the parish became a local municipality.

In 1665, Louis XIV decided to save his overseas investment and, once royal intervention produced some security, the colony stopped being a precarious experiment. For the next thirty years, a program of subsidized industrial development and immigration led to significant expansion of the settlements. By the end of the century the population had increased to 7,000, the cultivated areas had doubled and new industries had been launched.

Meanwhile, French explorers cut pathways over the Great Shield, or paddled southward in the direction of the Gulf of Mexico. In 1673, Jolliet and Marquette entered the Mississippi, tracing portages for LaSalle and others who followed the river as far as its mouth. In their wake, trading posts sprang up, creating a network of strategic points within the fur-bearing territory between the Ohio River and the upper Mississippi. The Frenchman, making a home on the banks of the St. Lawrence or pushing westward, was transforming himself into a Canadian.

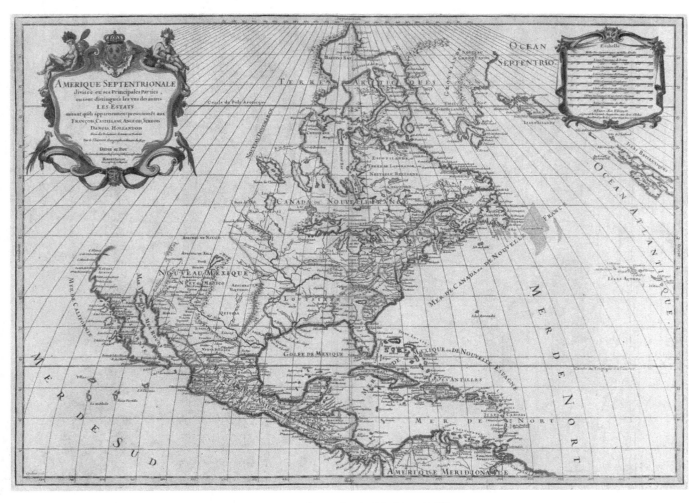

1694 map by Alexis Hubert Jaillot

Comte de Frontenac

Samuel de Champlain

BISHOP LAVAL

Cardinal Richelieu

Jacques Cartier

IBERVILLE

LA SALLE

JEAN TALON

MADAME
DE LA PELTRIE

Map of New France charted and drawn by Champlain

VII

Marsolet in New France

he life of Nicolas Marsolet, Sieur de St. Aignan, could easily be recorded in three distinctly different intervals. During his first 18 or more years in France he developed his personal skills and lived a bourgeois life in France's second largest city, Rouen. He then moved to New France where he adapted so well to the New World and its native inhabitants that he thrived. For 27 years, he lived in Tadoussac, serving as an interpreter and facilitator for the fur trade. He aided the Récollets' (Franciscan Friars) evangelization efforts while living in close proximity to the Montagnais Indians he loved. Finally, he married a French girl from Rouen, Marie Le Barbier, lived 42 years in Québec City and raised ten children. In a century when 40 was old, he died at 90 years of age. The last of the original *habitants*[1], he endured almost 65 years of life in New France and played a pivotal role in establishing a French presence in the New World. [2]

Nicolas Marsolet III, son of Rouen citizens Nicolas Marsolet II and Marguerite de Planes, was born about 1587, probably in Rouen. [3] Tanguay, Morrison, Parkman and other historians have established his birth to be 1601. This is probably due to their reliance on his record of baptism in 1601 at St. Pierre le Portier, Rouen, which was a Catholic baptism. We believe he was probably born and baptized Protestant in 1587 at Rouen[4]. There is strong evidence to suggest that his father, Nicolas II, was Protestant and that he too converted, like so many of the French, to survive the Wars of Religion. We know for certain that Champlain mentions Nicolas Marsolet by name as one of eight survivors of the first winter in Québec (1608). Reason tells us if he had been born in 1601 he would have been only seven years of age, which is hardly plausible.[5] From other sources we learn that Nicolas was several years older than Etienne Brûlé, who also was a survivor of the founding of Québec, and was estimated to have been 16-18 at the time.[6]

Some biographers place Nicolas's birth at Saint-Aignan-sur-Ry. Research has failed to uncover any link between Nicolas and the farming village of Saint-Aignan-sur-Ry about 35 kilometers east of Rouen or the closer Mount Saint-Aignan community.[7] There is no doubt that his family lived in Rouen for at least two generations prior to the birth of Nicolas III.

---

[1] This term was preferred by the colonists who wanted to differentiate their status from that of the peasant in France.

[2] Lemyre, Bizier, Others

[3] Sulte and Others

[4] Ibid

[5] Thwaites, *Jesuit Relations*

[6] Sulte

[7] Ibid

The Marsolet family owned property and lived in the southwest section of Rouen on rue des Bons Enfants and rue Cauchoise in close proximity to a hill that was called *Mont des Malades* because it was where the Plague hospital and cemetery were located. The hill and surrounding community were renamed Mont-St-Aignan probably about the time Nicolas was growing up.

Rue des Bons Enfants

rue Cauchoise with Mont Saint-Aignan in the distance

These same biographers believed that when he later adopted the noble title and became Nicolas Marsolet, Sieur de Saint-Aignan, he was adopting the name of that village or region. A better explanation for adopting the name may have been the proximity of Mont Saint-Aignan, a dominating terrain feature so close to where the family lived.[8] Additionally, at that time, homes in Rouen were named, not numbered. It is highly likely that the name St-Aignan was adopted and transferred from his home in France to his "home" in Québec.[9]

His father, Nicolas II, and his family were heavily involved in activities in Rouen at this time and are frequently mentioned in church documents in the local Rouen parishes of St-Pierre-le-Portier, St-Godard, Ste-Marie-la-Petite, St-Sauveur, St-Vigor and St-Maclou. Several of these churches were Protestant during this period. [10]

The Marsolets seem to have been a well-connected bourgeois family in Rouen at this time. They are closely tied to many of the leading Huguenots of the period which further establishes the possibility that the family may have been Protestant. Additionally, they owned property in a good section of Rouen, which was then the second largest city in France.

Guillebert Marsolet, Nicolas's uncle, was a Sergeant Royal in Rouen and was

---

[8] Campeau, Lucien, Cahiers D'Historie Des Jesuits, No. 2, 1974, Bellarmin: Montréal, p. 57
[9] Osselin, Anne, unpublished correspondence, maps, church records, customs.
[10] LeMyre, Danielle, Thwaites, Others

active on the periphery of the court of King Henri IV.[11] Nicolas's father, Nicolas II, and his mother, Marguerite de Planes, "were regular attendants at the French Court"[12] and they are reported to have carefully arranged to have Nicolas III selected by Henri IV to serve as a *Truchement* (interpreter). "At age 12, Nicolas showed promise with languages having enough natural ability to have learned Latin, Spanish, Italian, English and Dutch. He had a good temperament and demonstrated resourcefulness, endurance, courage and integrity, all key prerequisite for the challenging task he faced. His skills and talents, coupled with his father's faithful service were enough of a recommendation for King Henri IV to select Nicolas III as the first interpreter to sign with the *Compagnie de Montréal* in 1599."[13]

According to Sulte, the use of interpreters to gain inroads with the native population was not new. It had been used effectively in Brazil in the 1500's to secure wood trade, but without effective control, the traders eventually melted into the population that adopted them.

Champlain was a difficult taskmaster, demanding of his interpreters, keeping them under tight control and strict orders. As a consequence, they accomplished amazing things by gaining the confidence of the natives, acting as trade intermediaries, exploring the wild country and adapting to local traditions while spreading a civilized French influence throughout the countryside. For this, his interpreters received well-deserved but not always ardent praise, even from the Jesuits.[14].

Researchers of the earliest history of New France are both blessed and cursed by the plethora of information available in *The Jesuit Relations* which are clearly the foundation documents for research on New France for the early colonial period.

The *Jesuit Relations,* a series of letters, books, maps and reports, compiled by Jesuit Missionaries between 1610 and 1791, provides a comprehensive view of life in the colony and are the foundation of most research from that period. Although it has been proven to be authoritative and accurate, many view it as a politically correct, impassioned plea for martyrdom and sainthood. [15]

Generally, neither the Jesuits nor Champlain wrote or spoke well of people who did not support their position and they were always quick to present their position under the best light. Champlain's contempt for those who lived with the Indians, especially the interpreters, was evident in his writings and he personally intervened to prevent awards and promotions to some of his men. The Récollets (French Franciscans) were equally critical of the interpreters' behavior which they viewed as improper. The traders and

---

[11] "The feudal rank of sergeant, it will be remembered, was widely different from the modern grade so named, and was held by men of noble birth." Francis Parkman, *"Pioneers of France in the New World"* FN#14
[12] LeMyre, Danielle Duval, "Nicolas Marsolet de St-Aignan Interpretor (sic) to the Montagnais First Nation"
[13] Thwait
[14] Sulte
[15] Ibid

company representatives felt that the *coureurs des bois* were very important in maintaining strong ties with the Indians. The interpreters fared well eventually by occupying an important part of New France history.

Champlain, never quick to pass on a compliment, is reported to have told Brûlé and Marsolet… "You have been excellent young men in this position."[16]

Even the Jesuits, who were notorious for interfering with or tearing down anyone who didn't agree with them, were forced to say some good things in their writings, the *Relations*. In identifying those interpreters who had excelled in their mission, they said: *"The most conspicuous were Jean Nicollet, Jacques Hertel, François Marguerie, and **Nicolas Marsolet**. Doubtless, when they returned from their rovings, they often had pressing need of penance and absolution; yet, for the most part, they were good Catholics and some of them were zealous for the missions. Several of them were men of great intelligence and an invincible courage. They lacked restraint, had a love of the wild and adventurous independence. Although they encountered challenges and dangers equal to those the Jesuit is exposed to from religious zeal, charity, and the hope of Paradise. The interpreters faced it simply because they liked it. Some of the best families of Canada claim descent from this vigorous and hardy stock."[17]*

¹' Sulte

Extract from Pierre Descellier's 1546 Map of the World
- from Labrador to Mexico
One of the earliest representations of Canada
South is pointing up.

The New World

France was the last of the European powers to turn its attention to the New World. In fact as late as thirty years after the discoveries of Columbus, the French based their claims to the new continent on the work of another Italian explorer, Giovanni Verrazano, who sailed in the service of France. Shortly after his voyage in 1524, he published a map identifying an extensive portion of the North American continent as Nova Gallia (New France). Although Verrazano's discoveries were not the fabled route to Cathay, they were part of what would become a great empire and provide France with a claim to North America.

Francis I, the French King, was now anxious to focus the country on the new opportunity and called upon Jacques Cartier to complete the work of Verrazano.

Cartier departed St-Malo, April 20, 1534 and reached the coast of Canada in twenty days. Cartier was not the first to make this trip, Bretons, Basques, Portuguese and others had been fishing the outer banks for years. What distinguished this trip was that it was a voyage of discovery. He sailed primarily in the area of the Gulf of St. Lawrence and was dismayed that a passage to the Asian sea was not discovered. He arrived back in St-Malo on September 5, 1534, and received a commission for a second voyage.

His second voyage in 1535 introduced him to the St. Lawrence and Saguenay valleys and their peoples. From them he learned of the interior of the country and he pressed to see Hochelaga, the largest native settlement. He sailed up the St. Lawrence until the shallows forced him to shore. Cartier set out with about twenty men to view the town. He found the settlement without difficulty and marveled over its size and organization. The town was completely round with palisades throughout. There was a single entrance secured by bars with three tiers of timber. Cartier spent only a day there and returned to an anchor site near present day Montréal.

Because it was so late in the season and with the impending threat of ice, Cartier elected to spend the winter in what is now Québec. His men constructed a fort to guard against attack and prepared to face the long Canadian winter. No one knew that, besides severe weather, the French would face the dreaded scurvy.

One by one his men succumbed to the disease and they were beginning to question whether they would ever see France again. Cartier was reluctant to discuss the matter with the Indians since they might sense French weakness. Finally their Indian interpreter, Domagaya, inadvertently introduced the crew to the boiled bark of the white cedar tree. He had shown signs of the disease and cured himself. Cartier merely asked him what he had used and he immediately provided the recipe, within days the crew was cured. The elixir became known as *"arbor vitae"* or "the tree of life."

The voyage of 1535-36 had been much more fruitful than the previous trip from a geographical perspective. Cartier had discovered and explored the great St. Lawrence River, which would be the key to the French penetration of North America. He had ambitious plans for exploiting those discoveries.

Unfortunately, Cartier arrived back in France just as war was beginning to break out with the Spanish. For a variety of reasons, Cartier was unable to return until 1541 and then all activity seemed to come to a halt for almost 50 years.

Under rather obscure circumstances, *Seigneur* La Roche persuaded Henry III to found New France and join the other great European powers in establishing a presence in the New World. Under provisions of his commission, La Roche was permitted to go to the new lands and establish a new colony which he would govern as Viceroy. However, La Roche did not begin immediately because various merchant groups challenged his monopoly. In 1584, he finally attempted a colonization effort involving 300 settlers. The project was doomed, however, by the shipwreck of his primary vessel, thus ending his attempts at colonization.

That same year the merchants of St-Malo began to look with interest on a commercial expedition. In 1587, Henry III gave Etienne La Jannaye and Jacques Noel (a nephew of Cartier) a 12-year monopoly for Canada and adjacent territories to reimburse losses and carry on the memory of Cartier.

This was immediately challenged by merchants in La Rochelle, Honfleur, Rouen and Dieppe as unfair and was eventually modified by the King and further ratified by Henry IV. The new monopoly did encourage La Roche to establish a colony at Sable Island. He maintained the colony for four to five years but soon found himself brushed aside by Pierre Chauvin.

Chauvin had obtained a monopoly to trade in Canada partially as an "attempt at co-existence" between Catholics and Huguenots in accordance with the edict of Nantes. Chauvin had served Henry IV and was now an important merchant and ship owner in Honfleur. He gained the monopoly by offering to take 500 colonists to Canada "without cost to the King."

A virtual celebrity list of important persons involved in the future of New France were part of Chauvin's misadventures in the new world and they included Champlain, Pont-Gravé and De Monts.

François du Pont-Gravé, Captain of the Navies and close friend to King Henri IV, and his Lieutenant (second-in-command), Samuel Champlain, were busy in Honfleur preparing for their journey to New France when Nicolas joined them in late March 1608. Nicolas was about to embark upon a journey that would shape his life and make him a significant figure in early Québec.

Honfleur was one of several ports, as were La Rochelle and Dieppe, used as a jumping-off point for New France. Both Champlain and Pont-Gravé had worked hard to help the King's friend, Pierre du Gua de Monts, raise money to secure the fur monopoly for at least one more year.

De Monts was the Calvinist Governor of Pons Saintonge and was a close friend of Pont-Gravé who had fought for and supported Henri IV. He had been awarded the New France fur monopoly following the death of Aymer de Chaste, who had been an advocate of placing a permanent Huguenot colony in New France.

Pierre de Chauvin de Tonnetuit, a wealthy Protestant merchant from Honfleur, assisted them with their first attempt at placing a colony in Tadoussac, a well established trading and wintering site at the junction of the Saguenay and St. Lawrence Rivers.

Neither Pont-Gravé nor de Mont were happy with the site of the colony, but Chauvin prevailed in selecting that site. Instead of the fifty promised colonists, sixteen men were left there over the winter of 1600 and eleven died of scurvy. When the supply ship arrived that next spring, it found the remaining five survivors living with the Indians. The colony had failed.[18] Champlain was very critical of Chauvin for that failure and went so far as to assert that Chauvin had never intended to exercise this condition of the monopoly but merely "throw dust in the eyes of the government." This view runs counter to the prevailing opinion since Henri IV had a "great confidence in him which was earned by his excellent behavior when Governor of Honfleur."[19]

With Champlain's assistance, Pont-Gravé tried to establish a colony again in 1603. This time they started with 79 people on an island in the St-Croix River. The colony succumbed to scurvy almost immediately. Thirty-five died and another twenty were too sick to move about. In hindsight, the island was actually a poor site for the colony since it lacked many of the necessities, especially wood and game.

De Monts was among the first to recognize the merits of financing these colonization efforts with private Protestant money from St-Malo, Dieppe, Honfleur, Rouen and Paris. Merchants and noblemen were anxious to invest in these speculative programs because, if they were successful, a small investment could yield substantial rewards, reportedly up to 1,000 percent. Additionally, the investors believed that the King's monopoly on the fur trade was absolute and enforceable when, in fact, a major struggle was under way between free traders and monopolists. It was virtually impossible to establish and protect the monopoly.[20]

On the 1608 trip, de Monts appointed Champlain his lieutenant and gave him the job of finding the site for a new colony. Before he died, de Chaste had invited Pont-Gravé to inspect the St. Lawrence as far west as Montréal with an eye toward future settlements. Samuel de Champlain, mapmaker and former soldier, accompanied him.

Until that time, Champlain had recommended that any colonization attempts be directed towards the Maritimes because of the milder climate. It was also far enough

---

[18] Trigger and Others
[19] Biggar, H.P. p. 43
[20] Sulte

away from Tadoussac to not to interfere with the fur trade. The fight between the fur traders and the colonists for New France had begun.

Now Champlain realized that a permanent colony inland, at the narrows of the river (Kebec), was a way to curtail the illicit trade in furs while providing a rationale for supporting a settlement.

Despite losing 100,000 Livres the year before, de Mont managed to raise enough money from wealthy Protestant Rouen merchants to equip three ships. *Le Levrier*, with Captain Nicolas Marion had items to trade at Tadoussac. *La Champdore* with Pont-Gravé, was to re-supply the colony they had established at Port Royal. *Le Don de Dieu*, commanded by Champlain with Captain Henry Couillard, was carrying workmen, supplies, plenty of weapons, trade goods and materials for a "Habitation." Also aboard *Le Don de Dieu* was a contingent of interpreters, including Nicolas and his friend for life, Etienne Brûlé, who would go on to serve as interpreter for the Hurons, explore the Great Lakes region to Sault St. Marie and the Lake Superior region and the Susquehanna River.[21]

Le Levrier sailed from Honfleur, France on April 5, 1608, and *Le Don de Dieu* sailed eight days later. The latter sighted Cape St. Marie, Newfoundland, on May 26, 1608 and, after a good crossing, passed through the Cabot Straits and arrived at Tadoussac on June 3, 1608. On July 3, 1608 *Le Don de Dieu* landed in Quebec.

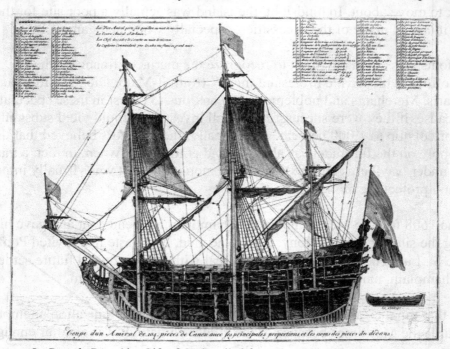

Le Don de Dieu (the Gift of God) sailed from the old harbor in Honfleur
on 13 April, 1608 and landed in Quebec on July 3rd
with Samuel de Champlain and Nicolas Marsolet

---

[21] Dione

The Old Harbor, Honfleur, Normandy, France

Champlain was immediately confronted with a problem. Captain Le Testu, Pont-Gravé's pilot, accompanied by a Basque seaman, rowed out to meet Champlain and told him Pont-Gravé had been wounded in a short battle when he had tried to exercise the monopoly trading powers which had been provided by the King. The Basques had been free traders for years and were not going to be told to cease their profitable trade without a fight.

The Basques had overpowered the French and stripped the ship of weapons. They offered to return the French weapons upon their departure and their leader, Captain Darache, was willing to discuss the current problem. After visiting the wounded Pont-Gravé, Champlain negotiated a settlement allowing the Basques to keep the furs and provided for the return of weapons. It was further agreed that the matter would be referred to French Courts upon returning to France. Knowing full well that the Basques would never voluntarily submit to French justice, Champlain allowed them to have their perceived victory because he had more pressing issues, the establishment of a colony.

After conferring with Pont-Gravé and transferring to a smaller boat, Champlain resumed his journey up river on June 30, 1608, accompanied by thirty men. He specifically named the following individuals: Nicolas Marsolet, Etienne Brûlé, Dr. Bonnerme, Jean Duval, Antoine Natel and La Taille.[22]

---

[22] Dionne, Bishop, Others

On July 3, 1608, Champlain arrived off Cape Diamond and looked for a campsite worthy of a cartographer and a soldier. He found one on July 8, 1608, and his site selection put the world on notice that the French were taking control of the river. He knew well the importance of finding a good defensive position and selected an area a little above water's edge, protected in the rear by towering cliffs. He immediately put his carpenters to work building his *"Habitation."* He had one group sawing trees, one digging and one was returned to Tadoussac to retrieve supplies left on the ships.

He was surprised to learn that his first defense would have to be against his own people. Captain Le Testu had arrived from Tadoussac with a full load of provisions. After the vessel was unloaded one of the plotters approached the Captain and advised him of a plot. The locksmith Duval was plotting to kill Champlain and turn the colony over to the Basque and Spaniards.

A Le magazin.
B Colombier.
C Corps de logis où font nos armes, & pour loger les ouuriers.
D Aitre corps de logis pour les ouuriers.
E Cadran.
F Autre corps de logis où est la forge, & artisans logés
G Galleries tout autour des logemens.
H Logis du sieur de Champlain.
I La porte de l'habitation, où il y a Pont-leuis.
L Promenoir autour de l'habitation contenant 10. pieds de large jusques sur le bort du fossé.
M Fossés tout autour de l'habitation.
N Plattes formes, en façon de tenailles pour mettre le canon.
O Iardin du sieur de Champlain.
P La cuisine.
Q Place deuant l'habitation sur le bort de la riuiere.
R La grande riuiere de saint Lorens.

Champlain quickly hatched his own plot. The four conspirators were invited to have some wine, and then were captured. They were sent to Tadoussac and tried before a jury consisting of Pont-Gravé, Le Testu, Champlain, Bonnerme, the mate and some sailors. Duval, their leader, was found guilty and sentenced to death. The other three were sent to France. Duval was strangled and his head was displayed on a pike in the most conspicuous part of the fort. [23]

Work continued on the *Habitation*, which now consisted of three two-story buildings each approximately twenty by fourteen feet, and a single story warehouse with a cellar. Around the continuous wall was a gallery for defense, a moat with drawbridge and elevated gun platforms rounded out the position. When the buildings were weather-tight, he had his men plant gardens. The Indians watched and wondered what would be

---

[23] Ibid

next. On September 28, 1608, Pont-Gravé sailed for France, leaving Champlain and twenty-seven men to face the approaching winter. Many Indians were camped nearby and proved to be a problem as winter set in. Brûlé and Marsolet used this time to try to sharpen their language skills.

Nicolas and the other interpreters were there to support both the traders and the colonists and, as we shall see, the evangelists. The *truchements,* or interpreters, were the most important of the arriving Frenchmen. Soon after their arrival, they were sent to live with the Indians to learn their language and customs. The interpreters gradually won the Indians' trust and respect. Nicolas was to deal with the Montagnais his entire life.

Dionne tells us, *"Étienne Brûlé and Nicolas Marsolet, who arrived at Québec with Champlain in 1608, acted as Interpreters, but at first they did not meet with much success. They were young, however, and intelligent and Brûlé soon acquired a knowledge of the Huron language, while Marsolet mastered the idiom of the Algonquin tongue. Brûlé spent nearly all of his life with the Hurons, who adopted him as a member of their family (Brûlé later died at the hands of the Hurons), while Marsolet accompanied the Algonquin to Allumette Island and became one of their best friends."*

Bishop tells us of Champlain, *"He had two bright boys with him; Etienne Brûlé about 15, and Nicolas Marsolet a little older. Without method, without labor they picked up the language. They adapted themselves to Indian life, joined the Indians hunting moose through the snow, and fishing through the ice with nets. They learned how to follow a true course through a strange forest, how to sleep though a freezing night and how to make wooden goggles against snow blindness."*

On November 18, 1608, a heavy snow blanketed the area four to five feet deep signaling a long and difficult winter. Soon scurvy and dysentery attacked the settlement. By February, all but four men had scurvy and most died of the ailment including the doctor. Surprisingly, Cartier's party had experienced similar scurvy problems years before and had overcome the problem using an Indian recipe making a tea from tree bark of the white birch. Unfortunately, word of this lifesaving solution never reached Champlain.[24]

During this period Champlain suspected the disease was caused by the lack of fresh meat and vegetables but did nothing to follow up. Soon the settlers would learn to slaughter animals as winter set in and hang the frozen meat in an icy cellar until it was ready to be eaten.

On April 8, 1609, as the snow suddenly melted and green buds were evident, the survivors began nibbling on the buds and the scurvy began to disappear. Of the twenty-eight men who watched Pont-Gravé's ship sail for France in September, Nicolas was one of eight Europeans to survive the first winter in Québec. From Champlain himself we know the names of four of the survivors: Champlain, Brûlé, Marsolet and La Route. Sixteen had died of scurvy while the other four died of dysentery that winter.

---

[24] Bishop, Dionne, Trigger

Coureurs des Bois

Nicolas Marsolet had faced many challenges and had overcome each of them. As spring dawned in Québec in 1609, Nicolas began his life in New France as a *truchement* or interpreter to the Montagnais Indians. Like other interpreters, he was sent to live with the Indians so that he could learn their language, customs and win their trust.

Les chifres montrent les brasses d'eau.

A Vne montaigne ronde fur le bort de la riuiere du Saguenay.
H Le port de Tadouſſac.
C Petit ruiſſeau d'eau douce.
D Le lieu ou cabannent les ſauuages quand ils viennent pour la traicte.
E Maniere d'iſle qui cloſt vne partie du port de la ri-

uiere du Saguenay.
F La pointe de tous les Diables
G La riuiere dú Saguenay.
H La pointe aux alouettes.
I Montaignes fort mauuaiſes, remplies de ſapins & boulleaux.
L Le moulin Bode.
M La rade ou les vaiſſeaux

mouillent l'ancre attendant le vent & la maree.
N Petit eſtag proche du port.
O Petit ruiſſeau ſortant de l'eſtag, qui deſcharge dans le Saguenay.
P Place ſur la pointe ſans arbres, où il y a quantité d'herbages.

Although Champlain did credit Nicolas with some positive achievements over the years, generally they did not get along. As a consequence, Nicolas tended to stay in faraway Tadoussac for most of the next 27 years. It was one of the busiest gathering places of the Indians, making it a desirable trading post. Other interpreters resided in Indian villages, in Québec or the Three Rivers area. [25]

---

[25] Trigger

The Montagnais Indian ancestral homeland was the northeast Atlantic region incorporating portions of the St. Lawrence lowlands, Appalachian highlands up to the Canadian Shield and the Saguenay River area. The Indians had sporadically traded with the French, Basque, Spanish, Dutch and English for at least 50 years from their gathering place, Tadoussac, at the mouth of the Saguenay River. Records indicate a flourishing trade with merchants from St-Malo sending five trading ships in 1583 and following up the next year when they doubled the number of ships. [26]

Noted historian, Bruce Trigger, tells us, "By the end of the Sixteenth Century, Tadoussac was clearly the most important fur trading center in North America. It stood at the head of a large number of native trade routes leading to the interior of the continent." Montagnais Indians were receiving furs from as far away as James Bay and western Ontario. Nicolas was thrust into this environment and prospered.

About this time the term, *Coureurs des Bois* (Runners of the Woods), began to creep into the lexicon to describe the lifestyle and activities of some of young men who had arrived in New France. It was clear that they were caught up in the sheer excitement of the moment. This was seen in their thirst for adventure, the attraction to the primitive life, the mystery of the wilderness and freedom in a country almost 20 times the size of France. All of this combined with the potential for great wealth created a new social order, the *coureurs des bois.* [27]

Many of the young French traders quickly adopted Indian dress, accustomed themselves to use canoes and snowshoes, hunted with Indian men and joined them in ritual steam baths. Most of them enjoyed greater sexual freedom since women were available and sexual behavior by young Indian women was uninhibited prior to marriage. Many of these young Frenchmen came from structured environments where they were often poorly treated or their chance for advancement was limited. With the natives, they were treated as honored guests and respected members of the community. Here was

---

[26] Trigger, Reindeau, et al
[27] Ibid

an opportunity to advance oneself through deeds and the possibility of accumulating wealth from being allowed to trade for furs with the Indians.[28]

Some historians were quick to assume that the early interpreters became deeply integrated into Indian society and adopted the lifestyle of a *coureur des bois*. Yet contemporary research indicates that this did not happen in early New France. As outlined previously, Champlain's interpreters were held to high standards. Brûlé was a much better businessman than was previously thought and Marsolet and Lintot became businessmen and landowners of importance in New France.[29]

Chauvin's House at Tadoussac

Nicolas's life with the Montagnais was certainly not that of an active *coureur des bois*. It is reasonable to assume that Nicolas did not reside in Indian villages on a continuous basis. In fact, he spent most of his time in Tadoussac. Records indicate he lived in a house Pierre Chauvin had built in his abortive colonization effort in 1600. Marsolet was a friend to the Montagnais and encouraged them to gather as many furs as possible for trade. They were the middlemen and control of them was critical. He wanted to ensure that they maintained their trader status. He served as a facilitator for trade transactions and was given praise for his evenhanded approach to the process. He maintained good relations with the Indians throughout his lifetime.[30]

---

[28] Ibid
[29] Trigger
[30] Sagard and Wrong

Etienne Brûlé, Nicolas's friend and fellow interpreter, worked with the inland Huron tribes. Brûlé traveled with the Hurons to French trading stations to act as an intermediary for the trade. He was also charged with the responsibility of keeping the Dutch from trading with the Hurons and circumventing the French trading network. This was an easy process since the Dutch did not possess sufficient knowledge of the interior to contact the Hurons and, in addition, the Mohawks would not allow such trading to take place. Because of the importance that was attached to expanding trade, the trading company paid Brûlé and the other interpreters very high wages for their services.

Brûlé was a favorite of Champlain and enjoyed his adventurous life. He was frequently called upon to travel. Although he explored the area as far west as Lake Superior and as far south as the Susquehanna in present day Pennsylvania, he was restricted from travel along trade routes in central Québec in fear of the fact that the French might strike a deal with neighboring tribes.

"Brûlé in his capacity had rendered many good services to his compatriots. Unfortunately, his private actions while dwelling with the Hurons were not above reproach.... Marsolet's case is nearly identical with that of Brûlé, although it is not proved that he was licentious during the time he lived with the Algonquins..... Nicolas Marsolet became a good citizen and his family alliances were most honourable."[31]

But the interpreters did develop some enemies and were caught in the cross-currents of the issues that prevailed in New France, not the least of which was religious zeal to convert the "Savages" to the Roman Catholic faith and the competition between the Récollets and the Jesuits to do just that.

The Récollets, it will be remembered, were an order of Franciscan monks that strictly adhered to the vows of poverty and self-denial of St. Francis. They had joined Champlain early and had hopes of working with the savages to bring them the "True Faith." Central to their philosophy for conversion was that the savages must adopt the European ways of life. The concept was that if the Indians were educated and adopted European customs, they would surely adapt to a new religion. To help in this conversion, the French colonists were expected to act as role models of Christian virtues. The *coureur des bois* hardly fit that mold.

Additionally, the friars believed that force might be required to make the savages abandon the most abhorrent aspects of their behavior and colonization would provide that. [32] The friars complained bitterly to Champlain about the issue and they accompanied him back France to make his case for colonization. During 1613 and 1614, efforts were made by several board members to demote or fire Champlain for his strident position on colonization, which was indicative of the continuous struggle between traders and colonists. Simply, Champlain's insistence on colonization gradually brought him into

_____

31 N.E. Dionne

32 Sagard

conflict with his employers who were looking for a return on their investment, not the added burden of colonists.

figures des montaignais   figure des sauvages almouchicois

David pelletier fecit

Champlain tried to get Montagnais families to farm, learn to speak French and convert to Christianity. He even attempted to meddle in Montagnais politics by involving himself in the selection of the chief by one of the bands of Indians. As a consequence, his relations with the Indians became increasingly acrimonious.

Champlain and the Récollets returned to France to argue again for more colonists. He took his case for colonization to the Paris Chamber of Commerce and provided a spectacular briefing outlining the benefits of the colony and mercantilism. They could offer no solution and the debate continued on the merits of colonization.

At this time the Jesuits entered the equation. With their strong financial and political support, they were anxious to begin conversions in New France. They were essentially religious zealots organized by a strict code which states in effect: "the ends justify the means." To them, the Church is infallible; they are predestined for heaven. They must be in control to ensure the natural order of things.

Their concept for converting the Indians was diametrically opposed to the Récollets; they believed the Indians needed to be isolated to ensure that they received the right teachings. In their view, the French should spend little or no time interacting with the Indian so they do not transmit the wrong message.

The Jesuits were quick to try to control the message by publishing and widely distributing *The Jesuit Relations 1625-1658*. It was a highly edited compilation of writing, poems and letters that described this period from the Jesuit viewpoint and had rapidly become the foundation for reporting the history of the period.[33] Several historians

---

[33] Morris

suggest that caution should be exercised when using this material because it was biased and, as one author had described, an impassioned plea for sainthood.

The same was true for the works of Gabriel Sagard, a Récollet Priest, who wrote one of the first accounts relating to New France, *l'Histoire du Canada*, printed in 1866 in Paris in four volumes. Sagard entered the order of St. Francis, (the Récollets, a very strict branch of Franciscans) at an early age. His friendship with Father Chapon, who was charged with sending the first Récollets to Canada, led to his assignment there. Upon arrival he was sent to help establish the Huron mission.

Departing from Dieppe, Sagard kept a journal and, in 1632, published an account of his voyage and Huron mission. In 1636, he published an expanded version of his *Grand Voyage* under the title, *l'Histoire du Canada*.[34]

Champlain sided with the Récollet philosophy for converting the Indians. He viewed them as citizens of the new colony and subject to his command. If they simply adopted European customs and traditions, they could be more easily governed.

Champlain, after all, was the son of a naval Captain, a soldier, statesman, and administrator and, as a devout Catholic, served as an example of Christian values. He had recruited the Récollets and was determined to see to their success in the colony and the conversion of the Indians.

In the end, Champlain's and the Récollets' high-handed treatment of the Montagnais undermined their relationship. His meddling, even in tribal matters, produced a growing hostility between the French and the Montagnais that eventually drove them to help the English capture Québec in 1629.

Although the Jesuits seldom spoke of people who opposed them, Nicolas Marsolet was often mentioned with honor, even though he did not conform to their writings, the *Relations*.

It was Gabriel Sagard, however, who in 1624 began to discredit Brûlé and Marsolet in Champlain's eyes. The Récollet friar denounced the wandering adventurers' loose morals and disclosed, moreover, that they were playing a double game, working at the same time for the administration of New France and for the fur merchants who were opponents of Champlain. A serious matter that will be discussed further.[35]

Colony or Trading Post

The central underlying issue affecting New France had always been trade. Free traders versus monopolists, traders versus colonists, Indians versus settlers, Récollets versus Jesuits, missionaries versus *coureur des bois*. Whatever the conflict, scratch the surface and the issue of trade was somehow connected.

---

[34] Biggard
[35] Sulte, Dionne

From the first day of colonization Champlain, was in conflict. On one hand, the traders believed and supported him because they felt he must have some form of colonial presence to establish territorial rights in the area and give them a springboard for exploration and trade. On the other, they didn't want him to go too far in "civilizing" the Indians in fear that they might abandon their villages and trap areas across the region. There was also concern that settlers might eventually contest their monopoly rights to furs.

Award-winning historian, Bruce Trigger, did not sugar-coat words when he challenged previous histories of the settlement of New France. "Many historians accept without question the interpretation of Champlain, the Récollets and the Jesuits assuming they have "noble" motivations and are disinterested men." Nothing could be farther from the truth. The often used quote that "Winners write the history" applies here.

Trigger continues his criticism by pointing out, "There is a serious imbalance in the traditional interpretation of early New France history. Too much attention has been paid to priests and officials; too little to traders and their employees." He adds, "It is clear that traders played a major role between natives and European people. The French traders were more altruistic than others and their desire for profitable trade made them more adept to look to the long term. Their desire for profitable trade led them to study Indian ways and made them adopt native conventions and become involved in native alliances when it was in their economic interest."

A classic example is Champlain's often cited decision to side with the Algonquin and Huron tribes against the Iroquois. His decision was criticized by many for making the French and the Iroquois enemies forever and, at a minimum, led to years of strife. But it also bonded the Montagnais, Huron and Algonquin to the French.

De Mont's monopoly expired and free trade was restored to the St. Lawrence area. As a result of increased competition, the cost of European goods went down, forcing many of the existing investors to lose interest in supporting either further exploration or settlement. Champlain had to return to France to lobby to get the fur monopoly reinstated and solicit new financial backing. At first Champlain had his feet

firmly planted in both camps. He recognized that trade companies would provide colonists in return for monopoly rights to the fur trade. He attempted to keep both sides happy, which was not an easy task.

With de Mont facing financial ruin, Champlain was successful in getting de Mont to cede his rights and he persuaded Charles de Bourbon, Comte de Sossions, Governor of Normandy, to have the King appoint him Lieutenant-General of New France with a twelve-year monopoly on fur trading. When Soissons died suddenly, his nephew, Henri de Bourbon, Prince de Condé and second in line to the throne, acquired the monopoly rights and added the title, Viceroy of New France. He made Champlain his lieutenant who, along with shareholders from St-Malo and Rouen, established the *Compagnie du Canada*.[36]

---

[36] Costain and Others

According to the new agreement, Champlain no longer worked for the trading company. He was a Vice Regal responsible for governing the colony. Part of his responsibilities was to enforce the monopoly and prevent infringements by free traders. Infringements by those who traded illegally were a constant problem from the beginning of the settlements. Indians were in favor of free trade because competition helped drive prices. Imposition of the monopoly meant higher costs for the Indians. The Montagnais attributed most of the problem to Champlain and were very angry. It is interesting to note that during this tense period, relations remained good with the interpreters who lived in the Indians' midst as agents of the trading companies.[37] Also, in spite of their anger at Champlain, the Montagnais always got on well with their interpreter, Nicolas Marsolet.

Perhaps this was related to reports that Marsolet had a Montagnais wife and Métis (mixed blood) children. A subject frequently mentioned by George Marsolais, the "Twister."

By 1613 the monopolists had triumphed over free traders and money was pouring into the trade companies' coffers. But those monopolies came with a price, namely colonization, which the traders were reluctant to carry out even to a modest extent. Champlain, in his capacity as a governing official, became an advocate for more colonization and there were several attempts to force him from office. Somehow, fate always seemed to intervene.[38]

Champlain had recruited and paid for Récollets (Franciscans) to come to the colony. This greatly offended Protestant shareholders and led to their defection. Champlain continued his colonization efforts and made frequent trips to France to secure financing and recruiting. During one visit, he married Helene Bouille, daughter of a wealthy Protestant; he was forty, and she was a child bride of twelve. Her dowry was an impressive 6000 Livres which no doubt helped Champlain at this time. His marriage was not consummated until she visited New France some years later.[39]

With the assassination of Henri IV in 1610 and the appointment of Marie de Medici as Regent (1610 – 1617), Champlain realized that the Protestants were losing power and that New France needed a strong Catholic protector.

Henri, Duc de Montmorency, Grand Admiral, purchased Prince de Condé's interests in New France. He appointed Champlain as his Lieutenant and gave a 15-year trade monopoly to Guillaume de Caen, whom he appointed General of the Fleet of the new company. In return, stipends were to be paid each year to Montmorency and Champlain. Additionally, the upkeep of six Récollets and the immigration of six families per year was a contract condition.

---

[37] Trigger
[38] Ibid
[39] Ibid

Guillaume de Caen was Protestant like his parents, who were important ship owners in Dieppe. He was a naval captain who had served with Montmorency. Although a native of Dieppe, he had settled in Rouen.

Emery de Caen was the Catholic son of Ezechiel de Caen, a wealthy merchant and shipowner from Rouen. Together with his cousin, Guillaume, they became prominent merchants and ship owners engaged in trade with North America and the East Indies.

When Guillaume, a Calvinist, was awarded the monopoly of fur trade in Québec, he formed the Compagnie de Caen with Emery and Ezechiel, which included both Roman Catholics and Huguenots. Along with other Rouen merchants, the company included the Chief of Royal Finances at Orleans, the Receiver of Finance at Limoge and the Counselor Secretary to King Louis XIII (1617 – 1643).[40]

As de Caen moved to exercise his monopoly through the *Compagnie de Caen*, he was challenged by the former monopoly holder *Compagnie de Marchands de Rouen et de St-Malo*. The former company refused to acknowledge the change in monopoly trade rights. The King finally had to intervene and allowed both companies to trade concurrently provided they contributed equally to upkeep. Under the new name, *Compagnie de Montmorency*, it was still headed by the de Caens and had a trade monopoly until 1636.

Henri II, duc de Montmorency now introduced the *Seigneurial* system to provide for the long-term growth of New France. Under this concept, parcels of land were awarded to a *Seigneur* with an honorable title. The recipient was responsible for the recruiting and placement of persons who could either work the property within some unique parameters or sell a specific service.[41]

About this time, Cardinal Richelieu became Chief Minister of France. He planned to impose a new monopoly on the colony and eliminate the Protestant influence. He recruited one hundred Catholic men of influence and wealth (One Hundred Associates) to make a covenant with the King to control New France. The new company excluded the Protestants completely. No rights would be given to Protestants or to non-baptized persons.

La Compagnie de Nouvelle-France or The One Hundred Associates

The de Caen Company had built some settlements and financed the reconstruction of the fort. Champlain, working for the Company de Caen, had imposed the monopoly reducing the number of ships allowed to trade. In 1624, 22,000 furs were taken, yielding a 40% return on investment. This was up substantially from an average year of 12,000 to 15,000.

Since other industries had failed to develop in New France, only the fur trade offered an opportunity for colonists to move up and acquire wealth. Although land-

---

[40] Dionne
[41] Gravier, Warburton

78

holdings were always a store of wealth, pride and long-term value, in New France furs were the medium of wealth. If the Protestants were prohibited from the fur trade, they would have no access wealth.

The Jesuits finally gained a foothold in New France with the arrival of five Jesuits in June of 1625. They were not well received in either the settlement or the fort. In fact, they were told to return to France or reach an accommodation with the Récollets. Out of compassion, the Récollets allowed the Jesuits to stay with them. These same Jesuits later worked to bar the Récollets from returning to New France.[42]

The Jesuits had arrived in country with the authority to order Brûlé and Marsolais back to France. These orders greatly angered de Caen since he believed the two interpreters were absolutely essential for the trading operation. Nevertheless, the interpreters were ordered to comply with the Jesuit instructions.[43] The interpreters' lifestyle, lack of assistance and refusal to teach the Indian language to the priests had been identified as the principal obstacle in converting the savages. As a consequence, they were being ordered back to France and were to be replaced by those who could be controlled.

The Jesuits complained that Calvinists were at Tadoussac and pushed to have all Protestants driven from New France. Soon the Huguenots were removed from all directorships within the Mercantile Company and the King's Council was petitioned to take the fur trade from the Protestant, Guillaume de Caen.

Cardinal Richelieu was now the Minister of France and a powerful figure. His trade philosophy was strictly mercantile. He felt that a colony existed to benefit the mother country and for exporting raw materials while importing finished goods. As a consequence, he was behind the formation of the *Compagnie de Nouvelle France*, commonly referred to as the One Hundred Associates. (See Appendix for list of names.) This plan was designed to solve many of the colony's problems in one stroke while conforming to his trade and religious philosophy.

The concept was modeled after the British and Dutch East India Company. Each investor purchased a subscription at a certain value (3,000 Livres) with limited withdrawal rights at the end of a period. The investors were issued a statement periodically and proceeds were divided among the participants. Only Roman Catholics were allowed to participate. To ensure that the One Hundred Associates were not just fur traders, it was stipulated that priests and members of the nobility might invest without a loss of status.

In return, the charter conferred upon the company virtually all of North America from Florida to the Artic with the exception of the Atlantic fishing areas, and from the Gulf of St. Lawrence as far west as Lake Superior with its associated watershed areas. They were given exclusive rights to the fur trade of that area for all time and were

---

[42] Gravier and Others
[43] *Relations,* Vol 4, Fr. Lallemant's letter to his brother

allowed to control trade with the colony for a period of fifteen years. Finally, full *seigneurial* rights were provided.

As decreed in return, the company was required to send three hundred colonists each year amounting to four thousand total. Additionally, the colony was required to provide support for three priests for a period of three years. Richelieu acted quickly and the Guillaume de Caen's charter was revoked.

Without knowledge of this, De Caen's ships had already sailed for New France. The de Caen Company had invested 165,000 Livres to send 400 colonists and supplies to New France. They were captured by the Kirke brothers off the Gaspé Peninsula. The Kirkes also captured Tadoussac and the French ships there. [44]

Kirke

The English and French were renewing hostilities when Charles I of England authorized the Kirke brothers, Lewis, Thomas, John, James and David to take possession of Canada. They took Port Royal and captured the French fleet of 18 vessels enroute to Acadia almost immediately.[45] Although Charles I was married to King Louis's sister, that did not remove all sources of dissension between the two monarchs. Charles encouraged the Huguenots and forbade the exercise of the Roman Catholic religion in England. In retaliation for the queen celebrating a Mass in her private chapel, he expelled her and her household. France retaliated by seizing all British goods and also seized the wine fleet at Bordeaux. As a consequence, Charles issued letters of marque authorizing the capture and confiscation of French ships and goods.[46]

Among those who applied was Jarvis Kirke, a London merchant, who outfitted three ships manned by 200 men and sailed to capture Québec for the English. He had raised his family in Dieppe having spent forty years there. He had raised five sons not only conversant in the language but also attuned to French politics. This outbreak of hostilities had convinced Kirke that this was an opportunity to secure a portion of the St. Lawrence for English trading interests.[47]

Under command of David Kirke, they captured the *Compangnie de Nouvelle France's* re-supply ships enroute to the trading post at Tadoussac. David Kirke was then sent to demand the surrender of Québec. Champlain refused to surrender. Kirke did not press the issue, waited at Tadoussac and captured the remaining supply ship and some fishing vessels near the island of St-Pierre. [48] With his prizes, now numbering 14 ships with 600 prisoners, he burned the poorest of the prizes and set sail for England. The remaining ships were eventually returned to France.

---

[44] Warburton
[45] Campeau
[46] Biggard
[47] Ibid
[48] Ibid

This first campaign against New France and Champlain was rumored to have been instigated by de Caen in retaliation for his loss of trading privileges. Cardinal Richelieu wrote of this to the French Ambassador in London. "Please examine his [de Caen's] actions. Being a Huguenot and having been much displeased with the new company in Canada, I have entertained a suspicion that he connived with the English. I have no sure knowledge but it will please me if you inform me of his conduct," he wrote. The suspicion was unfounded since de Caen had a personal loss of 40,000 ecus and had personally taken an active part in defending the colony.[49]

In 1629, Charles I of England declared a private war by giving permission to make prize of all French or Spanish ships or goods at sea or land. The treaty of Susa established peace between England and France; the terms of the Treaty were that all territory captured after the signing would be returned. The Kirke Company of Adventurers to Canada had already sailed when the treaty was signed and were unaware of the terms. The nine ships of the Company of Adventurers to Canada were under the command of David Kirke, a mixed blood English-French from Dieppe. He had orders to take possession of the French colony. With him were the Calvinists under Jacques Michel, Michel, having been expelled from New France, provided the English with details on the French position and current disposition. The Québec settlement was starving. Provisions of every sort were exhausted and the hunger of the *habitants* was being allayed by roots and wild berries gathered in the woods.[50]

Champlain had refused to surrender the previous year and the Kirkes had believed it was because he was in a position of strength. This time the English, through the Basque fishermen, asked if Champlain would surrender. The interception of their French supply ship at Tadoussac was the last straw; Champlain had little choice. He had no more than sixteen men at his command at this time. In reality, he had only one man holding the fort while the others were in the woods searching for food.

True to his reputation as a man of honor and legalities, Champlain surrendered only after all legal questions were answered: Did a state of war exist? Were the Kirkes authorized to act for England? Were these Kirke brothers duly authorized to proceed? As one author states, "It is a wonder he did not ask to study enemy log books."

---

[49] Dionne
[50] Biggard

He was allowed to wait at Tadoussac for his passage back to England. There he learned that Etienne Brûlé and Nicolas Marsolais had taken the English to Fort Québec. Champlain was outraged at what he thought was a betrayal by two of the premiere interpreters who had been with him since the first day in the colony. Both insisted they had been captured and forced to assist the Kirkes. Champlain gave them a severe tongue lashing and would not believe either of them. He would write a stinging summary of their actions. His one-sided account was published, as well as versions adapted by Récollets and Jesuits, all of whom were critical of the interpreters. These became the historical documentation for destroying the reputations of the interpreters.[51]

Champlain's" version of events is presented here:

"1629   The Eleventh Voyage
...At four shifty figures among the occupiers Champlain looked askance. These were Etienne Brûlé and Nicolas Marsolet and two other French renegades. Brûlé and Marsolet! The boys he had brought out in 1608, who had survived the first terrible winter in Québec, who had become the colony's best Interpreters, who had adventured so far and had suffered so much for France! So they had sold their honor, and the respect of their fellows, for some mean advantage with the English!

....He begged Louis Kirke to let him leave this scene of torture, to go down to Tadoussac and there await transportation to England. He asked again permission to take with him his two dear Indian girls, Hope and Charity. And Kirke, recognizing the troubled spirit and the innocent affection of the kindly old man, granted both requests. On July 24 the three left Québec in Thomas Kirke's flyboat.

...The English brought their prize into Tadoussac. Here Champlain was courteously received by the English commander, David Kirke, the eldest of the five brothers. He had a fleet of five large vessels of 300 to 400 tons, well equipped with

---

[51] Armstrong

82

cannon and fire throwers. His rear admiral was a French renegade, Jacques Michel, who was treated by his superiors and inferiors with barely concealed contempt.

...Here too were faithless Brûlé and Marsolet, down from Québec. Champlain treated them with lively scorn. 'God will punish you if you do not mend your ways,' he said. 'If you knew that what you are doing is displeasing to God and to mankind, you would have a horror of yourselves. To think of you, brought up from boyhood in these parts, turning round now and selling those who put bread in your mouths! Do you think you will be esteemed by this nation? Be assured you will not, for they only make use of you out of necessity, watching your actions closely all the time, because they know that if someone else should offer you more money than they are paying you, you would sell them even more readily than you did your own nation; and when they have become acquainted with the country, they will drive you away, because people only make use of traitors for a time. You are losing your honor; you will be pointed at with scorn on all sides, wherever you may be. 'These are the men,' people, will say, 'who betrayed their King and sold their country. Better would it be for you to die than to live in the world under such conditions, for whatever happens, you will always have a worm gnawing at your conscience.'

The pair was surly and defiant. 'Well we know,' they said, 'that if they had us in France they would hang us. We are sorry for that, but the thing is done. We must drink the cup, since we have begun, and make up our minds never to return to France. We shall manage to live, just the same.'

'Oh, what poor excuses!' said Champlain, and turned away in contempt and bitterness.

The renegades suffered the usual lot of the faithless, being scorned by their new masters as by the old. Hungry for favor, they abjured even their religion; they ostentatiously ate meat on Fridays, 'thinking thus to curry favor with the English, who, on the contrary, blamed them for it.'

...Shortly after, Brûlé left for Huronia, whence he was never to return.

...Marsolet took an opportunity for a private vengeance. Knowing how dearly Champlain cherished his two Indian girls, he attempted to seduce one of them, but was repelled by her violence, greater than his own. He then wrote a letter to General David Kirke, alleging that the Québec chiefs demanded the return of their girls. Champlain branded the letter a downright lie, prompted by Marsolet's malice and his lewd purposes. He persisted that the girls should accompany him to France, for their safety in this world and their salvation in the next. But the general was unwilling to discredit his own creature on the word of his prisoner. The girls, on learning of the general's obstinacy, 'were so sad and distressed that they could neither eat nor drink, but wept bitterly, so that I felt great compassion for them. 'Is it possible,' they said to me, 'that this bad Captain wants to prevent us from going to France with you whom we consider as our father, and from whom we have received so many benefits, even to taking the food you needed for your own life to give to us during the hard times, and keeping us clothed? We have such sorrow in our hearts that we cannot tell you. Would there be no way of hiding us in the vessel? Or if we could follow you in a canoe, we would do so. We beg that you will ask this wicked man once more to let us go with you; if not, we shall die of grief rather than go back with our savages. Thus did they express to me the sentiments of their little hearts.'

Champlain made another offer to keep them. He proposed that the value of his beaver skins, amounting to a thousand livres, be given to their tribesmen, to reconcile them to the loss of the girls. He would arrive destitute in France, but with two immortal souls. But no, even this offer did not sway the general. He had spoken; he had chosen his course; nothing would make him change. The girls must go back.

Those poor girls, seeing that there was no remedy left them, began to grieve and to weep bitterly, so much so that one fell into a fever, and went for a long time without eating, calling Marsolet a dog and a traitor, and saying: 'Since he saw that we wouldn't yield to his desires, he has caused us such distress that I can conceive of nothing like it short of death..'

One evening, as the General was giving a supper to the captains of his vessels, Marsolet being in the room, one of the two girls named Hope came in. Her heart was very sad and she was sighing. Noticing this, I asked her 'what was the matter,' whereupon she called her companion, Charity, saying: 'My sorrow is so great that I shall have no rest until I unburden my heart against Marsolet.' She then approached him, and looking him straight in the face, she said: 'I can have no peace of mind until I speak to you."

'What do you mean?' he asked.

'It is not in secret,' she replied, 'that I wish to speak to you. All who understand our language will understand my meaning well enough. All the savages know that you are a perfect liar, who never says what has been said to you, but you make up lies to get people to believe you. Remember that for a long time now the savages have owed you a grudge. You report to your captain things that were never said by the savages; but, villain, you were careful not to mention what moved you to invent such stories; it was that I wouldn't yield to your dirty pleasures when you asked me to go with you, and you said I wouldn't lack for anything, that you would open your chests and I could take out whatever I liked, but I refused. You tried to make some improper caresses, and I thrust you off, telling you that if you annoyed me further, I would make a complaint. After that you left me in peace, saying I was an obstinate creature. I assure you that I was not afraid of you. I want to go to France with Monsieur de Champlain, who has fed me and provided me with necessaries up to the present time, teaching me to pray to God, and many other virtuous things. I didn't want to destroy myself by staying here. The whole country had agreed to it, and my purpose was to go and live and die in France, and there learn to serve God. But, miserable creature that you are, instead of taking pity on two poor girls, you show yourself worse than a dog toward them. Remember that, though I am only a girl, I will procure your death if I can, and will do my best to that end, and I assure you that if you come near me again, I will plunge a knife into your heart, though I should die for it the moment after. Ah, traitor! You are the cause of my ruin; how can I look at you without weeping, seeing him who has caused my misfortune? A dog has a better nature than you; he follows the one who gives him his living, but as to you, you destroy those who have given you yours, without any proper gratitude toward your brothers, whom you have sold to the English. Do you think it was well done thus to sell your nation for money? But not content with that, you ruin us too by preventing us from learning to worship the God whom you disown, and who will visit you with death if there is any judgment in store for the wicked!' Thereupon she began to weep and could hardly utter another word.

Marsolet said to her: 'You have learned that lesson pretty well.'

'0 villain!' she said, 'you have given me plenty of cause to say more to you, if my heart could express it!'

Marsolet then turning to the other little girl called Charity, said to her: 'Won't you say something to me?'

'All that I could say to you,' she replied, 'my companion has already said. I will only say this in addition, that if I had your heart in my grasp, I would eat it more readily and with better courage than the meats that are on this table.'

Everyone thought highly of the courage and language of this child, who spoke not at all like a savage. That fellow Marsolet was greatly taken aback by the truth of these words coming from a child of twelve; but nothing could move or soften the heart of General Kirke.

No further argument of Champlain could avail. He had his own cloak and dressing gown cut up to make clothing for his charges. He told them to take courage, always to be good girls, always to say their prayers. He gave one a rosary, as Boullé did to her sister, 'for we could never give anything to one without the other having the same, on account of the jealousy existing between them.' He arranged with Couillard that they should live on his farm, under the eye of Mme. Hebert. Couillard promised to care for them as if they were his own children. The girls curtsied to Couillard, and said: 'We will not leave you any more than we would our own father, in the absence of Monsieur de Champlain. What will console us and help us to be patient is that we are hoping for the return of the French; and if we had to return to the savages, we should have died of grief.'

So, with many embraces and tears, Champlain parted from Hope and Charity.

...On October 20 the English ships reached Plymouth. And there General Kirke learned that peace between France and England had been proclaimed on April 29. So his conquest of Canada was illegal! There would soon be great work for diplomats and lawyers, restitutions, claims, and counterclaims! Kirke was greatly angered, notes Champlain with satisfaction.

The French were landed at Dover, to be repatriated to France...."

<u>Champlain: The Life of Fortitude, Bishop</u>

Upon arrival in England Champlain immediately pressed his case for the return of New France.

At Tadoussac, Brûlé and his fellow interpreter, Nicolas Marsolet, admitted it was their intention to remain in New France. "We have been taken by force," they maintained as an excuse to Champlain, "and we know very well that if we were held in France we would be hanged but it is done and we must drain the cup to the bottom...." The Kirke brothers claimed Québec for England and decided that those French who had any position of authority were compelled to leave. All others, especially interpreters were at liberty to remain.

Marsolet was one of the thirteen Europeans who stayed behind. Seven were interpreters to the various Indian Nations. This adventure with the three French-speaking Kirke brothers with whom he was a fast friend left a temporary taint on Marsolet's loyalty and reputation.

But Brûlé and Marsolet did not view the Kirke affair as seriously as Champlain. Marsolet had discussed the matter with Kirke and they were sure that the issue was to be quickly resolved. It was really a petty dispute involving the dowry associated with the marriage of Charles I of England and Henriette de France, the sister of Louis XIII. Marsolet indicated that a solution was nearly at hand. Besides, they were sure they had accomplished their mission by being allowed to remain in New France with their Indian charges.

> *"The population of Québec or of the whole country in July 1629 was divided as follows: Inhabitants, twenty-three; interpreters, eleven; clerks, fourteen; missionaries, ten; domestics, seven; other French arrived from Huron country, twenty. This makes the total number of eighty-five persons.*
>
> *The following probably remained at Québec: Guillaume Hubou and his wife; Marie Rollet, widow.... Étienne Brûlé, Nicolas Marsolet, Le Ballif, Pierre Raye, Oliver Le Tardif... Other coeurers des bois including Gross Jean of Dieppe had retreated to live with the Indians.*
>
> *....Since the year 1608 there had been only seven births, three marriages and forty deaths. One man had been hanged, six had been murdered, and three drowned....there had been sixteen victims of scurvy."* [52]

Marsolet's name was rehabilitated somewhat later as he was honored for his work with the Indians and for the company. He was designated Sieur de St. Aignan and presented with four *seigneuries* from a grateful government. He married, had ten children and was the patriarch of one of the oldest, finest and best-allied families in Canada.

"It may be interesting to recall the names of some of the notable citizens of Québec at that time, other than the high officials. There were Michel Filion and Pierre Duquet, notaries: Jean Madry surgeon to the king's majesty; <u>Jean Le Mire</u>, the future syndic des habitants; Madame d'Ailleboust, widow of a former governor; Madame Couillard, widow of Guillaume Couillard and daughter of Louis Hebert, the first tiller of the soil; Madame de Repentigny, widow of 'Admiral' de Repentigny, to use the grandiloquent expression of old chroniclers; **Nicolas Marsollet**, Louis Couillard de l'Espinay, Charles Roger de Colombiers, Francois Bissot, Charles Amiot, Le Gardeur de Repentigny, Dupont de Deuville, Pierre Denis de la Ronde, <u>all men of high standing</u>. …"[53]

Brûlé became a word meaning to give up French rule and live with the natives. Brûlé was eventually killed by his Huron tribe. Some suspect that Champlain was involved in plotting his death or at least condoning the killing.

After his encounter with Champlain at Tadoussac, Brûlé had retreated back to Huron country where he spent the remainder of his days. He seemed to have lost his spirit of adventure and was dejected. He settled in the village of Tonache on Penetanguishene Bay reported to be a place of great beauty. Several years later and shortly after

---

[52] Dionne
[53] Chapais, Thomas, "The Great Intendant, A Chronicle of Jean Talon, 1665 – 1672."

Champlain had returned to New France, Brûlé was suspected of attempting to establish a trading alliance between Seneca Indians and the French in order to atone for working for the English. He was overpowered, murdered and eaten by his tribe on the orders of several war chiefs who had reportedly had been assured that Champlain still considered him a traitor.[54] Even with those assurances there was much controversy and dissension among the Hurons. Guilty fears about this murder were to trouble the Hurons for years. In fact, they did not trade with the French for several years in fear of retribution. Additionally, later plagues and epidemics were all considered supernatural retribution for the death.[55]

"1633   *The Last Voyage*

    ...When official business was dispatched, Champlain inquired for his two dear adopted children, Hope and Charity. Ah, they had gone back to their people, to the life of the camp and woods, and their souls were lost, as they had well foreseen. We never hear of them again.

    Now the busy times began. Perhaps first of Champlain's tasks was to fulfill the vow he had made four years before: to raise a church to Our Lady of Recovery, if She would restore Canada to Her devotees.

He built the chapel on the high land near the fort. It was ready by autumn, and the Jesuits there sang high Mass every Sunday. Its site is sanctified indeed; upon its ruins rises the high altar of the Cathedral of Québec.
All available men were put to work clearing the site of the Habitation and building a new warehouse, with a platform for cannon. Everyone labored through the long summer days, driven by the will of Champlain.

    ...He turned actively to the promotion of the fur trade. A party of English, with shifty Marsolet for Interpreter, was encamped forty miles below Québec, offering competition in prices, offering drink. Champlain countered their move, not by fruitless battle, but by establishing his trading post thirty-five miles above the city..."
<u>*Champlain: The Life of Fortitude*</u>[56]

The Second Habitation – 1633
at Place Royale

---

[54] Thwaites
[55] Berry and others
[56] Bishop

Return to France

Nicolas Marsolet had gone to considerable trouble to stay on in Canada though changing his alliance to the English was not unusual if he needed to survive in his adopted homeland under a new regime. Although Champlain wanted Nicolas expelled from Canada after it was returned to French control, he had no real authority over him.

Nicolas chose the more prudent course of action and returned to Rouen on his own in the autumn of 1632. He reasoned that it was the best thing to do when the French regained control of Québec in May 1632. He anticipated Champlain's retribution and opted for time away from the colony.

Marsolet lived in Rouen, in the parish of Saint-Sauveur. Setting aside the attire of a *coureur des bois*, he took on the role of his deceased father, tending to his financial affairs, conducting business, recruiting new colonists and preparing to return to Québec for a fresh start.

On November 9, 1635, it was as a "bourgeois citizen of Rouen" that he entered into a transaction with his uncle, François Heugier, husband of Marie Marsolet. A month later, on December 25, Champlain died in Québec, rekindling Marsolet's desire to return to New France. [57]

During 1636 and 1637, still working with investors and recruiters for New France, he prepared for his return to North America. On March 19, 1637, he promised to marry Marie le Barbier, age 18, daughter of Henry le Barbier and Marie le Villain.

Of significance are the signatures of several witnesses of the marriage contract. The largest and perhaps most important is Emery De Caen, Captain of the Navies, Principal in the Compagnie De Caen, Associate to the Viceroy of New France and Jehan Rozee, Merchant and Member of the One Hundred Associates. Along with their witnesses, Emery de Caen, and Jehan Rozee, Nicolas and Marie signed the contract.

Nicolas III and Marie were married on March 26, 1637 at Saint Sauveur parish in Rouen, France. He was 50 years old, she was 18. Together they would spend forty years in New France and rear 10 children.

On March 28, Marsolet received the Bellechasse *seigneurie* as a wedding gift from the Company of New France.[58] Aside from the marriage itself, the attendance list contains many notables and certainly does not reflect someone living in disgrace after the Kirke incident. In fact, this tends show that those intimately involved in the business of New France took this in stride as part of the perils of doing business.[59]

When New France was returned to French control, there were no punishments. To the contrary, Marsolet was kept at his post, in all honor, and apart from Champlain's complaints, there were highly favorable reports years later.

---

[57] Bezier
[58] Osselin
[59] Roy

Marriage Contract

To attain the marriage agreement, which to the pleasure of God, will be done and celebrated before *our Mother, Holy Church*, between noble man, Nicollas Marsollet, son of deceased Nicollas Marsollet, living merchant of Rouen, and Marguerite Deplanes, his father and mother, of one part, and Marie le Barbier, daughter of deceased, honorable man Henry le Barbier, living notary-scrivener of said Rouen, and Marie le Villain, her father and mother, of the other part, is to be done by the accords, endowments and promises which follow; this is to inform that the said Marsollet, with the consent of his parents and friends, promised to take for wife and future bride the said le Barbier, to whom he has pledged the customary settlement of all his liens, furnishings and properties, present and to come, with his part of the communal property and acquired property, following the said customs of this country of Normandie; and on the part of the said le Barbier, with the consent also of honnorable man Artus Chrestien, her tutor, and of other parents and undersigned friends, has promised to take for her husband and future groom, the aforementioned Nicollas Marsollet, if God and *our Mother, Holy Church* thereby consent, to which the aforementioned tutor and parents are agreed to this which did belong to the said le Barbier, the future bride, of "all and each" the estate that she will receive, of whatever nature they be, the power to dispose, following the "ways and customs" of the said country and duchy of Normandie, and in case the said future husband would decease before the future wife without children coming from the said marriage, she will win, by préciput [right to a preference share of the inheritance], and before paying the debts and the charges, her complete bed, her clothing, her linen of her use, with her rings and jewels, and if there are children coming from the marriage, she will take only her complete bed, clothing and linen of her use, without being deprived of her rights, following the said customs; otherwise, this treaty will be considered null. Done at Rouen today the 18th day of March one thousand six hundred thirty seven.

The year one thousand six hundred thirty seven, the Thursday before noon the 19e day of March, in the office of the scrivener of Rouen, in front of the notaries of Rouen undersigned, was present the said sieur Marsollet, named to the attached contract, who "recognized" his signature on the said contract and promises that he will hold the promises and obligations, while pledging his position and inheritances, etc. Witnesses Nicollas Lefebvre and Théophile Lamort residing at Rouen.

Note: "...*our Mother, Holy Church*..." is Protestant.
"...*Holy Church Catholic Apostolic and Roman*..." is Catholic.
This was the Marriage Contract done at the Notary's Office on March 19, 1637.
The wedding ceremony was at St-Sauveur on March 26, 1637.

Pour parvenir au traicté de mariage qui au plaisir de
Dieu sera faict et celebré en face de notre mere ste eglize
entre nobl ho. Nicollas marseller filz de feu Nicollas marseller
vivant marchand a Honfl. et marguerite Deplanes son pere et mere
d'une part et Marie le Barbier fille de feu Honni. ho. Henry
le Barbier vivant notre tabellion a Honfl. et marin de villain
son pere et mere dand par ... ... saincte lle a condz.
d'autre et promesses qui ensuivent C'est assavoir que ledit
marseller du consentement de ... parentz et amys ...
a promis prendre a ... et future espouse lad. le barbier
et lad. ... a promis domaine constituer sur tous ses biens
meubles et immeubles p. et advenir ... a p... aux
acquestz et conquestz suivant les coustumes de ce pays de
normandie et de la part dolay le barbier du consentement
aussy de Honni. ... Arture chastitey ... tuteur et autres
... parentz et amys faictz ... a ... prendre prendre p.
son mary et future espoux ledit Nicollas marseller ... dit
... mere ... eglize ... contre ... aud. ledz futur ...
p... ... ... ce qui ... comporte et appartenir a lad.
le barbier future espouse ... de tout ... et ... les faire ... theur
a elle presentz ou a advenir de quelque nature que lion
somme q... par luy ... francs et disposer suivant lez et coustumes
du ces pays et duché de normandie et du ... le dy
future et pour a ... de ... a droitz aucun les future espouse
... defentz ... des mariage elle n... p... par p...
... de las des par... dit toute d'autre et ... les ...
a... les et... et ses ... aux her baigne et ...
et en cas q. y ... defentz ... des mariage elle
n... p... seullement ... les ... y ... et ...
... ce ... sera p... des her aux droitz suivant
les coustumes c... que les ... propre et autre

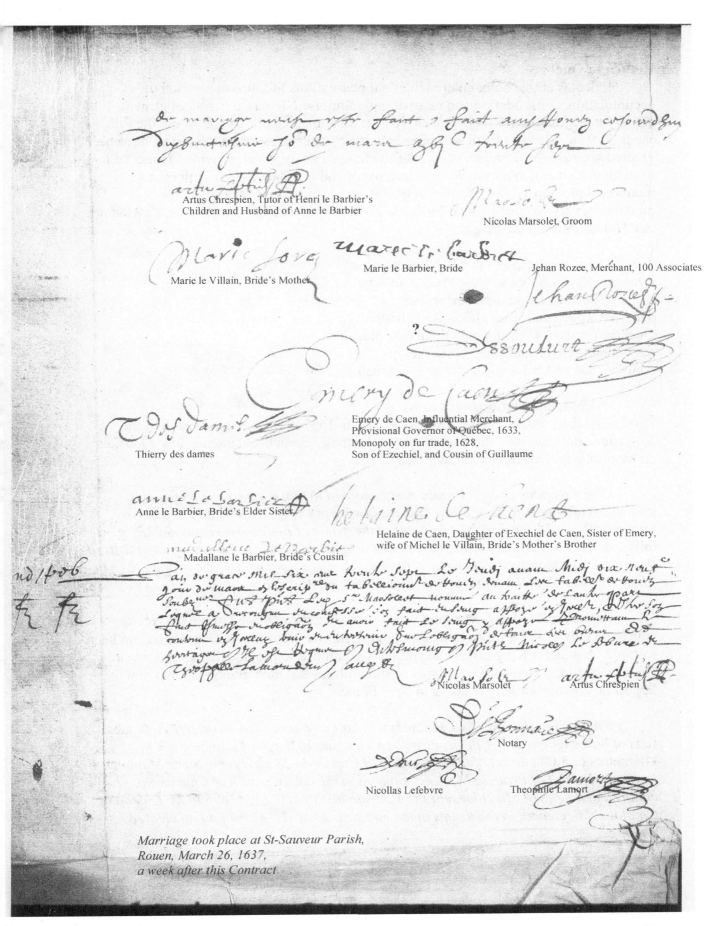

de mariage... fait... fait auy Houdy co fourdhuy dyxhuict Juin 55 de marc azby C fourcte Leze

Artus Chrespien, Tutor of Henri le Barbier's Children and Husband of Anne le Barbier

Nicolas Marsolet, Groom

Marie le Villain, Bride's Mother

Marie le Barbier, Bride

Jehan Rozee, Merchant, 100 Associates

?

Thierry des dames

Emery de Caen, Influential Merchant, Provisional Governor of Québec, 1633, Monopoly on fur trade, 1628, Son of Ezechiel, and Cousin of Guillaume

Anne le Barbier, Bride's Elder Sister

Helaine de Caen, Daughter of Exechiel de Caen, Sister of Emery, wife of Michel le Villain, Bride's Mother's Brother

Madallane le Barbier, Bride's Cousin

Nicolas Marsolet   **Artus Chrespien**

Notary

Nicollas Lefebvre   **Theophile Lamort**

Marriage took place at St-Sauveur Parish,
Rouen, March 26, 1637,
a week after this Contract

Return to Québec

Nicolas at this point entered the final phase of his life. It was a period of accumulation, consolidation and relative tranquility for Nicolas, a period of growth, activity and structure for New France. Also at this time, Nicolas began to use the title, Sieur de Saint Aignan. A title meaning honorable man bestowed on those who have been granted s*eigneuries*, a French version of the feudal system which provided blocks of land to individuals who, in return, were to improve it and populate it with settlers. As mentioned previously, the title probably was taken from *Mont St. Aignan*, the predominant terrain feature near his home in Rouen, a large hill formerly called *Mount des Malades* during the Plague.

After Champlain's death, Nicolas began arrangements to return to New France. In June the newlyweds, Nicolas and Marie, had departed Rouen and were at sea---destination Québec. On the 14th of that month, aboard ship, the young bride became the godmother of Antoine, son of Madeleine and Antoine Arnaux.

Nicolas and Marie arrived in New France and then settled in Québec. On October 6, 1637, they took possession of the *Seigneurie Bellechasse,* "the fine stream for hunting," at an event attended by Monsieur de Montmagny, Governor of New France.[60]

The Company of New France had conceded to him a quarter of a league (1 kilometer) *along the front of Saint-Laurent having one league and a half of depth* (6 kilometers)*, on the left hand (to the east) of the brook of Bellechasse* (totaling 2.2 sq. miles or 1,429 acres). *Marsolet guarded this seigneurie pending 32 years but never lived there and was, therefore, conceded of the land. It was abandoned 15 November 1672 to M. de Berthier. It is the seigneurie of Bellechasse or Berthier.[61]*

In November 1637, Marsolet was a witness at the marriage of his interpreter colleague Olivier le Tardif to Louise Couillard, further proof that his reputation had been restored. A grateful King Louis and company continued to provide thanks and rewards. His service to the kings of France was repaid with several land grants, making him the largest landowner actually residing in New France.

On the 5th of April 1644, the Abbey of La Ferte conceded an arrière-fief (sub-fief) *of half a league along the front with two leagues of depth* (4 kilometers x 8 kilometers or 8,000 acres) *of his seigneurie of Cap-de-la-Madeleine to Sieur Marsolet. It is the arrière-fief of Prairies Marsolet situated in the actual parish of Champlain. The children and heirs of Marsolet sold the 12.5 sq. mile tract 3 June 1696 to M. Gideon of Catalogne, lieutenant in the troops of the marines. As of yet, Marsolet had cleared nothing.*

---

[60] Bezier
[61] Ibid

92

The 16th of April 1647, the Company of New France conceded to Nicolas Marsolet a half league of land found on the river Saint-Laurent coast to the south, adjacent to the coast of the seigneurie of Francois Hertel and of the other to Pierre Lefebvre, with two leagues of depth. (2 kilometers by 8 kilometers or 3, 840 acres) *Marsolet did not occupy this seigneurie or the two others, which he had received in 1637 and in 1647. He sold this 6 sq. mile seigneurie 23 October 1671 to Michael Pelletier of the Prade. This seigneurie became part of the seigneurie of Gentilly a little later.*

On, 3 November 1672, the Administrative Officer, Talon, conceded to Nicolas Marsolet half a league at the front and a league and a half deep (1mile x 3.4 miles or 2,841 acres), *found on the river Saint-Laurent, near Three Rivers.* [62]

Even the acquisition of the Marsolet fief and land in Lotbinière and Québec failed to win over this man from Normandy. In 1646, after having been an interpreter, a clerk for the Company of One Hundred Associates, a merchant and a *coureur des bois*, he became the captain of a barque, *La Louise.*

His days in Tadoussac and in the Saguenay area were still his enjoyment. He had a healthy lifestyle and had developed deep friendships with the Montagnais people through the years whom he thought of as "his people." They loved him as much as he loved them. To many he was known as "*le petit roi du Tadoussac*" or (Tadoussac's little king).

Marsolet land holdings in Québec City included a prime piece of property atop Saint Genevieve. *"We continue to give the list of the colonists established along the route of Sainte-Foy at the end of 1636. The last that we have mentioned is Noel Pinguet. His neighbor to the west was Nicolas Marsolet, Sieur of Saint Aignan. The lands he possessed along the route to Sainte-Foy extended until the current rue Murray, to the summit of the hill Sainte-Genevieve towards the Grande Allee, on different depths* (roughly 2 sq. kilometers or .77 sq. miles). *The whole 494 acres, except two acres and a half, bought from Rene Maheu, had been conceded by M. de Montmagny in 1642.* The area contains what is today much of downtown Québec.[63]

---

[62] Roy
[63] Dionne

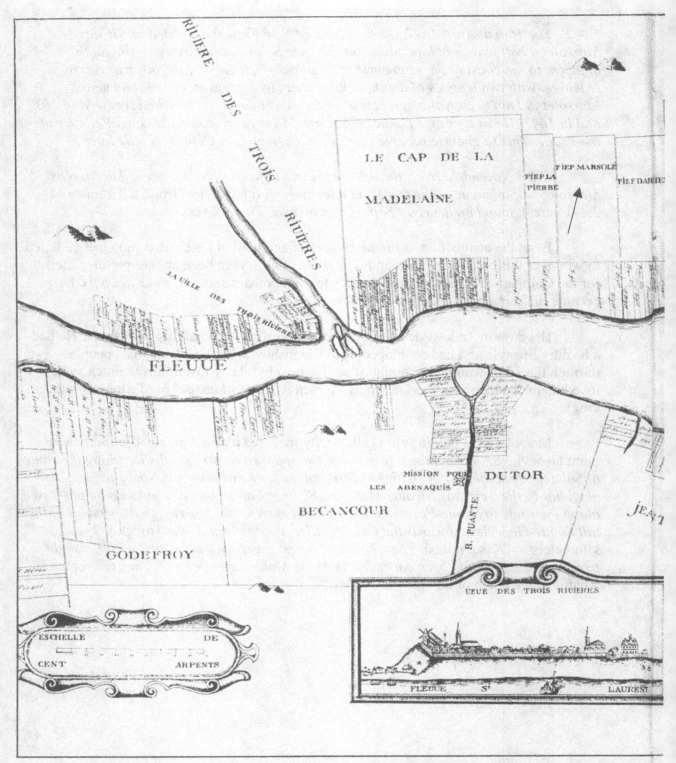

73 — Le peuplement seigneurial en 1709 : la région des Trois-Rivières (extrait de la carte plus haut citée)

Bien qu'ont ait commencé dès le premier tiers du XVIIe siècle à concéder des terres le long du Saint-Laurent, le peuplement ici, à mi-chemin entre Québec et Montréal, a été fort lent. Sauf aux environs immédiats des Trois-Rivières, le long de la Batiscan et de la Sainte-Anne, le peuplement seigneurial est à peine entrepris.

Noter une vue cavalière de la ville qu'entoure une palissade de bois.

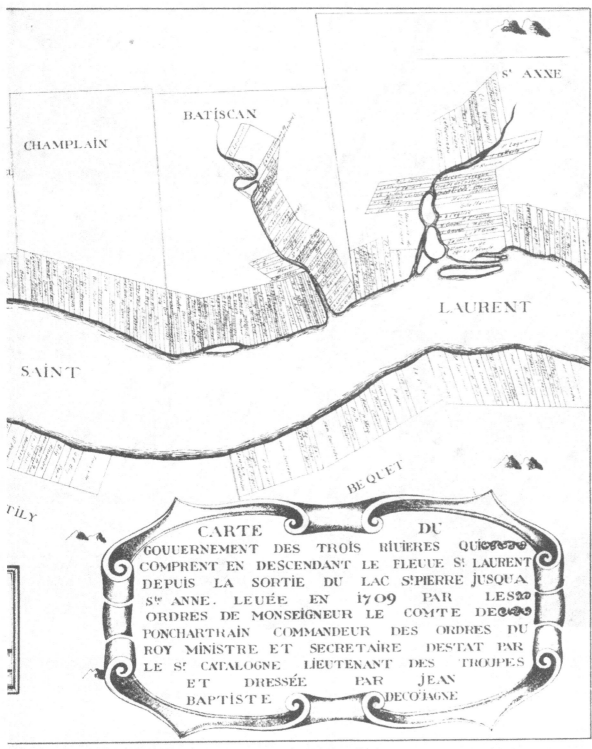

CHAMPLAIN

BATISCAN

St ANNE

LAURENT

SAINT

BECQUET

TILY

CARTE DU
GOUUERNEMENT DES TROIS RIUIERES QUI
COMPRENT EN DESCENDANT LE FLEUUE St LAURENT
DEPUIS LA SORTIE DU LAC St PIERRE JUSQUA
Ste ANNE. LEUÉE EN 1709 PAR LES
ORDRES DE MONSEIGNEUR LE COMTE DE
PONCHARTRAIN COMMANDEUR DES ORDRES DU
ROY MINISTRE ET SECRETAIRE DESTAT PAR
LE Sr CATALOGNE LIEUTENANT DES TROUPES
ET DRESSÉE PAR JEAN
BAPTISTE DECOÏAGNE

73—Seigniorial Settlement in 1709: The Trois-Rivières Region (part of the map cited above)

Although land concession along the St. Lawrence had started in the first third of the 17th century, here, midway between Quebec and Montreal, settlement had been very slow indeed; except in the immediate vicinity of Trois-Rivières and along the Batiscan and Ste. Anne Rivers, seigniorial settlement had barely begun at this date.

Note the crudely-drawn view of the wood-palisaded town.

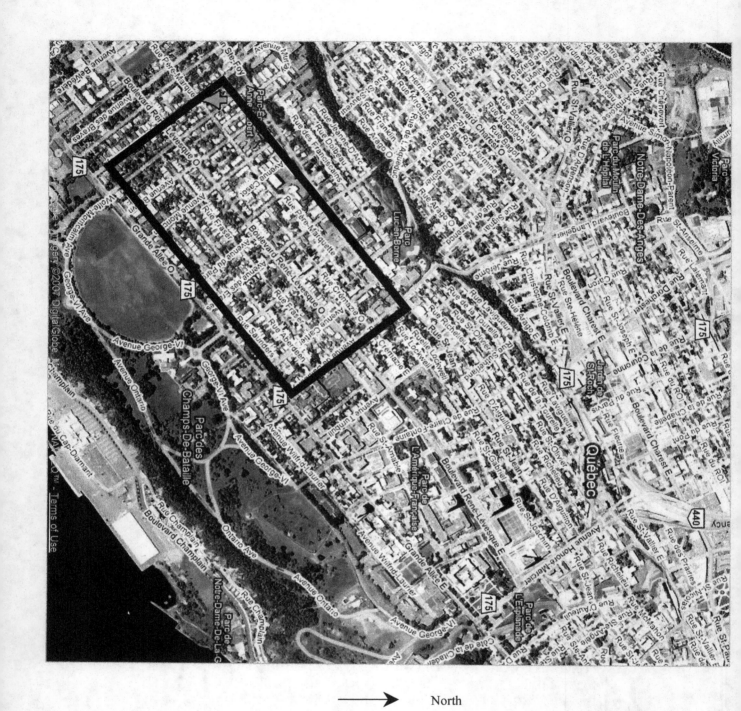

North

Approximate dimensions of the Québec City land owned by Nicolas Marsolet
along the Route Saint Foy.

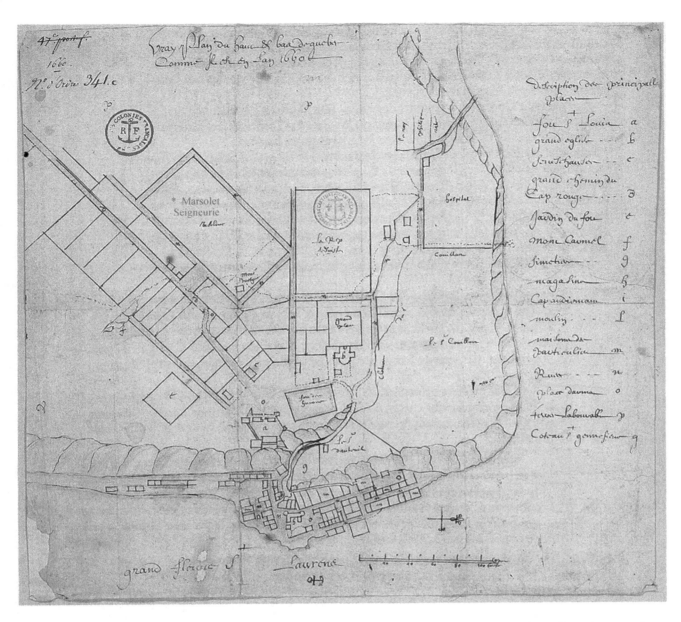

"Vray Plan du haut & Bas de Québec
Comme il est en l'an 1660";
[Jehan Bourdon]; measures 35.7 x 32 cm.

This map of Québec shows the two sections of the town: Lower Town, the centre of commerce, and Upper town, the centre of religion and government.
Archives nationals, Paris, France: Section Outre-Mer, Dépôt des fortifications des colonies, Amerique septentrionale, 341c.

*

"We continue to give the list of the colonists established along the route of Sainte-Foy at the end of 1636. The last that we have mentioned is Noel Pinguet. His neighbor to the west was Nicolas Marsolet, Sieur of Saint Aignan. The lands he possessed along the route to Sainte-Foy extended until the current rue Murray, to the summit of the hill Sainte-Genevieve towards the Grande Allee, in different depths. The whole, except two acres and a half, bought from Maheu, had been conceded by M. de Montmagny in 1642."

"In the censive (seigneurial area) of Québec Marsolet owned two other estates: 71 acres on the Sainte-Genevieve hill, granted by the Compagnie de la Nouvelle-France on 29 March 1649, and 16 acres on the Saint-Charles River. Only the land on the Sainte-Genevieve hill was brought under cultivation---and in 1668 Marsolet declared that the 71 acres were "now ploughed" and that on them he "had built two buildings and a barn': it seems, as is suggested by the farming lease made between Marsolet and Raymond Pagé dit Carcy, in 1656, that this land was chiefly worked by farmers."

Also, Nicolas Marsolet is included among the residents in the census of 1667 and 1668.

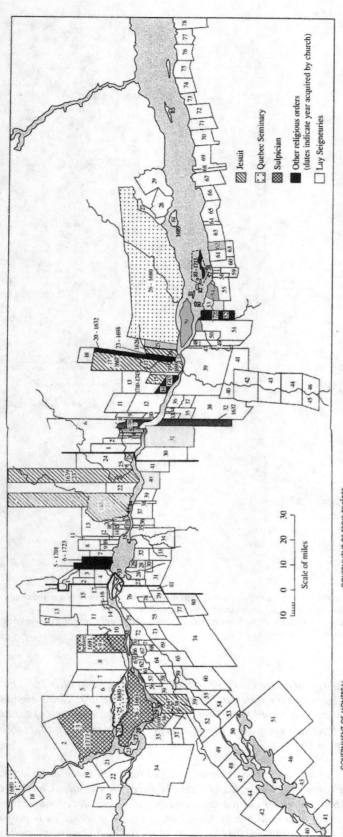

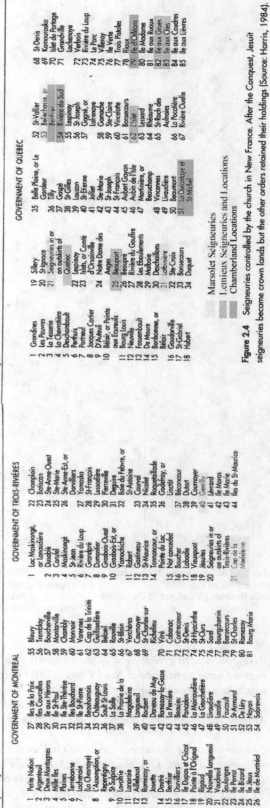

Figure 2.4 Seigneuries controlled by the church in New France. After the Conquest, Jesuit seigneuries became crown lands but the other orders retained their holdings (Source: Harris, 1984).

The Jesuit, Le June, wrote in 1633: "In all the years that we have been in this country no one has ever been able to learn anything from the interpreter named Marsolet, who, for excuse, said that he had sworn that he would never teach the savage tongue to anyone whomsoever." Only "Father Charles Lalemant won him."

Nicolas Marsolet was still harboring the inveterate distrust felt by the majority of the fur-traders towards the missionaries and the settlers, for they dreaded their influence over the Indians who supplied the fur trade." The "interpreter" reported by the *Relations* who spent the winter of 1625–26 with the Jesuits of Québec while incapacitated by pleurisy and who agreed to impart his linguistic knowledge to Lalemant was, with little doubt, Marsolet.

Excerpt of a Letter from Father Charles Lalemant, Superior of the Mission of the Canadas of the Society of Jesus, sent to Father Jerome Lalemant, his brother,
"…. *It is true their expenses are very heavy, as they keep here forty persons and more, who are paid and maintained; this in addition to the expense of the crews of two ships, which consist of at least 150 men, who receive their wages and food. These wages are not all the same. They are generally 106 livres, but some receive a hundred écus. I know an Interpreter who receives one hundred pistoles, and a certain number of hides which he is permitted to carry away each year. It is true that he trades them off as his own merchandise. Your Reverence will see him this year; he is one of those who have very effectively assisted us. Your Reverence will, if you please, give him a kind greeting; for he is going to return, and do great service here for Our Lord. It remains now to tell your Reverence what we have done since our arrival in this country, which was the last of June. The months of July and August passed by, partly in writing letters, partly in getting a little acquainted with the country, and in seeking a proper place for our settlement, that we might show the Reverend Récollet Fathers that we desired to relieve them as soon as possible of the inconvenience which we caused them. After having carefully considered all the places, and after having consulted with the French people, and especially with the Reverend Récollet Fathers, we planted the Holy Cross on the 1st day of September, with all possible solemnity, upon the place which we had chosen. The Reverend Récollet Fathers took part in the ceremony with the most prominent of the French, and after dinner all of them went to work. We have continued this work ever since, we five, uprooting trees and breaking the ground whenever we had time.*
    The snow intervened, and we were compelled to give up our work until spring. During the work, the thought of acquiring a knowledge of the language of this country was constantly in our minds; for it was said that we could expect nothing from the Interpreters. Nevertheless, after having commended the matter to God, I made up my mind to speak to the Interpreter of this Tribe, saying to myself that at the worst, I could only be refused as the others had been. So, after having striven by my exhortations and our conversation to correct the impressions concerning our Society that exist in this country, can Your Reverence believe that we have found here the "Anti-Coton," which was circulated from chamber to chamber, and which was finally burned, about four

months after our arrival?[64] Having, I say, tried to give other impressions, I applied then to the Interpreter of this Tribe and begged him to teach us the language. Strange to say, he at once promised me that, during the winter, he would give me all the help that I could ask of him. Now in this a special providence of God must be admired, because it must be observed that the General was ordered by his associates to send him back to France, or else to reduce his wages; and he [the Interpreter] begged him so earnestly to return the same year that we arrived, that the General was compelled to use imperative authority, and to tell him that his wages would not be reduced, to make him stay this year; and, in fact, he remained, to our great satisfaction. Secundo notandum; This Interpreter had never wanted to communicate his knowledge of the language to any one, not even to the Reverend Récollet Fathers, who had constantly importuned him for ten years; and yet he promised me what I have told you, the first time I urged him to do so, and he kept his promise faithfully during that Winter. However, as we did not feel certain that he would keep his word, and fearing the Winter would pass and we would make no progress in the language, I consulted with our Fathers as to the propriety of two of us going to spend the Winter with the Savages, far into the depths of the forest, in order that, by constant association with them, we might gain the knowledge we sought. Our Fathers were of the opinion that it would be sufficient for one to go, and that the other ought to remain to attend to the spiritual needs of the French. So this good fortune fell to the lot of Father Brébeuf. He left on the 20th of October and returned on the 27th of March, having been distant from us 20 or 25 leagues all the time. During his absence I reminded the Interpreter of his promise, which he did not fail to keep. I had hardly learned from him what I desired, when I determined to go and spend the remainder of the Winter with the first Savage who should come to see us. So I went off with one on the 8th of January, but I was compelled to return 11 days later; for, as they could not find enough for themselves to eat, they were compelled to come back to the French. As soon as I returned, I lost no time in urging the Interpreter of another Tribe to teach me what he knew; and I was astonished that he should do it so freely, as in the past he had been so reserved in regard to the Reverend Récollet Fathers. He gave us all that we asked for; it is quite true that we did not ask all that we would have wished; as we noticed in him a mind somewhat coarse, it would not have been to our advantage to have urged him beyond his depth. We were, however, highly pleased with what he gave us; and what is noteworthy, in order to better recognize the providence of God in this matter, this very Interpreter was to return to France the same year that we arrived, and this was to be done through the intervention of the Récollet Fathers and through our influence, as we deemed it necessary for the good of his soul; and in fact we carried the day over the head of the General of the fleet, who was resolved in any event to send him back to the Tribe whose Interpreter he was. So he arrived here where we are, with the French who were returning from the trading station, resolved to go back to France, the ships being on the point of leaving. The evening before his intended departure, he came to see us at the Reverend Récollet Fathers', to bid us Farewell. The great God showed his Providential designs very propitiously then; while he was with us he was taken with a severe attack of pleurisy and was put to bed, so

---

[64] *Anti-Coton*: a sarcastic pamphlet, published in September, 1610; it attacked the Jesuits, and especially Father Coton, the confessor of Henry IV., of whose murder the Jesuits had been accused by their enemies. Daurignac says (*Hist. Soc. Jesus*, vol. i., p. 295) that this pamphlet was attributed to Pierre Dumoulin, a Protestant minister of Charenton. This and other like attacks on the Jesuits had been circulated in Canada, and had prejudiced against them even many Catholics.

nicely and comfortably, that the ships were obliged to go back without him, and by this means he remained with us, out of all danger of ruining himself; for it was the fear of this which had caused us to urge his return. You will readily understand that during his sickness we performed every act of charity for him. It suffices to say that, before he recovered from this sickness, in which he expected to die, he assured us that he was entirely devoted to us; and that if it pleased God to restore his health, the Winter would never pass by without his giving us assistance, a promise which he kept in every respect, thank God....."

From the outset, there had always been two concepts regarding colonization of New France. On the one hand the merchants and their clerks, concerned solely with furs and wealth, were opposed to the establishment of a large French presence. On the other hand, Champlain and his associates were struggling to populate the colony and preach the gospel to the Indians. For years, Marsolet seems to have supported the merchants and traders.

Perhaps sensing a change of mood in France or because he was reconciled to live there, he was soon to abandon his position. By about 1636, it seemed that the movement towards populating and evangelizing the country would continue to grow unchecked. Although colonization was only beginning, Marsolet sided with the general opinion and resolved to settle down. From that point on Marsolet was regarded to have lived a generally peaceful life. In 1643, for example, the *Relations* spoke of him as a valued collaborator of the missionaries.

Thanks to his long experience of Indian questions and of the fur trade, Nicolas obtained a post as clerk to the Cent-Associés about 1642. But while he continued to act as an interpreter, an occupation which he never abandoned, he soon began to traffic on his own account. Although he was one of the founders of the organization, Nicolas was on bad terms with the directors of the *Communauté des Habitants*, disapproving of their luxurious living. He was one of the principals who incited a movement of protest against the directors in January 1646, which was swiftly suppressed by the Governor. From that point he had to rely on his own resources to carry through his commercial undertakings.

LE SIÈCLE DU GRAND ROI

Navires de commerce, par Pierre Puget. (Dessin du Musée du Louvre.)

By 1647 he was the owner of a boat, *La Louise,* which he utilized in his fur-trading trips to Tadoussac. Later, about 1660, he appears to have operated a shop at Québec. In December 1664, for instance, he was accused of retailing wine at 25 *sols* a jug, despite the rulings of the council. In 1663 he was one of the 17 settlers to whom Governor Davaugour had rented the Tadoussac trading concession for two years. This lease, however, was judged irregular and annulled shortly afterwards by the Conseil Souverain.[65]

The "little king of Tadoussac," totally engrossed in the fur trade, took scant interest, perhaps for lack of capital, in exploiting the numerous grants of land that had been given to him. Only the land on the Sainte-Geneviève hill was brought under cultivation – and in 1668 Marsolet declared that the 71 acres were "now ploughed" and that on them he had "had built two buildings and a barn." It seems, as is suggested by the farming lease made between Marsolet and Raymond Pagé dit Carcy in 1656, that farmers chiefly worked this land.[66]

Shortly before 1660, he began to devote more time to his business in Québec and he still acted as an interpreter if the occasion arose.

Company of One Hundred Habitants

One of Nicolas's final battles was the creation and management of the *Compagnie des Habitats.* He was one of the founders of the group that was established to handle the struggle against the One Hundred Associates which had been accused of abusing the monopoly of commerce it had for New France.

Champlain had wanted to make Québec an agricultural colony to provide some degree of independence but his efforts were thwarted by the succession of mercantile companies who cared only to develop the fur trade. The colonists had no way of cultivating the soil and had no industry to produce employment.

Sagard says that not even one arpent (roughly 190 linear feet) was cleared by the Company in 22 years of activity. The merchants even pressed Hebert, the only fulltime farmer in the colony and the only one to be able to support his family from the produce of the land, by compelling him to sell his produce and only at specified rates. In general, New France was the equivalent of a "company town." Its growth was regulated, the prices were controlled and the company reaped the benefits.

To understand what occurred when the *Compagnie des Habitants* was formed, we must review the history of how these monopolistic companies dominated New France:[67]

De Monts, friend to King Henri IV, received the first monopoly primarily using Protestant money but his monopoly was cancelled in 1609. He gave up claims to the colony and turned over his charter to Madame de Guercherville, financier to the Jesuits through Charles de Bourbon, Comte de Sessions. During that same period, Champlain transformed his position from an employee of the company to that of a lieutenant for the King, becoming responsible for the government of the colony. The colony itself was

---

[65] Vachon, Andre
[66] Ibid
[67] Thwaites, Jesuit Relations

sustained by private money primarily from Rouen, St-Malo, La Rochelle and Dieppe. Essentially, investment was open to all willing to take the risk and share the profits and losses. The La Rochelle investors withdrew after awhile when they determined they could make more money as "Free Traders" ignoring the monopoly extended by the King. This free trade problem would plague the colony throughout its history.

The Company of One Hundred Associates was formed between 1612-1613 with problems between Catholic and Protestant members beginning almost immediately. Champlain was almost relieved from his duties and his position remained in jeopardy until the Prince de Condé used his influence to expand the title and authority of the Charter. Now revalued, he sold the position to the Duc de Montmorency. With conflicts and quarreling evident in the organization, Montmorency formed a new company with de Caen at its head. The de Caen family straddled the religious issue by having both Catholic and Protestant members. They were wealthy and influential Rouen merchants actively involved in trade. Almost immediately, they were challenged by the old company concerning the de Caens' right to operate. The King, under the influence of Marie de Medici, had to intervene to apportion membership in a new company.

Shortly thereafter, Cardinal Richelieu dissolved the de Caen Company and established the One Hundred Associates or the *Compagnie de Nouvelle France*. As mentioned previously, the One Hundred Associates included some of France's leading figures: Cardinal Richelieu; Marquis Deffiant, Finance Minister; Claude de Roquemont, Commander De Razilly; Sebastian Cramoisy, a publisher; Louis Honel, Secretary to the King; Jean de Lauson, President of the Company and Intendant, and leading merchants of Paris, Bordeaux, Dieppe and Rouen including Jean Rozee, close family friend to the Marsolet. The new company was given trade authority from Florida to the Artic Circle and from Newfoundland to the Great Fresh Lake Superior.

Under the new company, only Catholics were allowed to participate or settle in the colony and Huguenots and foreigners were not allowed to enter Canada. The capture of the colony by the English broke up this monopoly but it resumed operations when Canada was returned to France. Under conditions of their charter, the company was obliged to send 4,000 colonists by 1643, to lodge and feed them for three years and give them cleared lands for maintenance. The high cost of providing this was beyond the capabilities of the company so, in 1645, after the *habitants* prodded and petitioned, the One Hundred Associates relinquished their monopoly on fur trade. The *Compagnie de Nouvelle France* or the One Hundred Associates was dissolved in 1647 although the investors retained their seigniorial rights. The scheme had encouraged the fur trade but not plans for colonial expansion.[68]

The losses to de Caen were heavy and some relief was provided by granting a monopoly for fur trade for one year. Emery de Caen was appointed Provisional Governor during the transition. The documents returning Canada and authorizing the operation was signed by Richelieu and exercised before the Treaty of St-Germain-en-Laye.

---

[68] Gravier, Dionne and Others

As time went on, the *Compagnie des Habitats* was formed to challenge the monopoly of the One Hundred Associates. It was made up of an alliance of prominent families joined by marriage under the leadership of le Gardeurs.

In the autumn of 1644, Pierre le Gardeur, Sieur de Reppentigny and Jean Paul Godefroy went to France as delegates of the *habitants*, hoping to gain some government intervention on the fur trade monopoly that the company had enjoyed. The One Hundred Associates had failed to live up to their contractual obligations. Additionally, they asked for Récollet priests to be allowed into the colonies to serve as parish priests since the Jesuits were primarily serving as missionaries.

The effort to bring in Récollets failed but they were successful in getting the company to cede the fur monopoly in return for supporting the government structure and providing the Governor with a 1000 pounds of pelts each year as seigniorial rent.

Inventories were taken and announcements were made and published. On October 29, 1644, the vessel sailed with 20,000 pounds of beaver skins for the *habitants* and 10,000 pounds for the general Company. The ownership of some pelts was in dispute so it was decided to spend the money derived from their sale on a church and clergy house.

The next season, the Hurons brought 32,000 pounds of beaver pelts representing a value of 320,000 Francs while leaving out 1000 pounds of pelts plus 150 hides as rent. The community garnered great wealth from the profitable trade. The colony had never seen so much money circulating and there were bound to be disagreements when jobs and money were parceled out.

After its organization, budgets were established in preliminary meetings and council members received considerable pay raises and rewards for their service. At least one board member stood against the indecent proposals and shocked the others to their senses. The public, too, was shocked at the high salaries. In spite of their attempts to take more than they deserved, they were retained in office. Nicolas had his say through René Robineau, a youth in the Governor's service.[69]

As previously discussed, although he was one of the founders of the organization, Nicolas was on bad terms with the directors of the *Communauté des Habitants* because he disapproved of their luxurious living. Nicolas Marsolet and Monsieur Maheu were identified at this time as the principal organizers of a group of angry *habitants* determined to overthrow the current government officials. They complained that many of the government and company officials were living in luxury on company money. As word spread of an impending uprising, the Governor stepped in to stop it by proposing stern punishments to participants and reasoning with Marsolet.

Although Nicolas did not have direct contact with many of the Hurons at this time, their story must be told as part of the history of New France. When Champlain and

---

[69] Thwaites, Jesuit Relations

the Europeans arrived in 1608, there were an estimated 30,000 Hurons organized into a powerful Indian Nation that dominated the fur trade. The Hurons were selected as a primary target of the Jesuits for conversion to the "True Faith." During the 40 years leading up to this juncture, over half of the Huron nation had been devastated by disease. Influenza, small pox, measles, and other contagious diseases had decimated their ranks. The Hurons felt that "the Blackrobes" had cast a spell upon them in retribution for Brûlé's murder. Sightings of a female spirit (Brûlé's sister) seeking revenge were frequently reported during later epidemics.

In 1648 and 1649 the final blows were dealt when the Iroquois attacked and massacred the Hurons. The Hurons had no European weapons (a French policy) and were divided by their Christian values (turn the other cheek). About 1,200 Iroquois destroyed the once powerful Huron Nation. Forty years after meeting and aligning with the Europeans, the Huron Nation had disappeared because of furs, wars and religion.[70]

Having defeated the Hurons, the Iroquois now had free reign to wreak havoc on the French. In just a few months they created chaos and over the next two years they shut down the entire fur trade and brought the colony to verge of economic collapse. Commerce in the colony was virtually at a standstill. It was then that the colonists petitioned King Louis XIV (1643 – 1715) to take control.

Louis XIV was newly crowned and anxious to create an empire. He was quick to understand that New France would not survive as a strictly commercial project. He abolished the One Hundred Associates and made the colony a royal property with all the government protections. Soon New France had French soldiers, a working government and new colonists arriving daily. The King instituted a program to  provide wives for the settlement called *Les Filles du Roi* (The King's Daughters). The King would provide a dowry for the poor or adventurous young girls who would immigrate to New France. The priests and notaries were on hand with the expectation that the girls would pick their husbands on arrival. The population of New France was finally growing and prospects for the future looked good.[71]

---

[70] Gillmore and Tuchette
[71] Ibid

Later Life

Until Marsolet's death years later, he would still come to the Indians' assistance whenever they needed him, which was often. At the age of 75 years old it is recorded that he went on a mission during the middle of winter to aid them and had no problem keeping up with the party.

"Nicolas's dedication to the Indians was evident in a meeting held February 10, 1664, in which he played a key role in determining the fate of Robert Hache, an Indian accused of drunkenness and the rape of a French girl, Marthe Hubert, the wife of Monsieur Lafontaine, habitant of the Ile de Orleans. Attending the meeting was an all-star cast of colony notables. In addition to members of the Conseil Souverain were the chiefs of the various Indian tribes in contact with the French. Attending were: Noel Tekerimat, Chief of the Algonquians of Quebec; Kaetmagenechis, Chief of the Nepissiniens; Gahykean, Chief of the Iroquois; Nauchapeith dit le Saumonnier, Chief of (tribe illegible); Pere Druillette, a Jesuit and Nicolas Marsolet who served as interpreter.

Noel Tekerimat speaking through Marsolet explained that 'the French and Indians' long history of friendship was being tested by this incident. Some of the youth, including the French youth, were acting badly and this had to stop. Additionally, it was unfair for Robert Hache to be facing death by strangulation (hanging), a penalty that was usually reserved for murder. He indicated that Hache was unaware until then that rape was punishable by death.' Marsolet presented the Indian case that 'in the interests of continuing friendship with the tribes and the fact that the French were not without fault, the death sentence should not apply in this case. Further, that the sentence could be applied in the future now that everyone was aware and to ensure that a record of the meeting should be made so that it will live on in posterity.'"[72]

Le Journal des Jésuits was, as its title indicates, a brief record, from day to day, of events occurring in the Jesuit residence at Québec, and written by the superior in charge. In January 1646, they wrote regarding Madame Marsolet:

"On the Sunday before Septuagesima (*the ninth Sunday before Easter, the third before Lent*), Madame Marsolet, having to prepare bread for consecration, desired to present it with the greatest possible display; she had it furnished with a toilet, --a crown of gauze or linen puffs around it. She wished to add candles, and quarter-écus at the Tapers, but seeing that we were not willing to allow her this, she nevertheless had it carried with the toilet and the crown of puffs. However, before consecrating it, I had all that removed, and blessed it with the same simplicity that I had observed with all the preceding portions, especially with that of Monsieur le Governor, ---fearing lest this change might occasion Jealousy and Vanity."[73]

---

[72] Tanguay, Cyprien, *"A Travers les Registres,"* Montreal. 1886, p. 46
[73] *Le Journal des Jésuits*

Nicolas and Marie LeBarbier had 10 children:

1.   *Marie*, born February 22, 1638, Quebec. Boarded at the Ursuline school in 1644. Married 1652, age 15, Mathieu d'Amours
2.   *Louise*, born May 17, 1640, Quebec. Boarded with the Ursulines from June 22, 1645, 5 years old, until 1646 and again from 1652, age 12, until 1653, for her First Communion. Married 1653, age 13, Jean Lemire, master carpenter
3.   *Joseph*, born 1642 and died before the census of 1666.
4.   *Genevieve*, born August 10, 1644, Quebec. Married 1662, age 18, Michel Guyon
5.   *Madeleine*, born September 27, 1646. Boarded with the Ursulines from May 12, 1652 until 1653. Married 1662, age 16, François Guyon
6.   *Louis*, born September 30, 1648, Quebec and died before the census of 1666.
7.   *Jean*, born 1651, *tonnelier*, married twice. His first wife, Marguerite Couture, the daughter of Guillaume Couture, who had been an interpreter to the Hurons. She died in childbirth. His second wife was Anne Bolduc, daughter of an advisor to King Louis XIV. He left no male heir to carry on the Marsolet name.[74]
8.   *Anne*, born June 9, 1653 and died February 27, 1677 in Quebec.
9.   *Elisabeth*, born September 29, 1655 and died before the census of 1666.
10. *Marie*, born July 20 1661, baptized at St-Vincent-de-Rouen, France. Boarded at the Ursuline school in 1669, age 6 years, returned in 1674, but left due to illness, and died February 22, 1677 in Quebec.

Their middle daughters, Genevieve and Madeline, married into the powerful Guyon family. Genevieve married Michel Guyon du Rouvary and François Guyon des Pres Dion married Madeleine, thereby establishing another important link. (Nicolas may have already been related to the Guyon family through his grandmother, Laurence Griffon.) The most prominent Guyon of the time was Jean de la Motte Guyon, probably a cousin through his grandmother, who was responsible for introducing "Quietism," a pacifist mysticism. She was eventually confined to a convent for undermining the influence of the King and the Catholic Church.

Marie Marsolet, their eldest child, was known as *la petite Marsolet*. After Marie boarded at the Ursuline school, the *Jesuit Journal* mentioned her strong will.

"Performances are given in the main hotel of the fledgling colony, "the store", i.e., the house of the Hundred Associates, the lords of the country, the Royal Palace of the capital, the elite Canadian society gives them appointments, the young people of college, the students of the Ursulines will accompany their parents; it admits even the main Chiefs, who love these shows, in order to attach themselves to the civilization and the French mores.

The Jesuits could hardly abstain from attending the evening of December 31, 1646, because they still lived, at that time, in a part of the same building, the house of the Hundred Associates, where the piece was played. They protested however, by their absence, against another spectacle, which took place at the same place a few weeks later,

---

[74] Roy

because the piece, this time, was mixed dances. I quote their journal:

The 27th of February 1647, there was a ballet at "the store": it was Fat Wednesday. Not one of our Fathers, nor our Brothers assisted, nor also the Daughters of the Hospital and Ursulines, except *la petite Marsollet*."[75]

Marie was married to Mathieu d'Amours, son of Louis d'Amours and Elisabeth Tessier on April 30, 1652 by the Archbishop of Rouen. Mathieu was 33 years old and Marie was 15. D'Amours was from a noble and influential family. His father, Louis d'Amours, was *Counseiller du Roi* or the King's Counselor. Mathieu was the brother of Pierre d'Amours, Grand Sénéchal de France. His half-brother, Gabriel, was Confessor to the King. Mathieu was a *Major des Troupes* (commander of troops) and served on the *Conseil Souverain* and was succeeded in that role by his son, Mathieu.

Marie brought an interesting and necessary dowry to the marriage: for three years, her father agreed to provide them with a house, some land, all necessities including food, two hired hands, a cow and two oxen. After exchanging his concession two years later, the family preferred to live with Marie's father, whose hospitality was never in question, until they bought their house in Quartier Petit-Champlain.

Mathieu d'Amours and Marie Marsolet had fifteen children, of which eleven survived, were well educated and were eventually titled:

1. *Nicolas*, born April 19, and died April 29, 1653
2. *Louis*, born May 16, 1655, Sieur des Chaufours, Seigneur de Jemseg, Acadie
3. *Mathieu*, born March 14, 1657, Seigneur des Chaufours da La Fresneuse et de La Morandiere
4. *Elizabeth/Isabeau*, born December 1, 1658, dame Claude Charbon de la Barre (her husband was Governor of New France in 1682.)
5. *René*, born August 9, 1660, Sieur de Clignancourt
6. *Charles*, born March 4, 1662, Sieur de Louvieres et Seigneur du Lac Matapedia
7. *Joseph-Nicolas*, born May 11, 1664
8. *Claude-Louis*, born January 18, 1666, Sieur des Chauffours, married on January 17 1708 in Port-Royal, to Anne Commeau, daughter of Jean Commeau and Françoise Hebert, but he died 5 months later, and she re-married to François Richard
9. *Bernard*, born December 14, 1667, Sieur des Plaines et Seigneur de La Fresneuse
10. *Daniel*, born December 2, and died December 20, 1669
11. *Madeleine*, born September 10, 1671
12. *Geneviève*, born August 22, 1673, dame Jean-Baptiste Celoron de Blainville
13. *Marie-Jacquette*, born October 13, 1675, dame Etienne de Villedonne
14. *Marguerite*, born November 30, 1677, dame Jacques Festard-Montmigny
15. *Philippe*, born February 6, 1679, Sieur de La Morandiere

Interestingly, the two oldest d'Amours brothers, Louis and Mathieu, married two of the Guyon sisters, Marguerite and Louise, in a joint ceremony in 1686 thereby, again, linking these two powerful families.

---

[75] Le Devoir, Montreal newspaper, 2008

In 1681, Louis de Buade, Count de Frontenac, had Mathieu d'Amours secretly arrested and put in prison to keep him from divulging some of his own activities. Mathieu's wife, Marie Marsolet, daughter of Nicolas, who had died four years before, took it into her own hands to have her husband released by bringing in physical proof of his innocence. After the facts were examined, Mathieu was exonerated and Governor Frontenac was relieved of his command and had to return to France[76] Again, Marie demonstrated she had as much determination as her father.

Hal Marsolais standing on the porch of Marie Marsolet d'Amours' house on rue Sous-le-Fort in Quartier Petit-Champlain, Quebec.

Plaque on the home of Nicolas Marsolet's daughter, Marie, and her husband, Mathieu d'Amours, on Sous-le-Fort, in Quartier Petit-Champlain in Quebec, which they bought in 1657 and moved into with their family.

It was Louise and her husband, Jean Lemire, who assumed the responsibility of continuing the Marsolet name. Jean Lemire, the son of Mathurin Lemire and Jeanne Vanier, was born about 1626 and baptized at St-Vivien parish in Rouen, France. He was a master carpenter and arrived in New France sometime between 1650 and 1653. He married Louise Marsolet, daughter of Nicolas Marsolet and Marie le Barbier de Bocage, in Québec on October 20, 1653. She was 13 years old. Jean and Louise obtained, after their marriage, land at Cap-Rouge, near Québec City, where they spent the rest of their lives. Together, they had sixteen children, of which seven died in infancy. As a master carpenter, Jean was in charge of important works at the Castel St-Louis, the fort was at the location of the current Chateau Frontenac. In 1663 and again in 1667, Jean Lemire was elected to the *Syndic* of the Inhabitants of Québec. The *syndic* was the mediator or arbitrator between the citizens and the *Conseil Souverain*. He died in 1684. Louise survived him by twenty-eight years and died in 1712.

Jean Lemire and Louise Marsolet had 16 children:

1. *Male Infant*, born and died December 28, 1655
2. *Male Infant*, born and died January 27, 1657
3. *Jeanne-Élisabeth*, born June 13 and baptized June 14, 1658, in Québec. Married Pierre de Gaumont (or Lyaumont) dit Beauregard, from St-Jean d'Angely, eveche de Xaintes, France. Mr. Gaumont married again in 1708 with Jeanne Bourgeois, from Paris.
4. *Marie-Madeleine*, born and baptized on February 3, 1660. Boarded at the Ursuline school in 1666, at age 6, and return on February 21, 1670 for her First Communion. Married on November 27, 1677, to Pierre Moreau, Sieur de la Taupine (Faussine) from St-Eric de Massa, Xaintes, France. They had thirteen children but many died young.
5. *Joseph*, born and baptized March 6, 1662 in Québec. His first marriage on April 1, 1685, was to Anne Hédouin. His second marriage was to Jeanne le Normand on November 4, 1690. His daughters and granddaughters were: Choret, Brien, Paquet, Carrier, Parant, Maillou, Chevalier, Colard, Gourdeau, Garneau, Chalifour. He left no male heirs.
6. *Anne*, born March 13, 1664, in Québec, was married three times. She married Laurent Tessier, bourgeois of Montréal, son of Urbain Tessier and Marie Archambault and was soon widowed. In 1689, she married the legendary Chevalier Pierre Jean d'Au-Jolliet and soon after his wedding he was sent on a mission as Ambassador to the Iroquois (Mohawks). Anne was married a third time on November 9, 1694, to Antoine de Rupalley, Sieur des Jardins, son of Jean Baptiste de Rupalley, *"1er Ecuyer de la fauconnerie du Roi"* and Anne de Gonneville, from Madry, eveche de Bayeux. Anne Lemire had a son from Sieur de Rupalley, named Henri-Charles, Sieur de Gonneville. Anne Lemire was interred in Montréal on June 22, 1750.
7. *Louise*, born and baptized May 10, 1666 in Québec. At the age of 15, she was married on the same day as her sister, Anne, on October 20, 1681, to Pierre Pepin dit Laforce, son of Guillaume Pepin-Tranchemontagne (*syndic de Trois-Rivières*, then judge of the Seigneurie of Champlain).
8. *Catherine-Éléonore*, born March 20, 1668. Married on November 4, 1686, in

Québec to Jean Raymond-Bellegarde who died in 1704. She was married again in Montréal September 11, 1707, to Louis le Cavelier. She was interred in Montréal on May 20, 1749.

9. *Marie-Anne*, born and baptized May 26, 1669, and her Godmother was Marie-Anne de Lauzon, daughter of *le Grand Senechal.* On August 11, 1690, Marie-Anne married Gedeon de Catalogne. They had 14 children, out of which five daughters and one son survived. French nobleman, Gedeon de Catalogne, was Cartographer and Engineer to the King. He left France during the religious persecutions, was shipwrecked, changed his faith in favor of Catholicism and married Marie-Anne. He was responsible for the plans and the building of the early Canal Lachine and the Louisbourg fortifications. He died there in 1735 alongside his son, Louis, during the English takeover of Louisbourg.

10. *Jean*, born February 22, 1671 in Quebec

11. *Charles*, born May 24 and died June 23, 1673 in Quebec

12. *Marie-Charlotte*, born April 6, 1674 in Petite Riviere St- Charles, Quebec

13. ***Jean-François Lemire-dit-Marsolet***,[77] born July 2, 1675 in Petite-Riviere St-Charles. He married Francoise Foucault in February 5, 1701, which spurred the population of Trois-Rivieres where Françoise lived with her parents, Jean-François Foucault who had arrived there in 1671 and his wife Elisabeth Prevost from St-Nicolas de Rouen in France. They had eight children: Jean-François (1701), Marie-Anne (1703), **Joseph (1705),** Jean-Baptiste (1707), Marguerite (1710 or 1711), Rene (1712), Alexis (1708), Pierre (1716).

14. *Jean II*, born and baptized September 6, 1676 also carried the dit Marsolet. He married in Montréal on July 30, 1703 to Elisabeth Bareau. They had ten children: Charlotte-Françoise (1705), Elisabeth (1707), Nicolas (1708), Marie-Anne (1710), Marie-Catherine (1714), Jean-Baptiste (1716), Charles-Antoine (1719), Marie Josephe (1722), Louis (1724) and Marie-Françoise (1726).

15. *Hélène*, born August 28, 1678 in Grande Allee

16. *Pierre*, born May 7, 1681 in Quebec

---

[77] The "dit" designation is a unique French feudal method of adopting a name, honoring or distinguishing a family. Literally translated into English, "dit" means "called" hence, Jean Lemire *"called"* Marsolais.

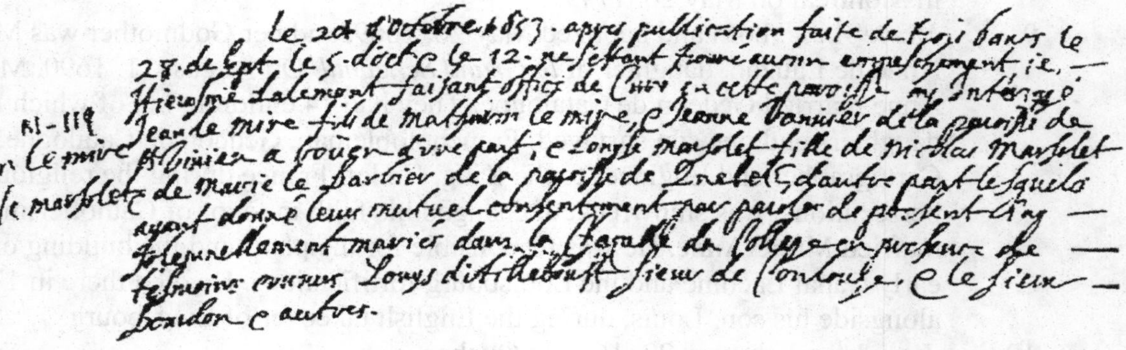

Jean Le mire
Louise Marsolet

Le 20 d'octobre 1653, apres publication faite de trois bans le 28 de Sept. le 5 d'oct. e le 12, ne s'estant trouvé aucun empeschement, ie, Hierosme Lalemant faisant office de Curé en cette paroisse ay Interrogé Jean le Mire fils de Mathurin le Mire, e Jeanne Vannier de la paroisse de St-Vivien a rouën d'une part, e Louyse Marsolet fille de Nicolas Marsolet e de Marie le Barbier de la paroisse de Quebek, d'autre part lesquels ayant donné leur mutuel consentement par paroles de present i'ay Solennellement mariés dans la Chapelle du College en presence de tesmoins connus Louys d'Aillebout Sieur de Coulonge, e le Sieur Bourdon e autres.

Jean Le mire
Louise Marsolet

October 20, 1653, after publication of three bans on September 28, October 5, and October 12, no one has found any impediments. Hierosme Lalemant, having the office of Curé in this parish has interrogated Jean le Mire, son of Mathurin le Mire, and Jeanne Vannier of the parish of St-Vivien at Rouen, of one part and Louyse Marsolet, daughter of Nicolas Marsolet and of Marie le Barbier of the parish of Québec of the other part, as they have given their mutual consent by their word, have been solemnly married in the Chapel of the College in the presence of known witnesses: Louys d'Aillebout, Sieur de Coulonge, and the Sieur Bourdon and others

Through marriages, the Marsolet were allied with many of the leading families of both France and New France. Those families include the d'Amours, Dion, Guyon, Lemire, Gendron, Pepin, Lemieux, Pelletier, St-Castin, Olivere, Rozee and de Caen to name a few.

From a bourgeois family with loose connections to the King's Court, he journeyed to the New World, weathered the first winter and learned the native languages to become a trusted friend of the Indians and one of the leading pioneers of New France. He was a major landowner, the captain of a barque, and a Québec shop-owner who helped establish the Company of the Habitants. He was the crucial link between the Marsolet and Lemieux families because of his recruitment efforts in the parishes of Rouen. His descendants went on to help form the foundation of New France and eventually found their way to settle in the United States.[78] He is truly the patriarch of all the Marsolais in North America.

Nicolas Marsolet died in Québec May 15, 1677, and was buried at Notre-Dame-de-Québec. In a century when 40 was old, he died at 90 years of age. Surely he died content, for he lived his life exactly the way he wished, with freedom, adventure and fame. The last of the original *habitants*, he endured almost 65 years of life in New France and played a pivotal role in establishing a French presence in the New World. At the time of his death, he was New France's largest landholder with approximately 19,000 acres. When he arrived in Quebec in 1608 with Champlain, there was not a single building. He was put to work building the first *Habitation*. When he died in 1677, Quebec was the flourishing political, religious and commercial capital of New France.

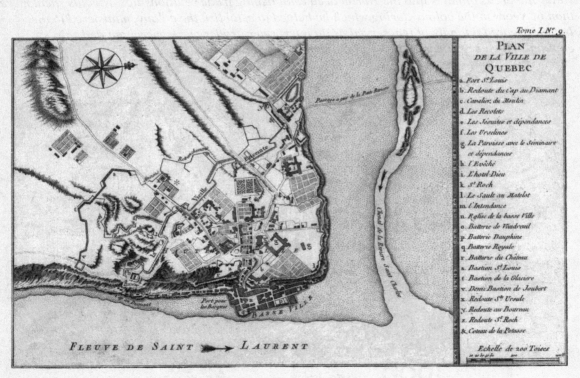

* Marsolet's property was still under cultivation

---

[78] Roy

A BIAS NOTE.........ABOUT BIAS

There are numerous discrepancies in dates and times concerning this period in published sources. We have sorted through the documentation to arrive at what we believe to be a credible timeline for Nicolas. Where possible, we have relied on documents in our possession or on the research of reputable authors. Although his work is impressive, many researchers do not like to rely on Champlain because as much as 20 years had elapsed before he hired a writer to help him chronicle the events. At the time he admitted his memory was not clear on specific dates when events may have occurred. As a consequence, when dates or details of events conflict, many researchers tend to rely more readily on the other source. Additionally, Champlain was notoriously biased; he felt Nicolas and the others led "dissolute lives, eating meat on Friday and drinking." He accused them of "betraying" the French to the English. Through research we now know that his view was not totally accurate.

Champlain was a great man and through his perseverance the colony of New France was established. Unfortunately, he never recovered from what he believed was the ultimate betrayal; Brûlé and Marsolet working for the English. His contempt for their lifestyle and desire for revenge was channeled into his memoirs which have survived these many years as a primary research source document for that period. That serves to diminish the historic accomplishments of both Brûlé and Marsolet. Although he certainly had the right to criticize, his narrative should be viewed in context. Champlain's final few months involved a massive stroke and dementia. In a last minute soul cleansing, he left his entire estate to the "Virgin Mary."

In fact, Champlain actually spent a limited amount of time in New France. He had retuned to France on at least twenty occasions and had endured a two year exile by Kirke. At best he spent a few productive years in the colony. By contrast, Brûlé had mastered the Huron language, explored as far west as Sault St-Marie and as far south as the Susquehanna River valley hundreds of miles into the Huron area establishing trade relationships. Nicolas spent more than 65 years in the colony during which he helped to establish the colony, ministered to the Indians, reared a family of ten, served as an interpreter, trader clerk, merchant and ship's captain. Which begs the question - who did more for New France?

First day cover commemorating Champlain's 1606 voyage.

Direct Descendants of Nicolas Marsollet III

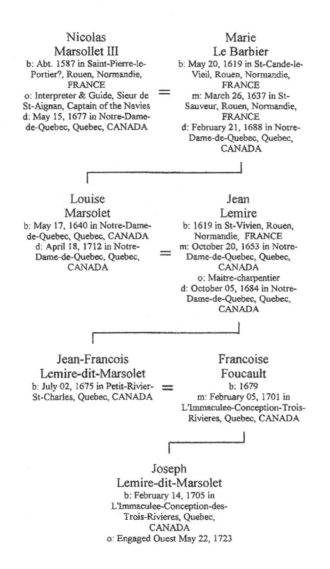

Nicolas
Marsollet III
b: Abt. 1587 in Saint-Pierre-le-
Portier?, Rouen, Normandie,
FRANCE
o: Interpreter & Guide, Sieur de
St-Aignan, Captain of the Navies
d: May 15, 1677 in Notre-Dame-
de-Quebec, Quebec, CANADA

=

Marie
Le Barbier
b: May 20, 1619 in St-Cande-le-
Vieil, Rouen, Normandie,
FRANCE
m: March 26, 1637 in St-
Sauveur, Rouen, Normandie,
FRANCE
d: February 21, 1688 in Notre-
Dame-de-Quebec, Quebec,
CANADA

Louise
Marsolet
b: May 17, 1640 in Notre-Dame-
de-Quebec, Quebec, CANADA
d: April 18, 1712 in Notre-
Dame-de-Quebec, Quebec,
CANADA

=

Jean
Lemire
b: 1619 in St-Vivien, Rouen,
Normandie, FRANCE
m: October 20, 1653 in Notre-
Dame-de-Quebec, Quebec,
CANADA
o: Maitre-charpentier
d: October 05, 1684 in Notre-
Dame-de-Quebec, Quebec,
CANADA

Jean-Francois
Lemire-dit-Marsolet
b: July 02, 1675 in Petit-Rivier-
St-Charles, Quebec, CANADA

=

Francoise
Foucault
b: 1679
m: February 05, 1701 in
L'Immaculee-Conception-Trois-
Rivieres, Quebec, CANADA

Joseph
Lemire-dit-Marsolet
b: February 14, 1705 in
L'Immaculee-Conception-des-
Trois-Rivieres, Quebec,
CANADA
o: Engaged Ouest May 22, 1723

NEW FRANCE
after map by
Jean Boisseau
1643

VIII

Lemieux in New France

ierre did not arrive in New France until mid-August, 1643. It is not known if the Saint-François was delayed due to poor winds, shipwreck or by attack from the Iroquois. Most ships arriving from France put in at Tadoussac before going on to Québec, which usually took two days. As Pierre arrived in Québec he would have seen a small community. Between the cliff and the river Champlain had rebuilt the company store on the site of the *Habitation*, which had been burned down by the Kirke brothers in 1629. The Jesuits and the *Société de Notre-Dame* of Montréal owned a storehouse. At the top, the Saint-Louis Fort had been under construction since 1640. The Company of the Hundred Associates had a house that was used as a chapel, a presbytery and a college. The *Hospitalières de l'Hôtel-Dieu,* sisters of the hospital, lived in cabins and the Ursuline nuns had a three-story stone house for teaching and housing the settlers' and Amerindians' daughters. The total population of the city was only 200 people, with 400 more, including women and children, spread along the

St. Lawrence River from Tadoussac to Montréal. Pierre would surely be anxious to end the voyage and begin his new life.

Until the middle of the 17th Century, three-quarters of the immigrants to New France were men with trades useful for the progress of the colony. They were surveyors, woodcutters, ploughmen, carpenters, cabinet-makers, masons, wheelwrights, blacksmiths and coopers, like Pierre Lemieux, who had signed contracts with recruiters. They were called *engagés*. Manpower was so scarce at that time that the *engagés* could not limit themselves just to their own profession or craft. The colony relied on these master craftsmen to clear and till the land, the construction of buildings or forts, as well as defensive raids to push back enemies, assist the existing settlers, haul materials and food by canoe, and contribute their skills for further development. As stated in Pierre's contract, "…serving the Messieurs of said company in his said trade of tonnelier and all other things that he finds himself capable."

When they decided to immigrate to New France, the average *engagé* was about 20 years old. Since the colony accepted only people who did not represent a burden, it was young people who were encouraged to sign contracts. The standard agreement stipulated that before embarking, the recruiter would advance part of the *engagé's* wages. The same contract guaranteed that upon arrival in the colony, the *engagé* would receive room and board and clothing, and that the annual wages agreed upon at the time of signing would be paid on the agreed dates. In case the *engagé* still had not decided whether he would remain in the colony after his thirty-six month stay, the recruiter had to commit to bearing the cost, not only of his voyage to America, but also his return to France. At the end of their contracts, many *engagés* decide to stay. They frequently made their home in the region where they had been living since their arrival, or elsewhere, depending on their interests and wishes. The decision to stay was often influenced by the possibility for the new settler to assume ownership of a parcel of land or a homestead which was granted by the *seigneurs*.

In New France these humble people found a freedom and dignity they did not have in the old *seigneurial* system back in France. They no longer tolerated being called "peasants." The *paysans*, countrymen, were now referred to as *habitants*, as were all the settlers in French Canada. These were hardworking tradesmen who earned this dignity while they were building a better life for themselves … and a new country.

The *habitants* were encouraged to build a support network that contributed to their permanent attachment to the land. Jacques Mathiers writes: "... *75% of those who succeed in establishing kindred relationships with their neighbours are here to stay. Those who leave their land are mostly bachelors with no relatives, and they more often leave within five years of the concession date. Discouraged by the hard work, unable to raise the money they need to buy equipment and animals, or without the support of the neighbours, they leave to try their luck elsewhere.*" Martin Grouvel's sponsorship of Pierre was key to their mutual success in New France.

On his arrival, Pierre settled in and worked closely with Martin Grouvel, who was a boatswain, a carpenter and lumber merchant. In 1645 Martin Grouvel and his wife, Marguerite Aubert, were granted a piece of land in Beauport where, with the help of Pierre, they settled, built a house and Pierre lived with them.

It makes sense that Grouvel and Pierre worked as a team shipping goods and supplies in casks or barrels between the Gulf of St-Lawrence (Tadoussac) and Québec. With Grouvel, the boatswain owner of his own boat, but could not sign his name, and Pierre, educated, Master Cooper and former ship's Valet, supervising the handling of those casks and barrels, their skills meshed perfectly.

Pierre completed his *engagé* contract in 1646. He was 30 years old, unmarried, and had remained working and living with the Grouvels at Beauport. The entire colony consisted of 85 families or about 600 people in conditions that can only be described as isolated and rough. Instead of deciding to return to Rouen, on 17 August 1647, Pierre signed a contract of marriage with Marie Besnard, 16 years old, the daughter of Denis Besnard and Marie Michelet, from the region of Palaiseau, now Île-de-France. Without the bride's signature, her father, husband and witnesses signed:

Contract of Marriage of Pierre Le Mieux and Marie Benard
August 15, 1647

By before Claude Lecoustre, notary Royal of New France, undersigned, in the presence of witnesses, hereafter native of Rouen, son of deceased Pierre named Mieux and Mary Luguen, his father and mother ... Ls Lemieux, to be married

Was present in person, Pierre le Mieux inhabitant of New France residing in Beauport, also Noël Juchereau, Sieur des Châtelets, ... Martin Grouvel also inhabitant residing in Beauport, Martin Prévost inhabitant of said place, Mr. Gabriel Le Mieux, brother of said Pierre, Jean Cochon, also inhabitant of this place, all friends of said Pierre Le Mieux, who has promised to take for his wife through the sacrament of marriage with ceremonies of the Catholic Church, Apostolic and Roman and accomplished (at the earliest opportunity) to Marie Benard, daughter of Denys Benard and Mary Michelet, her father and mother, inhabitants in New-France. And also in the presence of Sieur J. Benard and Marguerite Benard, children of said Benard and Michelet, and Louis Costé, and César Léger, inhabitants of Montréal, and the said Jean Bonard of Quebec, also relatives and friends of the said Marie Benard.
In favor
Mariage aforementioned engaged couple endowed and endows aforementioned future wife with the sum with five hundred livres for aforementioned to pay Le Mieux with the aforementioned

.... And the custom of Vicomté and prévosté of Paris the custom under which the people of this country are regulated and governed. Are the said (spouses declared) Community Property following the custom that .... Benard and Michelet to be obliged to provide the wedding dress of the future wife, their daughter.

Also to be prefixed ...... of the engaged couple..... also known as the future spouses, to the children resulting from their marriage the aforementioned engaged couple gave and gives by these presents irrevocably according to the custom.....furnishings, acquisitions and gains following the custom contents here above...............................
done and passed in the presence of the witnesses

Jacques Coquerel

Which relatives and witnesses have signed this Monday, the seventeenth day of August after midday
Of the said year one thousand 600 forty seven

	Marie Michelet	Bride's Mother
stated to know signed.......		
	Denis Benard	Bride's Father
Mark of		
Martin Grouvel	P Lemieux	Groom
Neighbor		
Jean Cochon	César Léger	Signed a marriage contract the same day to marry Marguerite Besnard, Marie's sister
Neighbor		
Gabriel Lemieux	Jacques Coquerel	Groom's Friend
Groom's Cousin		
	Martin Prévost	Neighbor
	Claude Lecoustre, Notary	

120

D Benard

P Lemieux

Mark of Martin Grouvel

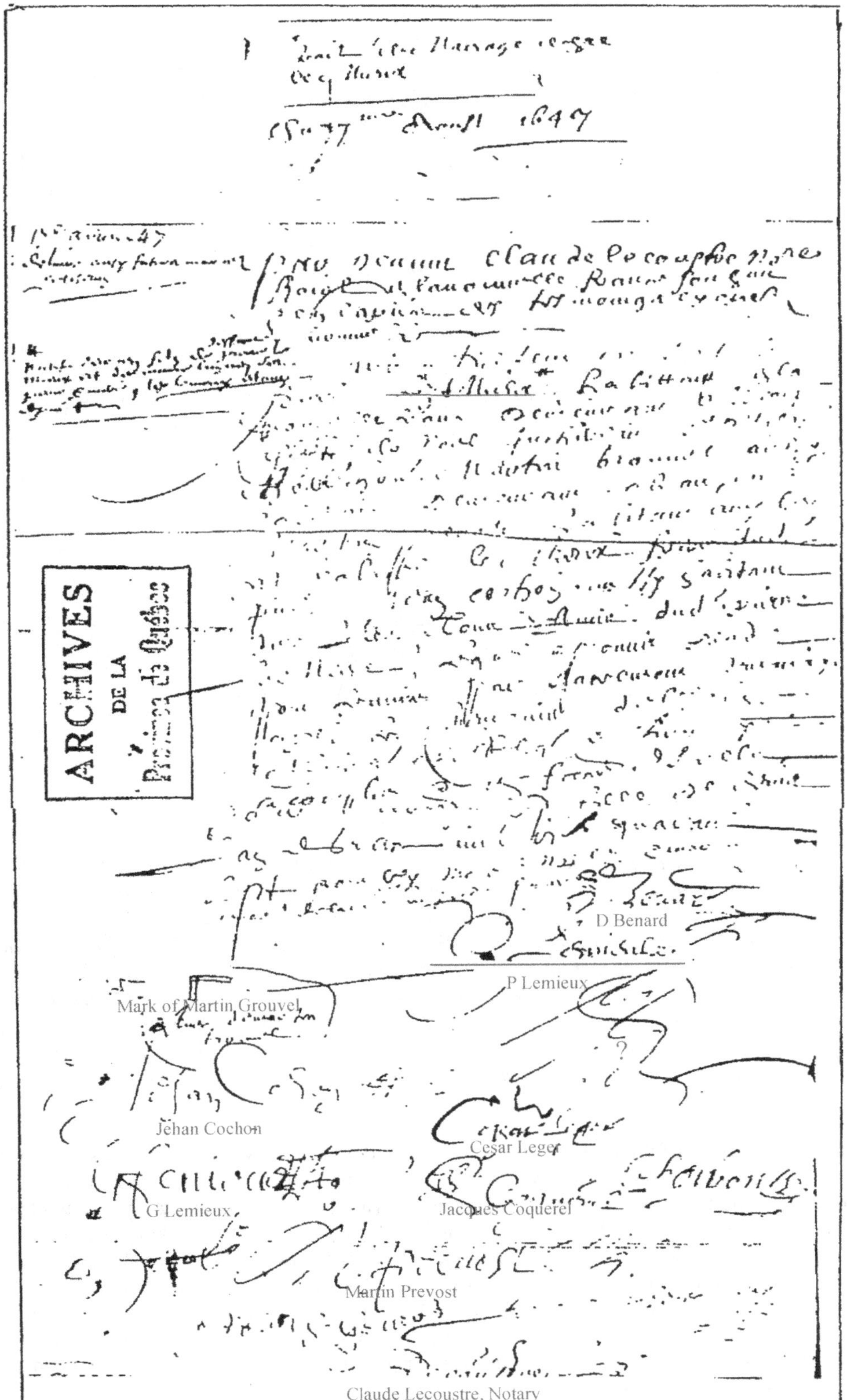

Jehan Cochon

Cesar Leger

G Lemieux

Jacques Coquerel

Martin Prevost

Claude Lecoustre, Notary

121

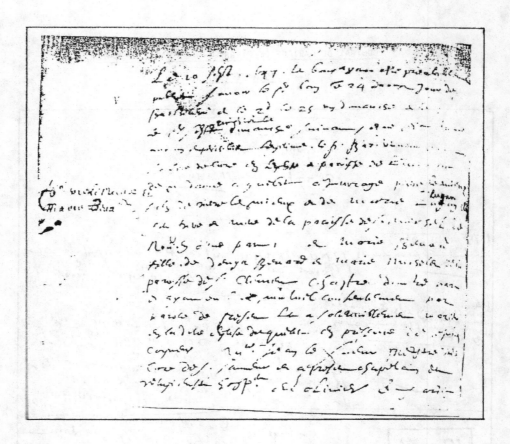

EXTRAIT DU REGISTRE DE N.-D. DE QUEBEC

10 SEPTEMBRE 1647

MARIAGE DE PIERRE II et MARIE BESNARD

P. Lemieux
M. Besnard
10 sept. 1647

Le dixième jour du mois de septembre de l'année mil six cent quarante sept les bans ayant esté préalablement publiés savoir le premier ban le vingt quatrieme d'aout jour de S. Berthelemi et le second le vingt cinquième un dimanche et le troisième, le premier de septembre quy etoit le dimanche suivant et ne s'estant trouvé aucun empeschement légitime le P. Bar. Vimont faisant l'office de curé en l'église et paroisse de l'Immaculée Conception de Notre-Dame à Québec a interogé Pierre Lemieux fils de Pierre Lemieux et de Marie Luguen ses père et mère de la paroisse de S. Michel de Rouen d'une part, et Marie Besnard fille de Denys Besnard et de Marie Michèle de la paroisse S. Clément Chartre d'autre part et ayant eu leur mutuel consentement par parole de présent. Les a solennellement mariés en la dite Eglise de Quebec en présence de tesmoins cogneus Mr. Jean le Sueur prestre jadis curé de S. Sauveur et a présent chapelain des religieuses hospitalières et Olivier Tardif.

The tenth day of September of the year one thousand six hundred and forty seven the banns were previously published, the first known ban on the twenty-fourth day of August from S. Berthelemi and the second being the twenty-fifth Sunday and the third on the first of September which was the following Sunday and has not found any legitimate impediment. Fr. Bar. Vimont, who holds the office of pastor in the church and parish of the Immaculate Conception of Notre-Dame in Quebec questioned Pierre Lemieux, son of Pierre Lemieux and Marie Luguen, his father and mother, of the parish of St. Michel of Rouen, of one part, and Marie Besnard daughter of Denys Besnard and Mary Michèle, of the parish of S. Clément Chartre of the other part, and having had their mutual consent by word of this, they were solemnly married in the said Church of Quebec in the presence of known witnesses, Monsignor Jean le Sueur, priest, former pastor of S. Sauveur and the present chaplain of the hospitalières sisters and Olivier Tardif.

Pierre and Marie were married on September 10, 1647. Barthélemy Vimont, a Jesuit priest, blessed their union in the parish of Immaculée-Conception de Notre-Dame de Québec, in the presence of Jean Le Sueur, priest, chaplain of the Hospitalières Sisters, and Olivier Le Tardif, interpreter and Procurer General of the Company of Beaupré. Of interest is the fact that Nicolas Marsolet was a witness at Le Tardif's wedding just ten years before, and Father Le Sueur was formerly from the parish of St-Sauveur in Rouen, Nicolas Marsolet's parish. Also, cousin Gabriel Lemieux was witness to the wedding.

Pierre Lemieux II and Marie Besnard had seven children:
1. *Guillaume*, born and baptized November 17, 1648 at the home of Martin Grouvel. He was baptized by Father Barthelémy Vimont, curé of Notre-Dame-de-Québec. His godparents were Guillaume Thibault and Marguerite Aubert, Martin Grouvel's wife. Guillaume married Élisabeth Langlois in 1669.
2. *Pierre, III*, born in Beauport on April 16, 1650, baptized April 24, 1650 in Quebec. At Beauport he was a domestic for Jacques Lehoux.

3. **Louis I**, born February 6, 1652, baptized March 3, 1652 at Québec by Joseph-Antoine Poncet de LeRiviere, Jesuit. His Godfather was Gabriel Lemieux (22 years old), his father's cousin, and Godmother was Jeanne Richer. Louis married on November 26, 1682 to Marie-Madeleine Coté, daughter of Louis and Élisabeth Langlois. They had **Louis II** on October 4, 1683 on Île-aux-Grues. He was baptized October 6, 1683 at Cap-St-Ignace, and married Genevieve Fortin in 1705. **Louis I** and Madeleine Coté also had Alexis on October 27, 1685.

4. *Marie*, born and baptized 14 February 14, 1654 at Quebec. Her godparents were Louis Couillard dit de Lespinay and Marie Bourdon. She was killed accidentally at age 4 by a rifle shot on June 7, 1658, and was buried June 8.
5. *Jeanne*, born March 20, 1656, baptized March 22, 1656 at Québec. Her godparents were Jean-François Bourdon and Marie Olivier Sylvestre Manitouabewich, wife of Martin Prévost. She probably died before the 1666 census.
6. *Marie-Françoise*, born April 21, 1658, baptized June 20, 1658 at Québec. Her godparents were Jean-Baptist le Sueur and Marie Giffard. She probably died before the 1666 census.
7. *Thomas*, born August 18, 1660, baptized August 30, 1660 at Quebec. His godparents were Thomas Touchet and Marie Giffard, wife of Nicolas Juchereau, Sieur de Saint-Denis. He probably died before the 1666 census.

As mentioned, Martin Grouvel was granted land in 1645. It was four arpents wide and located on the coast of Beaupré where the church of Courville now stands, around 2600 de la rue Royale. Pierre helped the Grouvels clear the land and build their house and still lived with them when he and Marie had their first child. On October 19, 1649 the concession of a piece of land was given to Pierre Lemieux, resident of Beauport, by Robert Giffard, Counselor of the King, ordinary doctor of His Majesty. It was the first piece of land east of Martin Grouvel's measuring two arpents on the St. Lawrence River (1.69 acres) and stretched back to the bend in the River du Sault Montmorency within the seigneury of Beauport.

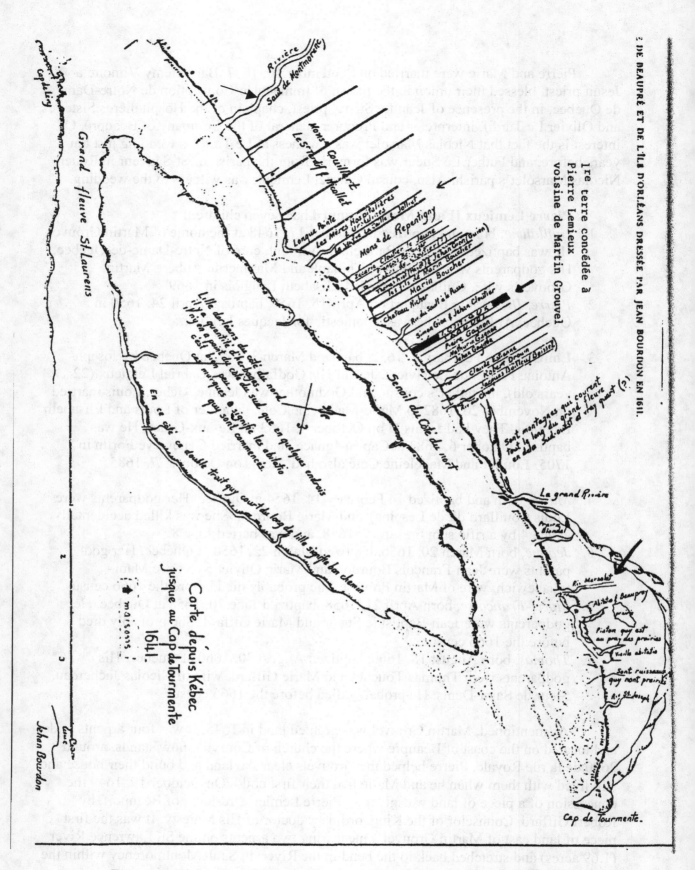

1re terre concédée à
Pierre Lemieux
voisine de Martin Grouvel

Top arrow: Riviere Sault de Montmorency. Second arrow: LaSalle and Jolliet's land.
Third arrow: 1st land given to Pierre Lemieux, neighbor of Martin Grouvel
Bottom arrow: Riviere Marsolet

On Jun 6, 1650, Olivier Le Tardif, procurer of the Company of Beaupré, conceded to Pierre Lemieux 6 arpents of land on the front (5.07 acres), located between Guillaume Thibault and Jean Cochon.

On January 10, 1655, the concession of land situated by Beauport from Robert Giffard, *Seigneur* de Beauport, was renewed for Pierre Lemieux, Master *Tonnelier* and *habitant* of the *seigneurie de Beauport,* measuring 2 arpents at the front (1.69 acres), between the rivers St. Lawrence and Sault Montmorency.

Thanks to deeds by notaries, census surveys and court records, we know the normal order of construction of farm buildings. The *habitants* began by building a basic shelter which would become a utility building once their house was built. Even though furniture was imported and woodworkers came to settle in New France, 17th Century pioneers such as Pierre, with his new wife, Marie, built their own furniture, mostly beds, cupboards, tables, chests, benches and chairs. They would then build a barn and a shed. If they could afford it later, they would also build a stable and a dairy barn.

The *habitants'* work was related to the seasonal cycle. In the spring, they would straighten fences and take their animals to pasture, either on their land or on the commons. They would plough and seed their land with oat, wheat, hay and barley and plant the vegetable garden. At the end of July, they would put up hay for the animals. One month later, they would harvest the cereal crop which they would take to the mill for grinding. In the fall, they would store the grain, bring in the animals, stack the wood, butcher, store provisions in the attic or cellar and prepare the soil for the next season's crops. During the winter, caring for the animals would take up most of their time, but they also had to heat their house and so had to cut trees and prepare a supply of firewood.

Adapting to the North American climate was essential for Pierre who had to get to know and overcome winter. His three years of commitment taught him how to live differently from his life in France where, as a rule, snow was rare and the cold was never so raw. His comfort and his health depended in part on the quality of the house he had built and how well it is heated.

By the same token, the cold forced him to change his wardrobe, and his way of getting from one place to another. To protect himself from the frost, he copied some of the Amerindian's clothing items, including *mitaines* on his hands and moose leather boots lined with beaver fur. Like the native people, and as was done in some cold European countries, he would wear a *pelisse*, a fur-lined coat. To walk in the snow, he would wear snowshoes and load his provisions on a toboggan to slide on snow and ice. He would hitch his horse to the sleigh and the cutter.

In times of scarcity, the *habitant* sometimes would go hungry, and even under the best of conditions, some farms did not produce enough to feed their families and animals between harvests. To maintain provisions in one's attic and cellar, one had to take seasons into account. After the fall harvest, reserves were plentiful, but in the spring, when the thaw threatened them, provisions were at their lowest.

Products imported from France were luxury items, and were more accessible to town residents than to the *habitant* who tried to produce his own everyday foods. His larder had to contain the essentials. A traditional farm provided cereal for the animals and wheat for making flour and bread. Poultry and livestock provided eggs, meat, cream, butter and cheese. The orchard and garden provided fruits and vegetable - especially turnips, cabbages, onions, leeks and beets. Nature could be abundant with wild fruits - blueberries, strawberries, raspberries, currants, blackberries and plums. As early as 1634, home-brewed beer and wines made from domestic fruits were commonly consumed. Barrels were always in demand.

If the *habitant* paid the *seigneur* a fee which authorized him to fish and hunt on his estate, he found what he needed to enrich his table closer to home. The country was filled with game birds: ducks, geese, partridge and passenger pigeons - and with fish: eel, pickerel, carp, smelt, sturgeon, herring, cod, salmon and trout.

As the flow of migration toward New France was very low, land development and occupation of new lands relied on the birth rate. In 1673 Louis XIV tightened the budgets he reserved for populating New France in order to concentrate on European wars, and instituted measures designed to encourage early marriage and population growth. Young men who married at 20 years or younger and girls who married at 16 years or younger each received 20 pounds on their wedding day. A yearly pension of 300 pounds was given to families of ten living children and 400 pounds to families of twelve or more children.

In New France, the family was a strong cell, closed in on itself, especially as the children did not have to leave their parents while they were still young to apprentice in a trade as was the custom in France. Colonial administrators attributed this family

126

solidarity to the Amerindian influence and they judged it as dreadful. In May, 1706, the administrator Jacques Raudot wrote: *"People in this country love their children madly, imitating in this sense the Savages, and this prevents them from disciplining them and forming their characters (honour)."*

LA SORTIE DE L'ECOLE

In the colony's earliest days — in this case, 1635 — the Jesuits opened a school for the sons of colonists. Over the years, they added a secondary level of education in their Classics course. In 1653, they had only 16 students, divided into two classes: one for grammar, the other for mathematics. Despite its modest beginnings, however, the Jesuit College in Quebec City remained the only one, during the entire French regime, to offer a complete primary and secondary education. The Jesuits taught catechism, French and arithmetic, then, little by little, the entire Classics course. During their studies, students of the college even presented philosophical theses at public events, which were attended by most of the lay and clerical elite of the colony.

In 1639, three Ursuline nuns from Tours and Bordeaux disembarked at Quebec City, under the direction of Marie de l'Incarnation, who had this school built to house the sisters and board the students.

At the request of the Jesuits and subsidized by Madame de la Peltrie, the Ursulines had come to convert native women and girls, and to instruct the daughters of early colonists. Their clientele was formed of boarders and day pupils from all social classes, including the Marsolet daughters and granddaughters.

Marie and Louise Marsolet boarded at this school for a year in 1644 and 1645 respectively. Neither of them were attending in 1650 when the school burned down.

INCENDIE DU PREMIER MONASTÈRE 1650

ÉGLISE ET PENSIONNAT DU SECOND MONASTÈRE
bâti en 1651   brulé en 1686

The church and school were rebuilt in 1651 and Marie-Madeleine Marsolet, age 5 1/2, and her sister, Louise, age 12, boarded here from 1652 to 1653. Louise made her First Communion and in October 1653 married Jean Lemire.

After Nicolas Marsolet died in 1677, Marie le Barbier gave some of their land to the Ursulines; this would contribute to the education of their granddaughters and subsequent generations. Children living in the main towns were fortunate to have education offered to them. Most of the French in Canada did not know how to sign their own name. Knowledge was transmitted by those mothers who were educated, especially when living in the wilderness like Pierre Lemieux, Marie Besnard and their children.

At the beginning of the eighteenth century, a constant drop in the numbers of native students led the Ursulines to devote themselves solely to the education of colonists' daughters. Over the years, they added new subjects to their program, including history, geography, music and the sciences.

The French who settled in New France were very clean and careful of their appearance, as was noted by several travelers who visited the country as tourists. In the main towns, the population followed the Parisian fashion and it was hard to differentiate between the social classes. In the rural areas, where people were not so extravagant and spent less on clothing, garments were more practical. Sundays and holidays were the occasions to wear ribbons and lace. Until flax was grown and looms built, all fabric was brought from France.

In New France, the home was the place most conducive to socializing. In France in those days, the peasants would meet at the stables and stay up late to listen to stories or sing together as they worked: *"The women card and spin the wool as their partners do the leatherwork."* In Canada, the *veillées* (evening gatherings) were exclusively recreational. People played cards, and even though musical instruments were scarce, there was singing and dancing.

The clergy did not tolerate dancing. In an order written on February 16, 1691, Monseigneur de Saint-Vallier, Bishop of Québec, *"urges the confessors to keep the parishioners away from popular dances which are gatherings of iniquity."* Even when they were vigorous, interventions from the Church did not prevent the *habitants* from dancing, especially at weddings and days when abstinence was not required (*jours gras*).

Entertainment of all kinds could not escape the vigilance of the Church. Games, dancing, balls, cabarets, theater and in some cases, music were often denounced by the Church authorities. The cabarets were also under close surveillance. The cabaret, sometimes the only other meeting place for villagers, could not in any way compete with the Church. Under the French Regime, there were several attempts at regulating the sale and consumption of alcohol and the opening of cabarets on Sunday.

Coming from the rigid French social structure, Canadians valued their freedom above all else. Land was everywhere and it was free. The revenue from the fur trade was open to any able-bodied man with complete independence from traditional channels of authority. Royal edicts, the King's Administrators and the *seigneurs* exerted relatively little control over the *habitants* who were spread out over two hundred miles along the St-Lawrence River. Even the Church's interdictions sat lightly on them. The French way of life had been transformed.

A concession dated May 24, 1659 gave Pierre a piece of land in Quebec City. Since the space between the cape and the river is very narrow, the property measured only twenty-four and a half feet wide and twenty-four feet deep (588 sq. feet). It was situated at the corner of Sous le Fort and rue Champlain at the bottom of "Breakneck Stairs." It was then the last piece of private property granted. In the concession it is mentioned that Pierre "will have the obligation to build a high wooden stockade." It is worth noting that this piece of property was neighboring a brewery owned by the Jesuits and named, humorously, The Holy Fathers' Brewerie. Good neighbors for a cooper.

Now Pierre and Marie had a pied-à-terre or a place of busines in town. They could always stay with Gabriel and Marguerite just down the street for the city life, for business or pleasure whenever they wished.

CONCESSION PAR PIERRE DENIS SR. DE LA RONDE
A PIERRE LEMIEUX
(Devant G. Audouart, N.P.)

le 24 mai 1659

Pardevant Guillaume Audouart Secretaire du Conseil estably par Le Roy a Québec Notiare en la Nouvelle France et tesmoins soubsignez fut present en sa personne Pierre Denis Escuyer Seigneur de La Ronde lequel a recogneu et confessé avoir ceddé transporté a Pierre Le Mieux habitant demeurant en la Coste de Beauport a ce present et acceptant une place conentant de front vingt quatre pieds et demy ou environ sur vingt deux pieds ou environ de profondeur Joingnant d'un costé a la place of the Charles Cadieu dit Courville et dautre costé aux terres non cence dez le tout suivant et conformenent au tiltre de concession quy en a esté baillé par Messire Pierre de Voyer Chevallier vicomte dargenson cy devant Gouverneur et Lieutenant General pour Le Roy en ce pais of the la Nouvelle france en datte du 28e octobre mil six cent cinquante huit signé P. de Voyer Dargenson et plus bas par Monsiegneur Gillet – Ceste cession transport fait par le dit Sieur de La Ronde au dit Le Mieux a condition d'en jouir luy ses hoirs et ayant cause a perpetuite Moyennant que the said preneur sera obligé de fermer et clarre un jardin de bons pieux qui est joignant La brasserie et qui va jusques a la maison du nommé Descarreaux, Ycelle closture estre faicte bonne et valable et sujette a visitte a la reserve de tenir par le dit preneur les chemins Libres qui seront jugés necessaries. La dicte cession et transport faicte sans autres charges debtes ny hypotheques quelconnues par le dit Seigneur ceddant au dit preneur pour en jouir luy ses hoirs et ayant cause a ladvenir en toute propriété sans aulcune charges de droicts seigneuriaulx deus de present et qui pourroient estre pretendus pour ladvenir en faisant la dite closture ainsy quil est speciffié cy dessus Et pour cet effect le dit Siegneur bailleur sest obligé de matter es mains du dict preneur Le contract et Tiltre de concession a luy donné concernant la propriété de la dicte place voulant &ca, qu'il en prenne possession &ca, Et pour cet effet a institué son procureur le porteur des presentes auquel il donne tout pouvoir de faire ce que requis sera le concernant et en faire revocation sur Obligation de tous ses biens presents et advenir Renoncant &ca, faict et passé a Québec en lestude du Notaire susdit et soubsigne Le vingt quatriesme jour de may mil six cent cinquante neuf en presence de Jean dutertre et Paul Vachon, tesmoins soubsignez avec les parties – Et la closture cy dessus mentionnez sera faite dans le jour et an des presentes sinon et a faute de quoy les presentes seront nulles et encore qu'il soit speciffié que le dit preneur ne sera tenu a aucune cens et rentes a lad. venir Ce neantmoins La verité est telle que le dit preneur s'oblige payer les cens et rentes qui se trouveront mentionnez aud. contract Car ainsy &ca,.

P. Deny
P. Lemieux
J. Dutertre
p. vachon
Audouart, Nott.

CONCESSION BY PIERRE DENIS, SIEUR DE LA RONDE,
TO PIERRE LEMIEUX
(Before G. Audouart, Notary Public)

24 May 1659

Before Guillaume Audouart, Secretary of Council, Notary for the King at Québec in New France and undersigned witnesses were present and in person Pierre Denis, Esquire, *Seigneur* of La Ronde who are recognized and have confessed to have transfer giving to Pierre Le Mieux, *habitant*, residing in the Cote de Beauport who is present and accepting a place consisting along the front of twenty-four and a half feet or approximately by twenty-two feet or approximately deep adjoining one side at la place de Charles Cadieu dit Courville and on the other side lands not ceded, all according to and conforming to the title of concession which is backed by Messire Pierre de Voyer, Chevallier, vicomte Dargenson who, before the Governor and Lieutenant General for the King in this place of New France on the date of 28th of October 1658 signed by P. de Voyer Dargenson and, beneath, by Monsiegneur Gillet – It is transfer given by the said Sieur de La Ronde with the said Le Mieux on condition that it is his to enjoy in perpetuity. With the help of the said taker will be obliged to farm and cultivate a garden from the construction stakes which adjoin La brasserie and which go to the Descarreaux house. That fence is to be done well and valid and subject to inspection to be held by the said taker the Free paths which will be judged necessary. The said transfer and transport to be done without other charges debts nor hypotheticals known to the said ceding *Seigneur* to the said taker for his enjoyment and having cause the said to come into all property without any charges of *seigneurial* rights, *seigneurial* dues to the present and which would spoil the claim for the said fence to come to be made thus as it is specified here above. And for this effect the said *Seigneur* financial backer is obliged with the matter at hand of said taker of the contract and Title of the concession to him given concerning the property of the said place wanting etc., that he takes possession etc. And for this effect to legatee his prosecutor the donor of these presents to whom he gives all to be able to do that which is required will be concerning and make revocation on Obligation of all these goods present and to come to renounce etc, done and passed at Québec in the study of the aforesaid Notary and undersigned the 24th day of May 1659 in the presence of Jean du Tertre and Paul Vachon, witnesses undersigned with the parties – And the fence here above mentioned will be done on the day and year of the presents and if not and at the fault of whomever takes the presents, will be null, and still that is to say specified that the said taker will be held to no taxes and rents to the said to come, nonetheless, the truth is such that the said takers' obliged to pay the taxes and rents which will be found mentioned in said contract because, thus, etc.

P. Deny
P. Lemieux
J. Dutertre
p. vachon
Audouart, Notary

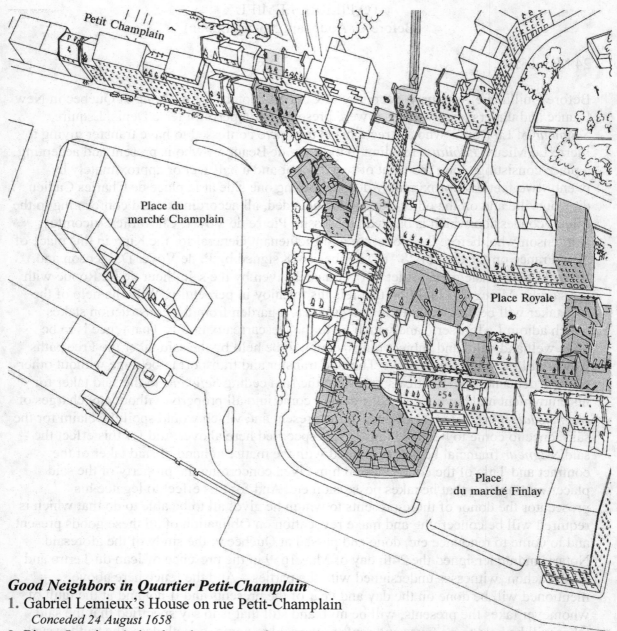

Good Neighbors in Quartier Petit-Champlain

1. Gabriel Lemieux's House on rue Petit-Champlain
   Conceded 24 August 1658

2. Pierre Lemieux's land at the corner of rue Petit-Champlain and Sous-le-Fort
   Purchased 24 May 1659

3. Mathieu and Marie (Marsolet) d'Amours's house on Sous-le-Fort
   Purchased 1657

4. Jolliet's house on rue Petit-Champlain
   Resided until his death in 1700

5. Joseph E. Lemieux's house on Place du marché Finlay
   Circa 1924

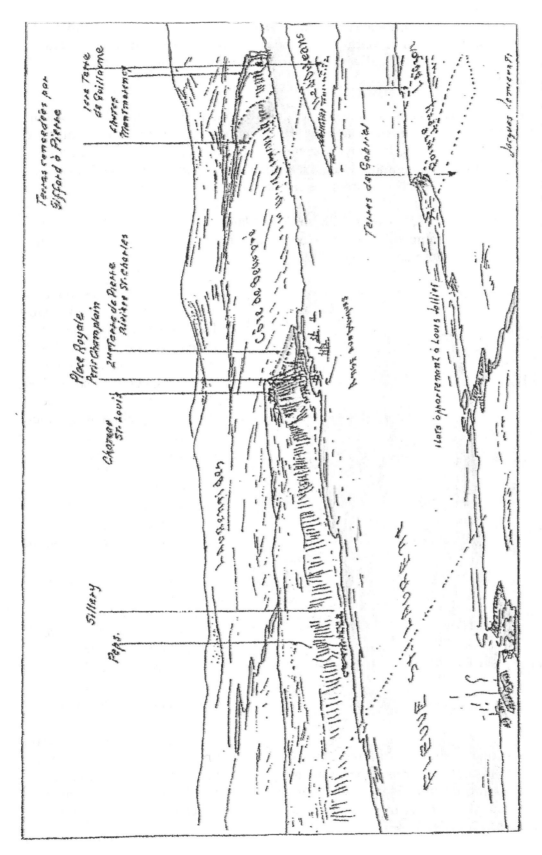

About the same time he bought the lot in town, Pierre acquired a piece of settled land at La Petite-Rivière (now the St-Charles River). It is doubtful that he found the time to move there since he would disappear in late 1661. And in the inventory of his estate on 18 July 1662, he was identified as a Master Cooper still living in Beauport.

Across the river are the lands of Gabriel at Pointe Levy and Lauzon.

The life of our ancestor, Gabriel Lemieux, was better known because of the events in which he and his wife, Marguerite Leboeuf, were involved. Gabriel Lemieux had come from Rouen by 1647 and witnessed his Cousin Pierre's marriage that year to Marie Besnard.

In 1655, he obtained the concession to a plot of land in the *seigneurie* of Lauzon across the St. Lawrence River at Pointe Levy. His neighbors were the potter, Nicolas Pré or Dupré, and Louis Begin, both fellow Normans. To be allowed to keep that tract of 3 arpents by 40, he must, among other things, remit to the *seigneur* "one sol poll tax per arpent, one-eleventh of all eels or salmon he catches and two live capons."

On September 3, 1658, Gabriel, 28, married Marguerite Leboeuf, who was born in 1640 in Troyes, in Champagne, France. His cousin, Pierre Lemieux, Martin Grouvel and Nicolas Pré were witnesses.

Claude Vollières

Gabriel was given a piece of property on 24 August 1658 situated where the house called "Maison Lemieux" is still located today, the oldest house in Québec. It stands near the stairway going from rue Petit Champlain to the former marketplace at the lower level, which stretches along the foot of Cape Diamond from the Coté de la Montagne toward Sillery to the west. Houses built on the southern side of the street were formerly on the very edge of the St. Lawrence in a small bay called *l'Anse aux Barques*, the Boat Caves. Indians were at the bay regularly because furs were brought there to be traded for all kinds of goods. Ships leaving and coming from France also anchored there.

Like his cousin, Pierre, Gabriel was a cooper who later became a merchant, having no doubt realized that it was more lucrative to sell full barrels rather than empty ones. On April 22, 1665, he appeared before the Conseil Souverain, along with his wife, to explain why they were selling jars of wine and alcohol for "more than 20 sols a jar." They were sentenced that day to pay a fine of ten ecus.

In 1666, while Gabriel was returning from France where he had gone to sell merchandise worth 2,400 livres, his ship was attacked and pillaged by an "English vessel enemy of the state" which returned him to France, where he had to borrow money to pay for his passage back to the colony.

Gabriel had just returned to Québec when his creditors demanded immediate payment from him, threatening to sell his furniture and throw him, his wife and children out of his house. Marguerite pleaded his case before the Conseil Souverain and won Gabriel a delay of three years to repay his creditors.

While Gabriel was away, Marguerite had leased a house at the bottom of the cliff from François Bissot. There she could run her business and help Gabriel return to Quebec and repay those whom had entrusted him with goods to be sold in France. He and Marguerite must have had a pottery business with their Lauzon neighbor, Nicolas Dupré, as they repaid part of his debts with pottery. It seems Marguerite also took the initiative of operating a cabaret close to the port. It must have been popular with sailors and *coureurs des bois* causing the neighbors to complain and accuse Marguerite of operating a house of ill repute. The Counseil Souverain intervened and dismissed the case knowing that the accusations came from Gabriel's enemies. Gabriel managed to repay all his debts by 1682 and bought an additional piece of land next to his.

During all this, Gabriel and Marguerite had five children:
1. Nicolas, born August 20, 1659
2. Helene, born 1661
3. Gabriel II, born September 4, 1663
4. Marie Madeleine, born around 1664
5. Marguerite, born January 21, 1666

Marguerite died in late 1669. On November 26, 1671, at 41, Gabriel remarried to Marthe Beauregard, 28, a "fille du Roi" (daughter of the King), daughter of Jean Beauregard, goldsmith, and Marie Desmarais of Saint-Xavier Parish in Rouen. Marthe's dowery was 400 livres and a gift of 50 livres, compliments of King Louis XIV, which improved Gabriel's financial situation.

Gabriel and Marthe had an additional five children:
1. Louis-Theandre, born August 31, 1672
2. Michel, born October 23, 1673
3. Marie-Marthe, born April 11, 1675
4. Marie-Charlotte, born April 13, 1677
5. Guillaume, born April 13, 1679

Gabriel died in Lauzon December 3, 1700 at the age of 70, and was buried at St-Joseph-de-Levi. Marthe lived with their son, Michel, on the farm until she passed away on October 21, 1728.

It is likely that Pierre and Marie continued to live also in Beauport so that Pierre and Martin Grouvel could continue to work together.

On June 12, 1650, Martin acquired a boat, most likely for fishing sea bass or commerce in general. Surely, Pierre accompanied him to supervise the containerized merchandise and they continued trading on the St-Lawrence River. In the beginning they traded toward the Great Lakes, but because of wars with the Iroquois, that market soon closed. They turned their attention toward Tadoussac, the Saguenay River and Lake St-Jean. They took part in setting up many trading posts which became towns such as Chicoutimi and Metabetchouan. It has been said that Chicoutimi was founded by de Granville and a few Lemieux. A quote from Louis Frechette reminds us that not so long ago those manning all the canoes shuttling between Québec and Lévis "were all Lemieux or Saint-Laurents."

In 1660, a full war with the Iroquois was raging and the colony was in serious danger. In 1661, harvesting was not possible due to constant Indian attacks. If there were no harvest, there was no bread---Pierre and Martin were sent to France to buy flour. Grouvel and Lemieux had always chosen to divide their time between the land and

Navires fuyant la tempête. (Bibliothèque Nationale, estampes.)

the sea. Grouvel, who skippered a small fishing boat, was said to have "been shipwrecked near the hills of Notre-Dame, in the Saint-Laurent River. His boat broke apart and he drowned with two of his crewmen" around 1661. It was about this time that Pierre Lemieux disappeared; this father of seven was never seen again.

July 18, 1662, the widow Marie requested an inventory of her goods. The tools and hardware of a tonnelier were sold to various buyers. Gabriel signed as witness on these transactions. Had Marie moved to Gabriel and Marguerite's?

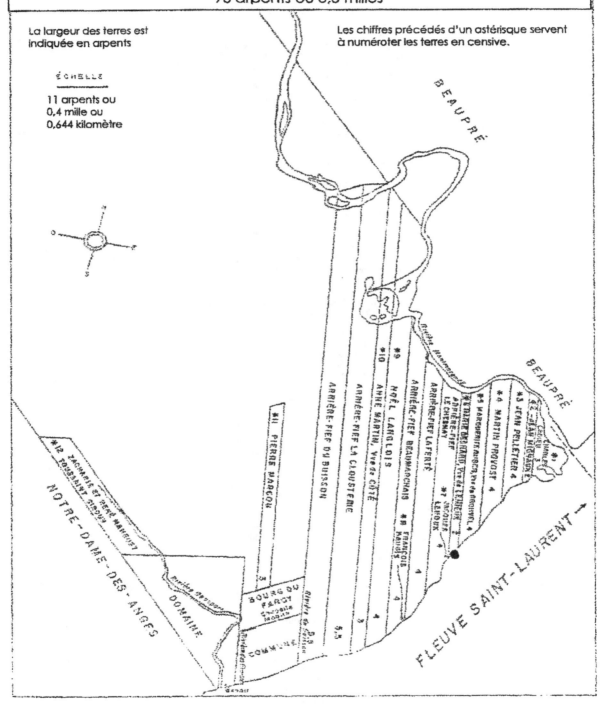

Pierre's lot in Beauport

This 1663 map shows that Marie Besnard, widow of Pierre Lemieux and next door, Marguerite Aubert, widow of Martin Grouvel still owned their lands.

On July 10, 1668 Marie sold her lands to Laurent Dubost.

In August 1668 Marie married Antoine Gentil.

Direct Descendants of Pierre Lemieux II

**Pierre
Lemieux II**
b: October 21, 1616 in
St-Michel-de-Rouen,
Normandie, FRANCE
o: April 10, 1643 (26 yrs)
Engaged from La
Rochelle; Maitre-
Tonnelier/Cultivateur
d: December 30, 1661 in
La Nativite-de-Notre-
Dame-de-Beauport,
Quebec, CANADA
b: January 01, 1662
La Nativite-de-Notre-
Dame-de-Beauport,
Quebec, CANADA

=

**Marie
Besnard**
b: 1631 in St-Clement-
de-Chatres, Paris, Ile-de-
France, FRANCE
m: September 17, 1647 in
Notre-Dame-de-Quebec,
Quebec, CANADA
d: Aft. 1685 in La
Nativite-de-Notre-Dame-
de-Beauport, Quebec,
CANADA

**Louis
Lemieux**
b: February 06, 1652 in
La Nativite-de-Notre-
Dame-de-Beauport,
Quebec, CANADA
o: Cultivateur/Trapper
d: December 30, 1693 in
Ile-aux-Grues, Quebec,
CANADA
b: January 01, 1694
St-Ignace-du-Cap-St-
Ignace, Quebec,
CANADA

=

**Marie-Madeleine
Cote**
b: September 18, 1663 in
Chateau-Richer, Quebec,
CANADA
m: November 26, 1682 in
St-Ignace-du-Cap-St-
Ignace, Quebec,
CANADA
b: August 25, 1689
Cap St. Ignace Parish,
L'Islet, Quebec,
CANADA

**Louis
Lemieux II**
b: October 04, 1683 in
l'Ile-aux-Grues, Quebec,
CANADA
o: Cultivateur, habitant
de la Pointe-aux-Foins

=

**Genevieve
Fortin**
b: November 19, 1686 in
St-Ignace-du-Cap-St-
Ignace, Quebec,
CANADA
m: February 11, 1705 in
Notre-Dame-de-
Bonsecours-de-l'Islet,
Quebec, CANADA
b: July 31, 1763
St-Ignace-du-Cap-St-
Ignace, Quebec,
CANADA

**Augustin
Lemieux**
b: February 04, 1709 in
St-Ignace-du-Cap-St-
Ignace, Quebec,
CANADA
o: Cultivateur
b: December 22, 1755
St. Roch, Quebec,
CANADA

140

On May 1, 1662 Guillaume, age 14, was confirmed and on March 23, 1664, Pierre III, age 13 and **Louis**, age 12, were confirmed at Notre-Dame-de-Québec.

A census was done in 1666 and did not mention the children Marie, Marie-Francoise and Thomas. We may assume that they were taken by epidemic or possibly the Iroquois. The older children Guillaume, Pierre and Louis took jobs at other homes. The 1667 census showed that Louis and Pierre were still at Beauport in the same jobs, but there was no mention of Guillaume. July 10, 1668, Marie sold her land to Laurent Dubost.

On August 27, 1668, there was a contract of marriage between Marie Besnard, widow of Pierre Lemieux, and Antoine Gentil, son of Adrien Gentil and Antoinette L'Angevin. Marie was 37 years old and Antoine was 26. Of her surviving sons, Guillaume was 19, Pierre was 18 and Louis was 16. Marie and Antoine bought a house situated on the route Champigny on December 26, 1671, and the census of 1681 shows they had 3 horned beasts and 14 arpents of land under cultivation.

A transaction between Antoine Gentil and Guillaume and Louis Lemieux took place on October 14, 1682. Possibly, Marie was dead and her dowry was being remitted to her sons. Her son, Pierre, was not mentioned.

The Lemieux family mingled in the adventurous life of the country. They were neighbors with notables such as LaSalle, Jolliet, Fathers Dablon and Marquette. All the important characters of New France's history lived thereabouts, including Nicolas Marsolet. Guillaume, Pierre III and **Louis** really were in the middle of the great adventures of the time. Due to the Iroquois threat in 1665, France finally sent the famous de Carignan Regiment to defend them. Since their soldiers had just fought the Turks, they were weak, ill and arrived in poor shape. Nevertheless, the regiment was sent to fight the Iroquois and force them to make peace. This is how Guillaume, Pierre and probably Louis ended up as soldiers in the French regiment. There they met Captain Granville and Captain Dupuis. Later these captains granted them land, first to Guillaume on Ile aux Grues (Crane Island) and Ile aux Oises (Geese Island) offshore from l'Islet.

In 1678, the two unmarried sons of Pierre and Marie, Pierre, 28 and his brother, Louis, 26, were stopped for having traded with the Temiscaming without authorization. On July 10, 1678, Governor Frontenac received an account of the capture of Pierre and Louis at Montréal and the seizure of ten packets of pelts by Jean-Baptiste Champagne dit Saint-Martin, *Sergent* of the Garrison of the Québec Castle. Pierre and Louis were imprisoned. On August 1, Governor Frontenac decided to question them himself because he had no confidence in Jacques Duchesneau, the new Steward of Provost Marshall or Philippe Gauthier, Lord of Comportment, or Charles Aubert, Lord of the Chesnay, all who would protect the *coureurs des bois*.

The Governor questioned Pierre, Louis and Nicolas Doyon, arquebusier, locksmith and gunsmith, as well as Claude of Xaintes, cutlerer, and others. On September 6, Pierre and Louis appealed. The following October 15, was their hearing. On October

26, they were convicted and fined for having traded with the Indians. November 2, the court, for reparation, confiscated the pelts and merchandise for his majesty and each was fined 2,000 livres, half for his majesty and half for the poor in the hospital L'Hôtel-Dieu de Québec. On November 18, Pierre and Louis pledged all their present and future goods until the fine was paid and they were released.

Pierre and Louis were young, and they continued their adventures. Jolliet hired them in 1679 to explore the North with him. Together they rowed up the Saguenay River and crossed Lake St-Jean, rode up the Assouahmachouan River, rode down the Rupert River and moved as far north as the Hudson Bay. Then, the expedition fell on terrible conditions. On arriving at Hudson Bay, they realized there was already an English fort erected, which was being used as a relay for fur trading. In fact, the English went for their furs through the north passage---unknown to the French. Pierre and Louis accompanied Jolliet back to Québec, and explained the situation to the Governor, who sent one of the best soldiers, Pierre Lemoyne d'Iberville, to Hudson Bay. Pierre and Louis returned to the north with Lemoyne to take part in the attack against the forts.

Lemoyne chose Pierre and Louis to take the command of Fort Albany, also named Chichicouane, which they maintained under harsh conditions from 1685-1693. One year, the ships responsible for providing the fort with fresh provisions did not arrive. The group was forced to hunt and forage in order to survive the winter. Morale during that period was very low, and one of the men lost his mind and killed some of the people of the fort while Pierre, Louis and other men were out hunting. On returning to the fort, they realized what had happened and the man was put in irons to await the return of the ships. But it was English ships that came that year with the objective of taking the French fort. Against impossible odds of two hundred to five, Pierre, Louis, and the others succeeded in holding the fort for three days....then they hastily began their escape to Québec. With only a canoe, they tried to row down the St. Maurice and St. Lawrence Rivers. The trip was so perilous and the men so weak and malnourished, only Pierre and Louis survived.

After returning from the expedition with Jolliet in 1679, **Louis** went to live at Isle-aux-Grues with his older brother, Guillaume and his wife, Elisabeth Langlois, widow of Louis Côté from Chateau Richer. On November 26, 1682 Louis married Madeleine Côté, 19 years old, daughter of Elisabeth Langlois. On April 26, 1683 Louis, *habitant* of Isle-aux-Grues, made a will giving all his belongings to Madeleine before departing for Outaouais (Ottawa). He returned in time for the birth of his first son, our ancestor, **Louis II**, on October 4, 1683.

On October 26, 1684 Louis bought a piece of land in Cap St-Ignace from Guillaume Thibault, which was five arpents wide and one league deep, still referred to as "la terre des Lemieux."

Their second son, Alexis, was born November 11, 1685 and four months later Louis left for Hudson Bay with d'Iberville. While Louis was trapped with Pierre at Fort Albany, Madeleine died at Cap St-Ignace on August 25, 1689 at the age of 26. Louis's prolonged stay at Fort Albany in miserable conditions, the difficult trip home in 1693, and the loss of Madeleine must have all contributed to his death on December 30, 1693 and the age of 42. Guillaume and Elisabeth took in the orphaned sons, Louis, 10, and Alexis, 8. Since Louis did not rewrite his will, the Intendant of New France awarded the "la terre des Lemieux" in Cap St-Ignace to Louis II. Alexis inherited from Guillaume the land at Pointe-à-la-Caille (Montmagny).

In 1705, Louis Lemieux II, cultivateur, married Genevieve Fortin, daughter of neighboring Charles Fortin, in L'Islet.

Chateau Richer with a View of Ile d'Orleans
A line of houses, eel traps, salt marshes, kitchen gardens; fields of wheat and peas; livestock and game; these were basic elements of the Lower Canadian landscape.

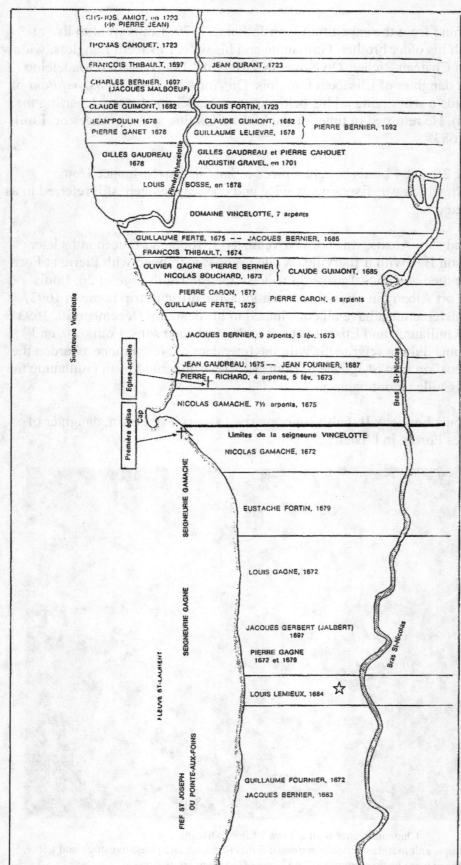

LES PIONNIERS
(Seigneurie VINCELOTTE)

GUS-JOS. AMIOT, en 1723
(de PIERRE JEAN)

THOMAS CAHOUET, 1723

FRANÇOIS THIBAULT, 1697 — JEAN DURANT, 1723

CHARLES BERNIER, 1697
(JACQUES MALBOEUF)

CLAUDE GUIMONT, 1692 — LOUIS FORTIN, 1723

JEAN POULIN 1678 — CLAUDE GUIMONT, 1682
PIERRE GANET 1678 — GUILLAUME LELIEVRE, 1678 — PIERRE BERNIER, 1692

GILLES GAUDREAU 1678 — GILLES GAUDREAU et PIERRE CAHOUET
AUGUSTIN GRAVEL, en 1701

LOUIS BOSSE, en 1678

Rivière Vincelotte

DOMAINE VINCELOTTE, 7 arpents

GUILLAUME FERTE, 1675 — JACQUES BERNIER, 1686

FRANÇOIS THIBAULT, 1674

OLIVIER GAGNE PIERRE BERNIER
NICOLAS BOUCHARD, 1673 — CLAUDE GUIMONT, 1685

PIERRE CARON, 1677
GUILLAUME FERTE, 1875 — PIERRE CARON, 6 arpents

JACQUES BERNIER, 9 arpents, 5 fév. 1673

JEAN GAUDREAU, 1675 — JEAN FOURNIER, 1687

PIERRE RICHARD, 4 arpents, 5 fév. 1673

NICOLAS GAMACHE, 7½ arpents, 1675

Bras St-Nicolas

Eglise actuelle

Première église

Cap

Seigneurie Vincelotte

Limites de la seigneurie VINCELOTTE

NICOLAS GAMACHE, 1672

SEIGNEURIE GAMACHE

EUSTACHE FORTIN, 1679

SEIGNEURIE GAGNE

LOUIS GAGNE, 1672

JACQUES GERBERT (JALBERT) 1697

PIERRE GAGNE 1672 et 1679

FLEUVE ST-LAURENT

☆ LOUIS LEMIEUX, 1684

Bras St-Nicolas

FIEF ST JOSEPH OU POINTE-AUX-FOINS

GUILLAUME FOURNIER, 1672

JACQUES BERNIER, 1683

☆ In 1705 Louis Lemieux II married Genevieve Fortin in L'Islet. Seigneurie Vincelotte is in the Notre-Dame-de-Bonsecours-de-L'Islet Parish. The crosses show that the first church washed away and the *actuelle* church's current location.

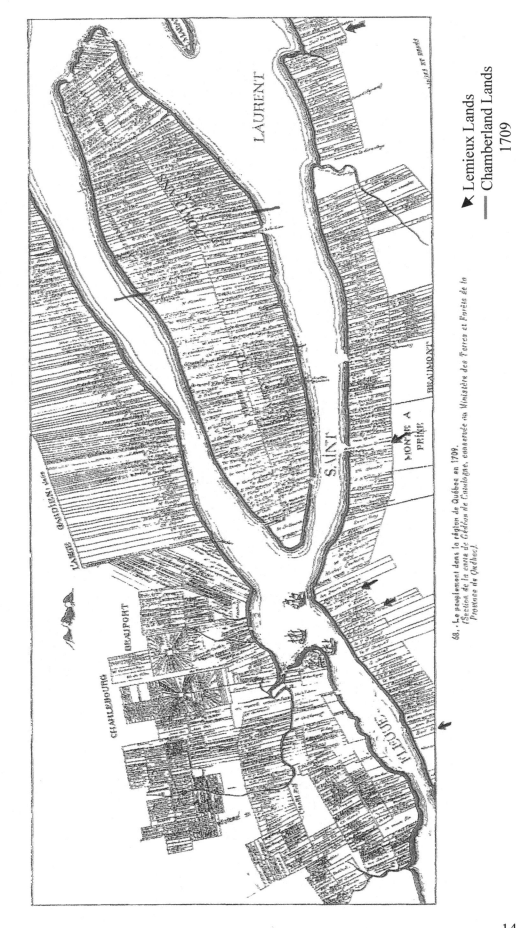

68. - Le peuplement dans la région de Québec en 1709.
(Section de la carte de Gédéon de Catalogne, conservée au Ministère des Terres et Forêts de la
Province de Québec.)

► Lemieux Lands
— Chamberland Lands
1709

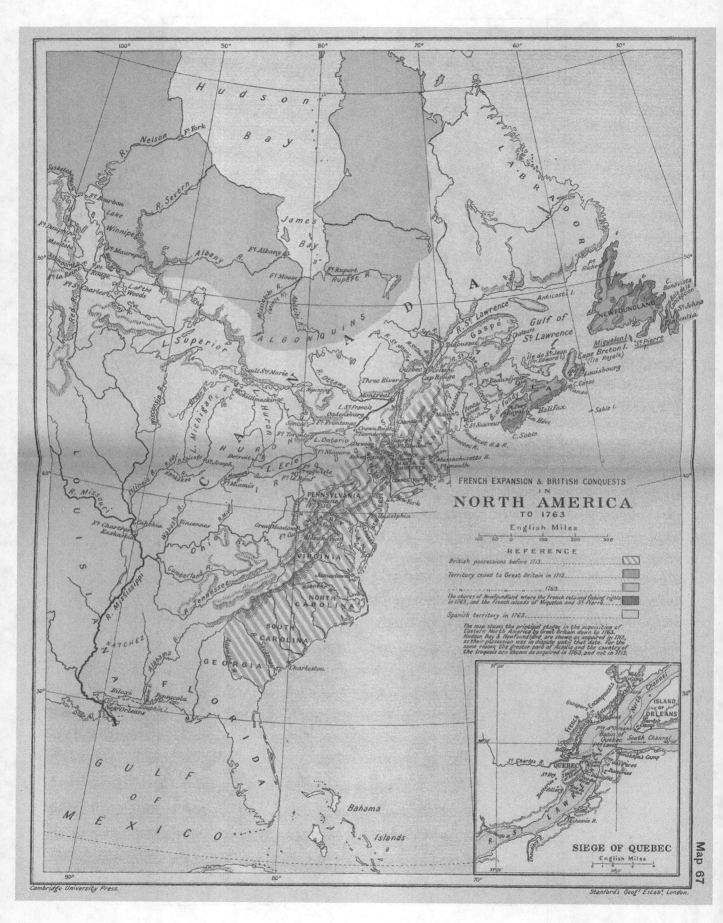

FRENCH EXPANSION & BRITISH CONQUESTS
IN
NORTH AMERICA
TO 1763

English Miles

REFERENCE

British possessions before 1713.................

Territory ceded to Great Britain in 1713.........

" " " " " 1763.........

The shores of Newfoundland where the French retained fishing rights
in 1763, and the French islands of Miquelon and St Pierre......

Spanish territory in 1763.........

The map shows the principal stages in the acquisition of
Eastern North America by Great Britain down to 1763.
Hudson Bay & Newfoundland are shown as acquired in 1713,
as their possession was in dispute until that date. For the
same reason the greater part of Acadia and the country of
the Iroquois are shown as acquired in 1763, and not in 1713.

SIEGE OF QUEBEC
English Miles

Stanford's Geog¹ Estab¹, London.

Map 67

146

IX

Canadian History

$\mathcal{B}$y 1690, Québec, the Rock, was the heart of the colony--a fortified stronghold frequently, but unsuccessfully, attacked. It was a seaport town and capital, with churches, parks, docks, warehouses, and public buildings. In the Upper Town, which stretched back from the great rock cliff, stood the residence of the Governor, the Chateau St-Louis. There also stood the Bishop's Palace, the Cathedral and the Convent of the Ursulines, all enclosed by a stone wall with three gates. Within this setting, the governor and citizens attempted to create as cultured a society as possible on the frontier.

In 1713, the French in Canada were outnumbered twenty times by English, Scottish and Irish, and the French community had little chance of survival. Meanwhile, France was beginning to show signs of decay that led to the Revolution, yet they made aggressive efforts to keep the British colonies out of the fur-bearing regions near the Great Lakes. Scattered fighting on the frontier broke out as early as 1750, and Voltaire was amused that the shot which heralded a major continental war was fired in the backwoods of America.

There was fighting on both continents. By September 1760, the surrender of Montréal sealed the fate of New France. Under the terms of the Peace of Paris, February 10, 1763, Britain took over the whole continent east of the Mississippi, except the town of New Orleans which was ceded by France to Spain.

French Canada seemed to face political, social, and cultural elimination at the hands of the enemy. Most of the administrative officers and educated bourgeoisie returned to France. The rest of the population turned to the few remaining clergy and the Church became the refuge for a deserted people. Although England was dealing with a people of equal civilization, it was one whose traditions and religion were hated. In England, no Roman Catholic could hold public office or be an officer in the military, and there were few Protestant French in New France. For the time, military governors made no effort to change the French Canadian customs or lifestyle. Later, it was insisted that the French Canadians should be protected in their ancient laws and customs, especially in matters relating to land tenure, and supported the use of French civil law in the courts. Gradually, a curious hybrid of French custom and English law developed.

In 1774, the Québec Act was passed. Because war was threatening in the south, the English went out of their way to be accommodating to the French in an effort to keep a contented colony within the empire. The old civil law was restored in its entirety. The *habitants*, while turning a deaf ear to the seductive invitations of the Americans, were equally reluctant to enlist in the British cause and remained neutral. In effect, the American Revolution contributed to the separatism enjoyed by the French Canadians.

While the Napoleonic Wars raged in Europe following the French Revolution, Canadians were involved in pioneer settlement. Due to primitive transportation, there was little growth of towns and local markets. Towns were far apart and roads were rough or nonexistent, apart from river highways which in winter could be used by sleigh. The British provinces stayed relatively undeveloped and inert until American embargoes stimulated clandestine trade over the borders, ushering in the War of 1812.

The Citadel of Québec, showing fortifications being rebuilt after the War of 1812, as part of the general defense against possible American attack.

The Treaty of Ghent ended an inconclusive war in December, 1814. Both sides were anxious to wipe out the past---the first significant hint of a new attitude to Anglo-American relations. Within four years, they were able to arrange an agreement for the limitation of armaments of the Great Lakes, settle the tangled in-shore fisheries question and establish Canada's southern boundary along the forty-ninth parallel from Lake of the Woods to the Rocky Mountains. Not until 1846 did the Oregon Treaty extend this line westward to the Pacific Ocean. From this point, people slowed the migration back and forth between the US and Canada, and settled near their preferred style of government.

While Britain and Canada were thrashing out the specific shape the Canadian government would take, there was a rebellion in Lower Canada in 1838. It had been felt that the only solution to the "racial" conflict was that French Canada must be submerged and thoroughly absorbed. Underestimating the tenacity of the *habitant*, the plan of merging the two cultures was as unworkable as it was unwise. French Canadian language and customs could be neither extinguished nor diluted. Though not without its rough periods, a government of compromise has existed since.

Most British Canadians were descendants of immigrants who had come in the nineteenth century, and their attachment to the mother country deeply affected their concept of Canada's role within the British Empire. But French Canadians, who had been North Americans for over three hundred years, and whose sentimental ties with France had been abandoned long ago, had no such divided loyalty. They were more supporters of the Empire because Westminster guaranteed their unique privileges as a minority within the Canadian nation. At the same time, they remained a prickly and highly self-conscious bloc, determined to resist any attempt to strengthen the connection with Great Britain.

In the 19th Century, Québec's agriculture underwent tremendous strains. With population growth, Québec's farmland had been systematically occupied, leaving thousands of landless farmers searching for fertile land mostly in peripheral regions, or gainful employment. Poverty, overpopulation, debt and infertile soils pushed French Canadians off their land. Farmers who left their land were naturally attracted to the huge textile factories of New England, as the U.S. had emerged as one of the most industrialized and prosperous nations on earth. During that period, the US/Canadian border was essentially open to the free flow of traffic in both directions.

French Canadians looked to the U.S. for their economic salvation and many migrated to the New England textile mills. Jobs were easier to obtain in the U.S. at better wages and frequently required no formal skills or education. The French Canadian immigrants left behind a traditional rural society with strong family ties and entered an industrial world, alien to them by virtue of its way of life, language and religion. They played a significant role in the industrial expansion of the New England area in the last half of the 19th Century. It was in this era that Joseph Siffroid Lemieux came to Michigan and on to Ohio. It is not certain that he ever was naturalized. Joseph Athanase Marsolais and his son, Joseph George, came to New York State, were naturalized and became U.S. citizens.

Stagecoach equipped with runners for snow

Marsollet, Lemire-dit-Marsolet, Marsolais

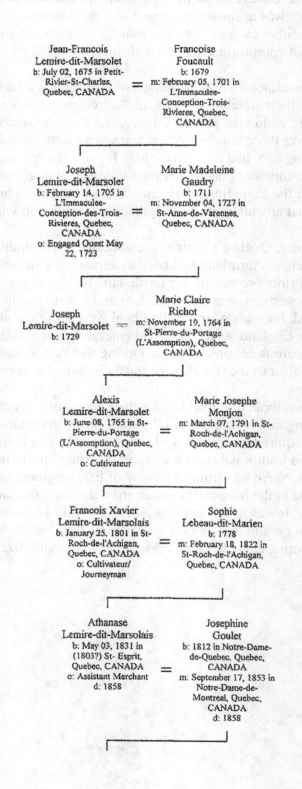

Jean-Francois
Lemire-dit-Marsolet
b: July 02, 1675 in Petit-
Rivier-St-Charles,
Quebec, CANADA

Francoise
Foucault
b: 1679
m: February 05, 1701 in
L'Immaculee-
Conception-Trois-
Rivieres, Quebec,
CANADA

Joseph
Lemire-dit-Marsolet
b: February 14, 1705 in
L'Immaculee-
Conception-des-Trois-
Rivieres, Quebec,
CANADA
o: Engaged Ouest May
22, 1723

Marie Madeleine
Gaudry
b: 1711
m: November 04, 1727 in
St-Anne-de-Varennes,
Quebec, CANADA

Joseph
Lemire-dit-Marsolet
b: 1729

Marie Claire
Richot
m: November 19, 1764 in
St-Pierre-du-Portage
(L'Assomption), Quebec,
CANADA

Alexis
Lemire-dit-Marsolet
b: June 08, 1765 in St-
Pierre-du-Portage
(L'Assomption), Quebec,
CANADA
o: Cultivateur

Marie Josephe
Monjon
m: March 07, 1791 in St-
Roch-de-l'Achigan,
Quebec, CANADA

Francois Xavier
Lemire-dit-Marsolais
b: January 25, 1801 in St-
Roch-de-l'Achigan,
Quebec, CANADA
o: Cultivateur/
Journeyman

Sophie
Lebeau-dit-Marien
b: 1778
m: February 18, 1822 in
St-Roch-de-l'Achigan,
Quebec, CANADA

Athanase
Lemire-dit-Marsolais
b: May 03, 1831 in
(1803?) St- Esprit,
Quebec, CANADA
o: Assistant Merchant
d: 1858

Josephine
Goulet
b: 1812 in Notre-Dame-
de-Quebec, Quebec,
CANADA
m: September 17, 1853 in
Notre-Dame-de-
Montreal, Quebec,
CANADA
d: 1858

Joseph A.
Lemire-dit-Marsolais
b: October 09, 1855 in
Montreal (Rockland),
Quebec, CANADA
o: Navagateur/Wagoner/
Fireman
d: November 19, 1928 in
Latham, New York, USA

Marie-Louise Emma
Laporte
b: December 10, 1861 in
LaValtrie, Quebec,
CANADA
m: November 28, 1882 in
St-Sulpice, Quebec,
CANADA
d: 1940 in Latham, New
York, USA

=

Joseph G.
Marsolais
b: December 31, 1883 in
Sainte-Brigide, Montreal,
Quebec, CANADA
o: Stationary Fireman,
New York State School
System
d: June 11, 1961 in
Leonard Hospital, Troy,
Rensselear County, New
York, USA

Matilda
Savois
b: April 04, 1883 in
Cohoes, Albany County,
New York, USA
m: Abt. 1902 in
Watervliet, New York,
USA
d: March 31, 1957 in
Gloucester Twp.,
Camden County, New
Jersey, USA

=

Harold George
Marsolais
b: June 17, 1920 in
Colonie, Albany County,
New York, USA
o: Bet. 1950 - 1975
Foreman, Republic Steel
d: February 13, 1985 in
Tampa, Hillsborough
County, Florida, USA

Viola Marie-Anne
Chamberlain
b: April 14, 1918 in
Cohoes, Albany County,
New York, USA
m: February 08, 1941 in
Church of Sacred Heart,
Cohoes, Albany County,
New York, USA
d: December 26, 1997 in
Hudson, Pasco County,
Florida, USA

Harold Raymond
Marsolais
b: March 10, 1942 in
Samaritan Hospital, Troy,
Rensselear County, New
York, USA
o: Army Officer,
Corporate Executive

Susan Kathleen
Lemieux
b: August 12, 1944 in
Fairview Park Hospital,
Cleveland, Cuyahoga
County, Ohio, USA
m: July 05, 1964 in 82nd
Airborne Divison South
Chapel, Ft. Bragg,
Cumberland County,
North Carolina, USA
o: Graphic Designer

=

Michelle Suzanne
Marsolais
b: May 05, 1965 in
Lakewood Hospital,
Lakewood, Cuyahoga
County, Ohio, USA
o: High School English
Teacher

William Thomas
O'Brien
b: January 10, 1962 in
Pittsburgh, Allegheny
County, Pennsylvania,
USA
m: November 05, 1988 in
St Joan of Arc Church,
Hershey, Dauphin
County, Pennsylvania,
USA
o: Hotel/Motel
Management

=

Emma Kathleen
O'Brien
b: October 18, 1992 in
Harrisburg, Pennsylvania,
USA

Le Mies, Lemieux

Louis
Lemieux II
b: October 04, 1683 in
l'Ile-aux-Grues, Quebec,
CANADA
o: Cultivateur, habitant
de la Pointe-aux-Foins

=

Genevieve
Fortin
b: November 19, 1686 in
St-Ignace-du-Cap-St-
Ignace, Quebec,
CANADA
m: February 11, 1705 in
Notre-Dame-de-
Bonsecours-de-l'Islet,
Quebec, CANADA

Augustin
Lemieux
b: February 04, 1709 in
St-Ignace-du-Cap-St-
Ignace, Quebec,
CANADA
o: Cultivateur

=

Catherine
Brisson
b: November 20, 1710 in
Riviere-Ouelle, Quebec,
CANADA
m: November 14, 1734 in
St-Roch-des-Aulnaise,
Quebec, CANADA

Francois
Lemieux
b: January 28, 1753 in St-
Roch, Quebec,
CANADA
o: Cultivateur

=

Marie Theotiste
Bernier
b: October 27, 1761 in
St-Ignace-du-Cap-St-
Ignace, Quebec,
CANADA
m: January 20, 1777 in
Notre-Dame-de-
Bonsecours-de-l'Islet,
Quebec, CANADA

Augustin
Lemieux
b: February 02, 1778 in
St-Ignace-du-Cap-St-
Ignace, Quebec,
CANADA
o: Cultivateur

=

Marie Therese
Jolbert
m: May 25, 1819 in
Notre-Dame-de-
Bonsecours-de-l'Islet,
Quebec, CANADA

Anselme
Lemieux
b: April 21, 1822 in
Notre-Dame-de-
Bonsecours-de-l'Islet,
Quebec, CANADA
o: Cultivateur
d: May 16, 1896

=

Vitaline
Bernier
b: in Notre-Dame-de-
Bonsecours-de-l'Islet,
Quebec, CANADA
m: April 19, 1852 in Cap-
St-Ignace Parish, L'Islet,
Quebec, CANADA

Joseph Siffroy Lemieux
b: July 10, 1867 in St-Ignace-du-Cap-St-Ignace, Quebec, CANADA
o: 1900 Saloon, 540 Gordon Ave.
d: May 12, 1935 in 23123 Center Ridge Road, Dover Village, Cuyahoga County, Ohio, USA

=

Maggie E. Haley
b: July 21, 1874 in Cleveland, Cuyahoga County, Ohio, USA
m: January 25, 1893 in Cuyahoga County, Ohio, USA
d: June 26, 1900 in 540 Gordon, Cleveland, Cuyahoga County, Ohio, USA

Alfred Joseph Lemieux
b: October 20, 1894 in 68 Penn Street, Cleveland, Cuyahoga County, Ohio, USA
o: Restauranteur
d: September 06, 1977 in Lakewood Hospital, Detroit Ave., Lakewood, Cuyahoga County, Ohio, USA

=

Helen Margaret Cushing
b: December 20, 1896 in 1793 Woodland Hills Ave., Cleveland, Cuyahoga County, Ohio, USA
m: June 09, 1920 in Holy Name Catholic Church, Harvard & Broadway, Cleveland, Cuyahoga County, Ohio, USA
o: 1920 Coal Clerk
d: April 22, 1964 in St. John Hospital, Detroit Ave., Cleveland, Cuyahoga County, Ohio, USA

Alfred Jean Lemieux
b: May 12, 1921 in St. Ann's Hospital, Cleveland, Cuyahoga County, Ohio, USA
o: U.S. Marine Aviator/Industrial Sales

=

Patricia Eileen Lape
b: January 11, 1924 in Canton, Stark County, Ohio, USA
m: November 15, 1943 in Morehead City, Carteret County, North Carolina, USA

Susan Kathleen Lemieux
b: August 12, 1944 in Fairview Park Hospital, Cleveland, Cuyahoga County, Ohio, USA
o: Graphic Designer

=

Harold Raymond Marsolais
b: March 10, 1942 in Samaritan Hospital, Troy, Rensselear County, New York, USA
m: July 05, 1964 in 82nd Airborne Divison South Chapel, Ft. Bragg, Cumberland County, North Carolina, USA
o: Army Officer, Corporate Executive

Michelle Suzanne Marsolais
b: May 05, 1965 in Lakewood Hospital, Lakewood, Cuyahoga County, Ohio, USA
o: High School English Teacher

=

William Thomas O'Brien
b: January 10, 1962 in Pittsburgh, Allegheny County, Pennsylvania, USA
m: November 05, 1988 in St Joan of Arc Church, Hershey, Dauphin County, Pennsylvania, USA
o: Hotel/Motel Management

Kelsey Elizabeth O'Brien
b: May 29, 1991 in Harrisburg, Pennsylvania, USA

153

Le Chateau Frontenac, Québec, about 1924
Jos. E. Lemieux's house, bottom, 2nd from left on the Place du marché Finlay
on the St. Lawrence River

X

Lemieux and Marsolais to Present

uring our families' remaining years in Québec province, we find their documents but little anecdotal material for them.

On February 5, 1701, Jean-Francois Lemire-dit-Marsolet, son of Louise Marsolet and grandson of Nicolas, married Francoise Foucault at the church of L'Immaculie-Conception-Trois-Rivieres. In 1705, they had a son, Joseph Lemire-dit-Marsolet who married Madeleine Gaudry on November 4, 1727 at Ste-Anne-de-Varennes. Their son, Joseph II, was born in 1729.

Also, in 1705, Louis Lemieux II, cultivateur, married Genevieve Fortin in L'Islet. On February 4, 1709, they had a son, Augustin, a farmer, who married Catherine Brisson at St-Roch-des-Aulnaise on November 14, 1734, and had Francois in 1753.

Notre-Dame-de-Bonsecours-de-l'Islet, Québec - 1768

Joseph Lemire-dit-Marsolet II, married widow, Claire Richot, at St-Pierre-du-Portage, L'Assomption, Québec on November 19, 1764. Their son, Alexis, was born in 1765, who became a cultivateur and married Josephte Monjon at St-Roch-de-l'Achigan on March 7, 1791.

Francois Lemieux married Theotiste Bernier on January 20, 1777 at L'Islet and had a son, Augustin, on February 2, 1778. He was baptized at Cap-St-Ignace.

Francois Xavier Lemire-dit-Marsolet, was baptized January 25, 1801 at St-Roch-de l'Achigan, who became a cultivateur/journeyman and married Sophie Lebeau-dit-Marien in the same parish on February 18, 1822. Their son, Athanase, was born May 3, 1831, and became an assistant merchant and married Josephine Goulet on September 17, 1853 at Notre-Dame-de-Montréal.

Augustin Lemieux, cultivateur, married Therese Jolbert at Notre-Dame-de-Bonsecours, L'Islet in 1819. Their son, Anselme Joseph, born April 21, 1822 became a farmer and on April 19, 1852 at Cap-St-Ignace married Vitaline Bernier from L'Islet.

Notre-Dame-de- Québec

Notre-Dame-de- Montréal

St-Roch-des-Aulnaise - 1849

St-Roch-de-l'Achigan

Cap-St-Ignace

St-Pierre-du-Portage-L'Assomption

Joseph Athanase Lemire-dit-Marcellais, born October 9, 1855 in Montréal, was a navigateur when he married Marie-Louise LaPorte at St-Sulpice in Montréal on November 28, 1882. Their son, Joseph-Georges-Leopold, was born in Montréal December 31, 1883, and became a wagoner. He was naturalized an American citizen on August 4, 1903, when there was a general amnesty. Settling in the Troy, New York area, he was called Alphonse Marsolais, retired as a stationary fireman, and died in 1928.

Joseph-Georges-Leopold Lemire-dit-Marsolet, known as George Marsolais, was naturalized in the general amnesty with his father, and was also a stationary fireman (a fancy name for a boiler operator). Around 1902 George married Matilda (Tilly) Savois in Watervliet, New York. They had five children, George, Arthur, Donald, Loretta and the youngest, Harold George, born June 17, 1920 in Colonie, New York. George, known for his sense of humor, was affectionately known as "The Old Twister" because of his ability to "twist" a story to gain a laugh.

Harold grew up in the Troy/Cohoes area and during the Depression he worked with the Civilian Conservation Corps in upstate New York. He was known as "Skinny" to his childhood friends who pinned the nickname on him. He married Viola Marie (Vi) Chamberland February 8, 1941 in Cohoes, New York. The Chamberland and Marsolais families were already related by the marriage of Vi's brother, Ernest (Red) Chamberland, to Harold's sister, Loretta. It was Red who changed the spelling to Chamberlain.

During WWII, Harold joined the "Seabees." After training at Norfolk, Virginia, he served with the 27th Naval Construction Battalion in the South Pacific and participated in campaigns on Guadalcanal, Tulagi and Emirau. He was honorably discharged in December 1945, and returned to upstate New York to hold a variety of manufacturing jobs.

Vi and Harold had four sons: Harold Raymond (Hal), born March 10, 1942 in Troy, New York; Dennis, born April 8, 1949, in Troy; Robert (Bob), born December 19, 1950 in Troy and Richard, born November 8, 1955 in Lorain, Ohio. Harold George had many occupations, but he settled with Republic Steel, and he was transferred to the Cleveland plant as a general foreman until his retirement in 1977. Harold, Vi and their sons moved to a new neighborhood in Sheffield Lake, Ohio in 1954. After retiring from Republic Steel, Harold and Vi moved to Hudson, Florida, where Harold enjoyed surf fishing whenever possible. Harold and Vi are buried together in Bay Pines National Cemetery in Largo, Florida.

Joseph Siffroid Lemieux, born July 10, 1867 in L'Islet, Québec, came to Michigan as a cook for a timber company, then to Cleveland, Ohio, but having found no naturalization papers, the date is uncertain. His first saloon was at West 98th and Lorain Road in Cleveland. At 41, Joseph married Maggie Ellen (Nellie) Haley, 19, in Cleveland on January 25, 1893 and they had two sons, Alfred Joseph (Fred), born at 68 Penn W. Street, Cleveland, Ohio, October 20, 1894, and John, born in 1897. At the age of 26, Nellie became sick with pneumonia, and was sent with her sons to a relative in Shelby, Ohio. Nellie died in Shelby June 27, 1900, after only 7 years of marriage. Alfred, 6, and

John, 3, stayed in Shelby temporarily. Joseph married Johanna (Hanna) Blumena in May 1903, and she helped him raise his family and run the newer Horse Shoe Inn. Fred Lemieux attended St. Ignacius College, where he was taught by Father Odenbach and studied Russian. Hanna died on June 18, 1918. Two years later, Joseph married to Mary (Mamie) Hoffman on April 12, 1920 and was married to her until his death on May 12, 1935, in Dover Village, Ohio.

Joseph Lemieux and his sons maintained the family restaurant business. When he was a young man, Fred conducted tour groups from Cleveland by boat up to the Chateau Frontenac in Québec, Canada, with Dick Storey, his future brother-in-law. During World War I, Fred joined the Army and attended flight school at Randolph Field in San Antonio, Texas. Exploiting Prohibition, the Lemieux prospered by making and selling bootleg liquor at the Horse

Shoe Inn, their restaurant at the time, transporting it in a florist truck. (Did he also have contacts to import liquor from Quebec?) Fred arranged with the Cleveland Electric Co. to run electric service out Center Ridge Road to the Horse Shoe Inn, guaranteeing $50.00 worth of revenues, at his own expense if necessary. He never had to pay more than his own bill because electrical service was welcomed by everyone on Center Ridge Road. During this time, Fred's brother, John, worked as a bailiff in the Tax Office in Cleveland, which was particularly beneficial for the Horse Shoe Inn. Whenever the police told John to write a warrant to raid the Horse Shoe Inn, he would do so and when the police departed, he would telephone Fred to warn him. When the police arrived at the Inn, they would find everyone peacefully playing cards.

Helen Cushing's father, Thomas Cushing, was a barber from Newburg who drank a bit and left when she was young. Her mother, Margaret (Aunt Mag), who took in any relatives arriving from Ireland, reared her. Helen lived with her sisters, Alice and Anna Mae, cousin Grace and the extended family. She only completed the eighth grade and at the age of about 14 went to work in a woolen mill making sweaters at 55th and Broadway in Cleveland. Subsequently, she went to work at Corrigan and McKinney Steel as a

switchboard operator and it was then that she met Fred Lemieux. They were engaged while Fred was in the Army during WWI and Helen would let her sisters, Allie and Anna Mae wear her engagement ring if they would answer Freddy's letters. During this time she also had engagement rings from a jeweler and a doctor. Helen was having a wonderful time and was not particularly interested in marriage yet, but, after the war ended, Helen's mother told her that Freddy was a good man and Helen should marry him. Fred and Helen were married in Cleveland on June 9, 1920, and returned to the restaurant business. Fred was very shy but he loved Helen deeply and was a good provider for his family. He was a sweet, gentle man who worked hard every day and when he came home, usually bringing coffee ice cream and one-pound blocks of butter, he liked to sit in his favorite chair and smoke cigars. His hobby was collecting clocks that he wound by key once a week. Every hour and half-hour, the basement rec-room would sound off with all their chimes. Fred and Helen had four children - Alfred Jean (Al), born May 12, 1921, Edward Joseph (Ned), born September 23, 1922; John, born May 6, 1924 who died of pneumonia in March, 1926 and Mary Jo (Mary), born May 17, 1929. The three surviving children spent their childhood in the Cleveland suburb of Rocky River. Helen was a wonderful wife, mother, grandmother and an important role model. Susan was able to learn from her by being able to spend time with her when she was making a beautiful home, watched her making her own slipcovers for furniture, gardening, cooking, baking, and making incredible doll clothes for the beautiful dolls Helen gave her. Helen was shy around strangers but was extremely generous and happiest with her family around her. Everyone loved her Irish sense of humor. Even though her formal education did not go beyond eighth grade, schooling was very rigorous then and Helen was so witty, smart, and full of common sense. She loved to read mystery novels and listen to the Cleveland Indians baseball games on the radio while working around the house. Whenever Helen needed to cheer herself up, she would go out and buy herself a new hat. She was very wise.

* * *

Alfred Jean Lemieux, 2043 Lakeview Road, son of Mr. and Mrs. Alfred J. Lemieux, has just received his wings at Corpus Christie, Texas. He graduated from River High in about 1939 and while there was a member of the track team, Hi Y, and other school activities. He enlisted in the Naval Reserve in July, 1942, was called to active duty in October and sent to Iowa State University for pre-flight training. He then went to Glenview, Illinois, for primary flight, and then to Corpus Christie for advanced flight training. Now that he is graduated, he has been sent to Daytona Beach, Fla., for assignment to a bombing or torpedo plane squadron, after which he will be stationed at San Diego, California. While at Daytona Beach, he was selected by the Marines and therefore is now in the Marine rather than Navy Service. It seems that the Marines do not have a flying training course of their own, and choose their men from Navy graduates.

Another son Edward J. Lemieux, who graduated from River High in 1940, where he was considered quite a baseball star, is now in the Merchant Marine Service having joined about a year ago. He is a pharmacist's third mate and at present in Detroit assisting in the present recruiting drive for Merchant Marine recruits. He will be home most likely tomorrow. His father, who is a resturanteur promises to have "Roast Beef", and his mother, a nice big Home Made Cake" for their son on his arrival. (How about inviting the neighbors?)

* * *

Al Lemieux joined the navy after the bombing of Pearl Harbor in 1941, and married Patricia Eileen Lape on November 17, 1943 in Morehead City, North Carolina before going to the Asian theater of World War II as a Marine aviator. Susan Kathleen was born in Rocky River August 12, 1944 while he was overseas. He participated in the War at Midway, the Marshall Islands, Guam and was at Naha, Okinawa, April 1, 1945. A year after his return, John Melvin was born on July 25, 1946. During Al's service in the Korean War, Alfred Carl was born November 17, 1951. Al was an industrial salesman after his military service. Elizabeth Ann (Liz) was born March 27, 1965. Al died of cancer on Saturday, September 6, 2008 at Liz's home.

Edward Joseph (Ned) Lemieux also joined the Navy during World War II, and married Virginia Mary (Dee Dee)

Roop on July 10, 1944. Ned worked for the C&O Railroad for 38 years until his retirement. Edward Joseph, Jr. (Joe) was born May 20, 1945; William Alfred (Bill) was born August 8, 1948; James Michael (Jim) was born April 30, 1950; and Mary Joanne (Mary Jo) was born November 9, 1953. Ned died January 21, 2005 in Tampa, Florida. He was a warm and wonderful man who, like his father, also collected clocks.

Mary Lemieux is the Godmother of Susan Lemieux and is still an ideal role model as a mother, wife, friend and person. She taught Susan how to sew, cook from a cookbook, paint with oil paints and many creative things. Mary Lemieux married Charles Kenneth (Ken) Koster on July 25, 1953 while he was finishing his medical studies. After his time in the Air Force, he opened his Ophthalmology practice in Lakewood, Ohio. Ann Marie was born June 14, 1954; Thomas James (Tom) was born January 15, 1956; Kathryn (Katie Cuddles) was born January 2, 1958; Edward Joseph (Neddy) was born September 7, 1959. His Godmother is Susan Lemieux Marsolais. Carl John II was born January 28, 1963. Mary and Ken made a wonderful home and family life with many friends and good times. They are always there to help those in need.

When Harold G. Marsolais moved his family to Ohio in 1954, it brought the Lemieux and Marsolais face to face again. Hal Marsolais was 12 years old and Susan Lemieux was 10 when they met. They had no idea their families had such a long history of close relationships.

Susan Lemieux graduated from Biloxi High School in Biloxi, Mississippi, where she was living with her aunt and uncle, Mary and Ken Koster, who were completing a tour of duty with the U.S. Air Force. Upon returning to Ohio in 1962 she renewed her relationship with the Marsolais family. Susan married Hal Marsolais, July 5, 1964 in the 82nd Airborne Division South Chapel at Fort Bragg, North Carolina. The families were finally joined. Michelle Suzanne was born on May 5, 1965, and H. Raymond Marsolais, Jr. was born May 11, 1967, both in Lakewood Hospital, Lakewood, Ohio. While rearing two children, Susan worked and studied fine arts. Interior decorating has always been her favorite interest, and during Hal's military career, the family was required to move frequently, providing Susan with many decorating challenges. They resided throughout the United States as well as Germany and Italy, giving the family and their wonder dog, Mighty Muffin, many adventures and wonderful memories. Susan was fortunate to live the life she always wanted. She married the boy she fell in love with at 10 years old, who grew into an amazing, successful man who loved her, too. She had two beautiful, healthy children, a daughter and a son, as she always wanted. She is proud that Shelly and Ray grew into intelligent, productive, successful adults with strong characters. She and her family traveled extensively, and lived a full, rich life. Because of this separation from the remainder of the family, Susan began researching genealogy to provide background information for her children. After 22 years of marriage, she found the historic link between the Lemieux and Marsolais.

Hal was an up-from-the-ranks military officer who completed his military career in 1982. He was a highly decorated veteran of two tours of duty in Viet Nam having served as an infantry paratrooper and helicopter pilot. The military not only provided a full and rich life, it also provided an opportunity for Hal for advanced education, including Bachelor's and Master's degrees in business. He is a Cum Laude graduate of the University of Southern Mississippi and holds a Master's Degree in Management from Webster University. He is an Honor Graduate of the U.S. Army Command and General Staff College. After retiring from his military career at the age of 40, he held a series of positions in the field of association management and retired as Managing Director (CEO) of the National Retail Hardware Association in 1994. Hal and Susan have now been married 46 years and are happily retired in St. Augustine, Florida.

John Lemieux married Lois Busch, November 3, 1983, in Cleveland. They had two children: John Louis who was born February 4, 1972, and Aaron Patrick who was born September 25, 1974, in Cleveland. John and Lois divorced in 1980 and he is currently married to Linda Soltis. After a tour in the U. S. Navy, John opened his own business selling pumps and filters to the nuclear power industry. He was involved in recovery operations after the Three Mile Island incident. John's son, John Louis, graduated from Michigan State University with a degree in law and established practice in Ohio. Aaron Patrick graduated the University of Toledo with a B.S. in Mechanical Engineering with a specialization in Biomedical Engineering and married the former Jill Graham from Indiana. Aaron LeMieux is the sole technology innovator and entrepreneur that invented, built and tested the first nPower (TM) device, Personal Energy Generator (PEG), to be released July 2010, and subsequently founded Tremont Electric LLC in May 2007, and holds multiple patents. One evening, John had cousin, Tom Koster, over for dinner. Standing out at the barbeque grill John said to Tom, "You never know when it's going to hit you, but one day you'll be walking down the street, and you'll light up a cigar and start collecting clocks." Tom pulled a cigar from his pocket, lit it, and said, "And I have five clocks in my house." The Lemieux men have inherited Freddy's gene.

Alfred Carl Lemieux was married to Linda Schneeberger November 1, 1980. After a tour in the U.S. Air Force he settled on the West Coast. Al is employed with the City of Long Beach, California. Sean Patrick was born December 21, 1982 and died March 2010. Jeanette Suzanne was born January 20, 1985 in Long Beach.

Elizabeth Lemieux married John Earl Emery September 30, 1989, in Rocky River, Ohio. John is a carpenter and a contractor. Shaylynn was born May 10, 1990. Kathryn was born February 17, 1995, in Cleveland and Annalise was born August 21, 1996, in Middlefield. They divorced in 2006. Elizabeth completed her Bachelor's Degree at Cleveland State University and went on to get a Master's Degree in Sociology at Case Western Reserve University in 2006 and works in an institutional Hospice Program. In October 2008 Elizabeth married Jerry Craddock in Chardon, Ohio and they divorced in 2009. In 2010 Liz, Kathryn and Annalise moved to St. Augustine, FL.

Dennis Marsolais graduated from Brookside High School in Sheffield Lake, Ohio and attended Bowling Green University. He served with the U.S. Army 1st Infantry Division in Vietnam and was wounded in action. He moved to the Pacific Northwest, attended the University of Idaho and settled in Bellingham, Washington, where he worked for a period as a commercial fisherman. He married Kris Browne on October 7,

1995. Kris is active in community affairs and was a volunteer for the Red Cross during the 2005 Katrina Hurricane crisis in New Orleans.

Robert Marsolais married Kathy Gibson. Their first child, Robert Allen, Jr. was born January 24, 1971 and their daughter, Jenny, was born October 6, 1973. They divorced shortly thereafter. Bob works as a tour bus driver. Bob and Carla Boyd were partners for years and had three children: Jeffrey on December 3, 1979, Michael on December 9, 1981, and Cheryl in May 1984. Bob married his current wife Anna Boyd in 1990 and they live in Vermillion, Ohio.

Richard Marsolais also graduated from Brookside High School and attended the University of Southern Mississippi. He is the Chief Meteorologist at WSFA television, an NBC affiliate in Montgomery, Alabama, where he has lived since leaving the university in 1975. He is a local celebrity, active in community affairs and is widely recognized for his work in providing storm warnings during periods of severe weather. In 2007, NOAA presented Richard the Mark Trail Award for his service. He has over 25 years of service at the station and works each day in a job he dreamed of as a youth.

Michelle Suzanne Marsolais was the first-born child of Harold R. Marsolais and Susan Lemieux. Shelly attended schools throughout the United States and Europe as the family followed Harold's military career. On November 5, 1988, Michelle married Bill O'Brien at St. Joan of Arc Catholic Church in Hershey, Pennsylvania. Bill's career is in the hotel and restaurant management and except for a short stint in Worcester, Massachusetts, he managed a number of properties in the Harrisburg/Hershey area. Michelle and Bill had three children. Their son, Sean Patrick O'Brien, died at birth, February 23, 1989 and was buried at Hershey Cemetery in Hershey, Pennsylvania. Kelsey Elizabeth O'Brien was born May 29, 1991, in Harrisburg, Pennsylvania and Emma Kathleen O'Brien was born there on October 18, 1992. Michelle went on to complete her Baccalaureate Degree with Honors at the Pennsylvania State University graduating with a Bachelor of Humanities Secondary Education/English in 1997. She entered the teaching profession in Elizabethtown, Pennsylvania. She later accepted a position at the Derry Township School District, Hershey High School as a Senior and Honors English teacher, where she prospered. Affectionately known to her students as Mrs. "O'B," she has been credited with being a student role model and confidant. She has served as academic advisor for the National Honor Society. She is an accomplished author with several published pieces. While maintaining her teaching position, she continued her studies at the Pennsylvania State University earning a Master's Degree in Humanities in December 2004 and went on to become head of the English Department. With Michelle's love of education and Bill's love of hunting and fishing, they are both excellent role models for Kelsey and Emma who love reading, writing, art and their studies. Both have taken piano lessons and have tried to master a variety of other instruments. They both are accomplished Irish step dancers, swimmers and travelers. Scholastic Magazine honored Kelsey at Carnegie Hall in 2006 with a National Silver Medal award in a writing competition. She had previously earned a Regional Gold Key in the same competition. Kelsey currently attends Marymount Manhattan College studying communications and loves living in NYC. Emma is a serious art student, hoping to attend

162

the Chicago Art Institute. Both Kelsey and Emma represent the future of the Marsolais…
…Could we see, "O'Brien-dit-Marsolais"?

H. Ray Marsolais has been singled out as the family's modern-day rascal. Known for his sense of humor with a sly grin and a twinkle in his eye, he has a penchant to do things his way, within his time frame. After graduating from Hershey High School, Hershey, Pennsylvania, he completed a tour of duty with the 3rd Battalion of the 68th Armor Regiment of the U.S. Army 4th Mechanized Infantry Division at Ft. Carson, Colorado. Upon completion of his military duties, he attended the University of Wyoming in Laramie studying Finance and Economics. While there he enjoyed the life of a *coureur des bois,* camping in the snow, rock climbing, exploring and mountain biking. He married Nicole Bryant August 30, 1997, in a beautiful rustic setting atop the Snowy Range Mountains near Centennial, Wyoming. She graduated from the University of Wyoming in Communications and is a descendant of pioneer family from Castle Rock, Colorado. After their marriage, they moved to Seattle, Washington, where Ray entered the shipping business and established a branch office in Bellingham, capitalizing on trade law changes with Canada. During this time Nicole worked for Western Washington University and went on to earn her Master of Arts Degree in Applied Behavioral Science from Bastyr University in Kenmore, Washington on December 13, 2004. They were divorced in 2010. With Ray's field of study in Finance and Economics, he accepted a position with a brokerage firm as a financial analyst and a

Fashioned after the *coureur du bois,* Ray, accompanied by his faithful dog, Dakota, is wearing the capote made by his mother, Susan, and designed to his specifications.

stockbroker, specializing in retirement planning. He was able to use his computer skills to assist in expanding the program nationally. Always interested in outdoor activities, he was determined to find a way to make the wilderness a career. He obtained his seaman's license and joined a firm that supplied fishermen, campsites and villages near the Artic Circle. His travels take him through the Inside Passage to the Gulf of Alaska, throughout the Aleutian Islands, and north across the Artic Circle to the 1,000-mile long Yukon River. His current position as Able Bodied Seaman Unlimited aboard the 143-foot, 199-ton, *Island Warrior* calls for ten trips each year from Seattle to Anchorage through the Inside Passage.

….and the saga continues. We welcome the next generations of Marsolais and Lemieux as they expand the accomplishments of our family. May they all live happily ever after…

Chamberland/Chamberlain

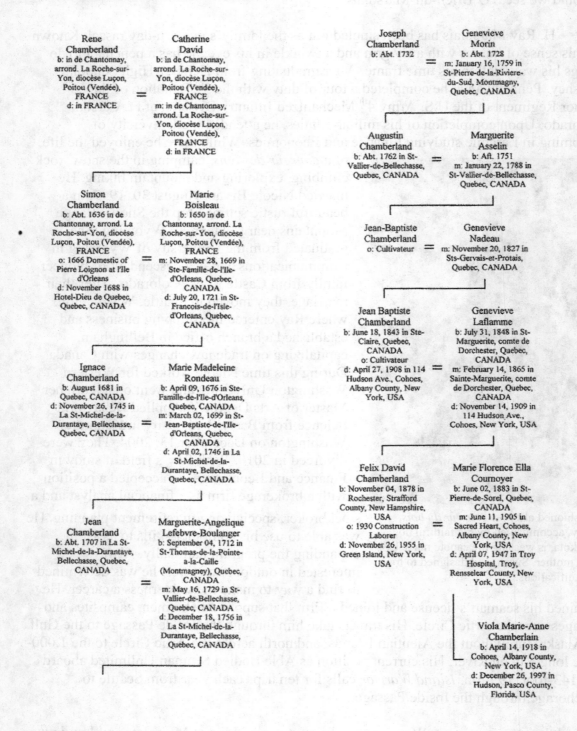

Rene Chamberland
b: in de Chantonnay, arrond. La Roche-sur-Yon, diocèse Luçon, Poitou (Vendée), FRANCE
d: in FRANCE

=

Catherine David
b: in de Chantonnay, arrond. La Roche-sur-Yon, diocèse Luçon, Poitou (Vendée), FRANCE
m: in de Chantonnay, arrond. La Roche-sur-Yon, diocèse Luçon, Poitou (Vendée), FRANCE
d: in FRANCE

Simon Chamberland
b: Abt. 1636 in de Chantonnay, arrond. La Roche-sur-Yon, diocèse Luçon, Poitou (Vendée), FRANCE
o: 1666 Domestic of Pierre Loignon at l'Ile d'Orleans
d: November 1688 in Hotel-Dieu de Quebec, Quebec, CANADA

=

Marie Boisleau
b: 1650 in de Chantonnay, arrond. La Roche-sur-Yon, diocèse Luçon, Poitou (Vendée), FRANCE
m: November 28, 1669 in Ste-Famille-de-l'Ile-d'Orleans, Quebec, CANADA
d: July 20, 1721 in St-Francois-de-l'Isle-d'Orleans, Quebec, CANADA

Ignace Chamberland
b: August 1681 in Quebec, CANADA
d: November 26, 1745 in La St-Michel-de-la-Durantaye, Bellechasse, Quebec, CANADA

=

Marie Madeleine Rondeau
b: April 09, 1676 in Ste-Famille-de-l'Ile-d'Orleans, Quebec, CANADA
m: March 02, 1699 in St-Jean-Baptiste-de-l'Ile-d'Orleans, Quebec, CANADA
d: April 02, 1746 in La St-Michel-de-la-Durantaye, Bellechasse, Quebec, CANADA

Jean Chamberland
b: Abt. 1707 in La St-Michel-de-la-Durantaye, Bellechasse, Quebec, CANADA

=

Marguerite-Angelique Lefebvre-Boulanger
b: September 04, 1712 in St-Thomas-de-la-Pointe-a-la-Caille (Montmagney), Quebec, CANADA
m: May 16, 1729 in St-Vallier-de-Bellechasse, Quebec, CANADA
d: December 18, 1756 in La St-Michel-de-la-Durantaye, Bellechasse, Quebec, CANADA

Joseph Chamberland
b: Abt. 1732

=

Genevieve Morin
b: Abt. 1728
m: January 16, 1759 in St-Pierre-de-la-Riviere-du-Sud, Montmagny, Quebec, CANADA

Augustin Chamberland
b: Abt. 1762 in St-Vallier-de-Bellechasse, Quebec, CANADA

=

Marguerite Asselin
b: Aft. 1751
m: January 22, 1788 in St-Vallier-de-Bellechasse, Quebec, CANADA

Jean-Baptiste Chamberland
o: Cultivateur

=

Genevieve Nadeau
m: November 20, 1827 in Sts-Gervais-et-Protais, Quebec, CANADA

Jean Baptiste Chamberland
b: June 18, 1843 in Ste-Claire, Quebec, CANADA
o: Cultivateur
d: April 27, 1908 in 114 Hudson Ave., Cohoes, Albany County, New York, USA

=

Genevieve Laflamme
b: July 31, 1848 in St-Marguerite, comte de Dorchester, Quebec, CANADA
m: February 14, 1865 in Sainte-Marguerite, comte de Dorchester, Quebec, CANADA
d: November 14, 1909 in 114 Hudson Ave., Cohoes, New York, USA

Felix David Chamberland
b: November 04, 1878 in Rochester, Strafford County, New Hampshire, USA
o: 1930 Construction Laborer
d: November 26, 1955 in Green Island, New York, USA

=

Marie Florence Ella Cournoyer
b: June 02, 1883 in St-Pierre-de-Sorel, Quebec, CANADA
m: June 11, 1905 in Sacred Heart, Cohoes, Albany County, New York, USA
d: April 07, 1947 in Troy Hospital, Troy, Rensselear County, New York, USA

Viola Marie-Anne Chamberlain
b: April 14, 1918 in Cohoes, Albany County, New York, USA
d: December 26, 1997 in Hudson, Pasco County, Florida, USA

XI

Branches

With the women's branches of the families, the Lapes, Rodgers, Cushings, and Chamberlains, there was less oral history to get started and, additionally, each state's archives provided a fresh, new challenge in obtaining records. But the July 2003, family reunion in Québec offered a breakthrough for the Chamberlains.

Chamberland/Chamberlain

Harold R. Marsolais's mother, Viola *Chamberlain* Marsolais, is also of French Canadian descent. In fact, the Chamberland family was among the early settlers of l'Ile-d'Orleans in New France, arriving before 1665. The French surname "Chamberland" is occupational in origin, derived from the Old French word "chamberlain" denoting one who was charged with the management of the private chambers of a sovereign or a nobleman in medieval times. The name was common in medieval France and is usually associated

Chamberland

with the Poitou area of the marsh country near La Rochelle, where it is still prevalent today. The surname also came into popular English usage as "Chamberlain" in the wake of the Norman invasion of 1066, when French influence prevailed throughout Britain.

Simon Chamberland arrived in New France before November 12, 1665, probably from La Rochelle, a major embarkation point. He was born about 1636 in Chantonnay near La-Roche-sur-Yon. His parents were Rene Chamberland and Catherine David. Simon settled on l'Ile-d'Orleans adjacent to the city of Québec where he married Marie Boisleau at St. Famille-de-l'Ile-d'Orleans November 28, 1669. Marie was a King's Daughter from an upper-class family. She was previously married to Pierre Chauvin in 1668 on l'Ile de Orleans. Marie and Simon had eight children, three girls and five boys. Simon died November 1688, in the Hotel-Dieu de Québec.

Simon's son, Ignace, was born in August 1681, in Québec. He married Marie-Madeleine Rondeau in St. Famille-de-l'Ile-d'Orleans, March 2, 1699. She was 23 years old. They had eight children, four girls and four boys. Ignace died November 26, 1745, at St-Michel, Bellechasse (the same *seigneurie* given to Nicolas Marsolet in 1637 as a wedding gift and which he owned until 1672). Marie-Madeleine died five months after her husband in April of 1746, a week before her 70th birthday.

Jean Chamberland was born about 1707, in St-Michel-de-la-Durantaye, Bellechasse. He married Marguerite-Angelique Lefebvre-Boulanger on May 16, 1729 at St-Vallier-de-Bellechasse. They had 15 children, seven girls and eight boys. Marguerite died December 18, 1756, and was buried at St-Michel-de-la-Durantaye, Bellechasse.

Joseph Chamberland was born about 1732, and married Genevieve Morin on January 16, 1755, at St-Pierre-de-la-Riviere-du-Sud, Montmagny, Québec. They had three children, a girl and two boys.

Augustin Chamberland, born after 1759 in St-Vallier-de-Bellechasse, became a farmer and married Marguerite Asselin from the same parish on January 21, 1787. They had four sons.

Jean-Baptiste Chamberland, born after 1787, married Genevieve Nadeau on November 20, 1827, at Sts-Gervais-et-Protais, Québec. They had a son and a daughter.

Jean-Baptiste, their son, was born June 18, 1843, at Ste-Claire, Québec. He married Genevieve Laflamme February 14, 1865 at Ste-Marguerite, compte-de-Dorchester, Québec. They had five daughters and six sons and made the move to the US, eventually residing in Cohoes, New York. Jean-Baptiste died April 27, 1908, in Cohoes, and is buried at St. Joseph's, Waterford, New York. His wife, Genevieve, died November 14, 1909, and is buried in the same cemetery.

Felix Chamberland was born in Rochester, New Hampshire on November 4, 1878. He and Florence Cournoyer were married in Cohoes, New York on June 11, 1905, and had four sons and four daughters. Florence Cournoyer was born in Trois-Rivières, Québec on June 1, 1884, to Felix Cournoyer and Mathilda Gregoire. Felix became a machinist/maintenance man and worked in the mills of Cohoes. Florence died in Colonie, New York, in 1947, and Felix died in Troy in 1955.

Two of Felix and Florence's sons, Leo and Raymond, moved to California shortly after WWII. Ernest Chamberlain became a senior executive at Firestone Tire and Rubber in Philadelphia and married Loretta Marsolais, Harold Marsolais's sister. They also had two daughters. Anna May married Peter Finger and Dorothy married Thomas Ryan. Both remained in the Troy, New York area. Of note, Thomas Ryan was a survivor of a kamikaze attack on the destroyer USS Lindsey in the Battle of Okinawa during WWII. Over one-third of the crew was killed in the attack and the ship was virtually cut in half. The surviving crew saved the ship and returned it to the United States.

Another daughter, Eva, was discovered during research. She had not previously been discussed by the Chamberlain family and was not recognized on the headstone at the cemetery. She was born October 15, 1907, in Schenectady, New York, and was deaf and mute. She spent seven years at home in the care of her family and was committed to the Rome State Custodial Asylum in December 1914. She spent almost three years there and died July 22, 1917, from seizures, at the age of nine years, nine months. She was buried the following day at St. Josephs Cemetery in Waterford, New York. Her name is now engraved on the Chamberland headstone.

Viola Chamberlain was born the sixth child on April 14, 1918 in Cohoes, New York. Her unnamed twin brother was stillborn. Viola married Harold G. Marsolais on February 8, 1941, in the Church of the Sacred Heart, Cohoes, New York and they had four sons. Harold became a foreman for Republic Steel and relocated to the Cleveland area of Ohio. They retired in Hudson, Florida where Harold died February 13, 1985 and Viola died December 26, 1997. They rest at Bay Pines Cemetery, Bay Pines, Florida.

Cushing and Rodgers

In attempting to research Al Lemieux's mother, Helen Cushing, there was little progress. The death certificate of Helen's father, Thomas Cushing, dated October 12, 1929, states he was a self-employed barber, born in Cleveland in 1871. His parents, Michael Cushing and Alice O'Connor were born in Ireland.

The death certificate of Helen's mother, Margaret Rodgers, dated September 24, 1943, indicates she was born in Cleveland August 20, 1874. Her parents, Edward Rodgers and Ann Cunningham were born in Ireland. Ann Cunningham Rodgers' (1844-1925) parents, James Cunningham and Catherine Devine were born in Ireland, as were Edward Rodgers' (1848-1916), Patrick Rodgers and Margaret Quinn. It is said that Ann and Edward Rodgers were born in Kilkeel, Northern Ireland, County Down, and married there February 28, 1865, but in writing to Belfast, Ireland, there was not enough information to acquire any documents.

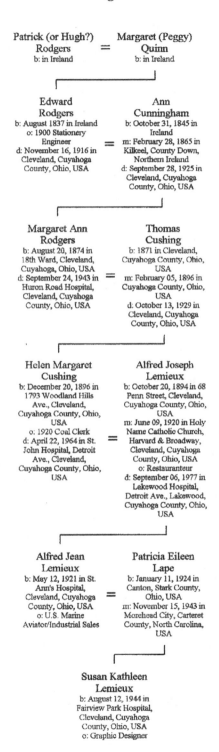

Rodgers

Patrick (or Hugh?) Rodgers
b: in Ireland
=
Margaret (Peggy) Quinn
b: in Ireland

Edward Rodgers
b: August 1837 in Ireland
o: 1900 Stationery Engineer
d: November 16, 1916 in Cleveland, Cuyahoga County, Ohio, USA
=
Ann Cunningham
b: October 31, 1845 in Ireland
m: February 28, 1865 in Kilkeel, County Down, Northern Ireland
d: September 28, 1925 in Cleveland, Cuyahoga County, Ohio, USA

Margaret Ann Rodgers
b: August 20, 1874 in 18th Ward, Cleveland, Cuyahoga, Ohio, USA
d: September 24, 1943 in Huron Road Hospital, Cleveland, Cuyahoga County, Ohio, USA
=
Thomas Cushing
b: 1871 in Cleveland, Cuyahoga County, Ohio, USA
m: February 05, 1896 in Cuyahoga County, Ohio, USA
d: October 13, 1929 in Cleveland, Cuyahoga County, Ohio, USA

Helen Margaret Cushing
b: December 20, 1896 in 1793 Woodland Hills Ave., Cleveland, Cuyahoga County, Ohio, USA
o: 1920 Coal Clerk
d: April 22, 1964 in St. John Hospital, Detroit Ave., Cleveland, Cuyahoga County, Ohio, USA
=
Alfred Joseph Lemieux
b: October 20, 1894 in 68 Penn Street, Cleveland, Cuyahoga County, Ohio, USA
m: June 09, 1920 in Holy Name Catholic Church, Harvard & Broadway, Cleveland, Cuyahoga County, Ohio, USA
o: Restauranteur
d: September 06, 1977 in Lakewood Hospital, Detroit Ave., Lakewood, Cuyahoga County, Ohio, USA

Alfred Jean Lemieux
b: May 12, 1921 in St. Ann's Hospital, Cleveland, Cuyahoga County, Ohio, USA
o: U.S. Marine Aviator/Industrial Sales
=
Patricia Eileen Lape
b: January 11, 1924 in Canton, Stark County, Ohio, USA
m: November 15, 1943 in Morehead City, Carteret County, North Carolina, USA

Susan Kathleen Lemieux
b: August 12, 1944 in Fairview Park Hospital, Cleveland, Cuyahoga County, Ohio, USA
o: Graphic Designer

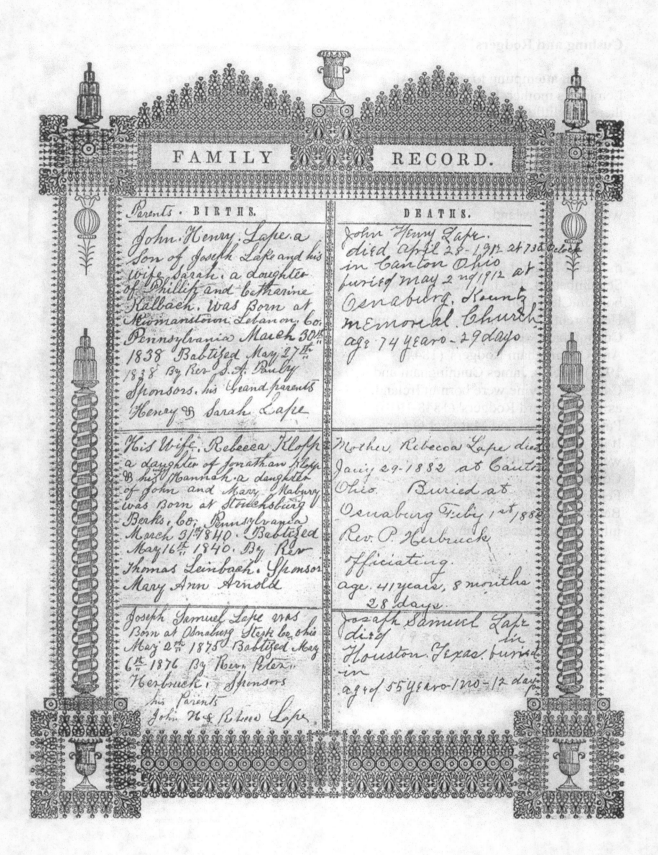

FAMILY RECORD.

Parents · BIRTHS.

John · Henry · Lape · a Son of Joseph Lape and his wife · Sarah · a daughter of Phillip and Catharine Kalbach. was Born at Niomanstown. Lebanon. Co. Pennsylvania March 30th 1838 Babtized May 27th 1838 By Rev. S. A. Pauly Sponsors. his Grand parents Henry & Sarah Lape

His Wife · Rebecca Kloss a daughter of Jonathan Kloss & his Hannah. a daughter of John and Mary Mabury was Born at Stouchsburg Berks. Co. Pennsylvania March 31st 1840. Babtized May 16th 1840. By Rev Thomas Leinbach. Sponsor Mary Ann Arnold

Joseph Samuel Lape was Born at Osnaburg Stark Co. Ohio May 2th 1875 Babtized May 6th 1876 By Rev Peter Herbruck. Sponsors his Parents John H & Rebecca Lape

DEATHS.

John Henry Lape. died April 28 1912 at 730 oclock in Canton Ohio buried May 2nd 1912 at Osnaburg Kountz Memorial Church age 74 years - 29 days

Mother Rebecca Lape died Jany 29 1882 at Canton Ohio. Buried at Osnaburg Feby 1st 1882 Rev. P. Herbruck officiating. age. 41 years, 8 months 28 days.

Joseph Samuel Lape died in Houston Texas buried in age of 55 years - 1 mo - 17 days

168

Loeb/Lape

In the case of the *Lapes*, who came from Pennsylvania, the Commonwealth Department of Health maintains vital records from the current date back only to 1906. From 1906 to 1893, records are kept in the county courthouse, and from 1893 back, one must go to the church records. Some churches unified, some split and sometimes there was only an itinerant minister. One must be inordinately lucky to obtain old records in Pennsylvania.

Obtaining a copy of the family record from the family Bible of John Lape, lets Rebecca (Klopp) Lape tell the family story in her own handwriting until she died in childbirth with her 13th baby. John Henry Lape, of Dutch descent, married Rebecca Klopp in her parents' home in Stouchsburg, Pennsylvania December 3, 1858.

Ullemann

Melvin Brosius Lape was their 11th child and was born March 8, 1878. He in turn married Amelia "Emily" Uebelhart in Canton, Ohio on June 12, 1902. Emily's family was of Swiss descent. Her grandmother, Marianne Allemann Ubelhart's ancestors, Benedikt and Jakob Allemann (Ullemann), were awarded a coat of arms for founding the first boy's school in Gut Nüchtern, Switzerland, northeast of Bern in 1820. Melvin and Emily lived in Canton, Ohio, in a house that was originally part of a farm, and Melvin also became a foreman in the Bendix plant. They had three sons, Carl Melvin, John Henry, and James Thomas. Their daughter, Margaret Lida, lived in the same house until her death.

On December 28, 1921, Carl Lape, 18, and Myrtle Eva "Becky" Tucker, 16, eloped in Pittsburgh---both were underage. During their marriage they had three daughters, Barbara Anne, Patricia Eileen and Beverly Jane. Carl and Becky were divorced in 1940. She was remarried in 1940 to Allen Doron, who died in 1945. After being widowed, Becky had a

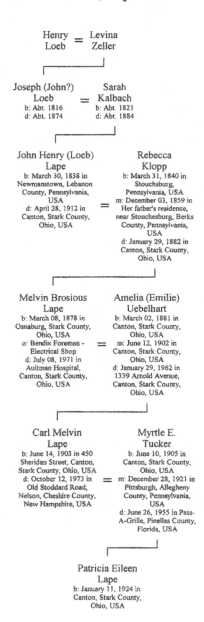

Loeb, Lape

Henry Loeb = Levina Zeller

Joseph (John?) Loeb
b: Abt. 1816
d: Abt. 1874
=
Sarah Kalbach
b: Abt. 1821
d: Abt. 1884

John Henry (Loeb) Lape
b: March 30, 1838 in Newmanstown, Lebanon County, Pennsylvania, USA
d: April 28, 1912 in Canton, Stark County, Ohio, USA
=
Rebecca Klopp
b: March 31, 1840 in Stouchsburg, Pennsylvania, USA
m: December 03, 1859 in Her father's residence, near Stouchesburg, Berks County, Pennsylvania, USA
d: January 29, 1882 in Canton, Stark County, Ohio, USA

Melvin Brosious Lape
b: March 08, 1878 in Osnaburg, Stark County, Ohio, USA
o: Bendix Foreman - Electrical Shop
d: July 08, 1971 in Aultman Hospital, Canton, Stark County, Ohio, USA
=
Amelia (Emilie) Uebelhart
b: March 02, 1881 in Canton, Stark County, Ohio, USA
m: June 12, 1902 in Canton, Stark County, Ohio, USA
d: January 29, 1962 in 1339 Arnold Avenue, Canton, Stark County, Ohio, USA

Carl Melvin Lape
b: June 14, 1903 in 450 Sheridan Street, Canton, Stark County, Ohio, USA
d: October 12, 1973 in Old Stoddard Road, Nelson, Cheshire County, New Hampshire, USA
=
Myrtle E. Tucker
b: June 10, 1905 in Canton, Stark County, Ohio, USA
m: December 28, 1921 in Pittsburgh, Allegheny County, Pennsylvania, USA
d: June 26, 1955 in Pass-A-Grille, Pinellas County, Florida, USA

Patricia Eileen Lape
b: January 11, 1924 in Canton, Stark County, Ohio, USA

restaurant/lounge/package store in Clearwater, Florida, called The Seahorse. Visits with her in Florida were unique. The day would start with a bag of peanuts to take out into the yard to feed the peacock, after breakfast, there was a stop at the restaurant to check on the day's business, then to go for a swim. In 1946, Becky married Albert Rogers and they later divorced. In 1955, Becky married Daniel Gallagher and she drowned 6 months afterward. She was an exciting role model of a lady entrepreneur who had a great deal of élan. She lived a stylish life of travel and adventure. Everyone loved her and she is still sorely missed.

During his life, Carl Lape attended the University of Pittsburgh, Youngstown Ohio Law School, Cleveland Advertising School and the University of Chicago. He was an engineer/inspector for the Panama Canal and in Cincinnati he owned a commercial laundry. In 1943, after the divorce from Becky in 1940, Carl married Ruth Schaettle in Milwaukee, Wisconsin. While growing up in Mondovi, Wisconsin, Ruth worked in her father's general store where she was primarily in charge of selling fabrics. She earned a B.S. in textile chemistry from the University of Wisconsin in 1927; she earned her M.A. from Columbia University in 1933, and attended the University of Washington for post-graduate studies in 1940. She was a member of several professional societies and associations and received many awards during her long and productive career. She was a high school teacher for 14 years, teaching Home Economics in England before WWII, and was a high school principal for 27. She was an incredible role model of a career woman and a wife who was highly professional and extremely gracious. Carl and Ruth lived in Cincinnati where Ruth consolidated all the city vocational programs into Central Vocational/Technical High School, and then was the Principal and Head of Curriculum there. Carl was a sales representative for a pest control company until he and Ruth retired to Nelson, New Hampshire. Even after retirement, Ruth was the only woman on national ad hoc committees on vocational education for President Kennedy and again in the 1970s. During the summer vacations Susan spent in Cincinnati, Ruth taught her how to sew, balance a career with a well run home, enjoy trying new things and so much more. It was interesting for Susan spending the days in the high school office, watching Ruth do her job, being allowed to run the switchboard at 12 years old, meeting the students in summer school, then coming home and helping to make a delicious dinner or going out to a restaurant. Carl, who died in 1973, is buried in Nelson and Ruth who died on April 27, 1997, is buried next to him.

Author's Note: This is where my story ends. Through this work, I have come to realize how much all of these people have enriched my life. I have always felt privileged that I knew my three grandmothers and two great-grandmothers and I still treasure the time we spent together. I have learned so much from the young, as well as the old, and feel fortunate for all they have passed on to me.

FAMILIES

Marsolais/Chamberlain

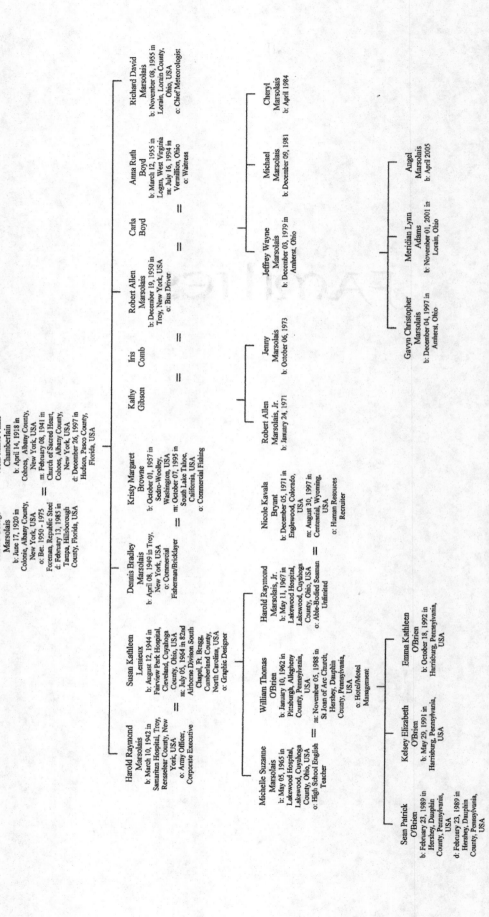

Ernest Chamberlain   Evelyn Marsolais

Harold George Marsolais and Viola Marie Chamberlain

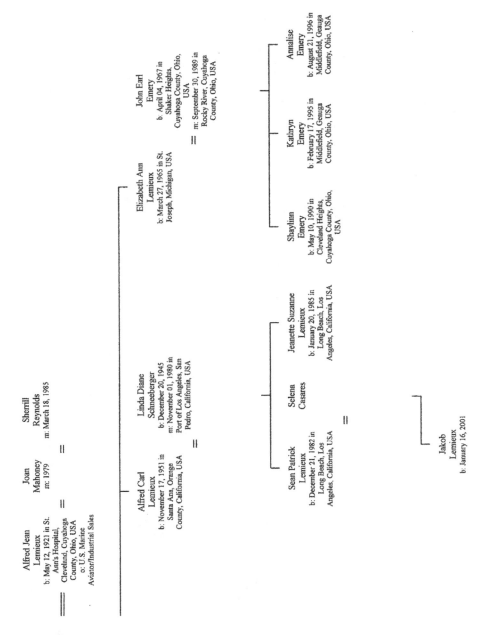

Alfred Jean
Lemieux
b: May 12, 1921 in St.
Ann's Hospital,
Cleveland, Cuyahoga
County, Ohio, USA
o: U.S. Marine
Aviator/Industrial Sales

==

Joan
Mahoney
m: 1979

==

Sherrill
Reynolds
m: March 18, 1985

Alfred Carl
Lemieux
b: November 17, 1951 in
Santa Ana, Orange
County, California, USA

==

Linda Diane
Schneeberger
b: December 20, 1945
m: November 01, 1980 in
Port of Los Angeles, San
Pedro, California, USA

Elizabeth Ann
Lemieux
b: March 27, 1965 in St.
Joseph, Michigan, USA

==

John Earl
Emery
b: April 04, 1967 in
Shaker Heights,
Cuyahoga County, Ohio,
USA
m: September 30, 1989 in
Rocky River, Cuyahoga
County, Ohio, USA

Sean Patrick
Lemieux
b: December 21, 1982 in
Long Beach, Los
Angeles, California, USA

==

Selena
Casares

Jeanette Suzanne
Lemieux
b: January 20, 1985 in
Long Beach, Los
Angeles, California, USA

Shaylinn
Emery
b: May 10, 1990 in
Cleveland Heights,
Cuyahoga County, Ohio,
USA

Kathryn
Emery
b: February 17, 1995 in
Middlefield, Geauga
County, Ohio, USA

Annalise
Emery
b: August 21, 1996 in
Middlefield, Geauga
County, Ohio, USA

Jakob
Lemieux
b: January 16, 2001

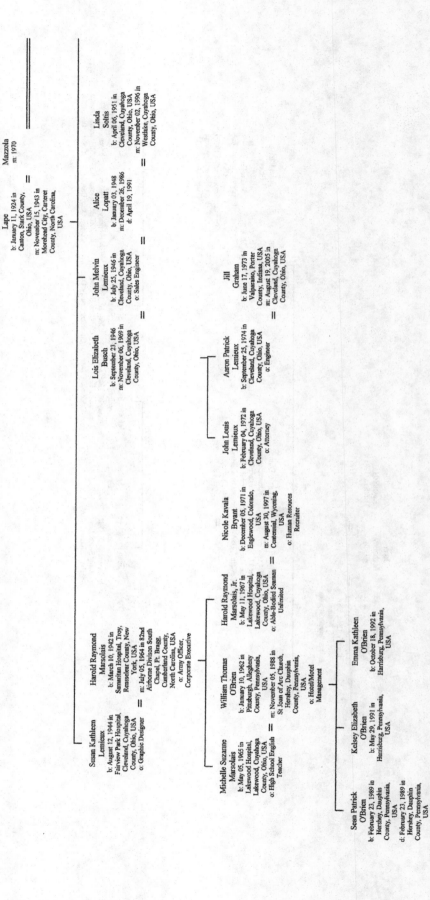

Lemieux/Lape

Patricia Eileen
Lape
b: January 11, 1924 in
Canton, Stark County,
Ohio, USA
m: November 15, 1943 in
Morehead City, Carteret
County, North Carolina,
USA

Rose Marie
Mazzola
m: 1970

=

Harold Raymond
Marsolais
b: March 10, 1942 in
Samaritan Hospital, Troy,
Rensselaer County, New
York, USA
m: July 05, 1964 in 82nd
Airborne Division South
Chapel, Ft. Bragg,
Cumberland County,
North Carolina, USA
o: Army Officer,
Corporate Executive

=

Susan Kathleen
Lemieux
b: August 12, 1944 in
Fairview Park Hospital,
Cleveland, Cuyahoga
County, Ohio, USA
o: Graphic Designer

John Melvin
Lemieux
b: July 25, 1946 in
Cleveland, Cuyahoga
County, Ohio, USA
o: Sales Engineer

=

Lois Elizabeth
Busch
b: September 23, 1946
m: November 06, 1969 in
Cleveland, Cuyahoga
County, Ohio, USA

Alice
Lopatt
b: January 03, 1948
m: December 26, 1986
d: April 19, 1991

=

Linda
Soltis
b: April 06, 1951 in
Cleveland, Cuyahoga
County, Ohio, USA
m: November 02, 1996 in
Westlake, Cuyahoga
County, Ohio, USA

=

Aaron Patrick
Lemieux
b: September 25, 1974 in
Cleveland, Cuyahoga
County, Ohio, USA
o: Engineer

John Louis
Lemieux
b: February 04, 1972 in
Cleveland, Cuyahoga
County, Ohio, USA
o: Attorney

Jill
Graham
b: June 17, 1973 in
Valparaiso, Porter
County, Indiana, USA
m: August 19, 2005 in
Cleveland, Cuyahoga
County, Ohio, USA

=

Harold Raymond
Marsolais, Jr.
b: May 11, 1967 in
Lakewood Hospital,
Lakewood, Cuyahoga
County, Ohio, USA
o: Able-Bodied Seaman
Unlimited

=

Nicole Kavaia
Bryant
b: December 05, 1971 in
Englewood, Colorado,
USA
m: August 30, 1997 in
Centennial, Wyoming,
USA
o: Human Resouces
Recruiter

Michelle Suzanne
Marsolais
b: May 05, 1965 in
Lakewood Hospital,
Lakewood, Cuyahoga
County, Ohio, USA
o: High School English
Teacher

=

William Thomas
O'Brien
b: January 10, 1962 in
Pittsburgh, Allegheny
County, Pennsylvania,
USA
m: November 05, 1988 in
St. Joan of Arc Church,
Hershey, Dauphin
County, Pennsylvania,
USA
o: Hotel/Motel
Management

Emma Kathleen
O'Brien
b: October 18, 1992 in
Harrisburg, Pennsylvania,
USA

Kelsey Elizabeth
O'Brien
b: May 29, 1991 in
Harrisburg, Pennsylvania,
USA

Sean Patrick
O'Brien
b: February 23, 1989 in
Hershey, Dauphin
County, Pennsylvania,
USA
d: February 23, 1989 in
Hershey, Dauphin
County, Pennsylvania,
USA

Patricia Eileen Lape and Alfred Jean Lemieux

Marsolais/Lemieux

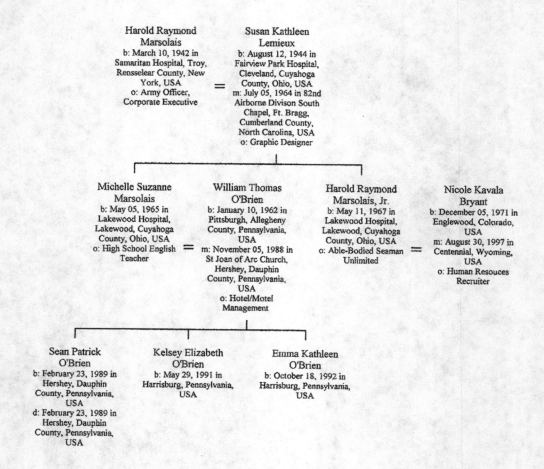

Harold Raymond
Marsolais
b: March 10, 1942 in
Samaritan Hospital, Troy,
Rensselear County, New
York, USA
o: Army Officer,
Corporate Executive

=

Susan Kathleen
Lemieux
b: August 12, 1944 in
Fairview Park Hospital,
Cleveland, Cuyahoga
County, Ohio, USA
m: July 05, 1964 in 82nd
Airborne Divison South
Chapel, Ft. Bragg,
Cumberland County,
North Carolina, USA
o: Graphic Designer

Michelle Suzanne
Marsolais
b: May 05, 1965 in
Lakewood Hospital,
Lakewood, Cuyahoga
County, Ohio, USA
o: High School English
Teacher

=

William Thomas
O'Brien
b: January 10, 1962 in
Pittsburgh, Allegheny
County, Pennsylvania,
USA
m: November 05, 1988 in
St Joan of Arc Church,
Hershey, Dauphin
County, Pennsylvania,
USA
o: Hotel/Motel
Management

Harold Raymond
Marsolais, Jr.
b: May 11, 1967 in
Lakewood Hospital,
Lakewood, Cuyahoga
County, Ohio, USA
o: Able-Bodied Seaman
Unlimited

=

Nicole Kavala
Bryant
b: December 05, 1971 in
Englewood, Colorado,
USA
m: August 30, 1997 in
Centennial, Wyoming,
USA
o: Human Resouces
Recruiter

Sean Patrick
O'Brien
b: February 23, 1989 in
Hershey, Dauphin
County, Pennsylvania,
USA
d: February 23, 1989 in
Hershey, Dauphin
County, Pennsylvania,
USA

Kelsey Elizabeth
O'Brien
b: May 29, 1991 in
Harrisburg, Pennsylvania,
USA

Emma Kathleen
O'Brien
b: October 18, 1992 in
Harrisburg, Pennsylvania,
USA

Harold Raymond Marsolais and Susan Kathleen Lemieux

Marsolais/O'Brien

Michelle Suzanne
Marsolais
b: May 05, 1965 in
Lakewood Hospital,
Lakewood, Cuyahoga
County, Ohio, USA
o: High School English
Teacher

William Thomas
O'Brien
b: January 10, 1962 in
Pittsburgh, Allegheny
County, Pennsylvania,
USA
m: November 05, 1988 in
St Joan of Arc Church,
Hershey, Dauphin
County, Pennsylvania,
USA
o: Hotel/Motel
Management

Sean Patrick
O'Brien
b: February 23, 1989 in
Hershey, Dauphin
County, Pennsylvania,
USA
d: February 23, 1989 in
Hershey, Dauphin
County, Pennsylvania,
USA

Kelsey Elizabeth
O'Brien
b: May 29, 1991 in
Harrisburg, Pennsylvania,
USA

Emma Kathleen
O'Brien
b: October 18, 1992 in
Harrisburg, Pennsylvania,
USA

Michelle Suzanne Marsolais and William Thomas O'Brien

Marsolais/Bryant

Harold Raymond
Marsolais, Jr.
b: May 11, 1967 in
Lakewood Hospital,
Lakewood, Cuyahoga
County, Ohio, USA
o: Able-Bodied Seaman
Unlimited

=

Nicole Kavala
Bryant
b: December 05, 1971 in
Englewood, Colorado,
USA
m: August 30, 1997 in
Centennial, Wyoming,
USA
o: Human Resouces
Recruiter

H. Raymond Marsolais, Jr. and Nicole Kavala Bryant

11. Reproduktion einer Landschaft mit einer Ruine (Brand)

PHOTO
ALBUMS

MARSOLAIS/
CHAMBERLAIN

Great-Grandfather Joseph Athanase Marsolais
Great-Grandmother Marie-Louise Emma LaPorte
1920
9 Maple Avenue, Colonie, NY

Chamberland Family Reunion - 1920s
Frank Chamberland's Home, Cohoes, NY
L-R: Florence Cournoyer, Uncle Messier, Evonne Chamberland, ?,?,?,?, Emily
Chamberland, Frank Chamberland, Aunt & Uncle Galarneau, ?,?,?, Aunt Messier,
Felix Chamberland. Standing: Uncle Tom Chamberland & wife, Elyse
Chamberland, Narcisse Marchand.

Florence Cournoyer and her sister

Florence Ella Cournoyer

Felix David Chamberland

Florence, Anna May and Felix
Chamberland

In Memory of Eva Chamberland
Deaf and Mute, Institutionalized, Deceased at Age 9
Almost Forgotten

1924

Halfmoon Beach, Crescent, NY
1924
L-R: Matilda (Savois) Marsolais holding Donald Marsolais, George Marsolais holding
Harold Marsolais, Loretta Marsolais in front of George, Ida (Foley) Marsolais standing,
Bertha (Simpkins) holding Wally, Grandma (LaPorte) Marsolais, Ellen Doran, Ralph
Marsolais, Alice Marsolais, Grandfather Alphonso Marsolais in front.
Mary Doran taking picture.

Ida, Mary
Grandpa, Grandma

Harold, Uncle Ralph, Aunt Alice
1925

Donald and Harold Marsolais
and Cousin Ellen Doran
June, 1924

Harold Marsolais
1925

Joseph George "The Old Twister" and Matilda "Tilly" (Savois) Marsolais

Grandmother Marsolais, Aunt Mary Doran,
George Foley, Aunt Ida Foley

Tilly, Donald & George Marsolais
and Gertie (Holmes) Marsolais

Uncle George Marsolais - 1951
Probably at Lake Champlain

Marion Marsolais, Dotty Chamberlain,
and Loretta (Marsolais) Chamberlain
pregnant with Sandra Chamberlain
1940

Donald and Marion Marsolais
1940

L-R: Richard Marsolais, Sandra (Chamberlain) Petrelli,
Hal Marsolais, Susan (Lemieux) Marsolais, Marion
(Marsolais) Patanian, Dennis Marsolais and Bill Patanian
Albany, NY - July, 2003

Wedding of Anna May Chamberland and Peter Finger
Standing: Ernest Chamberland, Peter Finger
Sitting: Cecilia Marchand, Helen Finger, Anna May (Chamberland) Finger, Agnes Galarneau
November 29, 1928 - St. Joseph's, Cohoes, New York

Wedding of Dorothy Chamberlain and Thomas Ryan

L-R: Donald Finger, Herman Gusty, Patricia Ryan, Thomas Ryan, Dorothy Chamberlain, Dotty King, Harold Marsolais, Ernest Chamberlain, Joan Chamberlain

October 12, 1947 - St. Josephs, Green Island, New York

American Legion Hall, South Troy, New York

Viola Chamberland
8th Grade
Back row, 2nd from R
Sacred Heart School
Cohoes, NY

World's Fair - NYC - 1939
Vi, Harold & Rita Hartley

Vi & Erma Clairmont
17 yrs old
1935, Cohoes

Vi & Harold - 1941

Florence & Felix's 41st Anniversary
Anna, Florence, Vi, Aunt Messier, Felix,
Janet, Hal, Ethel - 5 Arch Street - 1946

Art Collier, Viola Chamberlain,
Vicky Collier, Ray Chamberlain
Ray & Vicky's Wedding - 1930s

Loretta (Marsolais) and Red Chamberlain

Florence (Cournoyer)
Chamberland

Anna May, Dorothy, Viola, Felix and Ray
Chamberland

St. Joseph's Cemetery
Waterford, NY

Eva Chamberland was added
to the monument in 2004

Harold George Marsolais
U.S. Navy Seabees, WWII

Viola Marie (Chamberlain) Marsolais

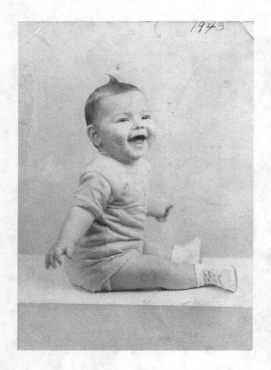

1943

Harold Raymond and Viola (Chamberlain)
Marsolais

A boy and (not) his dog…

…and (not) his cat.

NN29 14 TOUR=SANFRANCISCO CALIF 13 950P

VIOLA MARSOLAIS=

5 ARCH ST WATERVLIET NY=

945 NOV 14 . AM 7 23

ARRIVED FRISCO TODAY LEAVING FOR HOME FRIDAY PLEASE WIRE

MY FATHER AND LORETTA LOVE=

HAROLD.

Hal's First Communion
Troy, NY, 1949

Art & Hal Marsolais
Confirmation, Troy, NY 1953

George Marsolais

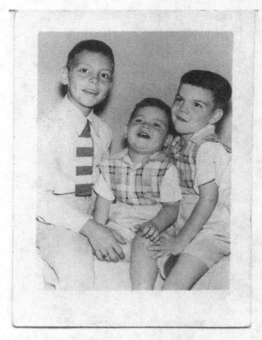

Hal, Bob & Dennis Marsolais

Bobby and Dennis Marsolais

Bob, Dennis, Richard and Hal Marsolais
Sheffield Lake, OH, 1956

Three Generations of Marsolais Men
Bobby, Hal, Harold and George Marsolais - 1956

Hal Marsolais
7th Grade
Troy, NY - 1954

Harold Raymond Marsolais
Graduation, 1959
Brookside High School
Sheffield Lake, OH

Dennis Bradley Marsolais
Graduation, 1967
Brookside High School

Dennis
U.S. Army Infantry
Viet Nam and Korea

Robert Allen Marsolais
Graduation, 1970
Brookside High School

Richard David Marsolais
Graduation, 1974
Brookside High School

Young Sheffield Lake Soldier Wins Decoration. With Valor

By BETSY WATSON
Staff Correspondent

SHEFFIELD LAKE — Because he disregarded his own safety to save the lives of his Army comrades, Pfc Dennis Marsolais, 20, has been awarded the Army Commendation medal with V device for valor.

The son of Mr. and Mrs. Harold Marsolais, 817 Irving Park, Pfc Marsolais was a rifleman on a reconnaissance mission north of Lai Khe, Vietnam, when his unit was suddenly hit by intense enemy fire.

With complete disregard for himself, Marsolais wove his way through the killing fusilage placing "devastating suppressive fire" on the enemy emplacements.

Then, continuing to ignore the barrage of automatic weapons and small arms fire and the danger created by Claymore mines, he gave emergency first aid to several of his wounded buddies and helped remove them to the medical evacuation zone.

"Dennis never said a word about this," commented his father with pride. "He probably got mad when the enemy struck and waded right in."

Marsolais, who was also awarded the Purple Heart for hand wounds suffered in another action, is the second member of his family to be decorated in the Vietnam war.

His brother 1st Lt. Harold Marsolais, was awarded the Bronze Star two years ago while serving as a paratrooper in Vietnam. Now a helicopter pilot, Lt. Marsolais has since chosen to make the Army his career and is now serving his second tour of Vietnam duty.

ALSO PROUD of his service record is the boys' father who served in the South

PFC. DENNIS MARSOLAIS

Pacific during World War II as a member of the Navy SeaBees. A third brother Robert is employed in The Journal mailroom while the youngest son, Richard, is an eighth grader at Sheffield Middle School.

A 1967 graduate of Brookside, where he was a first string guard for the Cardinals, Pfc. Marsolais began his Vietnam tour last December with Company C, First Battalion, 18th Infantry of the tradition proud First Division.

Two months ago he was re-assigned to duty in Korea and is now stationed about ten miles from the Demilitarized Zone. In January he expects to be returned to the States for discharge and at that time he hopes to return to his studies at Miami University.

Harold and Vi Marsolais
Hershey, PA
1983

Dennis, Hal, Harold, Vi, Richard and Bob Marsolais
Christmas, Hudson, FL, 1984

Richard & Vi Marsolais
Christmas at the Arbors
1996

Hal, Susan,
Dennis, Kristy (Browne),
Shelly, Ray and Bob Marsolais
Viola's Funeral, Hudson, FL
December 30, 1997

Hal, Richard, Dennis and Bob
Marsolais
Viola's Funeral
Hudson, FL
December 30, 1997

Step-Brothers
322 Fourth Street, Troy, NY - Revisited

Tom & Dot Ryan's backyard in Troy, NY
Richard, Dennis, Hal & Bob Marsolais
Family Reunion - July, 2003

The Cordova Times

Prince William Sound's Oldest Newspaper
Established in 1914

Guard helicopter rescues three from stormy ocean gulf

In a dramatic rescue late Monday afternoon, a Coast Guard helicopter hoisted three people off two gillnetters adrift in 30-foot seas between Cape St. Elias and Lemesurier Point on Kayak Island. The Mary C and the Persistence were only two of at least 16 small fishing boats caught in unsheltered waters off the Cape, when a storm swept in ahead of forecast early Monday, bringing up to 70-knot winds and 40-foot seas.

The chopper also dropped a pump to a third boat, the Annihilator, which managed to run to safety.

No lives were lost during the sudden storm, but a total of four gillnetters remain adrift or aground: The Mary C., the Persistence, the Bounty Hunter and the Sankris.

The Bounty Hunter reportedly flipped in the massive waves on the east side of Kayak Island Monday, throwing fisherman John Lorentzen into the water. Ron Bowen saw the accident and almost immediately was able to pull Lorentzen aboard his vessel.

The Sankris broke free of the anchorage in Barney's Hole on Monday, while owner Dave Belisle was in town. Other fishermen at the anchorage tried unsuccessfully to snag the drifting boat.

Commercial helicopters out of Cordova, the tender Harry B., two Coast Guard C-130's, and the

Coast Guard cutter Sweetbrier also responded to Monday's emergencies. On Tuesday, with winds down to 25 knots and seas to four feet, the C-130 out of Kodiak, the Sweetbrier, and the CG chopper from Sitka searched the Cape area in hopes of locating the vessels lost there.

Close to noon on Monday, the Coast Guard received word from Walt Raber, skipper of the Harry B., that the Mary C. had lost power and was taking on water off Kayak Island. Raber reported that he had several gillnetters rafted up behind his tender, in relative safety behind Kayak Island.

Commercial flying services in Cordova also picked up the emergency calls, and Chisum Flying sent a helicopter to the area. That chopper and one volunteered by Evergreen Helicopters of Anchorage stood by all afternoon at Katalla, but did not have hoist capabilities.

Chisum's Bret Fishell said that the two commercial 'copters could have picked up people out of the water with slings if necessary.

A Coast Guard C-130 circled over the Mary C., communicating with her crew, Jay Selix, 32, and Kristy Browne, 27. The two reported one of their engines out and the other running out of fuel.

(see GUARD..., p. A4)

GUARD...
(continued from p. A1)

At about 2:30 p.m., according to the Coast Guard, Mario Mikulich on the Persistence reported engine failure and requested assistance, also off Kayak Island.

The Coast Guard dispatched a helicopter from Sitka, which was airborne at 3:15 p.m. The helicopter based for the summer at the Cordova Aviation Support Facility at 13-Mile was in Kodiak for repairs, during a "scheduled non-deployment" period from June 15-30, according to the Coast Guard.

The helicopter based in Kodiak was involved in another mission at the time of Monday's emergency.

At 1 p.m, the Sweetbrier was diverted from a course that would have taken her across Prince William Sound to points south of Seward to participate in a U.S. Geological Survey project. The Sweetbrier came out Hinchinbrook Entrance in 80-knot winds and 30-40 foot seas, arriving at Cape St. Elias at 4 a.m. Tuesday.

The CG helicopter arrived at Kayak Island at about 5:45 p.m. and hoisted Selix and Brown from the Mary C. and Mikulich from the Persistence. They were flown to Cordova in good condition, arriving at 7:30 pm.

Lt. Commander John Glen from the helicopter crew reported that the seas at the time of the rescue were averaging 30 feet, with some up to 50 feet.

Glen said that the chopper located the Bounty Hunter

aground on the east side of Kayak Island Tuesday morning, but had not seen any of the other boats. The helicopter searched from the Copper River Delta down to Cape Suckling, Kayak and Wingham Islands on Tuesday morning, in fog with one-eighth mile visibility.

They were scheduled for another search Tuesday afternoon, of the shores of Hinchinbrook and Montague Islands, Glen said. Fishermen on the grounds reported that all other boats appear to be accounted for, he said.

The Sweetbrier is also searching the area on its way back to Hinchinbrook Entrance, to ensure that no other boats are in distress and incommunicado.

Dramatic rescue of Kristy Browne on June 19, 1985 off Kayak Island, Alaska.

Kristy Browne and Dennis Marsolais married October 7, 1995.

LEMIEUX/
LAPE

Joseph Siffroid Lemieux, Proprieteur
April 5, 1909
West 98th & Lorain Road, Cleveland, Ohio

Joseph Lemieux, Front and Center. Making liquor at his Horse Shoe Inn, 23123 Center Ridge Road, Lakewood, Ohio before and during Prohibition.

Alfred Joseph "Fred" Lemieux
Born October 20, 1894

John Dominic and Alfred Joseph Lemieux

Siffroid Joseph Lemieux

Johanna (Blumena), John Dominic, Alfred Joseph and Joseph Lemieux

Alfred Joseph Lemieux
First Communion

Helen Margaret Cushing
First Communion

Thomas Cushing
Father of Helen, Alice and Anna Mae Cushing

Margaret (Rodgers) Cushing
Mother of Helen, Alice and Anna Mae Cushing

Edward & Ann Rodgers' 50th Anniversary
4025 East 89th Street
Cleveland, Ohio 44105
About 1915

Top Row: Matthew Sloan, Sr. (Aunt Lucy's husband), William O'Rourke (Aunt Anne's husband), Millicent Rolland (No relation), Alice McGrath, Mary Gallagher Stringer, Rose McAneny Herbert, Coletta Rodgers Kehoe, Martin Gallagher

Third Row: Alice Cushing Percival (Aunt Allie), Helen Cushing Lemieux (Gram), Lily McAneny Hyland (In Ed Anderson's arms), Edward Anderson, John McCracken, Theresa (Tiny) O'Rourke (In John's arms), May Dixon McCracken, Grace Rodgers Percival, Anna Mae Cushing Storey (Aunt Anna Mae), Agnes McGrath Rodgers, Mike Gallagher, Pat O'Rourke (Aunt Delia's husband), Joe Whalen, Sr. (Aunt Kate's husband)

Second Row: Anne O'Rourke, Lucy O'Rourke Hamilton (On her mother's lap), Kate Rodgers McAneny Whalen, Joe Whalen, Jr. (On his mother's lap), Delia Rodgers O'Rourke, Betty O'Rourke Friedel (On her mother's lap), Lucy O'Rourke Smith (Blurred – Between her mother & Aunt Nell), Helen (Nell) Rodgers Gallagher, Catherine Gallagher Kelly (On her mother's lap), Ann Cunningham Rodgers (Great-great-Grandma), Edward (Ned) Rodgers (Great-great-Grandpa), William Rodgers, Edward Rodgers (On his father's lap), Margaret Rodgers Cushing (Great-grandmother), Lucy Rodgers Sloan, Matthew Sloan, Jr. (On his mother's lap), Mary McAneny Bettel

Front Row: Katherine McAneny Norman (White Dress), Anna Marie Sloan McNamara (Dark Dress), Margaret O'Rourke, Helen Gallagher Fleming, Nan Gallagher, Ellen O'Rourke Guarnieri, Ann (Sis) O'Rourke Telgron, Mary O'Rourke Murphy, William (Bill) O'Rourke, Sue Sloan Toomey

Edward and Ann (Cunningham) Rodgers
Maternal Grandparents of Helen Cushing

Helen
Cushing

Alfred Joseph Lemieux
U.S. Army Aviator, WWI

Freddy Lemieux - 1919

Grace Rodgers, Anna Mae Cushing, Dick Storey, Helen Cushing, ?, ?

Freddy Lemieux and Helen Cushing - 1919

Helen Cushing Lemieux

Alfred Joseph Lemieux

3 mo.   Gene   Aug - 1921

Al, Helen and Fred Lemieux
at East 89th Street, Newburgh, OH

May 30 23

Fred's floral truck for conveying liquor

Riverview Avenue,
Rocky River, OH

Al and Ned

July. 1 · 23
2 yrs.

Anna Mae Cushing, Fred and Helen (Cushing) Lemieux
Alfred Jean (Gene) and Edward Joseph Lemieux

2043 Lakeview Avenue
Rocky River, Ohio

Helen Lemieux and Mary Joan

Graduated Rocky River High School
1939

Mary Jo Lemieux

1939

Front Row
Sue Storey Looney
Mary Al Percival Powers
Lucy Ann Smith
Ed Smith
Grace Kehoe
Mary Lemieux Koster
Bob Storey
Pat Percival
Al Percival
Ralph Percival
Tom Kehoe
"Poochie" (Coletta?) Kehoe

Middle Row
Lucy Smith
Anna Mae Cushing Storey
Helen Cushing Lemieux
Margaret Cushing
Alice Cushing Percival
Ralph Percival
Bill Budd

Back Row
Dick Storey
Ed Smith
Al Lemieux
Alfred Lemieux
Grace Rodgers
Margaret Ann Storey
Richard Storey
Patsy Budd (O'Rourke?)
Coletta Rodgers Kehoe

Joseph Siffroy Lemieux

Margaret (Rodgers) Cushing

William Tucker
Spanish-American War

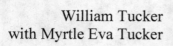

William Tucker
with Myrtle Eva Tucker

Grandmother Jones and
Myrtle "Becky" Tucker

Myrtle "Becky" Tucker,
12 years old,
and friend
July, 1917

Lape Family
Back Row: James, Carl Melvin and John
Front Row: Amelia (Uebelhart), Melvin Brosius, and Margaret (Lape) Fish
Canton, Ohio

Becky (Tucker) Lape,
Mrs. Carl Melvin Lape
holding Barbara Lape

Elizabeth (Jones) Tucker
holding Patricia Eileen
Lape with Barbara Lape

?, Barbara and Patricia Lape

Elizabeth (Jones) Tucker, Mildred Best, Myrtle
(Tucker) Lape, Iva (Jones) Best,
Beverly Jane, Patricia and Barbara Lape
Bayview Drive, Bay Village, Ohio

Graduated Rocky River High School
1942

Patricia Lape & Al Lemieux - Blind Date
November 1, 1941 - Art Club Halloween Ball

Alfred Jean Lemieux
Marine Aviator, WWII and Korea

Helen (Cushing) Lemieux, Paternal Grandmother,
Patricia (Lape) Lemieux, Mother, Myrtle (Tucker)
Lape Doron, Maternal Grandmother, Susan
Lemieux.
Rocky River, Ohio, September 17, 1944

Susan Kathleen Lemieux
Christening

Mary Jo Lemieux, Godmother,
holding Susan Lemieux

Susan and John Lemieux
Ethel Avenue, Lakewood, Ohio
1947

Susan, John & Al Lemieux
Ethel Avenue, Lakewood, Ohio
1947

John and Susan Lemieux
Philadelphia
1950

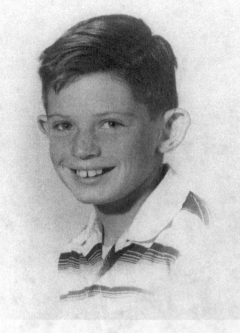

John Melvin Lemieux
through the years

Susan Kathleen Lemieux
through the years

1952

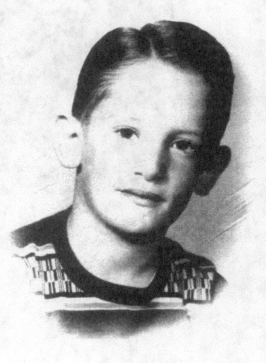

Alfred Carl Lemieux
through the years

Helen and Fred Lemieux
with Edward Joseph Lemieux, Jr.
1945

John Dominic and Alfred Joseph Lemieux

Allen Pearl
Doron
and
Myrtle
"Becky"
(Tucker)
Lape
Doron
1940 -1945

Daniel Gallagher and
Becky (Tucker) Lape Doron Rogers Gallag
1955

Minister, Elizabeth (Jones) Tucker, Albert Rogers, Becky (Tucker) Lape Doron Rogers, ?,
Patricia (Lape) Lemieux, Susan Lemieux, Mary Jo Lemieux, the rest unknown.
1946

Patricia (Lape) Lemieux,
Carl Melvin Lape,
Ruth (Schaettle) Lape,
Barbara (Lape) Griggs,
Jaci (Lape) Holtkamp

Amelia (Uebelhart) and Melvin Lape
50th Anniversary
1952

Elizabeth (Jones)
Tucker Wilkinson,
Paul Wilkinson
and friend

Lemieux Family Reunion
July 21-23, 1995
Nemacolin Woodlands, Pennsylvania

Back Row:
Bill Lemieux
Enrico DelPuppo
Tony DelPuppo
Scott Ackland
Carl John Koster
Tom Koster
John Emery
Kathryn Emery (in John's arms)
Josiane Lemieux
John Lemieux
Emma O'Brien (in Hal's arms)
Hal Marsolais
Syd (Savage) Lemieux
Alfred Carl Lemieux
Jim Lemieux
Ned Koster
Tom Fabek

Partial Row:
Ken Koster
Robin (Bale) Koster
Jack Koster (in Robin's arms)
Ann (Dreher) Koster

Middle Row:
Katy Ackland (Syd's sister)
Bill O'Brien
Kelsey O'Brien (in Bill's arms)
Shelly (Marsolais) O'Brien
Charles Kenneth Koster II (in Shelly's arms)
Elizabeth (Lemieux) Emery
Alfred Jean Lemieux
Mary (Lemieux) Koster
Edward Joseph Lemieux
DeeDee (Roop) Lemieux
Patricia (Lape) Lemieux
Susan (Lemieux) Marsolais
Ann Marie (Koster) Fabek

Kneeling:
Kathryn (Koster) Franklin
Benjamin Koster (on Kate's lap)
Mary Jo (Lemieux) DelPuppo
Jeanette Lemieux
Genna DelPuppo
Joe DelPuppo
Alison Lemieux
Chris Lemieux
Sean Lemieux
Alex Lemieux
Gordon Ackland
Linda (Schneeberger) Lemieux

Sitting:
Norah Fabek
Shaylinn Emery
Reed Fabek
Paul Fabek

L-R: Back: Alfred Carl Lemieux, Sean Lemieux
Second Row: John Emery, John Lemieux, Linda (Soltis) Lemieux
Third Row: Elizabeth (Lemieux) Emery, Louie Lemieux, Patricia (Lape) Lemieux,
Michelle (Marsolais) O'Brien, Jennifer Lemieux
Front Row: Shaylinn Emery, Kathryn Emery, Annalise Emery, Emma O'Brien, Kelsey O'Brien,
Susan (Lemieux) Marsolais
Wildflowers   Summer of 1999

Elizabeth (Lemieux) Emery, Center
Shaylinn, Annalise and Kathryn Emery
2006

Jaci (Lape) Holtkamp Milner,
Barbara (Lape) Griggs Hellwege, Patricia (Lape) Lemieux
Taken by Frank A. Griggs

MARSOLAIS/
LEMIEUX

Our Wedding Day – July 5, 1964
L-R: Bobby, Brother; Don Winslow, Best Man;
Hal, Groom; John P. Nix, Friend

Honor Guard, 82nd Airborne Division
Chapel, Ft. Bragg, NC, July 5, 1964

The night before Hal's Departure for Viet Nam - 1964

Harry, Hal & Norris
ready to jump.
Vung Tau, South Viet Nam

Hal in parachute jump
Doing it the hard way

Hal waiting to be picked up from LZ White

173rd Airborne Brigade
1965-1966
Near Bien Hoa
Hal deciding to become
a helicopter pilot

Susan (Lemieux) Marsolais holding daughter, Michelle Suzanne, born May 5, 1965
Susan's mother, Patricia (Lape) Lemieux, holding Susan's new sister, Elizabeth Ann, born March 27, 1965
1240 Thoreau Avenue, Lakewood, OH

Hal asked for a full-length picture of Susan.
He carried it through the year in Viet Nam

Shelly and Susan living on
Thoreau with her parents
while Hal's in Viet Nam…

…when Harold's not teaching
her to walk or climb stairs.

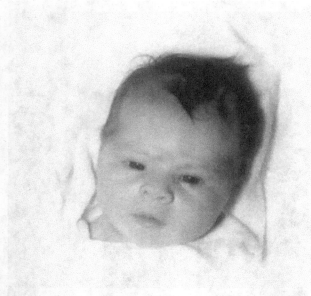

Michelle Suzanne Marsolais is born on May 5, 1965, at 8:53 a.m., 8 lbs., crawls, is two, three, and rides a pony.

H. Raymond Marsolais, Jr. is born on May 11, 1967,
at 10:04 a.m., 7 lbs. 8 oz.,
crawls, is 6 months, two and rides a pony.

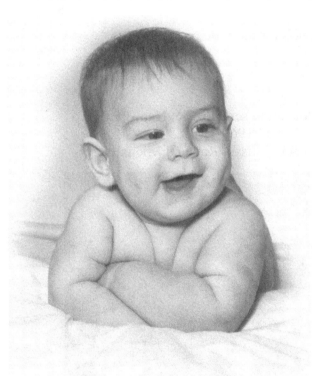

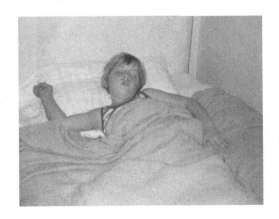

Flight School - Part One, Ft. Wolters, TX

Lunch for the little ones in Texas

Flight School - Part Two
Formal Ball, Ft. Rucker, AL, 1969

Family Portrait to send to Viet Nam-Part Two
1969-1970
Elizabeth, Susan, Ray and Michelle

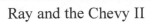

Snapshots for Dad in Viet Nam
The Enterprise year
107 Kate Street, Enterprise, AL

"Show me your muscles."

Ray and the Chevy II

Christmas 1969 with the Kosters
<u>and</u> the Marsolais…enough fun to wear
you out!

Hal's Christmas 1969 - Phu Loi, Viet Nam
Night Hawk Helicopter weapons system 67001

Red Dog
3 Alpha

Distinguished Flying Cross for heroism in Viet Nam is presented to Cpt. Harold R. Marsolais by BG Robert N. McKinnon on 1 October 1970 at Ft. Wolters, TX

Cpt. Harold R. Marsolais is presented a 3rd Bronze Star by Maj. John Carroll on 27 May, 1970 at Ft. Wolters, TX

Travels in Old Mexico

The Marsolais Family
Fort Wolters, Texas - 1971

"I hear sleigh bells!" Shelly actually saw Rudolph pulling Santa's sleigh across the sky on Christmas Eve 1970.

300 Patrick Street, Wolters Village, Ft. Wolters, TX

"I see by your outfit that you are a cowboy."

Ray is pirate in front of devil,
Hal is Superman,
Shelly is gypsy between Hal and skeleton

306C Lumpkin Road, Ft. Benning, GA
1972

Sheffield Lake Native Wins 3rd Bronze Star

H.R. MARSOLAIS

FT. WOLTERS, Texas — a third Bronze Star Medal, was awarded to Capt. Harold R. Marsolais, son of Mr. and Mrs. Harold G. Marsolais, 817 Irving Park Dr., Sheffield Lake, for outstanding performance of duty in Vietnam with the Army's 11th Cavalry Regiment.

Marsolais returned from a combat tour in April and is currently assistant operations officer in the Army Parimary Helicopter School's academic department here.

His other decorations include 11 awards of the Air Medal (one for heroism, the others for a minimum of 25 missions flown each) and the Army Commendation Medal. He has served overseas in Okinawa and again on a previous tour in Vietnam.

A 1959 graduate of Brookside High School, he attended the University of North Carolina and Kent State University prior to entering the Army in 1961.

He and his wife have two children.

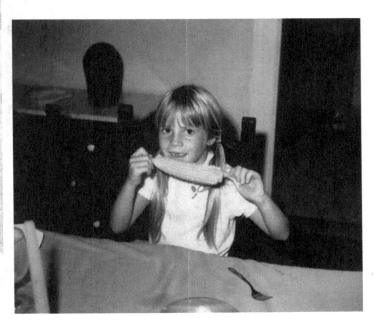

425 Royal Oaks Apartments
Hattiesburg, MS
1972-1974

Nick Risk, Ray Guy
and Hal on the radio
for Hattiesburg JCs

Bachelor of Science Degree
in Business, University of
Southern Mississippi,
Hattiesburg, MS
1974

Classe della Neve, Monte Bondone, Dolomiti, Italy

Clay Rosser, Shelly, Nancy Cottingham, Hal & Ray
Rothenburg, Germany

New Year's Eve 1976 in London

Ski lift, Pinzolo, Italy

55A State Street, Wildflecken, Germany
38A Villagio della Pace, Vicenza, Italy
1974 - 1977

London, New Year's Eve 1976

First Communion, Vicenza, Italy 1977

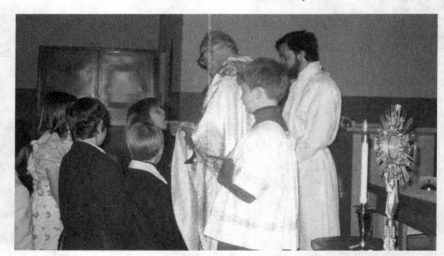

…to see
Pope Paul VI…

May 1977
To Saint Peter's in Rome…

…and to each throw a coin in the Trevi Fountain.

It was a beautiful time

Earthquake Rescue Mission 1976
Udine, Italy Epicenter

Meritorious Service Medals awarded by
MG Putnam, SETAF Commander

Dogs that we have known and loved:
Fearless Fred (Above Left)
Jacques, the Wonder Dog (Above)
and Mighty Muffin (Left & Below)

1105 Rustic Ridge Road, Auburn, AL
1977 - 1979

CGSC Student Quarters
and 19 Rose Loop
Ft. Leavenworth, KS
1979-1982

Ray's Happy Birthday

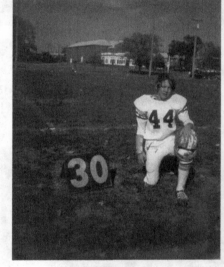

Football Season

New Year's Eve 1979, Atlanta, with Odoms

Ed Fenlon and Shelly - Prom 1980

Shelly's Confirmation by John J. Cardinal O'Connor, Ret. Rear Adm., Vicar to the U.S. Military

Whispering Sands, our 900 lb. pet.

Our Hero

Sophie Magnan de Bornier visits from Paris
July, 1981

Michelle Suzanne Marsolais
Leavenworth High School
Graduate
1982

Sheikh & Mrs. Mohamed hal-Marsolais

Superman and Lois Lane

Executive Director, MDRHA

Christmas Eve 1982
Going to Midnight Mass
1817 South Knox Avenue
Minneapolis, MN

Christmas 1984, making chili sauce

Managing Director, PASHA
Briarcrest & 611 Barrington Court
Hershey   Palmyra, PA

Kauai, Hawaii 1984 with Peggy and Steve Meyers

Ray stationed at Colorado Springs, CO

H. Raymond Marsolais, Jr.
U.S. Army
4th Infantry Division, 3rd Bn, 68th Armor
Fort Carson, CO 1985 - 1989

Michelle Marsolais & William O'Brien
marry on November 5, 1988

Managing Director
National Retail Hardware Association
Indianapolis, IN

International Hardware Convention, London

International Hardware Convention, Copenhagen

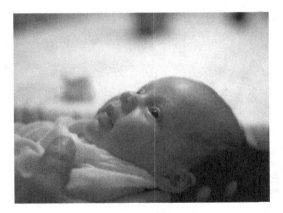

Kelsey Elizabeth at 2 weeks

Hal, Susan, Ray
William O'Brien, Shelly (Marsolais) O'Brien and
Kelsey Elizabeth O'Brien

Emma Kathleen at 3 months

Vows Renewed July 5, 1991
St. Augustine Cathedral

Vilano Beach Sunset

…with Uncle Ray

1994 - Ray discovers Seattle!

Ray discovers Nicole Bryant!

Treasure Hunts at Vilano Beach

Counting off the paces…

…digging up the treasure!

X Marks the Spot!
More pirate maps and buried treasures found at
Vilano Beach! Kelsey and Emma are the only
girls to find all those X's in the sand!

1. Look what I found!

5. Let's see!

2. It was over there.

6. We should start back here.

3. What is it?

7. We have to count off the paces.

4. It's a pirate's treasure map.

8. We dug up the pirate's treasure!
(And we look adorable in our Tinkerbell bathing suits.)

Commercial Fishing 1995

Seattle Apartment

Nicole and Ray kayaking in Bellingham, WA

Nicole Bryant and Ray Marsolais
marry on August 30, 1997

Like father…Like son.

Ray and Nicole at Oregon Coast

Ray and Nicole
at Lindsay Meyers and Troy Ritchie's wedding
Hal and Susan

Ray at work at Piper Jaffray, Seattle
Fun with Finance – 2003
Office with view of Space Needle

Grill Team
Don McCauley dit Marsolais (Cousin "Dit"),
Dennis, Hal and Ray Marsolais
Bellingham, WA

Good to see you.

Four Generations
Patricia (Lape) Lemieux, Susan Kathleen Lemieux,
Elizabeth (Jones) Tucker, Myrtle (Tucker) Lape Doran
19901 Roslyn Drive, Rocky River, OH - 1944

Five Generations
Susan (Lemieux) Marsolais, Kelsey Elizabeth O'Brien, Patricia (Lape) Lemieux,
Michelle (Marsolais) O'Brien, Emma Kathleen O'Brien, Ruth (Schaettle) Lape
Old Stoddard Road, Nelson, NH - Christmas 1993

Kelsey and Emma O'Brien, Rose Garden, Hershey Hotel, PA
After *A Girl with a Watering Can* by Renoir

Natural Beauties

Lots of Disney trips….

Dinner at the Brown Derby
Disney World – 1995
30th Anniversary

Lots of
Gingerbread
Houses…

Lots of
growing
up…

'92 NRHA Palm Desert
with new friends

Hawaii '84

…Lots of travels with family & friends,
for business & pleasure.

'96 PIA Biltmore Hotel
Coral Gables

'99 Soave

Picnic on German bunker at Omaha Beach, Normandy, with Ken Koster, Peggy & Steve Meyers, Hal & Susan Marsolais and Mary Koster

September 1997

Picnic on German bunker at Omaha Beach, Normandy, with Bill O'Brien, Nicole & Ray Marsolais, Hal Marsolais and Michelle O'Brien

July 2002

'97 La Mere Poulard's, Mont St-Michel

'99 Caffè Florian,
Piazza San Marco, Venezia

Shelly and Bill O'Brien

Shelly graduates from Penn State
December 1997
Bachelor of Humanities,
Secondary Education/English

Emma and Kelsey - Natural Athletes

On Hal's retirement from the Professional Insurance Agents of Florida in 2001, the Board of Directors showed their appreciation for his contributions to the Association by dedicating the building to him.

Ken Koster, with tremors, pouring champagne for Hal, with tremors, at Kosters' house in Provence. The only waiter in France who could pour wine for Hal without a drop being spilled.

Proud parents of the Groom
Ray and Nicole's Wedding

Family Reunion in France
and 38th Anniversary
July, 2002
Hal and Susan (Lemieux) Marsolais
Nicole (Bryant) and Ray Marsolais
Bill and Michelle (Marsolais) O'Brien

Marsolais origins in Bec-Thomas, Normandy

Lemieux ancestral
home, *La Mieuserie*,
in Cantaloup, Normandy

Adventures with Roxie
at Discovery Cove
Orlando, Florida
Summer 2004

Family Reunion, Lanthier's Grove - Cohoes, NY - July 13, 2003

L- R Back Row: Mike Petrelli, Roger Finger, James McCormick, Janet (Chamberlain) McCormick, Don McCauley-dit-Marsolais, Don Greenspan, Harry Reynolds, Dennis Marsolais, Jeffrey Gibson, Rich Marsolais, Mary Joan (Marsolais) Schneider, Harold Brooks, Dee (McCabe) Brooks, David Brooks, John Schneider, Bruce Marsolais, Ed Tanski

Middle Row: Robert Marsolais, Anna (Boyd) Marsolais, Mary Tompkins holding Connor, Steve Tompkins holding Bailey, Tiffany Reynolds, Kristy (Browne) Marsolais, Susan (Lemieux) Marsolais, Michelle (Marsolais) O'Brien, Hal Marsolais

Front Row: Martin O'Neill, Kelly (Reynolds) O'Neill, Linda (Ryan) Reynolds, Jeffrey Marsolais, Gavyn Marsolais, Joan (Chamberlain) Costello, Sandi (Chamberlain) Petrelli, Michael Marsolais, Dotty (Chamberlain) Ryan, Tommy Ryan, Emma O'Brien, Kelsey O'Brien, Bill O'Brien, Betty (Chamberlain) Tanski, Sharon Ryan

Children standing in front: Makenzie Tompkins, Anthony Reynolds and Tanner Tompkins

Joan (Chamberlain) Costello, Sandi (Chamberlain) Petrelli, Dotty
(Chamberlain) Ryan, Betty (Chamberlain) Tanski, Linda (Ryan) Reynolds,
and Sharon Ryan
Family Reunion, Troy, NY - July 13, 2003

Saratoga Springs - Hal's Favorite Spa
Kelsey, Dennis's hat, Shelly, Don, Bill, Kris & Hal
July, 2003

Family Reunion - July, 2003
rue Petit Champlain, Québec

L-R Back Row: Hal Marsolais, John Emery, Dennis Marsolais
Middle Row: Bill O'Brien, Michelle (Marsolais) O'Brien, Kristy (Browne) Marsolais, Don McCauley-dit-Marsolais
Front Left: Emma O'Brien, Annalise Emery, Kelsey O'Brien

Gabriel Lemieux's house and front door on rue Petit Champlain, Québec

Jacques Lemieux & Susan (Lemieux) Marsolais - Lunch at Chateau Frontenac, Québec - July, 2003

Dinner at the Restaurant aux Anciens Canadiens

Shopping in Québec

Joseph E. Lemieux's house still stands near the harbor beneath the Chateau Frontenac

Hal, Kelsey & Emma
on the balcony
of our Paris apartment,
November 2005

Around town…

Adventures in Paris
and Versailles
November 2005

2005 Exploring Paris on our own

2005 – Lunch at Aude's apartment in Paris:
Peggy & Steve Meyers, Aude & Jacques Magnan de Bornier
Hal & Susan, Monique Magnan de Bornier

Michelle O'Brien's Master's Degree
in Humanities from Penn State
University - December 2004

Boy Scout Troop 240 and other members of the youth group at Hershey Ward of The Church of Jesus Christ of Latter-day Saints honored 21 middle and high school teachers during the Students' Choice Awards Night. The teachers were from Feaser Middle School in Middletown, Hershey Middle School, Hershey High School and Lower Dauphin High School. Front row from left are Kristen Shaffer, Kevin Little, Michelle Garrett, Ellen Min, Judith Heckert, Jennifer Klos, Diana Armitage, Renee Owens and Klaura Hunt. Back row from left are Susan Frankeny, Michael Gustantino, Richard Bittinger, Jim Seip, Michelle O'Brien, Mark French, Charles Etter and Carol Miller. Honored but not pictured were Robert Finkill, Tom Hanninen, Glenn Nissley and Michael Warfel II.

Milestones and New Friends...

Kelsey O'Brien's Silver Medal from
the Scholastic Writing Award
June 2006 at Carnegie Hall, NYC

Capucine (above) & Ombeline (below) Choupin

Ray onboard the Island Warrior at Cook Inlet
- pancake ice in the background - 2006

Island Warrior
Specs: Gross Tons: 191
Length: 143
Horsepower: 3600

Ray & Nicole's Wedding at St. Alban's
Chapel, Medicine Bow National Forest near
Centennial, Wyoming

Dakota and Nicole

Nicole Marsolais's Master's Degree in
Humanities from Bastyr University
December 2004

- Germany 1975 -
Hal & Susan Marsolais, Bob & Toni Odom, Henry & Peggy Rosser
- St. Augustine 2006 -

…a bit of growing older.

Christmas 2006 - Cruise to the Bahamas
…and they sailed away
and lived happily ever after…

RENDEZVOUS 2008

MARSOLAIS-CHAMBERLAIN-LEMIEUX

MARSOLAIS-CHAMBERLAIN-LEMIEUX REUNION
Celebrating Quebec's 400th Anniversary Jubilee, July 2008

A dream come true, introducing our ancestors to our family and making history and geography come to life in a personal way.

Le Saint-Paul Hotel

Cartier claims to be the most important one to the history of Quebec because he came first in 1534.

Champlain claims to be the most important because he founded Quebec in 1608, and Nicholas Marsolet came with him to be a translator.

The Boating of the Luncheon Party

The Marsolais, Chamerlains, Lemieux, Bottinos, Cioncis, Connellys, Costellos, Emerys, Fabeks, Hogans, Julianos, Kosters, Petrellis, Tanskis, ---one, big, happy family!

Working toward rewarding careers:

The beautiful and talented
Kelsey Elizabeth O'Brien
Senior picture 2009
Sophomore at Marymount Manhattan
College, NYC - 2010
Award-winning writer

The beautiful and talented
Emma Kathleen O'Brien
Favorite picture 2009
Senior at Hershey High School
Hershey, PA - 2010
Professional artist

APPENDICES

Legend for end pages map of Rouen 1655, by Gomboust from an atlas
Legend faxed from Rare Books Section, Library of Congress

TOPOGRAPHIA
ALLIÆ,
Sive
DESCRIPTIO
DELINEATIO FAMO-
ORUM LOCORUM IN POTEN-
no Galliæ: partim ex ufu & optimis Scriptoribus
rum Linguarum, partim ex Relationibus fide
nis per aliquot annos collectis, in ordinem
redacta, & publico data,

Per
MARTINUM ZEILLERUM.

FRANCOFVRTI,
impendio Caſpari Meriani.
Anno M DC LV.

(new output 1970)

NEUE AUSGABE 1970

Ohne die Texte von Martin Zeiller

Mit einem Nachwort herausgegeben von Lucas Heinrich Wüthrich

BÄRENREITER-VERLAG KASSEL UND BASEL

TOPOGRAPHIA GALLIAE

III. Band

Mit Generalregister für die Bände 1-3

Faksimile der Teile 5-15 der lateinischen Ausgabe von 1657/1661
(Wüthrich 74 + 76)
1. Deutsche Ausgabe 1657/1661 (Schuchhard 75-83; Wüthrich 73 + 75)

Gesamtherstellung Willy Fischer, Strasbourg

Plätze/Palläste/Kirchen/Clöster vnd dergleichen/so in der Statt Rovan sich befinden: Vnd in dem Kupffer-Stück mit den Ziffern hin vnd wider an-gedeutet.

1. Logis du Roy.
2. Ab. S. Oven.
3. Saincte Croix.
4. S. Oüen par.
5. M. Poussin.
6. Les Minimes.
7. } Les P. P. Iesuistes
8.
9. Seminaire de Joyeuse.
10. } Rouge marre.
11.
12. Marche aux chevaux.
13. Manege.
14. Les Benedictines.
15. Les Carmelites.
16. Les Filles de Saincte Marie.
17. Religieuses S. Claire dites Gravelines.
18. Iardin de M. le Page.
19. Jardin des Arquebu-siers.
20. S. Nicaisse par.
21. Cimetiere S. Vivien.
22. Hostel de biaulieu.
23. Les Ursulines.
24. Capucins.
25. Seconde Maison des Filles Marie.
26. Saincte Claire.
27. Religieuse de la Non-ciad.
28. Les Penitents.
29. Filles Penitentes.
30. Les Celestins.
31. Tour du Coulombier.
32. Grand Bureau des Pauvres Valides.
33. Cimetier des Hugue-nots.

34. Hospital S. Vivien.
35. Sainct Vivien par:
36. Novitiar des Iesuistes.
37. } La matesquerie.
38.
39. } Iardin du Blanc.
40.
41. Viviers.
42. Tannerie.
43. S. Marc Clos du Puy.
44. Tuerie.
45. Bouteille.
46. Augustins.
47. S. Maclou par:
48. } Le ruissel.
49.
50. Cimetiere S. Maclou.
51. M. Dambray.
52. M. Galman.
53. S. Amand Ab. & par:
54. L'Archevesche.
55. M. le premier Presi-dent.
56. S. Denis par:
57. La Vieille Tour.
58. Halle au bled.
59. Lieu ou se leve la sier-te.
60. La Basse Vieille Tour.
61. M. Dire.
62. Sucrie.
63. S. Candre le Vieil par:
64. Ho:delisieux.
65. S. Martin par:
66. Hostel Dieu.
67. Magdelaine.
68. La Calandre.
69. Nostre Dame.
70. College de l'abbane.

71. Prison.
72. Chambre des Com-res.
73. College du S. Esprit.
74. M. Brice.
75. College du pape.
76. Sainct Nicolas par:
77. College d'Ernestal.
78. M. d'Amonville
79. les Carmes.
80. M. de Beneville.
81. M. de Miromesive
82. M. de Caumont.
83. la Croue.
84. M. du Mesnu Cotte.
85. Hospital du Roy.
86. Peres de l'Oratoire.
87. Ma:de Berniere.
88. M. Proc: Gnal:
89. M. d'Estalleville.
90. Murs S. Oven.
91. M. Briee.
92. le Cocq.
93. M. de Hautenas.
94. M. de S. Austin.
95. S. Godart.
96. Proche S. Godart.
97. S. Laurens.
98. M. de Couronne.
99. M. de S. Arnoul.
100. Bureau des Cuirs.
101. M. Bigot.
102. M. de lamperien.
103. Hostel S. Vandrille.
104. M. Bouchart Bonni-face.
105. S. Philbert Chap:
106. Host: de Iumiege.
107. Poterne.
108. S. Lo-

---

35. Jean Lemire – Baptized – 1619
63. Marie Le Barbier – Baptized – 1619
145. Marie Luguen – Baptized – 1598
159. Nicollas Marsollet III – Baptized – 1601
162. Nicollas Marsollet III – Married Marie Le Barbier – 1637

167. Gilles Lemieux – Baptized – 1586
     Pierre Lemieux – Baptized – 1594
     Pierre Lemieux II – Baptized – 1616
172. Nicollas Marsollet II – Baptized – 1570
174. Nicollas Marsollet I – Died – 1586
     Laurence Griffon – Died – 1600
213. Laurence Griffon – Residence – 1500s

239 R. des Minimes.	288 R. des Camayets.	338 R. du Caperon.
240 R. des trois poisson.	289 R. Postes aux rats.	339 Pont a brenaude.
241 R. des Marqueux.	290 R. Cauchoise.	340 R. des Celestins.
242 ⎫ R. de la levrette.	291 R. des Beguines.	341 Moulin.
243 ⎭	292 R. de la Prison.	342 R. Caumont.
244 R. de la loge.	293 R. Saincte Croix.	343 R. du bon Espoir.
245 R. de flandre.	294 R. du petit puy.	344 Moulin.
246 ⎫ R. S. Nicaise.	295 ⎫ R. de la grosse hor-	345 ⎫ R. Martinville.
247 ⎭	296 ⎭ loge.	346 ⎭
248 R. Lambert.	297 R. S. Jean.	347 R. du Figuier.
249 R. de la Mouche.	298 R. des Corets.	348 Pont d'auberre.
250 R. des deux Anges.	299 R. Escuyere.	349 R. S. Marc.
251 R. du petit Mailleutier.	300 R. Senecau.	350 R. de la Cheure.
252 R. du Grand Mailleu-	301 R. Perciere.	351 R. Nostre Dame.
tier.	302 R. S. Lo.	352 R. de la Grosse Cour
253 R. Caillon.	303 R. Boudin.	du Tor.
254 R. des Minimes.	304 R. du Bec.	353 R. du porc.
255 R. des Carmelites.	305 R. aux Juifs.	354 R. des Grottes.
256 ⎫ R. Beauvoisine.	306 R. des Carmes.	355 R. des Avirons.
257 ⎭	307 ⎫ R. de l'aumosne.	356 R. Tuvache.
258 R. d'Escosse.	308 ⎭	357 R. Malpallu.
259 R. du Cordier.	309 R. de la Chaisne.	358 Moulins de la Ville.
260 R. Prince dos.	310 R. S. Nicolas.	359 R. des Bonnetiers.
261 R. de la Seille.	311 R. de la Croix de Fer.	360 R. de l'espicerie.
262 R. des Carneaux.	312 ⎫ R. de l'Archeve-	361 R. S. Denis.
263 R. Boudin.	313 ⎭ sche.	362 R. du Bac.
264 R. des Arsins.	14 R. des Chanoines.	363 R. des Tapissiers.
265 R. Coupegorge.	315 R. des Cinq Cerfs.	364 R. Porarr.
266 R. de l'escolle.	316 R. des Sauetiers.	365 R. de la Magdelaine.
267 R. de l'escurevil.	317 Moulin.	366 R. Grand Pont.
268 R. des Hermites.	318 Moulin de la fosse.	367 R. du petit Salut.
269 R. S. Laurens.	319 R. de la Miette.	368 R. aux Ours.
270 petite Rue S. Godart.	320 R. des haurmariages.	369 R. du fardeau.
271 ⎫ Grande Rue S. Go-	321 R. du Rosier.	370.371 ⎫ R. S. Estienne.
272 ⎭ dart.	322 R. Pinton.	372 ⎫ R. des Charette.
273 ⎫ R. de Bouyrevil.	323 Pont de robee.	373 ⎭
274 ⎭	324 ⎫ Eau de robee.	374 R. du Crucifix.
275 R. de Matan.	325 ⎭	375 R. de la Bourse.
276 R. Doqueville.	326 Pont de l'arque.	376 R. de la Harangue.
277 R. du Bourel.	327 R. du Corbeau.	377 R. de la Vicomte.
278 R. du Baillage.	328 R. Neuve.	378 R. Ancrier.
279 R. du Sacre.	329 R. du Chaudron.	379 R. des Cordeliers.
280 R. des Maillots.	330 R. des rats Visez.	380 R. Massacre.
281 ⎫ R. de la Renelle.	331 R. du Ruissel.	381 R. des belles femmes.
282 ⎭	332 R. de la Glaure.	382 R. S. Andre.
283 R. du petit Muse.	333 R. de la Vigne.	383 R. du Merrier.
284 ⎫ R. S. Patrice.	334 R. du gredil.	384 R. Herbiere.
285 ⎭	335 R. des trois Cotners.	385 R. S. Eloy.
286 R. Estouppee.	336 R. de la poulie.	386 R. du Panetet.
287 R. du Gredil.	337 R. du Gredil.	387 R. du Vieil Palais.

* 2 388 Rue

290. Nicollas Marsollet's residence - 1613

388 Rue Neufue.
389 R. de la pie.
390 R. aux chevaulx.
391 ⎫
392 ⎭ R. des Iacobins.

Folgen die Vorstätte.

393 Fauxbourg S. Gervais.
394 Chemein du Mont aux Malades.
395 S. Gervais pri: & par:
396 Hospitaux pour la peste.
397 ⎫
398 ⎭ Cour.
399 l' Hospital S. Roch.
400 ⎫
401 ⎭ Cour.
402 l'Hospital S. Loris.
403 Jardin de M. de Guenonville.
404 Corderie.
405 R. d'Ionville.
406 Fauxbourg Cauchoise.
407 S. Andre parois.

408 Cimetiers pour les pestiferez.
409 S. Maur.
410 M. Dauvray.
411 Fauxbourg de Bouvervil.
412 Val de Grace.
413 Carmes. Deschauffes.
414 Rocolets.
415 Champ du Pardon.
416 Fauxbourg S. Hilaire.
417 S. Hilaire par:
418 Chemin de Darnetal & des Chartreux.
419 ⎫
420 ⎭ Riviere de robec.
421 Prez.
422 Fauxbourg Martinville.
423 Augustins dechauffe.
424 Moulin.
425 Lavanderie.
426 Martinville Banclon.
427 Petite Rivier d'Aubette.
428 Grande Rivier d'Aubette.
429 Moulin.
430 Fontaine Iacob.

431 Haute Iustice.
432 Vieux fort Sainct Catherine razé.
433 S. Paul p:
434 Pre au Loup.
435 Quay de Paris.
436 Quay la Romaine.
437 Pont de Pierre rompu.
438 Pont de Batteaux.
439 Fauxbourg S. Sever.
440 S. Yues Chap.
441 Chauffee.
442 les Iacobines dites les Amureés.
443 Emandreville.
444 Pre aux Aanglois.
445 S. Sever. p:
446 la Verrire.
447 M. Schalcq.
448 Nre: Dam de bonnes nouvelles Ab.
449 la petite Chauffe.
450 Iardin de M. Chappelle.
451 Iardin de M. Tillij.
452 la Gabelle.
453 Maison de Claquedent.
454 Grammont Ab.

NAMES OF THE HUNDRED MEN

who first formed

The Society of New France[1]

Armand, Cardinal Richelieu, Minister of Navigation and Commerce.

Antoine Ruzé, Chevalier of the King's Orders, Marquis d'Effiat, King's Counsellor and Treasurer of France.

Isaac Martin de Mauvoy, Counsellor of the Most Christian King and Intendant of the Marine.

Jacques Castillon, citizen of Paris.

François St. Aubin.

Pierre le Blond.

Martin Anceaume.

Louis d'Ivry.

Simon Clarentin.

Jean Bourguet.

Louis Houel, King's Counsellor and Controller-General of the salt-marshes at Brouage.

François Derré.

Adam Mannessier, citizen and merchant of Havre de Grâce.

François Bertrand, Sieur du Plessis.

Martin Haguenyer, notary of the Chatelet de Paris.

Adam Moyen, citizen of Paris.

Guillaume Nicolle, advocate to the Grand Council.

Gilles Boyssel, Sieur de Seneville.

André Daniel, medical doctor.

Charles Daniel, captain in the navy.

Jacques Berruyer, Esquire, Sieur de Mauselment.

Pierre Boulanger, King's Counsellor, *Esleu* at Montevilliers.

Jean Feron.

[1] In translating these names from the Latin use has been made of a manuscript list in the Public Archives of Canada, MSS Series, Colonies F2, vol. i, pp. 19-24. A published list is to be found in *Collection de documents relatifs à la Nouvelle-France* (Quebec Legislature, Quebec, 1883), vol. i, pp. 80-5. The names of Adam Mannesier and Simon Dablon are not on the MS list, but are included in the *Collection*. The MS list gives the name of Nicholas Blondel's widow as Nicole Langlois and adds nine names not in Du Creux's list; presumably they are later additions.

Claude Potel, merchant of Paris.

Henri Cavelier, merchant of Rouen.

Jean Papavoyne, merchant of Rouen.

Simon le Maistre, merchant of Rouen.

Jean Guénet, merchant of Rouen.

Claude de Roquemont, Esquire, Sieur de Brison.

André Ferru, merchant of Paris.

François Castillon.

Antoine Reynaut, Esquire, Sieur de Montmort.

Hugues Cosnier, Sieur de Belleau.

Jean Poncet, Counsellor of the King in his Court of Subsidies, Paris.

Sébastien Cramoisy, printer of Paris.

Guillaume Prevost, merchant of Paris.

Gabriel Lattaignant, former mayor of Calais.

David du Chesne, counsellor and magistrate at Havre de Grâce.

Michael Jean, advocate of Dieppe.

Nicholas le Masson, King's Counsellor and Receiver of Subsidies in the
    Eslection of Montivilliers.

Isaac de Razilly, Chevalier of the Order of St. John of Jerusalem.

Gaspar de Loup, Esquire, Sieur de Monssan.

René de Bethoulat, Esquire.

Jean de Fayot, King's Counsellor and Treasurer at Soissons.

Jean Vincent, Counsellor and Magistrate of Dieppe.

The widow of Nicholas Blondel, Counsellor and Magistrate of Dieppe.

Jean Rozée, merchant of Rouen.

Samuel Champlain, Esquire, sea-captain.

Nicholas Ellyes, Sieur du Pin, Lieutenant-general in the high court of
    justice of Mauny.

Jean Tuffet, merchant and citizen of Bordeaux.

Georges Morin, of the household of the duc d'Orléans.

Paul Bailly, Counsellor and Almoner of the King, Abbé of St. Thierry
    at Mont d'Or, Rheims.

Louis de la Cour, chief clerk of petty accounts.

Ythier Hobier, Counsellor of the King and Treasurer in Provence.

Simon Alex, Counsellor of the King and Secretary.

Pierre Robineau, King's Counsellor and Treasurer of the Light-armed
    Cavalry.

Jacques Paget, King's Counsellor and Receiver of the King's taxes at
    Montdidier.

Jean Le Saige, King's Counsellor and Receiver of the King's taxes at Soissons.

Charles Du Fresne, Secretary of the officer in charge of the King's galleys.

Charles Robin, Sieur de Coursay.

Charles Robin, Counsellor of the King and Master of Woods and Waters for Touraine.

Thomas Bonneau, Sieur du Plessis, Counsellor and Secretary of the King.

Jacques Bonneau, Sieur de Beauvais.

Raoul Huillier, merchant of Paris.

Charles Fleurian.

René Robin, Sieur de la Rochefarou.

Mathurin Bandeau, citizen of Paris.

Robert Godefroy, Counsellor of the King and Treasurer-general of special military expenditure.

Claude de Bragelogne, King's Counsellor, Superintendant and Commissary-general of supplies for France.

Jacques Bordier, Counsellor and Secretary of the King.

Claude Margonne, King's Counsellor and Receiver-general for Soissons.

Jérôme de Saintonge, King's Counsellor and Treasurer for Champagne.

Étienne Hervé, citizen of Paris.

Jean Verdier, Counsellor and Secretary of the King.

Bertrand de Champflour, Secretary of the King.

Pierre Féret, Secretary of the Archbishop of Paris.

Antoine Cheffault, Advocate of the Parliament of Paris.

Barthélemy Quantin, Sieur de Moulinet.

Prégent Proust, citizen of Paris.

Pierre du Ryer, Counsellor and Secretary of the King and of his finances.

Jean Potel, King's Counsellor and Secretary of the Privy Council.

Nicholas le Vasseur, King's Counsellor and Receiver-general of his revenues in Paris.

Octavio Mey, citizen of Lyons.

Bonaventure Quantin, Sieur de Richebourg.

Pierre Aubert, Counsellor and Secretary of the King.

Guillaume Martin, Sieur de la Vernade, King's Counsellor.

Aymé Sirou, King's Counsellor and Treasurer-general of Paris.

Claude Girardin, merchant of Rouen.

Simon Dablon, Syndic of Dieppe.

Jean Chiron, merchant of Bordeaux.

Jean David, merchant of Bayonne.

Étienne Pavillon, King's Counsellor and Treasurer for War in Xaintonge.

Jean Pontac, citizen of Paris.

Claude le Myre, citizen of Paris.

Didier le Myre, citizen of Paris.

Pierre Desportes, Sieur de Ligneres.

Guillaume Vernière, residing in Paris.

Claude Chastelain, special commissary for war.

Jean de Jôuy, residing in Paris.

Pierre Fontaines, Sieur de Neuilly.

Jean Pelleau, Counsellor and Secretary of the King and Usher in the Chancellery of Guienne.

Antoine Nozereau, merchant of Rouen.

François Mouret, merchant of Rouen.

Jacques du Hamel, merchant of Rouen.

Jacques Douson de Bourran, Senator in the High Court of Bourdeaux, in charge of Inquiries.

Jean Douson de Bourran, Senator in the High Court of Bourdeaux in charge of Memorials.

Jacques de la Ferté, King's Counsellor and Almoner, Abbé de Saincte Madelaine of Chasteaudun.

With seven additions. [1]

[1] The manuscript list in the Canadian Archives (referred to on p. 11, n. 1 above) includes the following nine names, which do not appear on Du Creux's list: Thomas du Mantet, Bertrand de Gombault, Emmanuel Huelga, Thibault du Mas, François de Lauson, Gabriel de Pontac, Olive de l'Estonnac, Simonne Gautier, Gilles Guerin.

APPENDIX C

Some Wonder, Some Wander......

1. 16 Mike Street
Fayetteville, Cumberland County, NC
28314
July 1964 – December 1964

2. 817 Irving Park Boulevard
Sheffield Lake, Lorain County, OH
44054
December 1964 – March 1966

3. 3324 Matilda Lane, Apt. 10
Columbus, Muskogee County, GA
31907
March 1966 – May 1967

4. 2413 Norton Drive
Augusta, Richmond County, GA 30900
November 1967 – July 1968

5. #4 Jenkins Trailer Court
Mineral Wells, Palo Pinto County, TX
76067
July 1968 – October 1968

6. 107 Kate Street
Enterprise, Coffee County, AL 36330
October 1968 – March 1969

7. 300 Patrick Street
Ft. Wolters, Palo Pinto County, TX
76068
March 1970 – January 1972

8. 306C Lumpkin Road
Ft. Benning, Muskogee County, GA
31907
January 1972 – November 1972

9. 425 Royal Oaks Apartments
Hattiesburg, Perry County, MS 39401
November 1972 – May 1974

10. 55A State Street
Wildflecken, West Germany
July 1974 – January 1976

11. 38A Villagio della Pace
Vicenza, Italy
January 1976 – July 1977

12. 1105 Rustic Ridge
Auburn, Lee County, AL 36830
June 1977 – June 1979

13. 19 Rose Loop
Ft. Leavenworth, Leavenworth County,
KS 66027
June 1979 – May 1982

14. 1817 South Knox Avenue
Minneapolis, Hennepin County, MN
55403
June 1982 – June 1983

15. 7250 York Avenue South, Apt. 207
Edina, Hennepin County, MN 55435
June 1983 – June 1984

16. 310 Townhouse, Briarcrest Gardens
Hershey, Dauphin County, PA 17033
June 1984 – June 1985

17. 611 Barrington Court
Palmyra, Lebanon County, PA 17038
June 1985 – June 1987

18. 2063 Oak Run South Drive
Indianapolis, Marion County, IN 46260
June 1987 – March 1994

19. 115 South Lake Circle
St. Augustine, St. Johns County, FL
32084
March 1994 - Present

1.

12.

9.

13.

10.

14.

11.

19.

BIBLIOGRAPHY, BY TITLE:

A Concise History of France by Douglas Johnson published in 1971 by Viking Press, NY. and illustrations.

A Concise History of Canada by Gerald S. Graham published in 1968 by Viking Press, NY. and illustrations.

Champlain: The Life of Fortitude by Morris Bishop published in 1948 by Alfred A. Knopf, NY.

Other published material on Marsolet La Famille Marsolet de St-Aignan by Pierre-Georges Roy published in 1934 by Levis, Montreal; and Memoires de la Societe Genealogique author and publisher unknown.

Les Lemieux 1384-1984 by Jacques Lemieux published by The Lemieux of America in 1984 in Canada, translated by Susan Marsolais; and from The Lemieux of America Journals.

The Lemieuxs of America, A single Norman lineage, by Guy Lemieux, 2007

Haskins, C.H., The Normans in European History, Fredrick Ungar Publ. Co., NY 1915

Simons, G., Barbarian Europe, Time-Life Books, 1968

A History of Canada, Volume One: From its Origins to the Royal Regime, 1663, Gustave Lanctot, Harvard University Press, 1963

The White and the Gold, the French Regime in Canada, Thomas B. Costain, Doubleday & Company, Inc., 1954

The Jesuit Relations and Allied Documents, Travels and Explorations of the Jesuit Missionaries in North America (1610-1791), Edited by Edna Kenton, the Vanguard Press

The Jesuits in North America in the Seventeenth Century, France and England in North America, Part Second, Francis Parkman, Corner House Publishers, 1970

Samuel de Champlain - Father of New France, Samuel Eliot Morison, Little, Brown and Company

Rouen, Patrick Beghin, Editions Jean-Pierre Gyss, 1984

The Great Book of Normandy, Noel Broelic, Editions Minerva/Solar, Geneva, 1988

Family Biography of Lemire and Others. Danielle Duval LeMyre, www.geocities.corn/Heartland/Bluffs/6403/marsolet.html

Nicolas Marsolet de Saint-Aignan. Interpretor to the Montagnais First Nation, Danielle Duval LeMyre, www.geocities.corn/Heartland/Bluffs/6403/marsolet.html
The French Canadians in New England, Prosper Bender, www.cdl.library.cornell.edu

Making of America, www.library5.library.cornell.edu/moa

Resources, Documents and Studies on the History of Franco-Americans and the Emigration of French Canadians to the United States, Claude Belanger, Department of History, Marianopolis College, www.marianopolis.edu/quebechistory/frncdns/links.htm

The Makers of Canada Series, Anniversary Edition: Champlain, N.E. Dionne, Oxford University Press, London and Toronto, 1926

Medieval Panorama, Edited by Robert Bartlett, J. Paul Getty Museum, Los Angeles, 2001

ᵮᵻᴃᴌᵻᴑᴳᴿᴀᵽᴄ, ᴃᵧ ᴀᵾᴄᴄᴑᴿ :

Armstrong, Joe C.W., *Champlain*, 1987 Canada: Joe Armstrong

Berry, Gerald. *Champlain, Father of New France,* 1967 Canada: Penguin

Biggar, H.P., *The Early Trading Companies of New France*, 1965 New York; Argonaut Press, LTD. (First Published 1901)

Bishop, Morris, *Champlain: A life of Fortitude,* 1948: New York: Knopf

Bizier, Helene–Andree, *Histoires de Famille: The Marsolet*: Collections Civilization

Campeau, Lucien, *Biographical Dictionary for the Jesuit missions in Acadia and New France 1603-1654,* Translated by William Long, S.J. and George Topp S.J., 200: St Mary's; Halifax (100 Copies)

Campeau, Lucien- Cahiers, *D'Historie Des Jesuits No. 2, Les Cent-Associes et le Peuplement dela Nouvelle-France (1633-1663)*, Lucien Campeau; 1974 Le Edition Bellarmin: Montreal

Champlain, Samuel, *Voyages du Sieur Champlain*, reprint 1971, University of Toronto Press, Toronto.

Choquette, Leslie, *Frenchmen into Peasants: Modernity and Tradition in the Peopling of French Canada* 1997 Cambridge Mass, Harvard University Press

Costain, Thomas B*., The White and the Gold, The French Regime in Canada*: 1954: Garden City, NY

Dionne, N.E., *Samuel Champlain,* 2 Vols: 1891-1906: Québec: Cote

Douville, Raymond & Casanova Jacques, *Daily Life in Early Canada*, Translated by Carola Congreve, 1968. London: George Allen Ltd
Fischer, David Hackett, *Champlain's Dream*, 2008, Simon & Schuster, NY, NY

Garneau, F X*, L'Histoire du Canada*: 1864: Québec: C. Darveau

Gillmore, Don & Turgeon, Pierre, *Canada, a People's History*, 2 Vols., 2002 Toronto: McLelland and Stewart

Gravier, Gabreil, *Vie de Samuel Champlain,* 1900: Paris

Jette, Rene: *Dictionnaire Genealogique des Familles de Québec des Origines 1730* Geaton Morin, Editor*:* 1944 ; Québec2003 print

Jurgens, Olga: *Etienne Brule*, 2000, Toronto: University Of Toronto: Univ. Press

LeMyre, Danielle Duval *Nicolas Marsolet de St Aignan Interpretor (sic) to the Montagnais First Nation*, 2004: currently Unpublished: Listed on the Internet

Lanctot, Gustave, *History of Canada, Vol 1, From Origins to Royal Regime 1663:* 1963 Montreal fides

Lemieux, Guy, The Lemieuxs of America, A single Norman Lineage, Quebec, 2007

Lemieux, Jacques, *Un lingage Normand de France en Amerique, Les Lemieux - de 1384 a 1984, Working Paper, Québec*

Lescarbot, Marc, *The History of New France, 3 Vols,* Translated by W. L.Grant; Champlain Society; Toronto

Morison, S,E., *Samuel Champlain: Father of New France* 1972: Brown and Co.

Osselin, Anne, *Genealogy of the Marsolet and Lemieux Families,* Unpublished Working Papers, Rouen: 1988/1990

Parkman, Francis, *Pioneers of France in the New World,* Internet Copy 2003:Gutenberg Project

Parkman, Francis, *The Jesuits in North America in the Seventeenth Century* Facsimilie 2003:Gutenberg Project originally 1867: Boston: Brown Little

Reideau, Roger, *A Brief History of Canada*, 2000: New York; Facts on File

Roy, Pierre-George, *The Marsolet Family of St Aignan*, 1934 Levis

Sagard, Gabriel. *Histoire du Canada*, 4 Vol., 1866:Paris.

Sulte, Benjamin. *Histoire des Canadiens-Francais, 1608-1880*, 1882-4: Montreal:Wilson

Thwaites, R.G: *The Jesuit Relation and Allied Documents 73 Vols*; Facsimilie Cleveland/Burrows Brothers

Tanguay, *Genealogical Dictionary for Canadian Families,* 7 Vols: CD: 2001 Global Heritage Press, Québec

Trudel, Marcel *The Beginnings of New France 1524-1663,* 1973; Toronto: McClelland and Stewart
Trudel, Marcel: *Champlain, Samuel de, 2000*; Toronto: McClelland and Stewart

Trigger, Bruce G. *Natives and Newcomers, Canada's Heroic Age Reconsidered,* 1985: McGill, Queens, Québec

Warburton, George; *The Conquest of Canada;* 1849: London: Bentley

Vachon, Andre, *Nicolas Marsolet, Seiur de St Aignan*, a Biographical sketch for The Dictionary Biographical for Canada.

Les Voisins
(The Neighbors)
Quartier Petit Champlain
Quebec City